THE HEART TASTES BITTER

Víctor del Árbol was born in Barcelona in 1968 and was an officer of the Catalan police force from 1992 to 2012. In 2006, he won the Tiflos Best Novel Award for his book *The Weight of the Dead*, and his next novel, *The Sadness of the Samurai*, was awarded the 2011 Best European Crime Fiction Prize. His novels have been translated into a dozen languages, and in 2016 he was awarded the prestigious Premio Nadal literature award.

D0307467

For Aurelia
From wherever you are, watch over us, the way you did here
during the short miracle called Life

THE
HEART
TASTES
BITTER

VÍCTOR DEL ÁRBOL

TRANSLATED BY LISA DILLMAN

SCRIBE
Melbourne • London

Scribe Publications
18–20 Edward St, Brunswick, Victoria 3056, Australia
2 John Street, London, WC1N 2ES, United Kingdom

First published in English by Scribe 2016
Originally published in Spanish as *Respirar por la Herida*
by Editorial Alrevés 2013

Copyright © Víctor del Árbol 2013
Translation copyright © Lisa Dillman 2016

All rights reserved. Without limiting the rights under copyright reserved
above, no part of this publication may be reproduced, stored in or
introduced into a retrieval system, or transmitted, in any form or by any
means (electronic, mechanical, photocopying, recording or otherwise)
without the prior written permission of the publishers of this book.

The moral rights of the author and translator have been asserted.

Typeset in Dante MT by the publishers
Printed and bound in the UK by CPI Group (UK) Ltd, Croydon CR0 4YY

Scribe Publications is committed to the sustainable use of natural resources
and the use of paper products made responsibly from those resources.

9781925321159 (Australian edition)
9781925228441 (UK edition)
9781925307306 (e-book)

CiP records for this title are available from the National Library of Australia
and the British Library.

scribepublications.com.au
scribepublications.co.uk

LONDON BOROUGH OF WANDSWORTH	
9030 00005 2733 2	
Askews & Holts	20-Oct-2016
AF THR	£8.99
	WW16012297

The only possible radical experience you can count on is death.

JOSEP FORMENT,

Arthur Rimbaud, *The Beauty of the Devil*

(Alrevés, 2009)

PREFACE

The landscape doesn't lie. It's our perspective that disguises it — as if what we see is merely a reflection of our frame of mind, the same place looks different every time.

A faded sign on the side of the Toledo highway pointed the way into town. It wasn't a pretty town — in fact, it couldn't even boast the Romanesque church that all ugly towns seem to have. But it was there on the map and it existed. Its existence was hinted at from a distance, a brownish stain there amid the nothingness, flanked on all sides by vast expanses of golden fields. Eduardo turned up the volume on the radio and lost himself in the music of Miles Davis, as though 'Blue in Green' had been composed solely so that he could enjoy that carefree moment. The whistling of the melody and the crackle of tobacco burning close to his nose afforded him a sense of wellbeing — and that was more than he managed most of the time. The half-empty bottle of whisky rolling around under the seat had done the rest. But there's no way to live inside a song, just as there's no way to live inside a car that smells of tobacco and has a glove compartment full of expired parking tickets, which he kept forgetting to toss.

He cracked the window a few inches and threw out his cigarette butt; then, downshifting, his heart began to pound. On the other side of the highway he took a road that seemed to lead nowhere. The asphalt gradually disappeared under thicker and thicker layers of dust, and after a few yards the road's surface simply vanished — as though swallowed up by the earth — and turned into a cart path riven with deep potholes. And then that road vanished too. Beyond it was nothing, nothing but a swathe of uncultivated earth from which shrubs sprouted up like cathedrals. Judging by the desiccated furrows and the weeds growing at will, it had been quite some time since anyone had bothered to cultivate the land here. And rounding off this portrait of abandon was an old tractor with a discoloured slip-scoop, its thick flat tyres rutted in the earth. At the edge of the field stood a fence, and beyond that a rambling old house. House

1

and barren field eyed each other indifferently from a distance, forming part of an indivisible unit, like painting and frame.

Eduardo closed his eyes. It smelled of countryside. *Oh, how smells deceive, how landscapes lie*, he said to himself, swallowing spit. He took the bouquet of dahlias from the passenger seat, smoothing the onionskin paper that held them together. They had no smell, and even their colour seemed washed out, as if the closer they got to the destination the more fictitious it became. Eduardo struggled out of the car with difficulty and massaged his knee.

Night was falling and birds flew close to the ground in search of insects hovering near the surface of the creek, which ran parallel to the access road. A few blackberry bushes were still dripping like sheets hung out to dry, swaying beneath the reddish sky, the peaks of the sierra visible in the distance. Eduardo made his way down a small incline separating the road from the creek. The place was uninhabited and silent, and after a few yards the creek curved sharply to bypass a reed bed and a large boulder from which the silhouette of Madrid's suburbs could be seen, far off in the distance.

This is where it had all happened.

He took off his shoes and deposited them on the shore, then rolled his pants halfway up and stuck his bare feet into the stream's gentle, freezing waters. The shocking cold made blood rush to his head. Wading a bit further in, until the water was up to his knees, he felt hundreds of miniscule shards of glass pricking his skin, but he managed to withstand it for a few minutes, staring vacantly at the reeds on the other side. He tried to find some vestige of the accident, but found nothing. Nothing, not a chunk of windshield, or a tyre track, or a stain — it was as if the earth and stream had simply swallowed up the evidence of what had happened and then kept right on flowing with the calm of centuries. Eduardo cupped some water into his hand and let it dribble out between his fingers. It no longer had the crimson tinge of fourteen years ago. 'The only possible radical experience you can count on is death,' he murmured, recalling the words of consolation spoken by a friend at the funeral. There are words of consolation that don't console, friends who stop being friends. Landscapes that erase all traces of tragedy. Dahlias with no scent, no colour.

2

A day like any other day, a single second identical to the one before it, a second that in no way had presaged that it would be the last moment of happiness in his life. It was an absurd thought, but had he known — had he had even an inkling — although he couldn't have avoided it, he could at least have hugged them tighter, said things that weren't as pointless and ridiculous and trivial as arguing. There is always something left to be said when there's no longer any time left to say it.

Thunder rumbled, stirring the air, and fat raindrops began to fall, creating expanding ripples around him. Some drops bounced like rubber balls off the shoulders of his coat, others slid down his forehead and onto his cheeks. It was getting late and he'd gone too many miles out of his way. He had to go back. There was no place for him to go — that was certainly the truth — but he couldn't stay here any longer. 'I have to get back,' he said to himself as he dried the tears forming in his red eyes.

Sometimes people only weep their sorrows on the inside.

He dropped the bouquet of dahlias, the flowers Elena had loved so much, and for a few minutes stood and gazed at the stream as it swallowed them up. Then he returned to the car and drove away without looking back.

1

Six months earlier, January 2005.

Eduardo walked over to the window. The playground on the other side of the street was deserted: it was odd, to see swings swinging with no children, wet wooden benches with no grandparents, puddles in the sand with nobody splashing through them. Rainy days only accentuated his conviction that an insurmountable distance separated him from the things that seemed to matter to others. And nothing could diminish that feeling.

He turned his head back to the inside of the office: Formica shelves, overflowing filing cabinets, forensic medical texts. In one corner a ceramic pot with a moribund geranium.

He closed his eyes. On opening them, Martina was still sitting there behind her desk with an inscrutable expression. Her face could be deceptive, looking sweet or fragile. You felt an immediate fondness for her smile — but Martina seldom smiled. The light cast from a desk lamp softened the severity of her pursed lips.

'Are you planning to write down everything I say?'

She nodded, crossing her arms.

'That's what the pen and pad are for.'

'Why don't you just sign the report, write me out a prescription, and we'll part amicably? We both know these little chats are a waste of time, Doctor.'

Martina pushed up the bridge of her glasses. The pen between her fingers trembled imperceptibly. What kind of perfume was she wearing? There was definitely something citrusy to it, very understated. Certainly not the type of fragrance that revealed anything about her.

'I disagree entirely. Personally, I actually care — quite a bit, in fact — about what we do here.'

Eduardo knew she was lying. In order to lie convincingly, the first thing you have to learn is how to control your facial expressions, and not everyone can do it: the doctor's eyes betrayed a look of scepticism. She didn't like him. A simple question of empathy. Their relationship had been tense from the start; they were like an ill-disposed couple forced to spend a few hours together each month without arguing, during which time they both behaved fittingly.

He stroked the table's smooth surface, tracing the winding course of an imaginary river in the thin layer of dust.

'Alright, then. What do you want me to tell you this time?'

Martina zeroed in for a moment on the scars on his wrists. Noting this, Eduardo tugged at the cuffs of his shirt, hiding them.

'How're you adapting to everyday life?' the doctor queried, not straying from the script.

'Everyday life' — now there's an expression, Eduardo thought. For him, death was a matter of slowly breaking the habit of life.

'I'm living in an apartment building on Calle San Bernardo, the rent's cheap, and the landlady is a good woman. She doesn't ask questions. I'm doing a few commissioned portraits I got through Olga, earning enough to get by. So, not bad, I guess.'

'And what about your feelings?'

'My feelings are where they need to be, don't you fret.'

'And where is that?'

'In a safe place.'

Martina made a note and then laced her fingers on top of the notepad, staring at him in curiosity. Possibly feigned, possibly genuine.

'And what about your nightmares?'

Eduardo pressed his thumbs into his eyelids.

'Listen, Doc, are you seriously planning on keeping this up?'

'Why don't you tell me what your dreams are about?' Martina insisted.

Eduardo gestured vaguely.

'I don't know, they're all different.'

'Tell me about the most recent one.'

'I wouldn't even know where to begin.'

'At the beginning.'

Dreams have no beginning and no end, Eduardo thought.

In his, there was a boy in the rain. His face was blurry, like the sketch for a portrait that's been smudged with a damp sponge that makes the colours and shapes run. Maybe seven or eight years old. He was on a muddy road, barefoot and shirtless, wearing only a frayed pair of trousers. You could see his ribcage sticking out beneath dirty skin and a network of veins running like the branches of a tree from his legs to his neck. They were all throbbing at once, an underground river of magma, and the boy was looking up at the top of a hill, anticipating something that was about to happen, from one moment to the next.

From the fog emerged a man — running, stricken with panic. He was being chased by two huge, slobbering mastiffs with spiked collars and yellow in their eyes. The man ran, turning to look back, and even though he was taking great long strides, the dogs were gaining on him. They'd catch him at any moment.

Finally, after racing desperately down the hill, the man stopped and spread his arms, as though he could do nothing else — or perhaps he was tired of fleeing. That was his way of saying he had given up, he wasn't going anywhere. The dogs, surprised maybe, slowed their pace and advanced like prowlers. They growled at him, baring their teeth. The man and the beasts took measure of each other from just a few yards' distance, and then the dogs' instincts sprang into action — all at once they leapt upon him, and he simply held his hands up like a useless shield that might somehow fend off their attack. The force of impact knocked him to the ground and the dogs launched into a frenzy of carnage — jaws, snapping bones, flailing legs, screaming.

Within a few seconds he'd been torn to shreds, but was still breathing. A stream of blood spurted from his mouth, glistening in the rain. The man looked up at the sky and, although he was dying, he smiled benevolently; he reached out a hand and spread his fingers, before clenching them into a fist. Not a threatening fist, but more an attempt to grasp at the air, to use it to keep breathing.

'Satisfied? Can I have my prescription now?'

'How do you interpret that, Eduardo?'

He shrugged.

'You're the expert, that's what it says there on your diploma. I'm just the guinea pig.'

Martina glanced discreetly at the clock. Five more minutes till the end of the session, and thankfully her next patient was already in the waiting room. She was grateful to be getting rid of the guy. Eduardo made her exceedingly uncomfortable.

Scribbling out the prescriptions with administrative efficiency, Martina adopted a neutral tone, warning him not to drink too much on Risperdal. Eduardo made no comment, but the doctor caught a glimpse of something troubling in his eyes. Sometimes Eduardo's expressions were like a fist punching her right in the pit of her stomach.

'That's it for today. See you next month.'

'Maybe. Good afternoon, Doctor.'

Through the window, Martina watched him cross the street, limping on his right leg.

'I should have chosen another goddamned line of work,' she said under her breath.

Returning to her desk, she glanced over the notes she'd taken, gently biting her lower lip, struggling for the necessary calm to order her thoughts. With a firm hand, she wrote:

Eduardo Quintana, seventh follow-up. After eight months the patient continues to exhibit the same symptoms: anxiety, denial, self-destructive thoughts. Conclusion: unstable.

'Gooooood morning, Madrid. It's seven o'clock on this cold, foggy Sunday morning. Rain's falling hard and you're listening to Onda Ciudad. So of course I'm going to play — you guessed it — Peter White's "Another Rainy Day".'

Eduardo flicked on the nightstand light and gazed at the psychedelic shapes the lampshade cast on the ceiling. He sat on the bed, elbows on his thighs, and let his sleepy gaze drift around the room.

It was a modest apartment, but it had all the basics: a TV, a reasonably comfortable bed, a few characterless paintings on the wall, a double-armoire with full-length mirror, a mini-refrigerator with a single gas burner next to it, and a shower and leaky sink. The thing was, despite the fact that the place lacked none of the essentials, it still wasn't comfortable. The problem was that there was a sadness in the air, one that all impersonal places seemed to exude, with the lack of detail they reveal about those who inhabit them. Eduardo could die right there and the following day all they'd have to do is change the sheets — and that would be enough to completely erase all trace of his presence.

Most of his stuff was still packed up in the same cardboard boxes that Olga had helped him truck over from the storage unit where they'd spent the past fourteen years. In one corner lay a heap of no-longer-consulted books on painting and his prized record collection, alphabetically organised beside his record player. Those records were the only things he still felt somewhat attached to. Jazz, blues, and soul formed the soundtrack of his childhood, although it wasn't until his father died and bequeathed him the collection that he truly learned to appreciate it. Childhood was no longer Eduardo's home, and never again would be, but at the very least that music was still *his* music.

He groped for a cigarette, lit it. The first puff burned his lungs. Then he reached out a little further and his fingers touched the rutted shape of a near-empty vodka bottle. There was a finger of booze left in it, and he downed it in one, feeling as though his head was about to explode. It stopped its spinning for a few seconds, and Eduardo closed his eyes and focused on the Peter White solo on the radio. It wasn't peace, but something akin to it — although his father would have said that nothing compared to Dexter Gordon's sax in 'It's You or No One'. But his father wasn't there.

The hangover made his stomach lurch and he felt the urge to vomit. His liver was killing him, though not fast enough. All he wanted to do was lie in bed and listen to old records, let that day fade away like all the others, without a trace. But that couldn't be. He had to get up, drag himself to the toilet, struggle with his constipation, clean himself up, make some breakfast — at least eat the apple that was starting to shrivel in the wicker fruit basket — and maybe spend a little time straightening up the apartment, airing it out, emptying ashtrays, cleaning the garbage out of the sink. With a little luck, he might even find it in himself to work on one of his commissions for Olga.

He took off his pyjamas and carefully folded them before placing them into the hamper and turning on the shower. The plumbing groaned and grumbled, but after a few seconds there emerged a stream of relatively warm water, which wouldn't last. The building was old and in dire need of repairs that no one seemed willing to take on — water was heated by a communal boiler, so you could easily find yourself out of luck mid-lather; if anyone in a neighbouring apartment happened to turn on their shower at the same time, that was it.

Eduardo stood leaning against the cracked wall tile beneath a sickly trickle of water as soap bubbles slid down his legs, making their way to the drain. He rubbed his right knee, swollen as a wineskin. A huge scar ran clear from one side to the other and, although over the years the skin had grown back around the wound, the flesh had been sucked down underneath it like an earthquake faultline.

Touching the mound of dead flesh was like rubbing up against a time he no longer wanted to remember.

He stayed in the shower until the plumbing groaned, in a sort of death rattle, and the water stopped flowing. When he slid back the screen that served to separate the bathroom from the bedroom, he saw that Graciela had slid a note under his door.

I heard music so I assume you're up. There's fresh coffee if you feel like having insomnia together.

Graciela was his landlady, although Eduardo suspected that wasn't her real name. Inventing a name was an easy way to invent a life — but either way, it was none of his concern.

He dressed slowly, pulling on a pair of polyester pants and a wrinkled shirt. The overall look, when he glanced in the mirror, made him frown. Not bothering to shave, he simply smoothed his hair with one hand before walking out the door. Eduardo wasn't trying to impress anyone. Not anymore.

Graciela's apartment was at the end of the hall. For most tenants it constituted off-limits territory unless Graciela granted them permission to venture there — and there was never a reason to grant it. The landlady needed her own space, a place she could be herself — or be the part of herself she didn't show in public.

The door was ajar. In the front room was an armchair with an open book on it and, a little further on, a side table with a half-empty glass of wine in which floated a couple of cigarette butts, one of them lipsticked. A pair of high heels stood guard at the bedroom door, a bunched-up dress on the floor beside them. Eduardo had heard Graciela with a stranger the night before. They'd sounded happy, the stranger had laughed a lot, his laugh like some odd kind of hiccup, and Graciela had kept shushing him, though she sounded gleeful. After awhile they'd stopped. Perhaps it had been a long night that had ended — like all of the landlady's dates — in tragedy.

'Hello?' he called, raising his voice to be heard.

But Graciela didn't hear him. She was in the bathroom, standing before the mirror with a towel wrapped around her. Eduardo had guessed she was in her late forties, though he'd never asked her age and she'd never offered it. At any rate, she wasn't beautiful and probably never had been, but now she seemed to have succumbed to the evidence. There must have once been a time when she got the urge to put on make-up, or go to the hairdresser's once in a while, a time when someone gave her the pre-date jitters — choosing an outfit, shoes, jewellery, trying out different smiles, thinking up topics of conversation in case of a catastrophic mid-dinner silence. But that time, if ever it was, was history.

Now Graciela gave off the air of undesired solitude; she'd reached the point of no return and it was too late to redirect her life and avoid a dead end. The lines on her forehead bore the scars of bad decisions, misunderstandings and lies, the disappointments and insecurities that had pushed away the men in her life one by one. She seemed resigned to her role as landlady, overseeing the old building, killing time behind the desk in the lobby, dreaming — even if her dreams inevitably ended with an ashtray full of butts and wrinkled napkins.

Through the half-open bathroom door, Eduardo watched her remove the towel carefully, as though it were stuck to her skin and painful to peel off. Graciela ran a hand across the steamed-up mirror, gazing at a deep pink scar that looked neat and clean. There was no breast where the cut had been made. For a few moments, she gazed at herself — examining herself, really — as if she were having difficulty getting used to the breast's absence. She stroked the wound as though trying to remember what it felt like, how it felt to possess that missing organ. Then she buried her face in her hands and wept, elbows on the porcelain sink.

Eduardo's first instinct was to go into the bathroom, but Graciela's sobbing stopped him. What could he possibly say? What right had he to interrupt this moment of intimacy? He knew almost nothing about her aside from the fact that they had something in common: different forms of loneliness.

He retraced his steps and was about to silently take his leave, but before walking out of the apartment, he sensed eyes on the back of his head, and he stopped. Sara, Graciela's daughter, was eyeing him from the hallway. Eduardo raised a hand and the girl imitated him, returning his greeting, each tacitly accepting that none of this was happening.

'Today's not a good day,' Eduardo said.

The girl shook her head.

'No, it's not.'

Strolling the deserted streets of Madrid at that hour of indecision — when everything is on the verge of happening but nothing yet has — redeemed the city, concealing its misery, creating a false sense of benevolence. Eduardo walked slowly, feeling free to go wherever he liked without the shouting and chaos that he was not yet re-accustomed to, after fourteen years of absence. He recognised all the streets, but in a way he felt like a foreigner.

What d'you say we go off in search of treasure? his father used to say, his voice hoarse from the endless cigarettes he smoked, and which had eventually taken him to the grave. Going 'off in search of treasure' meant spending the Sunday rummaging through the stalls of El Rastro — Madrid's flea market — among the torrents of people who streamed out of the metro, spilling down Calle de Roda and Calle de Fray Ceferino, toward Plaza de Cascorro and then down to Ribera de Curtidores. Once old tributaries leading to Río Manzanares, these were a noisy, delightful chaos, where people wandered between makeshift stalls and cosy taverns, back and forth from little second-hand treasures to *chatos* of wine and tapas.

Those crowds had been so exciting when he was a kid. He'd listen wide-eyed as his father told him the story of the soldier Eloy Gonzalo, left as a baby on the doorstep of an orphanage and later to become one of the national heroes of Cuba; or told him how cattle had been slaughtered in the old abattoirs, their blood running down the steep streets and staining them red. Eduardo was fascinated and could easily envision the stalls set up by the travelling barbers, auctioneers and second-hand dealers, the tanneries, the municipal slaughterhouse — things that no longer existed but that somehow still formed part of an atmosphere that was palpable there at the market. *It's our very own medieval medina*, his father used to say proudly, holding his son's hand tightly to keep the human river from sweeping him away.

But everything had changed: the things, the scenery. His perspective.

He walked into a bar close to Parque de El Retiro. It was still early and the tables were empty. At the bar stood a couple of customers who looked like they'd had a long and not particularly prosperous night. A bored waiter watched the television, hanging from the ceiling in one corner, absently. Eduardo ordered a whisky, straight up. It was just past eight in the morning, but the waiter seemed nonplussed — no doubt seasoned to these battles.

'A lot to forget, huh?'

Eduardo smoothed his hair nervously. Prickly grey-speckled stubble was growing in around his loose jowls and small mouth. A pale-skinned man, he smiled too much when he was uncomfortable, which essentially meant any time he was forced to carry on a minimally drawn-out or unwanted conversation. His eyes — darting, evasive, sleepless — were like those of a rat trying to make itself invisible. Occasionally some tiny little thing attracted his attention and his eyes glimmered with a dim light that, for an instant, hinted at the man he had once been. But soon the black cloud that hung over everything engulfed him once more.

'No matter what's upsetting you, friend, your liver doesn't deserve this kind of punishment.'

Eduardo made a face intended to banish the intruder. He downed his drink and made his way slowly up Cuesta de Moyano until he reached the fountain of The Fallen Angel, and took a break at the octagonal granite pedestal supporting the sculpture.

'His pride had cast him out from Heaven, with all his host of rebel Angels ... round he throws his baleful eyes, that witnessed huge affliction and dismay, mixed with obdurate pride and steadfast hate', he recited quietly, recalling an old Fine Arts professor who'd encouraged his students to study the bronze body that was being strangled by an evil snake — especially its facial expression, filled with dramatic intensity; it was an exact reflection of the verses of Milton's *Paradise Lost*.

13

Everything about it was still: the space, the time, the sculpture itself.

Eduardo knew that feeling: the exasperating and perpetual stillness, the certainty that nothing is mutable. He could order his legs to walk one metre to the right — or two, or three — and come up against a wall; he could do the exact opposite and yet still butt up against the same wall, he was sure he wasn't getting anywhere, that he was just like that petrified sculpture. The lack of trivial everyday thoughts and the obsession with one repetitive, grotesque, all-consuming thought was what his therapist called insanity.

But he wasn't insane. He was just dead.

He strolled slowly toward the Crystal Palace in Parque de El Retiro. Somehow, his steps always seemed to lead him there. He liked to sit for hours by the huge pond, gazing at the bald cypresses; he was fascinated by those tall, slender trees able to take root in the muddy earth.

He thought about the last time he'd been there with Elena and Tania.

Elena had looked beautiful, wearing tight jeans rolled up to mid-calf and a spaghetti-strap top with black and white splatters that looked almost random.

'What made you fall in love with me?' Eduardo whispered, embracing the memory. He had asked Elena that question often, and she had always responded with a happy, sincere laugh, and kissed him on the lips without answering. She never gave him a reason; what she did do was make him the happiest man in the world.

He picked up a small rock and hurled it out across the pond's placid surface, trying to make it skip. The smooth stone skipped twice and then sank, leaving an expanding ripple that soon disappeared as well. Eduardo smiled, recalling the stone-skipping contests he used to have there with Tania. She always won — her pebbles made it from one side of the huge pond all the way to the other. His daughter was a girl ill-at-ease with the changes taking place in her body, on the verge of becoming something that both scared and perplexed her. Tania was fourteen years old, and her wide eyes already showed signs of rebellion, which came out in simple ways — truculence, back-talking, being contradictory — that he didn't know how to handle. Had she been given the chance, she'd have eclipsed her mother both in beauty and wilfulness.

A different type of tree — hardy horse chestnuts, rooted deep

14

in the soil — lined the shore to the right of the great pond. Looking up, Eduardo saw a woman sitting under the latticework of leaves and branches, smoking absently beneath the dripping leaves, gazing at the surface of the pond. Her head was turned to one side and she looked as though she'd just emerged from deep reflection. Faint disappointment or sadness puckered her lips, like they were the tip of the iceberg of her thoughts. Her face was thin, drawn, as though she'd had a prolonged illness and was still convalescing. A brown raincoat lay draped across her thighs — matching her skirt, sweater and high heels — and she had thick, intensely black hair that tumbled messily over her shoulders in girlish disarray.

For a long while Eduardo watched her. He knew an exceptional face when he saw one. From his bag he pulled a sketchpad and charcoal pencil, and with quick strokes roughed out her profile, before her true expression had a chance to disappear. Unaware of being observed, the mysterious woman offered him a tiny cove of sincerity, an insight into who she was that she never would have shown, even posing nude on the divan in his bedroom. When people feel examined, even if their intentions are true, the seed of a lie is born.

As soon as she realised she was being watched, that woman's naive expression — her sincere modesty — would vanish, and he'd never be able to get it back. And with it would go the image of Elena that Eduardo had just evoked. Elena was dead. And yet the more he contemplated that woman's silhouette, the more perplexed he felt, the more flustered by her presence. Because, in a way, that woman was a precise reflection of his wife, her exact image distorted, like the other side of an invisible looking glass. As if her skin had been ripped off and placed on another body, allowing her to keep living.

The mirage lasted a few more precious moments, until the woman tucked a few strands of hair back with a relaxed gesture — but on looking up, her eyes met Eduardo's. For a split second she was still herself, as if her pupils were still fixed on the pond without having seen him, brimming with warmth and tenderness. But that look evaporated almost immediately, giving way to a chaotic jumble of allegations. Brusquely, she picked up her raincoat and made off into the trees.

Eduardo went to where the woman had been sitting, looked out where she had been looking, breathed in the air in case she'd left the trace of a fragrance. Nothing.

When he got back to his apartment, he pulled out a canvas and set it up on his easel. It had been a long time since he'd felt that sense of urgency — that need to capture something before it disappeared, aware of the fact that with each passing second it would slowly evaporate like smoke.

The next morning, he returned to the Crystal Palace in the hopes of seeing her again. He waited for hours before finally accepting that she wasn't coming, and then he left, scoffing at himself, at the loneliness that had driven him to seek the warmth of someone he'd invented.

Eduardo walked to the closest metro stop, intending to forget all about it. The station had Schubert piped in the background. He could see the glimmering tracks of the rail leading into a long curve in the dark tunnel. The only people on the platform were Eduardo and a young man with Asian features sitting on the other end of his bench. The man wore a small backpack over one shoulder and held one of those brightly coloured plastic cats they sell in Chinese discount stores — 'lucky cats', they call them. The young man was dressed in black from head to toe; a trench coat accentuated the pallor of his oval, almost childlike face. His fingernails were painted black and he was wearing a thin stripe of black eyeliner on his lower lids. His hair matched, too; it was as dark as his clothes, and tousled just so, in a purposefully messy style. The most striking thing, however, was that the kid would not stop staring at him.

Eduardo stared back, regretting the fact that he'd actually selected this bench himself, given that he had the entire platform to choose from, and suddenly he felt as if the young man were addressing him in some private reproach: *those scars on your wrists look old. So — what happened? Has the urge to commit suicide subsided? From what I hear it takes an iron will to actually go through with it.*

Eduardo blushed. He stood, intending to walk away, to put some distance between them.

Why don't you just mind your own business? he thought, staring daggers at the kid.

The young man seemed unperturbed by this reaction. There is an

16

odd silence between strangers, one that seems to say so much without pronouncing a single word.

'Do I know you?' Eduardo finally asked.

The boy didn't nod, didn't bat a single eyelash on his face. But his statuesque calm gave Eduardo the answer he was searching for.

The train stopped at the platform. The boy's eyes flitted momentarily toward the cars, and he stood. Smiling as though bemused by the middle-aged man, a man who despite his age seemed unable to make sense of something obvious.

Eduardo watched him walk to the car's open doors. He didn't realise, until the train had already pulled out of the station, that the boy had left his Chinese cat there on the bench.

He found Graciela behind the desk in the lobby of their building. She sat reading a fashion magazine by the light of a small lamp, its reflection giving her face a nocturnal-butterfly air. Dressed in worn jeans and a wrinkled, short-sleeved shirt with a tiny coffee stain at the collar, she had her legs crossed and was jiggling one clog back and forth in the air. When she saw Eduardo walk in, she raised her pointy chin and put the magazine to one side.

'I waited for you, so we could have our coffee.'

Eduardo fidgeted pointlessly with the collar of his shirt. The memory of Graciela's amputated breast troubled him.

'Sorry. Olga asked me to go see her at the gallery. She wants me to do a series of sketches — the anonymous faces of Madrid.' In the fictional world he'd invented for others, Eduardo was still a somewhat renowned painter, preparing a monograph he was planning to exhibit at one of Olga's galleries. Sure, it was a lie, but one credible enough to hold up, provided people didn't ask too many questions.

'Have you had dinner? I could make something. I don't feel like eating alone, and you shouldn't go to bed without some hot food inside you,' she dove right in, not giving him time to think it over.

Eduardo tried to act friendly. Graciela didn't interest him in the slightest, he had no intention of becoming yet another of her failures. But there was no need for sincerity. Sometimes the truth is nothing but an excuse to be cruel.

'I'm really tired. All I want is to go to bed.' In actual fact, he was thinking of the half-empty bottle on the dresser in his bedroom. 'Maybe another night.'

Graciela rubbed her forehead wearily. Her hair was cropped short, the colour faded, roots growing in, revealing the grey she was trying to hide. She sighed, flaring her red-veined nostrils.

'You've been drinking, haven't you? That's no way to solve whatever problem you're trying to solve,' she remarked.

Eduardo had no desire to argue with Graciela, so he changed the subject.

'So. How's Sara doing?'

'She had a bad night, but she's asleep now. It's funny — the first thing she did when she got up this morning was to ask about you. I don't know why, but she's really fond of you. You should stop by more often.'

Eduardo nodded. He, too, felt something like fondness for his landlady's daughter. She was thirteen, just a year younger than Tania had been when she died.

'Give her this when she wakes up.'

'A Chinese lucky cat?' Graciela asked, surprised.

Eduardo shrugged.

'This weird guy left it on the metro. I thought Sara might like it.'

She glanced at the figure with little interest.

'I suppose so; you both seem to like weird things. Come on over if you change your mind.'

Eduardo wasn't going to change his mind. They both knew that.

2

The gallery was located in the basement of an old building where the smell of wet ashtray and old furniture hung in the air. A few people were poking around, looking at the works on display. Olga was wandering, not showing much real interest in any of the paintings. The most she did was purse her lips in curiosity if one of them caught her attention, which, truth be told, seemed somewhat scattered.

Where the fuck are you, Eduardo? she thought. He was the damn artist, for God's sake, he was supposed to be there. When he finally walked in, thirty minutes late, she shot him a look — half-annoyed, half-aghast. Eduardo had arrived in shirtsleeves, unshaven. His hair was a mess and the bags under his eyes looked like two bottomless pits.

'You look like crap. And you're late, to boot.'

'Isn't that to be expected from drunks?' he replied sarcastically. Sarcasm was a luxury he afforded himself only with his dealer.

'Don't act all wounded with *me*,' she scolded, expelling a puff of air from the corner of her mouth as if she was smoking.

To some men, a woman as smart, beautiful, and as sure of her beauty as Olga was off-putting; it made them insecure, and they found it distasteful. Olga was the embodiment of all male fears. At five-foot ten, her tight pants revealed narrow hips and strong quads. She was an active woman with an air of self-sufficiency, and a certain masculinity about her. The virility in her look led many people to profile her, assuming she was a lesbian. She was a sci-fi brunette, with a somewhat robotic expression that was accentuated by her haircut — very short, almost shaven at the back, but with long bangs that hung down in front and covered her eyes; her hair colour changed in the light, sometimes grey and sometimes blue, and she had the inscrutable face and slightly irked countenance of those prone to frustration. The overall impression she gave off was one of aloofness.

Eduardo looked at the people nosing through the paintings. Just a handful of loafers who'd sought refuge from the rain and were waiting for it to abate.

'Maybe you shouldn't have taken me on. It seems my paintings aren't exactly wowing the public.'

Olga frowned.

'It's been a while. People need time to remember who you were.'

Eduardo stared at his hands as though someone had just sewn them onto his wrists. At some point, a permanent disconnect had formed, a gulf separating his fingers from his brain, like a short circuit inside him.

'Wholesale portraits, that's my thing now, Olga. I get paid by the canvas, you sell them to department stores. That's my deal, I just produce them like churros on an assembly-line.'

For some reason, Olga was intent on trying to coax Eduardo back to a stage of his life he was never going back to.

'You've still got it, you still have the urge to create something important.'

That wasn't true. His time had passed. And the exhibition, showcasing older works that Olga had tracked down, was his swan song, his final moment of inspiration.

At the time he'd done these canvases, the top art critics had been so taken by the portraits. Everyone seemed to swoon over what they saw as a hot young talent, barely twenty years old and capable of producing such groundbreaking work. They swore they'd never seen anything like it. Claimed nothing about it was traditional, hand-me-down, derivative, copied. It was all part of some indecipherable personal mythos. In these paintings, Eduardo had laid himself bare in a way that seemed brazen — even the feverish titles of his works were proof of that. *Demiurge*: God, in an apartment on the Costa Brava, overlooking the Gulf of Rosas, slitting his wrists with a razor. *Hippocampus*: a cross-sectioned brain pinned open, laid out on a dish before a television set. *Zephyr*: a naked woman, in a distorted heap at the bottom of a cliff … They were disconcerting, almost as disconcerting as the attraction the public seemed to feel for them back then, stunned at the depth of his sorrowful depiction of the models, their visceral pain reproduced in broad charcoal strokes that were as thick as the darkness of their expressions, their contorted bodies, all intensely depressing and black as night. Everyone wanted to know where on earth that painter had come from.

Olga pointed to a small oil painting hanging in an out-of-the-way corner beneath a poorly illuminated arch: a woman hanging from a rope, eyes cast down at the chair she'd used to hang herself from a wooden beam. She looked desperate to put her feet back on the chair, repentant for what she'd just done. You could see the panic on her face, but it was too late. The painter refused to save her.

'I think that one's got a lot of promise. I'm going to try to sell it to an English art house. They find it quite suggestive. What do you think?'

Eduardo focused on the painting: it was dramatic — the predominant use of ochre tones added to the sense of drama, as did the depth of the woman's expression, the torque of her body. Emotions translated into irreversible acts by desperation and sorrow. A painting no one would ever buy.

'People still wonder why you suddenly just stopped painting. You haven't lost your exceptional talent; you have a phenomenal hand — so plastic, so exact. These paintings, the visions they capture, they're so beautiful that they're ...'

'Repulsive?' Eduardo finished the sentence for her, with resignation.

'Sometimes you really are a pain in the arse, you know that?'

'Yeah, I do.'

Olga pulled out a business card and showed it to Eduardo. It was printed on roughly textured, expensive paper, in a calligraphic font, with plenty of curlicues.

'I think I've got something that's going to be really good for you this time. A very important woman willing to pay what your talent merits. Interested?'

Eduardo nodded, but it was half-hearted. The truth of the matter was, he earned enough to get by just doing the commissions, and he had no further aspirations. He was assiduous, but not passionate, about doing what Olga asked of him; he delivered his canvasses on time and didn't charge too much — so one way or another he was muddling through.

He read the card: *Gloria A. Tagger*.

'Who is she?'

'Seriously? You don't know? Doesn't it even ring a bell?'

But she could tell from Eduardo's expression that he was in the dark on this one.

'Only one of the most prestigious violinists in the world. And she's married to Ian Mackenzie, the film director. You know, the guy who made *What Your Name Conceals*. Documentary about the post-World War II Jewish diaspora; they say it was inspired by his wife's life.'

'Sorry to say, classical is not my cup of tea. I'm quite happy with the record collection I have already. And as far as film goes, I've been out of circulation too long.'

Olga stared at him like he was an extraterrestrial.

'Gloria A. Tagger showed up at the gallery in person a couple of weeks ago. I was closing, but I offered to help her. I felt this force of attraction from the first moment; she walked into the gallery and suddenly she just commanded the entire space, you know what I mean? She's the kind of person who fills everything with her presence, without saying or doing a thing — an act of will, and class. You can tell she got used to having people admire her a long time ago. When I asked what she was looking for, so I could help point her in the right direction, she seemed a little disappointed, took a disinterested glace around and refused to have a seat or even take off her coat.'

'Did she at least buy something?'

'No. She'd actually come to see you — see your work, I mean. Asked specifically to see your most recent portraits and I showed her some that hadn't yet sold. She seemed to have an expert eye; examined them closely, though I was pretty sure she wasn't a professional. But she asked the right questions about technique, focus, then asked to see the photos of the actual models. Thirty minutes later, she told me she wanted to hire you.'

'Did you tell her I'm off the market?' Eduardo asked, adopting a sarcastic tone that did little to conceal the anxiety in his voice.

Olga's tight, frozen expression said that she'd been interrupted before she finished.

'This is someone who could give you a second chance, Eduardo. Ever since you got out of Huesca you've done nothing but drink and squander your talents on people who couldn't tell a Velázquez from a "Monkey's Anisette" poster. You can't carry on like this. It's gone on too long. Fourteen years is penance enough.'

Eduardo made no reply, simply gazed off at some vague point in the distance. And Olga didn't know how to read his hazy look.

'So what did she propose?' he finally asked, cautious.

'She didn't say, just that it was a portrait. I'm telling you the woman really dug her heels in, kept repeating you were the only one she would talk to. But she gave me her card, and I promised you'd go see her first thing in the morning.'

'Why would you make a promise you have no idea whether or not I'll keep?'

Olga smiled indulgently and raised both palms like a wall, fending off his predictable protests.

'Because she left you an advance, and it was pretty damn substantial.' She pulled an envelope from the pocket of her trousers and showed him the cheque, dangling it between two fingers. 'You know how much money this is? A shitload — and it's just the first advance.'

'You took her money? Why?'

'Because I told her that you were a good professional, and that, whatever it was she wanted, you'd be up to the task.'

'Then you lied.'

Olga leaned close and pressed her lips to Eduardo's jowly cheek. Cold lips that left an overly thick lipstick mark.

'No. I didn't. You're very good, and you're going to prove it to that filthy rich, high-society jezebel. And now, if you don't mind, I have to get to work,' she said, scooting away. A Japanese couple, obviously tourists, were in need of her attention and so off she went to talk to them about one of Eduardo's paintings.

He silently commended the couple on their good taste. They were examining *Strolling the Shore of Your Eyes*. It was, no doubt about it, a beautiful canvas, one in which Elena strolled along a beach, one that captured the sea breeze in the movement of her dress.

In his mind, he reached a hand out to stroke the memory of that August afternoon spent in Cadaqués: the north winds blew hard that day, hard enough to make walking on the beach problematic, and swimming any distance from the shore dangerous. The scent of wicker from the fruit basket blended in with that of lemons, espadrilles and the saltwater of the sea, as did the sound of the waves with the laughter of children playing ball games on the shore. After lying in the rocky cove, Elena strolled a few yards away, staring out at the ocean. She must have been lost in the horizon, trying to capture it in the silence, her often headstrong silence.

They could have gone on like that forever, Eduardo thought, watching her: immersed in their own easy silence, no friction, protected by the magnificent sun, the pine trees, the cove, their complicit quiet, each in their own world, feeling sheltered by the other. Naturally, that desire was impossible from its very conception, but still it was marvellous to contemplate.

'Eduardo? You okay?' Olga's voice was as corrosive as turpentine. He was standing at the door, hand on the knob, but hadn't yet managed to leave, his eyes glued to the lithograph, which still lay on the counter — but now the image of Elena had gone still once more, and the Japanese tourists had disappeared.

No. He wasn't okay — but he forced a smile before saying goodbye.

'I'll go see her tomorrow, but I'm not making any promises.'

He downshifted shortly before reaching the turnoff to the back road. Off to the right, beyond the shoulder, he could see an overturned truck, its tyres spinning in the air — the dust had not yet settled. The accident must have taken place just a few minutes earlier. If Eduardo had been driving any faster, he surely would have been involved in it. Coincidence had always played a decisive role in his life.

'What happened?' he asked the traffic cop.

'What — you can't see?' the officer replied grudgingly.

The truck had been transporting a load of hogs headed for the municipal slaughterhouse. When it overturned, they had gotten trapped in the tangled steel of the cages, or thrown out and crushed in the surrounding vicinity. The worst thing about it, though, was the sound of the squealing of those dying pigs. Their cries were atrocious, and they pierced Eduardo's brain like knives cutting right through his nerves.

'For the love of God, can't you shoot the poor animals and put them out of their misery?'

The cop eyed him, his face the picture of impotence.

'We have to wait for the company's vet to arrive. If we do it ourselves, we'll almost definitely be reported for destroying *merchandise*.'

'That's absurd.'

The man shrugged in defeat.

'We live in an absurd country.'

'How long is traffic going to be stopped?'

Now he glanced carelessly at his watch.

'Hour. Maybe two.' He may as well have said a month, a year.

Eduardo opened the glove compartment and pulled out a piece of paper, which he showed the officer.

'I'm looking for the Mayoral complex, a house on Calle Doctor Ochoa.'

The officer glanced at him with slight surprise, just a flutter of the eyelids that morphed into his enunciating more clearly, adopting a slightly more formal demeanour, suddenly straightening his shoulders, setting his chin. The rich always make the poor uneasy — and even though the guy didn't look like a banker, you could never tell.

'It's not far. If you take that dirt road, you can cut across a hill where you'll see a few holes from the golf course. When you get to the guard's booth they can tell you exactly where the street is. Thing is, you'll have to walk. That road's got sinkholes like you wouldn't believe and you'll never make it in that SUV. Either that, or you wait for traffic to get moving again — the turn-off to the complex is less than two kilometres away.'

Eduardo took stock of his patience: he couldn't stand the stench of burning flesh or the agonised shrieking of the pigs another minute.

'I'll leave the car at the turnoff and walk from there. Thanks.'

The cop nodded, looking up at the sky.

'You don't get a move on, you're going to get caught in a downpour.'

'I'll take my chances.'

He parked at the turnoff to a very steep dirt road and started to climb up, his breath coming in quick panting rasps, stopping every few feet to catch his breath again. He hadn't yet made it a third of the way when it started to rain. It began as intermittent drizzle, so Eduardo kept going, but within a few minutes, sheets of water were coming down so thick that it was hard — almost impossible — to see the road. Soaked clear through, with mud splattered all the way up to his teeth, he gave up on the idea that seeking refuge might do any good and simply kept walking, no longer in a hurry, both resigned and vexed. Filthy and drenched to the bone, he wasn't exactly going to make a great impression on this Gloria A. Tagger woman.

He almost didn't make it to the complex entry's high, red-ivy-covered fence. He looked around until he found a buzzer by the main gate, where a sign warned him how ferocious the guard dogs were. Hidden in the ivy was a tiny security camera — Eduardo saw its lens blink like a bionic eye, inspecting him.

'What do you want?' a metallic voice barked through the intercom.

'I'm here to see Mrs Gloria A. Tagger — she lives on Calle Doctor Ochoa.'

Eduardo was then subjected to harsh, relentless grilling as he stood there in the rain. He was ordered to give his first name, both surnames, national identification number, and a cursory explanation of how it was he'd managed to turn up in such a sorry state, with no vehicle of any sort. When the invisible guard seemed to feel he had enough details, he ordered Eduardo to wait. Didn't say how long, didn't say what for. And it didn't stop raining.

Fifteen minutes later a broad-hipped woman with strong arms appeared, under a huge black umbrella. Her sleeves were rolled up and she wore an apron that went almost down to her bootlegs.

'Are you the painter from Madrid?' She shouted to be heard above the rain. Eduardo nodded and the woman used a remote control to open the gate and then motioned for him to follow.

The entire complex was a huge, terraced golf course, complete with little bridges and artificial lakes, rolling green hills dotted with luxurious, modern mansions, each with their own stone wall. Atop one lone hill stood an old country manor. It wasn't hard to imagine that in another time it had been a farmhouse, and that what was now a golf course had originally been its fields. Perhaps the old owners had struck it rich, selling their land during the years of wild speculation.

The woman led Eduardo to a raked-gravel courtyard with a pool, its water overflowing, the rain beating down like a drum. Behind it he could see part of the facade and leaf-covered steps that led up to the front door, covered by a porch with several columns. In the pounding rain, the whole of it had a sort of ephemeral quality, like some sort of fantasy. The sound of drops falling was the only thing to pierce the silence, the only thing that made it seem real.

They walked in through an annex that looked as if it had once been a stable or pantry of some sort. It was cosy inside: a slow fire burned in a huge fireplace with soot-blackened walls, whistling as the bark of the cork-oak firewood expanded and burned, providing a much-welcomed warmth. A huge mirror over the mantelpiece multiplied both the space and Eduardo's pathetic reflection.

'I look dreadful,' he muttered.

The woman provided bold confirmation, nodding vigorously.

'You need to get those wet clothes off or you'll catch pneumonia. I'll bring you something to put on.'

Despite her instructions, Eduardo didn't dare undress once he was left alone. He simply placed his jacket on a wrought-iron footstool and inspected the room carefully. Five minutes later the woman was back with a clean towel, a pair of wool socks and some thick-soled hiking boots. She also brought him a thick blue woollen turtleneck and a pair of worn corduroy pants.

'What on earth are you waiting for? Do you want to freeze to death?' she scolded sharply. 'This should do. These are Señor Ian's clothes, but the Señora insists you put them on, he won't mind. I think they're going to be big, but there's no other option. Clean yourself up a little and get warm. There's a sink over on the right if you want to wash up, and don't worry about your clothes — I'll take care of those.'

Eduardo only had time to mutter a brief thanks. He inhaled the scent of clean clothes — worn but high quality, soft and pleasing to the touch — and washed his face in the stone sink before removing everything but his underwear. The clothes were too big, especially the pants, which were far too long — Ian must have been two full heads taller than him — but the sweater was comfortable, and when he pulled on the dry socks and boots he sighed in relief. Once he'd dressed slowly he sat down to wait.

After a few minutes the woman returned and scrutinised him carefully. Judging by her expression, Eduardo looked pretty funny in those borrowed clothes. What she said, however, was, 'That's better. The Señora is waiting for you upstairs. I'll take you.'

They traversed a large entrance hall with Toledan-style furniture; a few bronze sculptures stood waiting in corners, not having had places found for them yet. The walls were decorated with portraits, people with defiant faces, complicated, hard-to-decipher looks. They were done in faint, pale colours that gave them the impression of being spectres whose lives had been erased, with only their shadows remaining, imprisoned in those gold-leaf frames.

The woman took quick little steps, opening a series of doors that led to equally ragtag spaces. The more doorways they crossed, the more meaningless time became, as though clocks would be an unbearable blasphemy in such a place. It smelled stale, and sad. And it looked like a lifeless museum.

'Señora Tagger lives here?'

'They bought the house and land from a bankrupt developer several years ago. But they're gone most of the year so the house is closed up.'

Eduardo didn't ask any more questions — but he was thinking, *buying a house doesn't make you its owner*. A house has to be lived in to become a home, and that place definitely wasn't. What was the point of buying a house and filling it with art, if not to live in it? He assumed a woman like Gloria A. Tagger had to find a place that gave her meaning, a place that made things make sense.

Finally they came to a huge room. The woman motioned for him to wait there and then walked out, leaving the door ajar.

It was a comfortable room, nothing excessive about it. Atop a desk lay several scores of marked-up sheet music and a jar of coloured pencils. On the other side of the room was an enclosed area, made by a screen that was sealed on all four sides, creating a soundproof booth. Inside it was a window, a stool and a soundboard, several sound systems, speakers, and a computer screen. An ashtray was still smouldering, as if someone had been working there until just a moment earlier.

A large painting especially drew his attention. It wasn't an ordinary portrait but an oil painting depicting a scene that seemed to hint vaguely at some ambiguous form of violence. A woman stood facing a large window overlooking a garden in which only a few orange and myrtle branches could be glimpsed; her narrow eyes looked red, watery, utterly exhausted — perhaps as a result of the pregnancy suggested by the hand on her belly. Her husband gazed at her, priest-like, as if the woman's pregnancy was a sin to be purged, one that he was displeased by but had forgiven.

'Do you know that painting?' asked a voice behind him.

Eduardo turned.

He blinked as though dazzled by the sun. It took him a few seconds to realise that the woman standing behind him was the same one he'd seen in Parque de El Retiro. But — and this was the most surprising thing — though she looked the same, she seemed totally different — a distorted version, a different dimension.

She showed no signs of recognising him.

'I'm Gloria A. Tagger,' she said. 'Is something the matter? You've gone pale.'

'No, no. I'm fine.'

'Do you like it?' Gloria asked, gesturing nonchalantly at the painting, slowly approaching Eduardo until her shoulder brushed against him. She wore a charcoal grey rollneck sweater that was tight across the chest, giving her a sculpted appearance. From beneath her clothes emanated the scent of a quite a bit of delicate perfume. Although he couldn't put his finger on it, it aroused his senses. She was exceedingly thin and her fingers trembled, a cigarette dangling between them.

'*The Arnolfini Marriage*. Jan van Eyck. Flemish painting is certainly beautiful, no doubt, but it's never really moved me,' Eduardo confessed.

'I especially detest this painting in particular,' Gloria agreed, and her eyes zeroed in on Eduardo's somewhat perplexed face, as if X-raying his insides. That woman spoke through her eyes, her quick little blinks serving as punctuation.

'Maybe the reason you dislike it is because it doesn't transmit anything positive. Look at the woman: her life is a tragedy, a mediocre existence she fixates on; she's full of a desire to be free the way she once was, before she got pregnant perhaps. See the way she's gazing toward the garden just barely visible behind her husband? She lives trapped between those walls, hearing everyday sounds, the sounds of the world, but without taking part in them, cloistered like a nun, subjected to dreary routines — breakfast, toilette, bed; it must be unbearable. Now look at the husband: his expression is demented, perhaps he suspects the child is not his, that she cheated on him. He might almost be hatching plans, conceiving ways to make her pay for that affront. The rendering of each detail is so concise it's disturbing: the double-edged lace of the wife's headdress, the rings worn above her knuckles on the ring and index finger, the folds of the husband's black shirt, the clearly uncomfortable fur-lined frocks they both wear, the earthy opaque colours of the mystics, that cadaver-like stoicism on their faces that seems also to be suggestive.'

Gloria stared at Eduardo with ill-concealed admiration.

'Do you paint portraits or write them?'

Eduardo smiled.

'Maybe the brush and the pen are not so different as people think.'

Two plush armchairs sat by the window, between them a small table with a coffee pot, two cups and a small steaming pitcher of milk. Gloria invited him to take a seat.

Outside it was still raining, and the room itself was quite chilly although there must have been a radiator on somewhere. Gloria poured coffee and they both sat and drank it in silence. She smiled and was friendly enough — her manner cordial — but deep down she seemed not even to be present; it was as though her smile and expression were the hollow remains of a soulless presence, like the first time Eduardo had seen her sitting by the Crystal Palace.

'I hope you won't think me indiscreet, but — what happened to your leg?'

'Car accident.'

Gloria gave him a look that displayed no emotion whatsoever. For a moment her face remained alert, as though waiting for Eduardo to add something to those two words — words that were not untrue, but were certainly incomplete. And yet he said nothing more, and Gloria's face relaxed with a hint of disappointment.

'Does it still hurt?'

'Actually, yes it does, even though the doctors assure me it's just somatic pain.' He himself wasn't so sure. In theory the nerve endings were dead and he shouldn't be able to feel anything, but that wasn't the case. When he touched his scar he could almost reconnect to the same horrific pain he felt when it happened.

Gloria glanced briefly, wordlessly at Eduardo's hands resting on his knees. Then she carefully placed her coffee cup down on the side table, turned her beautiful head toward a small French bureau with a record player on it, and looked back to him once more.

'Do you mind if I put on some music? It helps me to think and relax.'

She removed a record from its dusk jacket with great care, holding it by the edges so as not to touch the grooves. Lowering needle onto vinyl, she

30

stood for a few seconds and watched it spin, her back to Eduardo until the first notes rang out and she confirmed with a nod that indeed the contraption was working. She turned down the volume and the melody was reduced to a low, pleasant background noise.

'Do you like this? It's *Bruch's Concerto for Violin in G minor, Opus 26.*'

Eduardo listened to a few bars, his eyes half-closed. It struck him as a deeply romantic yet happy melody.

Gloria passed him the dust jacket. A young girl was pictured on the cover, seated cross-legged on a bench, one hand resting on her thigh and holding a violin, the other absently fingering a fine gold necklace with a pendant.

'That's you.'

'Hm. Actually we're different people but we happen to share the same life, you know? The girl on the cover isn't me — it's just my body at a time when it belonged to a different Gloria, one twenty years younger. That was a special recording for the Budapest Orchestra. The truth is, I was twenty years old and had no business accepting the challenge — I wasn't prepared. But of course, nor was I prepared to admit I wasn't ready and act accordingly.'

'Classical music is not my strong suit, but I'd say this piece is superbly performed.'

Gloria smiled indulgently.

'Listen closer. In every creation, the artist leaves a piece of his or her soul. And if you search for mine here, you simply won't find it.'

Eduardo had a hard time getting into the depths of the piece, which at some points seemed solid as a rock and then turned almost liquid, like the drops of rain hitting the window. It began with an *allegro vivace*, then moved into a long interlude, and slowly, delicately faded out. But maybe he could, in fact, sense a slight irritation in the violinist — almost as though she didn't feel comfortable, or as though each bar, each measure were on the verge of exceeding her abilities, putting her to the test again and again. Still, the longer it went on, the less obvious the performer's hand became, seeming to grow more relaxed and to be swept away, the violinist losing awareness of herself until the piece ended.

Gloria took the record off with such care that she could have been handling a newborn. She gently wiped a cloth across the record's surface and slipped it back into its sleeve.

'Well?'

'I think I understand,' Eduardo said, watching Gloria roll a cigarette between her index and middle fingers. Each of her gestures seemed to contain something different to any other woman he'd ever met. It was like she was performing a dance that commanded the will of others.

'You do?' Gloria held out her exquisite fingers and contemplated them against the light, like appendages that had just appeared out of nowhere and might reach through the air to touch the melody. 'I earn my living through music, but I've never stopped feeling like an impostor; I appropriate that which does not belong to me and distort others' creations by infusing them with my own desires. I've never composed a single score in my life.'

'My art dealer told me you were interested in commissioning me for something special.'

'*Something special*. That's certainly one way to put it.'

'I saw the advance you left. That's a lot of money — and I have a feeling you knew when you left that cheque that I'm no longer a professional painter.'

'Yes, I know.'

'So, if you know I'm no longer sought after, what do you want from me?'

Gloria didn't reply, at least not with words. Instead she simply gave Eduardo a calm, piercing, silent look. Then she got up, opened a dresser drawer and took out a recent photo. She gazed at it for a moment and her eyes shone.

'This is my son. What do you think?'

Eduardo examined the photograph, which she held out to him.

Most people are inhibited in front of the camera, their faces turning mummy-like, hard as a shell reflecting the light; or they ham it up, flashing ridiculous, infantile smiles. Either way, they look fake, forced. But the boy in this photo was different. Though not as beautiful as his mother, he gave off an air of certainty that made the camera fall in love with him. There was a clearly visible tension in the photo, a battle being waged between lens and subject, a struggle to see who would overpower whom. And from that tension emerged the image of a young man with brown hair, far thinner than looked healthy with something ungainly

32

about him — gangly, as if his body had grown disproportionately, with long arms and bony legs. He was wearing a khaki-coloured duffel coat with a frayed collar and a Dire Straits *Walk of Life* patch on the right shoulder, worn jeans, with cheek bones as prominent as mountain peaks, and so little facial hair that it could never be considered an actual beard, no matter how long he went without shaving.

'He's certainly a good looking kid.'

Gloria took the picture back and her pupils flickered, like a flame reflected on glass.

'He was seventeen, and brilliant. He had a promising future. My son died four years ago.'

Four years ago, the news on the radio warned drivers near Plaza de Oriente that several streets had been closed to traffic due to a horrific accident; a Mercedes had ploughed straight into the window of a boutique specialising in wedding attire. City police prevented traffic from circulating so that ambulances and fire trucks could get through. The driver, who'd caused the accident, reeked of alcohol. He seemed dazed and was bleeding profusely from a gash on his forehead, but his condition was stable. A fireman used heavy-duty hydraulic rescue cutters to saw through the car roof and a SAMUR emergency services doctor carefully placed a neck brace around him, cradling his head as though it were a priceless porcelain vase from the Ming dynasty, or a vial of nitroglycerine. The top half of a mannequin dressed in groom's attire was jutting out of the window display, its head broken, contorted awkwardly down on his shoulder, wig on the ground. From a distance it all looked very real. There were clothes everywhere: on the hood of the car, in puddles on the sidewalk. Wedding dresses, shiny vests with upholstered buttons, delicately pleated trousers, jackets with backstitching yet to be sewn.

Two feet could be seen sticking out from beneath the car. One was missing a shoe, a bare foot becoming soaked in the rain. The car had struck the person, crushing him between the bodywork and the shopfront. It was a young man, who was now attempting to say something as he stared at the driver being stretchered off to an ambulance — but all he managed was to spit bloody bubbles.

A few metres from the scene, a city policeman knelt in the middle of a crosswalk over a small figure, lying face-up. The officer's body blocked the view, making it impossible for onlookers to determine what the shape even was. From a distance it could have been a medium-sized dog. But no cop would give a dog mouth-to-mouth, or attempt desperately to restart its heart with cardiac massage. Several witnesses' hands flew to their mouths in dismay when the officer, visibly distraught, finally gave up and called for a thermal rescue blanket with which to cover the body. A sudden gust of wind lifted the blanket for a moment, revealing the pale face — peaceful as could be, no signs of violence — of a girl barely six years old, who looked merely to be asleep.

A medical team transferred the body of the trapped young man to an ambulance. On the ground were a brownish pool of blood, and a torn shoe.

Someone asked if the boy's condition was serious. He was dead, was the reply, like the girl.

Both of them, dead.

When Gloria received the news over the phone, she politely thanked the police, her voice not reflecting what she'd just been told, as if she hadn't quite understood, but was afraid to ask for details. She remained seated on the edge of the bed, staring vacantly at the night-table phone before finally placing the receiver — its dial tone now buzzing — back in the cradle. Her gaze, stunned and disconcerted, came to rest on a fruit basket on the kitchen table, visible through the half-open bedroom door. She went to the window, perplexed because her entire body had suddenly begun trembling, because it was nearly impossible to remain standing, as if all at once her bones had suddenly shattered. She contemplated the pedestrianised street, the people walking up and down, the sounds of distant traffic, the overcast sky, the roofs shimmering in the rain. Just another day, like any other day. And suddenly everything pained her terribly. Absolutely everything.

'Losing a child is like having a limb amputated, a vital part of you. It's no longer there, but it keeps hurting as if it were still part of you. Like the somatic pain in your knee's nerve endings; you feel it, even though they're dead. I'm sure you know what I'm talking about.'

Gloria measured the effect her words had on Eduardo, and allowed them to sink in, let him process what she'd said and then wither.

Eduardo got the feeling that she was very far away, and that no matter what happened he'd never get much closer to her than he was right now. Two lonely people colliding for a brief moment, only to grow distant once more. Though it was absurd, the intuition saddened him.

'I'm so sorry.'

Gloria closed her eyes, and when she opened them again it was as though an explosion had occurred inside her at that precise moment.

'You're *sorry*? Is that all you have to say, Eduardo?'

'What else can I say?'

Suddenly Gloria's expression grew sharp as flint.

'Honestly, I didn't think I'd have to explain it to you.'

'What are you talking about?'

'I've done some investigating. You lost your wife and daughter fourteen years ago in a car accident, too. You and I are both living corpses. That's why I asked you to come. That's why I want to hire you to do a portrait, a portrait that only you can paint.'

Eduardo grew pale and stroked the back of his neck.

'Trying to do an honest portrait of a person who's no longer here is like painting a landscape you remember from the past. It's not the landscape, just a mirage distorted by memory.'

Gloria went to another drawer and pulled out a newspaper clipping, from a financial paper, four years old. It showed the photo of a handsome executive with broad shoulders and a mass of red hair.

'It's not my son that I want you to paint. It's his killer.'

3

Arthur had taped a photograph taken on his honeymoon beside the metal headboard of his prison-cell cot. A young couple in love, arm in arm, smiling with the glee exclusive to those who believed in the wiles of the heart, at a time when happiness was a world open to hope, to the future.

The future: something that had ended before it ever arrived.

Arthur at twenty-five — tall, determined, a mane of red hair whipping in the wind, his quartz-like eyes peeking out from beneath long wisps. And Andrea, nearly ten years older — though age had not yet erected a barrier between them — her head thrown back, laughing at something Arthur could no longer recall. He was funny back then, he knew how to make her laugh, feel good. She clung tightly to his arm to keep from falling over with the giddiness of what must have seemed to them both like a dream.

The future: feelings that develop, atrophy, oscillate.

Arthur wondered what feelings he might still have for his wife. That joyful snapshot told nothing of the secrets a lover hides from his beloved, the things he never shared with her. Not everything can be shared, there are always private worlds that no other human can penetrate. In the end, theirs was a relationship that survived by virtue of the periodic distances between them, and of silence. Without Aroha — the one thing that united them — their relationship had finally broken.

In the background stood Algiers *la blanche*, the glimmering buildings of the Kasbah rising up, overlooking the sea. The Mediterranean, by contrast, looked almost indigo blue. Arthur missed the hibiscuses, the rose bushes, the magnolias of his house in Bab el Oued, with its whitewashed facade and wooden shutters painted blue. It was small and uncomfortable, but it had gorgeous views over part of the port, on a promontory, and out back there was a lovely spot by a eucalyptus where he spent hours just reading and writing poetry. Or not doing anything at all, simply leaning against the tree trunk for ages, absently gazing out. If someone interrupted him he'd turn with a jolt, a look so disconcerted and lonesome it was startling.

Arthur was not an easy man to understand. He had a permanently helpless air, as though having been the youngest of four siblings left to fend for themselves — no one worrying about them or playing with them — had scarred him. His thick wild hair, including red eyebrows and the hint of beard peeking out on his chin, he'd inherited from his father, a man he barely remembered. But his father's looks — he was almost the spitting image, in fact — were not the only thing he'd inherited from the man. He'd gotten his character, too.

Arthur was a *pied-noir*, a European born in Algeria just a few months before the Évian Accords, under which De Gaulle granted Algeria independence from France and put the National Liberation Front in power. His father — a Frenchman of Spanish origin — had seen it as an unforgivable betrayal. Arthur's grandparents had moved to France in mid-1938, fleeing Franco's army when the Second Spanish Republic fell. And Luis Fernández, his father, had been born in Algiers, where he celebrated the liberation of Paris with a French flag in one hand and a Spanish flag in the other. His father had had the privilege of being the first to reach the Champs-Élysées, in a tank called the 'Guadalajara', manned entirely by Spaniards.

Years later, as a lieutenant with General Massu's paratroopers, he'd been on the front line in the Battle of Algiers in 1956 and 1957 — a dirty guerrilla war in which the National Liberation Front carried out terrorist attacks on civilians and military alike, and General Massu and his men responded in kind, meting out torture and summary executions that forever changed his father's character. When De Gaulle handed over the 'province' (for his father, as for many French, Algeria was not seen as a protectorate like Morocco but another province of the Fifth Republic), Lieutenant Fernández joined the OAS insurrectionists, went underground and fought for General Salan.

Arthur recalled his childhood, running barefoot through the labyrinthine streets of the Kasbah, past the three clock towers, the fruit stands and stalls of Triad market, and the doorways of the Palace of the Dey; his escapades in and around the old artificial port where merchants flew French flags and supplied the city each day. Every place he went, despite the fact that he had been born in an independent Algeria, the OAS's initials could be seen, and for years it was not uncommon to see a mule, loaded with explosives, blow up in the middle of a crowded area; for a seemingly random pedestrian to be murdered right in Plaza de los Mártires, a bullet to the back of the head, by dissidents — militiamen like his father, or one of the Corsican hired-assassins or mafia men employed by the government to get rid of the much-feared *barbouzes*. Arthur recalled seeing a civil servant killed in a drive-by shooting, machine-gunned down on his way back from the main post office, lying in a heap by the minaret of Jamaa el Jedid mosque. Before he died, the man had used his own blood to write on the mosque's immaculately white wall: *France will never abandon her children*. Maybe France would not, but Arthur's father had, leaving his family defenceless and destitute. In 1964, when Arthur was barely two years old, his father was arrested by police and extradited to France to serve a prison sentence, convicted of terrorism.

Arthur never saw him again.

Years later, on honeymoon with Andrea, back at the old house in Bab el Oued, Arthur visited that mosque. Algiers had changed a lot — the port had grown, the old town of Kouba had been swallowed up with the city's expansion, and everywhere he looked, residential communities, villas, and new homes had sprung up. His old neighbourhood went from the Kasbah to beyond the river port, and although some of the old colonial style remained, most of its charm had been lost once it became the capital's most *chouchouté,* or upmarket, neighbourhood. The mosque had undergone renovations, the boulevard was now full of lush floral arrangements, fountains and tall palm trees. Other graffiti — recent graffiti, which workers rushed to cover with a thick layer of whitewash — had superseded the civil servant's blood, on the wall of the mosque. The enemy was no longer the OAS but Al-Qaeda in the Islamic Maghreb, or any another terrorist group. The names and the blood splattered on the wall changed, but Algeria was still bleeding, as always.

At the same time, though, it was a country full of opportunities for those who knew how to take advantage of them — and he'd known exactly how to do it.

Arthur had gotten rich in the oil and gas industry. Algiers was now a city of entrepreneurs, five-star hotels, and the Lycée Français; friends sent their kids to Turkish schools, Egyptian schools, Saudi schools; nightlife was teeming with private cabarets and clubs whose doors were guarded by off-duty policemen who earned extra income by moonlighting as bodyguards or part-time chauffeurs; there were private beaches at Club de Pins and the Moretti. There were huge receptions full of important men asking Arthur for favours, women trying to seduce him, and lots of riding around in convertibles. A place to get caught up in it all, to have fun.

To Arthur's cellmate, however, it was a very different city. Ibrahim listened incredulously to Arthur talk about the wonders of Algiers. He was Algerian, too, and that prompted a degree of complicity between them, but Ibrahim had been born in Annaba, a world apart from the executives of Algiers. The city he knew was one of industrial blight that had expanded, devouring old towns and neighbourhoods while simultaneously allowing centuries-old homes in the historic centre to be torn down, forsaken to the will of speculators while the rich moved out to the suburbs of El Sahel. A sad city, chaotic and at the same time nostalgic. But also the city of *bouqalate,* a sort of game in which girls recited improvised verses in a call-and-response — and of *chaabi* music, of old men in Dar el Djirane exchanging proverbs as a game. Ibrahim's father had been one of the greatest living Turkish *ney* reed-flute players. His fame throughout the Arab world had once rivaled that of any Western pop star. Sometimes, from their cell in the afternoons, they could hear the *ney* — the most important component of Mevlevi Sufi sacred music — being played, in recordings that filled the silent hall with their sound, bringing heartrending tears to the eyes of even the hardest man in prison.

From amid that mishmash of contradictions, the two men had formed something akin to a friendship. Arthur did not belong in jail. He was just passing through, and that was obvious in everything he did and said on the inside. He knew the rules, and obeyed them always, but he made no attempt to curry favour with the guards or other prisoners. Diana, the person he most trusted, was on the outside, working hard for his release; it was simply a question of holding out a little longer and not getting himself into trouble. The lawyer she'd hired for the appeal had told him that a pardon would be granted in a matter of weeks. It wasn't long, but after three seemingly endless years, each additional minute seemed like an eternity.

Ibrahim was his only form of support. An old scar ran the length of the man's entire face, splitting his left eye in two and giving him a terrifying look completely at odds with his demeanour, which was always discreet, impeccable. Ibrahim was one of the few men who, rather than fear, commanded the inmates' respect. Arthur admired him. And as long as they didn't discuss politics, Ibrahim protected him from the other prisoners. He didn't ask for anything in exchange, he did it for a reason only he could comprehend.

'You need to get back to your wife,' he'd respond laconically whenever Arthur asked him why he helped him so much.

Still, Ibrahim's domain was not extensive enough to keep Arthur safe from all evil.

In the cafeteria that night, Ibrahim barely lifted his head from his plate. They were having zucchini soup, and a dish made of some sort of fowl in thick, flavourful sauce. Arthur ate heartily, but Ibrahim drank only water, watching in disgust as the other prisoners at the table wiped their plates clean.

'You haven't said a word, and haven't even tasted your food. What's going on inside your head?' Arthur asked.

Ibrahim smiled faintly, exposing a rotted, gaping hole in his gums between two yellowed teeth whose days looked numbered. He had the teeth of a pirate and didn't often smile; when he did, he looked doubly fearsome.

'The older one gets, the less one eats, sleeps and, worst of all, lives. Music is the only form of pleasure left to the old, and even that drifts slowly from our grasp.'

Despite his words, Ibrahim was far from the helpless, pathetic figure he pretended to be. Though nearing sixty, he was agile, sinewy, his body hard as bamboo. No one knew much about him, but there were plenty of rumours and stories that people neither bothered to corroborate nor disprove; of course that served only to increase the air of mystery surrounding him. He was seen as easygoing, had no vices, was almost ascetic in fact; and on the prison yard, he mixed little with the other inmates, never getting into trouble. Nevertheless, Arthur had seen him fight in the showers. A younger prisoner had once tried to stab him with a homemade blade after some dispute over prison code.

Perhaps the young man had taken offense at a slight or a look, something that would hardly have registered on the outside — but in prison everything was overstated, extreme. More than likely the kid was trying to move up the ladder by challenging Ibrahim, who was both respected and also old, and that may have made him seem like easy prey. It didn't take long for the kid to see that it was a fatal mistake: Ibrahim disarmed him with his bare hands with astonishing ease, downing the guy with a sharp knee to the balls, and then smashed his face repeatedly into the cement floor until all those present saw several of the poor man's teeth go flying. Ibrahim could easily have killed him in cold blood, on the spot — and if he didn't, it wasn't because someone had stepped in to intervene, but because he simply decided not to.

That night in the dining room, Ibrahim was only half-listening to Arthur. The rest of his attention was divided among the people and objects surrounding him; he looked a bit like a prowler with no clear objective. Suddenly he struggled to his feet, resting his hands on his knees. He tottered unstably and Arthur thought he was about to lose his balance, but he managed to straighten out. Ibrahim liked to pretend he was defenceless.

'You better get ready; the Armenian's here,' he said under his breath, leaning over Arthur's ear. His breath stank of rotting gums.

Arthur shot a quick glance to the other side of the cafeteria.

'There are a lot of them.'

Ibrahim nodded. He took a quick count of the men before him and calculated that their chances of making it out of the small dining room unscathed were slim indeed, if the Armenian's thugs decided to attack. Inconspicuously, he reached down to touch the familiar grip of the handmade blade he'd fashioned in his cell, the one he kept — always — tucked inside his pants. It wasn't much, but maybe if he managed to really slice up the first few, the others would retreat, giving them a chance to escape. He knew how to use a knife. Knew the way you had to twist the handle, making circular motions in order to lacerate the flesh without tearing it too much. Knew it because he'd experimented on his own skin. His memories of childhood were filled with the screams to prove it. Remembering those cries, his muscles flexed, preparing for the fight.

The Armenian sat regally among his men, like an evil-eyed Caesar protected by a cohort of Praetorian Guards. From up close the man actually looked somewhat harmless. Rail-thin, his tendons stuck out like thick cords connecting muscle to bone, and his head was always shaved and bare. He used little reading glasses that were invariably tucked into a shirt pocket, and though he wasn't especially tall, nor was he noticeably short. The Armenian was known for being slow, deliberate, a lover of the finer pleasures. Some thought those little conceits were explained by age; others swore he'd always loved being served and pampered. There were also those who disdained his custom — an open secret — of 'protecting' young new arrivals who happened to be handsome; the protection he provided was not free, of course: the boys paid for it by becoming his private prostitutes. Word was, though this was only ever whispered, that he'd become an old satyr, disgusting even to himself but generous to his ever-younger lovers. The entire prison was controlled at his whim — and he absolutely despised Arthur.

The man had a debt outstanding, and he'd sworn to take Arthur's life as payment.

Ibrahim's presence, though, made him cautious. Nothing transpired that night, nor those that followed either.

Arthur wanted very badly to convince himself that the danger had passed.

'Maybe he's decided to forget,' he ventured.

'And the Arabian Sea is about to dry up,' said Ibrahim, disabusing him of that fantasy. 'You killed his daughter, a six-year-old girl. If it were my daughter I'd never forget the man who did that, not even if he was dead, not in a thousand lifetimes.'

Arthur was sorrier about that death than anything else on earth. He relived it again and again. But he couldn't go back and change what was already done.

'It was an accident, and I'm paying for it.'

Ibrahim scrutinised him, taking in every detail. Sometimes he looked like nothing could escape him. Slowly he stroked the deep gash in his cheek, as though exploring it. He'd never spoken about how it happened.

'Fate is an excuse, Arthur. It doesn't change the fact that we live with our mistakes because we, and no one else, are the ones who made them. And regardless, the fact that you didn't do what you did on purpose is not enough in the Armenian's eyes. Sooner or later he'll come after you.'

'I was drunk. It was raining. I lost control of the car.'

Ibrahim's expression altered slightly. It might have looked scornful, but in fact he was simply fed up. His eyes instinctively sought the photo Arthur had taped to his headboard. He contemplated Andrea at length, his eyes softening before they closed. *Destiny has a strange sense of humour,* he thought, evading answering Arthur.

Aside from haunting memories, the stars were the only consolation they had inside those walls. Looking up, when your feet were dragging, was a marvellous thing. They liked to sit and share a smoke, gazing out their window at the little patch of sky above the barred and fenced cellblock, contemplating the almost violent beauty of the stars twinkling above their heads. When confronted with the grandeur of creation, human pettiness, regret, even the most heinous of crimes seem meaningless. All of those things matter little when you realise that it all comes down to a series of chain reactions, sunspots, novas, icy meteorites, minerals, atoms, energy, matter and antimatter. We all form part of the universe. There is no love, no hate, no emotion, no feeling or predetermination in our existence. We're nothing but a coincidence that might never have happened, an improbable mathematical projection.

That was how Arthur passed the time, discussing things and chatting with Ibrahim, reading poetry, on the lookout for any movement of the Armenian's men, taking refuge in his memories, awaiting news from the lawyers Diana had hired to get him out of there. In the meantime, he curled up with his notebooks.

During what had so far been three years of captivity, he'd started writing again. It was hard at first, like turning on a tap that hasn't been used for years and waiting impatiently for the water to flow, when all that trickles out are a few drops; likewise, his first verses were awkwardly constructed, with unclear images, and then little by little the old spirit returned to his mind and the wheels of poetry began turning once more — first timidly, and then with increasing courage. After a few weeks, the young poet whose life Arthur had too soon cut short emerged from the ashes. He struggled to satisfy his hunger with what was available in the prison library, so he had part of his personal collection brought in, savouring especially the poetry of Rimbaud.

Ibrahim observed that slow, silent invasion of space, overtaken by an army of books and notebooks, with a faintly disconcerted smile.

'I'd never have guessed you were such a poet,' he admitted.

Arthur nodded.

'In one way or another, we all carry within us the totality of all men. Why we allow some to thrive and kill off the others is an unsolved mystery.'

Finally he got word. The request for pardon his lawyers had lodged with the Ministry of Justice was being processed by the Council of Ministers, but in order for it to be ruled upon they were requesting a hearing.

Before leaving the cell, Arthur perfunctorily adjusted the knot of his tie, sneaking a look at his reflection in the window. He felt strange in those clothes, after so long. The stiff collar of his shirt rubbed against the stubble at his Adam's apple, and he felt the weight of the jacket on his hunched shoulders. He'd decided to wear a good suit, even though his lawyer had advised against it — especially the tie. 'It projects an air of arrogance, and that's one thing judges and prosecutors do *not* like.' The lawyer had also asked him not to shave that morning. Bags under his eyes and the grey growing in on a three-day beard would help make him look vulnerable, distraught, as though he'd spent the night tossing and turning, worried about his immediate future. Arthur had refused to follow any of that advice. He flicked an inexistent speck of dust from his lapel with the back of his right hand, and for a moment his eyes rested on the white-gold band on his ring finger.

He looked like a different person. Everyone looked different. But they were all still the same, and that must have given him the courage he needed as he held the metal door handle, momentarily unable to turn it.

'It's going to go well,' said Ibrahim. He'd helped him dress and was now calming his nerves.

'You think so?'

The Muslim man nodded, displaying his gum disease.

'Of course. It always goes well for the rich, and you're rich, right? Well then, nothing to worry about.'

Arthur embraced Ibrahim.

'You're a real friend.'

Ibrahim made no reply, but his hooded look did it for him. He diverted his attention to the half-open cell door.

'You have to make a good impression on the outside.'

His court appearance had been scheduled for eleven o'clock, but the transfer was taking place more than an hour ahead of schedule to avoid his being mobbed by the press.

'This isn't going to be easy,' his attorney warned him, already gowned. His prominent cheekbones stretched the pale skin on his face taut, giving him the air of an edgy anorexic. The man was constantly flicking his hair back with a nervous gesture, jiggling his expensive watch as though it were a bell bracelet. Lefthanded, he wrote with a gold pen, and exuded a subtle lemon scent with the faintest hint of coffee and blonde tobacco. He spoke slowly, enunciating carefully as though he were at a business meeting, going over each agenda item one by one. He had them all written down in his planner and followed the list with the tip of his pen as he spoke.

'That's what you're getting paid for, to *make it* easy,' Arthur replied. The lawyer's affected mannerisms and excessive theatricality annoyed him.

'The fact that the deceased were both so young — especially the girl — goes against you, Señor Fernández. What's more, just today I was informed that the boy's mother's lawyers lodged an objection to the pardon. The mother is asking that you serve your entire sentence.' He periodically glanced at Arthur over his stylish glasses, to ensure his client understood what he was trying to say. He wasn't really seeing him. Arthur was just an object, a problem to be solved in the most brilliant way possible.

Arthur tightened his jaw.

'So what do I have going for me?'

The attorney cleared his throat.

'To begin with, the fact that I'm defending you. With a little luck, I'll get the judge to impose some precautionary measures and you'll be able to leave prison until the final ruling is issued. As shocking as the case is, these were indeed accidental deaths — involuntary manslaughter — and you've served three quarters of your sentence.'

The lawyer tossed his head for the nth time, forcing his wayward hair into place, and gave a little shrug, as if he'd forgotten one minor detail.

'Another thing that might play in your favour is mentioning the Aroha situation — only if it's strictly necessary, of course.'

'Not a chance,' Arthur whispered, eyes boring into the attorney. 'I thought I made that very clear. My daughter is off limits.'

The lawyer gave Arthur a disconcerted look, as though he didn't understand why the man was unnecessarily complicating the situation.

'Listen, you want to get off, right? That's why you're paying my firm's retainer, which isn't cheap, and that's why they asked me to represent you here today. The judge might need to be reminded of your pre-existing circumstances, of what led to the fateful day of the accident.'

'Forget it. End of subject,' Arthur repeated, unyielding.

The lawyer shook his head in resignation. *Whatever*, his expression seemed to say.

The courtroom was small, with creaky wooden floors and a long prefab table at which sat the judge, prosecutor, and a court clerk. To the left a young woman was taking notes and consulting a small red book that must have been the penal code. She was the lawyer involved in the private suit being brought by Gloria A. Tagger, the dead boy's mother. Representing the six-year-old girl, Rebeca, who had also died in the accident, there was no one. Her father, the Armenian, had sent the judge a letter stating that he didn't believe in the justice of the state, he believed in his own justice. And one way or another, he was going to see that it was served.

At an identical table sat Arthur's lawyer and an intern, whispering something into his ear and casting glances around like a conspirator. They were all wearing the long black gowns designed to instill fear or imbue authority, or both. On the wall before them hung a picture of the king formally opening the judicial year, and two flags. It was all clinical, silent, procedural. There was almost no one in the public gallery: a couple of kids who might have been law school students, spiral notebooks at the ready so as not to miss a single detail of the show.

The hearing began, opening statements were heard, and when it was Arthur's lawyer's turn, he addressed the judge with a somewhat condescending smile. He removed his glasses slowly, with exaggerated theatricality, and tut-tutted, looking annoyed.

'My client was sentenced to four-and-a-half years for the deaths of Ian Mackenzie Tagger and Luján Montes, and has already served well over half that time, with favourable recommendations from the parole board.

He has paid the millions imposed as compensation to both of the families affected by the tragic fatal accident, which he caused and for which he was charged with involuntary manslaughter on 18 January 2001. My client is a respected member of society, a well-known entrepreneur with no prior convictions. He has a permanent address and sufficient funds to meet any guarantee this tribunal might require — whether handing over his passport, paying any bail the court might set, or accepting other control measures imposed upon him. My client has most definitely, profusely and publicly, made known the remorse he feels. For all these reasons — bearing his personal circumstances in mind — it is our consideration that his appeal for pardon be granted by the Ministry of Justice. Thank you.'

After this statement came others, for and against. Expert opinions were given — findings presented by psychiatrists and psychologists — and guarantees of further compensation to the families of the deceased. The court noted the objections made by the lawyers for the family opposed to granting a pardon, then came a recess and the closing statements. Both sides spoke in legalese, which was like a monotonous drone, the words enunciated with zero emphasis by either party. No one cared about anything but the fastidious following of procedure.

Arthur closed his eyes, trying to escape. He didn't feel nervous, nor was he heavy-hearted. Sitting there on the wooden bench between the two police officers guarding him, he got the impression that nothing happening there had anything to do with him. It was as if, despite being the protagonist of the whole event, the bit players had stolen the show, discarding him, and the final outcome didn't depend on him in the slightest. He gazed at the photos the experts had taken the day of the accident, numbered and pinned on a corkboard, which an officer had wheeled in and positioned so that everyone could see. Specialists spoke of mathematical formulas, calculating trajectories and braking distances, offering hypotheses and numbers that some then refuted and others confirmed, depending on their need to demonstrate his guilt or innocence.

None of it had anything to do with him. None of them was even close to understanding what had truly happened that rainy morning.

Two hours later, the hearing was over, the ruling made.

Arthur's lawyer smiled on the way out, as though the two of them had just enjoyed a picnic on the beach together.

'That went well. If I were you, I'd start packing my bags.'

He was trying to be funny, but the glint in Arthur's eyes froze his smile.

'Why are you so happy, counsellor? I killed two people, and now they're going to set me free. Isn't the idea that people go into law because they believe in the justice system?'

'Exactly. I do believe in the system. It was an accident. You were drunk, it was raining hard, and the street was in a terrible condition. Those kids started crossing the street before the light at the crosswalk had turned green. It was all a series of unfortunate coincidences that resulted in tragedy.'

'Is that the conclusion you've come to, after all your reflections?' Arthur asked sarcastically, pointing to the attorney's planner. 'I read the appeal, there's no need to parrot it back to me. I'm not the judge so you don't have to keep playing your role on my account. Come on, you can do better than that. You think you can walk in here with a holier-than-thou air like you're above good and evil and *absolve me of my sins* just because you questioned me a couple of times?'

He could see his attorney was growing increasingly uncomfortable.

'I'm not judging you. That's what the judge does. I acted impartially.'

'You don't have a fucking clue.'

'There's no need to be vulgar, Arthur.'

'Oh, yes, there is. It's the only civilised thing I can do.'

His last few nights in jail, Arthur could hardly sleep. Every minute of every hour was like a re-enactment of those other nights — the terrible ones when he thought it would never end. He talked and smoked with Ibrahim, bestowing guilt-ridden affection upon him, tainted by the evidence that Ibrahim's words were true: Arthur's money and influence were indeed getting him out of there much sooner than the wheels of justice would ever turn for his cellmate. They never brought up the reasons they were in prison, never tried to proclaim their innocence or guilt. On the inside, certain things were simply not talked about — and when they were released those same things would lose all meaning, so there was no need to express them verbally to begin with.

Dawn often took him by surprise, having lain awake all night. And that particular morning — red clouds in the distance — was going to be stormy. The floodlights on the perimeter wall were trained on the empty prison yard and benches lining the wall. A cat prowled the ledge slowly, knowing it was still his domain for a little while longer. To the right, casting his flashlight back and forth, was the swaying silhouette of the guard on duty. There was one hour left until the siren would blare and the world of artificial serenity would vanish into thin air. Other sounds, the everyday sounds that slowly enveloped him, gave it all an air of normality: the clanging of gates on the cellblock, the orderly's footsteps, the coughing of prisoners in nearby cells … even the sound of a transistor radio filtering under the metal door like a distant murmur.

Arthur sat on the edge of the cot and placed his bare feet on the green cement floor. Someone must have thought that painting in that colour would make it seem like a meadow. The ground was cold. Ibrahim's body was barely visible in the dark, an arm wrapped around his pillow. Arthur heard him sigh before turning over and going back to sleep, and he took advantage of the solitude that afforded him to write a letter.

He'd been contemplating it for days, and the need he felt to write it had intensified when he found out he was going to be freed. Common sense told him that whatever words he might scribble were uncalled for, might even be counterproductive. It makes no sense to stir things up once the dust has settled, unless you want the dust to rise once more. He had no desire to reopen wounds that hadn't even scarred over. So what was it that he was trying to do? He himself was unsure of his intentions, as he leaned toward the window to capture what little light he could from the weak glow of the searchlights and put pen to paper. He could have done it after he was out of jail — but by then the impulse would have faded. He had to do it there, between those four walls, by the barred window, with the smell of incarceration permeating their sheets, their clothes, their skin; he had to do it before it all faded away, vanishing as if it had never occurred.

He wrote for twenty minutes, hardly even pausing to consider his words, simply transferring them onto paper as they gurgled forth chaotically, like haemorrhaging blood.

When he was done he felt no better. He slipped the paper into an envelope and collapsed onto his cot, eyes open. He could still get an hour's sleep.

But something made him sit up. He heard the metallic sound of the bolt in the cell door sliding back.

Arthur turned to the small square of light on the floor and suddenly knew that something was wrong. This was not the time for a headcount, and even if that's what it was, no guard showed up inside a cell without announcing his arrival. Silently, he woke Ibrahim and pointed to the door. In the crack of light coming in, they could see someone's shadow.

Slowly, cautiously, as though attempting not to be heard, the intruder pushed the metal door ajar. The enormous figure in the doorway, its shadow projected onto the cot, was certainly not a guard: guards aren't skinheads, guards don't have spiderweb tattoos on their faces. The man held something in his right hand — an icepick or sharpened piece of glass. He must have been thrown off by seeing his target standing there before him, and that brief moment of hesitation was enough to allow Arthur to dodge the man's first thrust. After lunging at the air, his attacker froze for a split second.

This fleeting moment of hesitation allowed Arthur to reach the man's side and, before he had a chance to react, punch him in the kidneys — hard. Like some surreal scene out of a silent movie, the attacker's hands flew to his side and he opened his mouth wide in a silent howl. A blow like that would have felled a normal man, but the giant wasn't about to submit. He clenched his teeth and charged Arthur, pinning him to the wall. Arthur was bigger than most of the other inmates in the cellblock but looked a wimp compared to this guy. He pummelled the man's head, punching his ears and trying to jam his fingers into his eyes, but it did nothing to diminish the strength and impact of this brute, who was grunting like a wounded boar, thrusting his blade at Arthur's face as Arthur tried desperately to dodge him.

And then, suddenly, his attacker opened his eyes wide, his pupils dilating as if something inside him had exploded. He gurgled briefly and spat a sludgy clump of blood onto Arthur's face before collapsing sideways, lifeless on the floor. From the other side of the cell, Ibrahim watched the slow death rattle wrack the man's body, an icepick sticking out of his neck. Ibrahim trembled with the exertion of that thrust still coursing through the muscles in his neck. He wiped bloodstained fingers across his face — for a moment making the dry hollow of his scar look like a crimson river — and crouched beside the body to check his vitals.

'Is he dead?' Arthur asked, panting.

Ibrahim nodded, thinking fast.

'The guards will be here any minute, we need to get rid of it somehow, and quick. If they connect you to this, you can forget about walking out through the big door.'

They quickly hatched a plan. Acting in total silence, they lifted the motionless body, put it down on a sheet, and then dragged it outside their cell. The cellblock had three corridors forming a U-shape, and theirs was in the third. Each of them overlooked the same light shaft, into which prisoners threw cans, cigarette butts and other rubbish. So Ibrahim rolled the body out and then pushed it off the third floor, like a sack of potatoes being dropped onto a cart. Then they went back to their cell, taking care to not make any noise.

'That must all have been caught on tape,' Arthur said, devastated. He cared nothing about the man they'd just tossed out like garbage. The only thing he cared about right then was his freedom.

'I doubt it,' Ibrahim said, calming him. 'That was one of the Armenian's henchmen, so the boss probably bribed the nightshift guard, who must have flipped the switch to let our cell be unlocked. He wasn't from our block, so the guard will be waiting for him to come out before he turns the cameras back on.'

'But what will happen when they discover the body?'

Ibrahim shrugged. He was annoyed by Arthur's naiveté, his thin skin, too delicate to survive in the prison world on his own.

'Nothing will happen. Nothing ever happens. They'll fake an investigation for the sake of appearances, maybe find a scapegoat, but more than likely it will all just be forgotten about. Either way, by that time, you'll be long gone and no one will be able to tie you to anything that went down — so relax.' Ibrahim was at the sink washing the blood off his hands; then he bundled up the sheet he'd used to drag the body out and stuffed it down at the bottom of his mattress. Suddenly he was moving with surprising vigour. He seemed to know just what to do and how to do it.

'You saved my life. When I get out of here I'm going to do everything in my power to return the favour.'

Ibrahim made a face, and his scar deepened.

'Yes, I'm sure you will.'

By that morning everyone knew what had happened, absolutely everyone: from the guard who'd been bribed to open the cell, to the newest inmate, who'd been watching through the slats of a barred window when Ibrahim and Arthur dragged the corpse down the corridor and hurled it into the light shaft. They knew that that bear of a man had been one of the Armenian's enforcers. But no one would say a word. There would be no whispering, no gossip. But there are always currents flowing beneath the surface. Currents that flow like the truth but are never stated, currents comprised solely of sidelong glances, half-gestures, unspoken understandings. The guards searched each cell top to bottom; Ibrahim was brought in for questioning, brought before the prison warden to make a statement; then came Arthur, and other prisoners. No one said a word. Everyone was playing dumb. And slowly, a superficial sense of normality returned to the cellblock, a tense waiting game in which inmates placed bets on Arthur and Ibrahim's days, which were surely numbered. Only someone incredibly naive could actually believe that what had happened would have no consequences. And in jail there's no such thing as naiveté.

On 3 February, a female civil servant led Arthur to the administrative block. The warden wanted to see him. Ordóñez was, at the time, one of the youngest prison wardens in all of Spain. He was seen as a man of few words, a hard worker with little fanfare, discreet and efficient, honest and just, but intransigent — a man with very clear ideas and the determination to bring them to fruition, regardless of whose feathers he might ruffle. In addition to all that, he was an exceedingly elegant man. When Arthur walked into his office, the warden was looking over some papers, leaning against a bookcase. He shot Arthur a quick glance — gauging, sharp — and extended a hand toward a chair as he motioned for the civil servant to take her leave.

'Take a seat.'

Arthur remained standing for a minute, hands in his trouser pockets. He wondered what kind of relationship he might have had with Ordóñez outside those walls; they'd probably never have been friends, but there might have at least been some degree of mutual respect.

'Please, take a seat,' he repeated, this time less peremptorily.

Reluctantly, Arthur perched on the edge of the chair.

'I suppose asking you about the inmate found dead in your cellblock again would be of no use.'

Arthur glanced at the ceiling; it had been recently painted and the office still smelled of fresh paint. He glanced around the room, the metal bookshelves, the files in various coloured folders, the phone on the desk nestled between a portrait of the king and a photo of the warden posing with two little girls so fair they looked albino. *Just a regular guy*, Arthur thought. 'A guy with twin daughters, a guy who eats orange candy,' he said to himself, noting the ashtray full of wrappers.

'I'm so broken up about it I can't sleep, if that's what you mean.'

The warden's neck flexed involuntarily. He didn't like sarcastic types. He didn't like Arthur.

'Don't be an ass. You're not in the block now, there's no need to be cocky.'

'I know nothing about it, I already told you that, and I told the investigators that. I know absolutely nothing about the death of that thug, all I know is that he was one of the Armenian's. Why are you so concerned about that sack of shit? He was one serious motherfucker — the man raped little girls, shoved glass up their vaginas. The world's a better place without pigs like him on the loose.'

'I'm concerned because someone threw that "sack of shit" down my light shaft. I, better than anyone, know the records of all the inmates, so I don't need you to remind me of what he did, much less lecture me about it. It just so happens that, whether I like it or not, that man was under my custody, he was my responsibility. I'm not willing to let this facility turn into the Wild West, with every man taking justice into his own hands. I know what happened — I know it, I just don't have proof, so I have to accept things as they are. But don't for a minute think I'm a fool, Arthur.' The man clearly didn't have a clue about certain forms of subtlety. 'Throughout your incarceration we've tried to protect you as much as possible, especially from the Armenian — but there's no such thing as absolute safety, and I have another thousand inmates to worry about, so, frankly, I'll be glad to see the back of you. One less headache for me.'

'See the back of me?'

'Your pardon just came through from the ministry. You've got friends in high places, Arthur.' Ordóñez loosened his tie — blue silk that matched his spotless shirt perfectly. Without asking if Arthur minded, he lit a cigarette and leaned against the edge of his desk, pulling over a crystal ashtray with a few butts in it. He slowly exhaled a dense cloud of smoke, not taking his eyes off him. Arthur realised that Ordóñez was tired of men like him, and that he was making the effort to be polite regardless, which was truly laudable.

'I don't think I need to warn you about the Armenian. You'd be dreaming if you thought that when you walk out that gate, you'll be out of that man's reach. Quite the contrary, you're more exposed on the outside than you are in here: the man's got very long arms. Take your precautions, get a private bodyguard or something — and watch your back.'

'I appreciate your concern. I'll keep it in mind.'

The warden nodded, unconvinced, and then glanced down at his watch like a busy executive.

'Very well. Sign these forms and then you can head to the locker for your personal effects. You'll spend the night in the access block and tomorrow they'll transfer you to the Castilla courts. And one more thing — slip up again, no matter how small, and you're right back here.'

Arthur signed the papers and made for the door. He had the feeling the warden was watching his movements, and turned suddenly to face him.

'You think I'm an arsehole, too, don't you? You think if it weren't for my money I'd be rotting in here for what I did. Right?'

Ordóñez examined Arthur curiously. He smiled faintly, as though it were a funny question. Funny in a sad kind of way.

The same woman accompanied Arthur back to the prison's communal area. Walking by the open gate of one cell, he caught sight of the Armenian, side-on, leaning over his windowsill. Sensing that he was being observed, the man turned his head, slowly. His eyes met Arthur's coldly.

The Armenian smiled. Yes, he already knew. Of course he'd heard about the pardon already. But he didn't seem bothered by it.

'See you around,' he said.

4

'She wants you to do a portrait of the man who killed her son?'

Eduardo nodded, his gaze fixed stubbornly on the cup of coffee Olga had offered him. She was sitting on the marble countertop, legs crossed, jiggling one bare foot. Her hair was messy, curtaining her eyes in a series of corkscrew curls. A blue silk nightgown had slipped off her right shoulder, and he could see the gentle slope of her breasts, although Olga seemed unconcerned by this detail. She was smoking, and exhaling the smoke toward a sink piled high with dirty dishes from the night before.

'That's what she said.'

'That's nuts, don't you think?' Olga asked, smiling skeptically, though much less caustic at that hour — sans lipstick or any other make-up — than she would be a few hours later.

Eduardo set his cup down on the counter.

'Doesn't seem that way to me,' he replied, staring now at the back of the chair, from which a bit of stuffing was trying to escape.

Olga gave a low whistle of admiration.

'When you die, make sure to donate your brain to science. It must be as complex as Tagger's.'

'Very funny.' Eduardo felt uneasy. He always did around Olga.

'I'm being serious. It's perverse.'

Eduardo took Olga's reproach stoically, despite the fact that it was coming from a thirty-something with dyed hair — today's highlights were auburn — and waxed eyebrows. *What was the point of waxing your eyebrows if you were just going to pencil them back in afterward?* he wondered. Suddenly he felt like he'd been foolish to tell her he'd accepted Gloria's assignment. In theory she should have been thrilled; after all she was going to earn a hefty commission. But rather than celebrate, she had moved down to the floor, where she sat half-dressed, smoking and staring at him like he was either insane or an idiot, and debating whether to be pissed off or make fun of him.

'It doesn't seem that hare-brained to me.'

Olga tugged between her knees at her nightgown, which was short enough to reveal her shapely legs.

'Well then explain it to me, because I sure don't get it. If someone had killed my son, the last thing I'd want to have is a portrait of the killer. Kill the guy, maybe, rip him to shreds, or erase him from my memory entirely, but I certainly wouldn't want his face permanently on hand.'

Eduardo let his gaze drift down to the worn, grey floor tiles. Olga's bright red stilettos, cast off in a corner, seemed out of place with the filth crusted into the grout.

'You don't have kids, so you can't lose them. That's why you don't understand.'

Olga smiled nastily, the snarl on her face discredited by teary eyes.

'You don't have to be a dick. I'm fully aware of the fact that I don't have kids and never can. Besides, I'm your agent and I'm planning to earn a bundle on this — I got you the job, so it's not like I'm questioning your actions, just trying to understand them.'

'This isn't just any old portrait, that wouldn't do the trick. What Gloria's looking for is for me to give that man a soul, to map out his personal geography so she can overcome her son's death.'

'Tell her to get a self-help book, do some yoga or something, for God's sake ...'

'She needs to understand everything about him, no holds barred — don't you get that? And in order to paint him, I'll have to get to know him, get close to him in a way Gloria never could.'

Olga remained pensive. She understood enough about painting to pick up on the tricks Eduardo employed in order to sell optical illusions — not what his clients actually saw with their own eyes, but what they wanted to see. Eduardo helped them believe whatever they wanted to believe. If a plain-faced daughter was looked upon with a mother's love, he could achieve that same effect with no clear alterations to the model's appearance; by adding a glimmer to the beloved's dull eyes, he made her seem rapt, instilling physical beauty in an unattractive subject, elevating the play of shadows to an art form and thus always delivering the desired results. The portrait Gloria wanted, however, was entirely different. She was asking Eduardo to lock a man inside a cell made of brushstrokes, a man who would surely struggle to rebel against the painter and jump out of the canvas.

She looked away. She had a feeling Eduardo was judging her with his eyes, mocking her feigned indifference. She wanted to say something but couldn't find the words to do it. After thinking it over for a minute, Olga faltered, like someone who's decided to jump into a river without knowing whether they'll be able to swim their way out, leaving their fate to chance.

'You like her, don't you? Gloria,' she murmured, as though asking herself the question, then she leaned onto her knee and struggled to stand.

Eduardo blushed, visibly uncomfortable.

'That's not any of your business.'

'Yes, it is. You were very good when painting was the most important thing in your life, and you got even better when you met Elena. But this woman you're inventing, Gloria — whatever it is you're trying to do, it's not real. Elena's dead, and no optical illusion is going to bring her back.'

Eduardo glowered, furious.

'So you want to psychoanalyse me, too? Fine, you can come to my next appointment with Dr Martina on Thursday and expound all of your theories.'

Olga waved her hands in front of her as though to erase what she'd said.

'Calm down, would you? I just think there's something insincere about that woman; there's something fishy, too many coincidences. First you run into her at the park, then a few days later she shows up at my gallery ...' Ever since she'd seen Gloria A. Tagger walk into the gallery, Olga had had a vague presentiment hanging over her, the sting of long-forgotten danger. Objectively, there was no reason for the knot in her throat, the heaviness in the pit of her stomach, but something — something strong — told her not to let her guard down.

She felt uncomfortable, or maybe silly, like she regretted having brought up certain subjects with Eduardo.

'Does she know you lost Elena and Tania in an accident?'

'Yes, she does, and I assume that's why she wants me to be the one to paint the portrait. I've been through the same thing, so she's hoping I can help her make it through a dark tunnel.'

'And can you? Have you yourself even made it out of the dark tunnel?'

'I really don't feel like talking about this anymore,' Eduardo said.

'Well you've got to talk to someone about it. It's been fourteen years since they died. You spent the last thirteen locked up, and I don't just mean physically. You've been trapped, reliving the accident. You think you're over it? Shit, Eduardo, you're not even close, and now you tell me you're going to be some kind of beacon of hope for that woman. It's absurd.'

Eduardo fished around in his trouser pockets and he came out with a wrinkled cigarette. He smoothed and lit it, attempting to calm down, and then anxiously glanced around as though searching for something. Olga followed his eyes and realised what it was.

'It's eight o'clock in the morning, Eduardo.'

'Life is short,' he replied.

'If you say so.'

She had glasses somewhere, but wasn't sure where. Eventually she unearthed a grimy tumbler. She rinsed it in the sink and poured Eduardo a vodka — no ice, no lemon. He downed it in one, spilling a few drops on the floor, hands trembling. Suddenly he got that shifty look that made others avoid him.

Olga was now standing by the window. She looked distressed. Fourteen years on, she still felt like she owed Eduardo something. She worried about him, brought him clean clothes — often leaving a couple of hundreds on his table on the way out — and once in a while even agreed to drink with him in run-down, sordid dives that stank of old smoke, just to keep him company. In exchange for all that, she expected just a modicum of consideration, of appreciation. And he categorically refused to give it to her.

'I'm worried about you, Eduardo.'

Eduardo had poured himself another shot. This one he sipped, feeling less desperate. Shielding himself behind the scratched rim of the glass, he eyed Olga. He still wondered who she really was, why she'd suddenly appeared in his life. Without the commissions she got him, Eduardo would have ended up as a night watchman in an underground parking lot, reading bad novels, eating pre-packaged pastries, drinking vending-machine coffee and smoking his life away. She'd also been the only one who showed any concern for him when he was locked up in the prison's psych ward in Huesca. She had come see him on visiting day, each of them spending the twenty-minute communication period in silence, sitting facing each other, separated by a thick, dirty glass panel inevitably smudged with the fingerprints and breath marks of those who couldn't touch the person on the other side. They'd found nothing to say, barely daring to glance at one another. That same ritual was repeated month in and month out, same day, same time, neither one expecting anything from the other, neither asking anything of the other. From time to time she sent him cigarettes, magazines, art books, new clothes. And then, one fine day, she'd just stopped coming, and slowly her packages stopped arriving, too. She didn't tell him why and he didn't ask. He simply let it happen. But when he got out, thirteen years later, Olga was there, waiting for him in the parking lot. And still Eduardo didn't ask why.

'Look, I don't need you to worry about me, or feel sorry for me, or protect me. I'd be happy if you just left me alone.'

Olga attempted a look of disdain, hidden contempt she actually felt for herself.

'You're right. The next time you decide to slit your wrists, you can find someone else's door to knock on. If you've made up your mind to screw up the rest of your life, or fall in love with some illusion, that's none of my business. And now, if you don't mind, I'd like to be alone for a while.'

She walked Eduardo to the door, placed her hand on the knob and turned it, but as she stood in the doorway she turned sideways.

'You never asked why,' she said, eyes flashing beneath her lashes, which were thin as a little girl's without mascara.

'What do you mean?'

'I could have gone to the cops, but instead of heading for the nearest police station, I told you. You never asked me why that was what I did. You never asked me why I started visiting you at the clinic — or why I suddenly stopped. You weren't even surprised to see me waiting for you in the parking lot the day you got out … You never asked a single thing.'

Eduardo pondered coldly how to reply. From among the multitude of tangled thoughts and suspicions swirling in his mind, he came up with a few words by way of response.

'Maybe I never wanted to know the answers.'

It was very late by the time Eduardo managed to get to sleep, as usual. He never slept deeply and his dreams were always a struggle from which he awoke utterly exhausted. But this time it wasn't his nightmares that awoke him but the cries coming from the other end of the hall. Horrific, animal-like howls. He knew, however, that those blood-curdling shrieks were not coming from an animal. Eduardo had grown accustomed to hearing them every once in a while.

He turned on the light and found his slippers. Walking to the door, he knew no one else would come out into the hallway. Despite the racket, not a single other tenant would come to help, no one would admit to knowing what was going on; if anything, the incident would simply serve to fan the flames of gossip whispered by those spying from the other side of their peepholes.

Graciela was at her apartment door, which stood ajar. They looked at each other and said nothing. She pulled her hair back in exasperation, lips trembling.

'She woke up.' Her eyes implored him to help.

Eduardo heard Sara's frenzied cries. Graciela was attempting to pacify her daughter, cooing and speaking softly through the crack in the door without letting go of the handle, but Sara's voice grew louder and louder, finally erupting into a crazed blend of laughter and tears, incomprehensible insults and threats. He heard banging, more shouting, objects being smashed, and finally Eduardo pushed Graciela aside and opened the door in alarm. Sara was totally out of control, her eyes glassy and glimmering wildly, like a blind man staring directly into the sun. As soon as she saw the door open, she hurled herself at it in an attempt to escape. The girl was desperate to make it out onto the street, fixated on the idea of running away.

Graciela held her arms, but Sara broke free, kicking her and biting at the air. She was as strong as an adult, especially during these fits of rage. Eduardo managed to avoid her snapping jaws twice, but not the kick that got him right in his injured knee. He repressed a cry of pain and wrapped both arms tightly around Sara like a beast, so she couldn't shake him off, despite her writhing like a snake.

'Call an ambulance!' he shouted to Graciela, who had suddenly gone motionless, as though she'd lost all her strength. 'Graciela, for God's sake, call an ambulance!' he repeated, short of breath.

Forty minutes later, Sara was in bed, sleeping deeply, at the hospital. Her thin fidgety body, so like that of her mother, could be seen breathing easily beneath the sheet. There was no sign of the snake-spirit that had whipped through her a few minutes earlier; it seemed never to have happened. She was just a normal girl, perhaps a little on the pale side, the tiny veins on her eyelids too pronounced, her mouth a bit too tense. Listening carefully, you could hear the sound of her teeth clenching and grinding as she dreamt, but that was it. The little bedside lamp projected the shape of her defeated body onto the wall.

'The sedatives will make her sleep for hours, but they won't stop the frantic thoughts churning in her mind. She's boiling, I can feel it. It's like a river of lava beneath her skin, and her brain is on fire,' Graciela said, one hand on her daughter's sorrowful forehead, smoothing away a few sweaty strands of hair.

In the morning, Sara would wake up and it would be like part of her body was still on the other side of that dream; it would be days before she returned completely.

'The nurses will take good care of her. You heard the doctor. It's better for her to spend the night, for observation,' Eduardo said.

She nodded absently. Eduardo studied her, watching as she performed mechanical movements: opening the armoire, taking out a toiletries bag, a clean change of clothes, hanging them up on the hanger … Each action required superhuman strength just to keep her from collapsing — she looked so fragile. Eduardo took the small overnight bag — the one that was always packed and ready to go, in case Sara had a fit — from Graciela, just before it fell from her hands.

'It's okay, I'll take care of it.'

And she began to cry. But not even then did her tears flow as she'd have wished — freely, torrential, liberating. Instead they were constrained, released in small, measured doses. Without knowing why, Eduardo stroked her lips with the tip of his thumb, as though attempting to erase her sorrow and provide the kiss his lips could not give. She cleared her throat, and then shook her head the way people do in India, a yes that looked like a no.

Graciela pulled away from his touch, drying her eyes with the back of a hand.

'It's been like this for years. I can't take it anymore, I'm exhausted. Sometimes I feel like she's hijacked my life, but then I realise that's not true. The fact is, I gave up long before she was born.' She was speaking softly, wearily, not thinking about what she was saying but also not keeping the words from streaming from her mouth.

'What about her father?'

Graciela waved a vague hand through the air.

'Her father was ... very handsome.' She laughed at her own quip, exasperated. 'Isn't it sad that that's the only thing I can say about the man who got me pregnant? I've always had a weakness for green-eyed arseholes who refuse to grow up. He held out for a month, maybe two, promised he'd take care of Sara — and I know he really did make an effort to accept it when the doctors told us she'd never be a normal girl — but in the end he couldn't hack it, and that's what counts. He started cheating on me pretty quick, and maybe at first he felt guilty — he must have felt at least a little remorse, with some random girl sucking his dick in the doorway while I was tearing my hair out upstairs, desperate because I had no idea what was the matter, up all night because Sara couldn't get to sleep and wouldn't stop crying. But he got over that pretty fast. One day he just took off. Didn't say goodbye. Erased us from his lives. Some people are just like that, you know?'

'You'll find someone,' Eduardo replied, mostly because he assumed that was the kind of response he was supposed to give. Graciela deserved better luck than she had. But in the end, he was convinced that luck had nothing to do with the choices people made.

Graciela accepted his insincerity with a forced smile.

'There have been other men since then, of course. There always are, as long as you're prepared not to be too picky ... Did you know I had a mastectomy six months ago?' She asked this, staring straight into his eyes, emptily, as though talking about some trivial matter. Eduardo blushed slightly and said nothing. 'Most guys get scared the second I take out the padding, even though I warn them. They can't help but look bereft as soon as they see the scar. Some of them get over it, but very few think it doesn't matter. And when they meet Sara, even those guys get scared — the kind words get stuck in their throat — and they can't run away fast enough when they realise what the prospects are. Honestly, I've given up hope.'

Everyone hopes for something, until they give up, Eduardo thought, unsure how much of what Graciela said was resentment, and how much was an attempt to conceal secret optimism.

'You're not scared, though,' she said, eyeing him curiously. 'I know you saw me in the bathroom. The truth is, I wanted you to. And you don't get freaked out by Sara's attacks, you know how to handle her. She likes you, it's so obvious that she's fond of you.'

Eduardo asked her to stop right there. But Graciela went on. She took his elbow to keep him from moving away, trying to trap him with her eyes, her pained expression, her desperate hands.

'I know you lost your wife and daughter, and I know that all these years you haven't wanted to be with anyone. But we all have a right to start over, Eduardo. You're a good man — and I'm not quite ready to feel like my life is totally over yet.'

Eduardo gently but firmly pulled her hand from his elbow.

'I'm not a good man, Graciela. Really, you know nothing about me.'

'I know enough.'

'No, you don't. Now let's drop it, please. I have to go; tomorrow I've got to be up early.'

Graciela nodded, her eyes full of sadness. Sadness for herself, for Sara, for him. She tried to hide it, repositioning a vase on the shelf.

'A bouquet of dry flowers is as close as we get to knowing the ephemeral, don't you think?'

Eduardo eyed the flowers. They were roses, freshly cut. And they'd been cut for the express purpose of dying in a vase, their agony contemplated by others.

'Give Sara a kiss when she wakes up.'

'I will.' Graciela brushed her cheek against his, feigning a quick air kiss. The layer of foundation she was wearing made her skin feel like velvet.

She let him go, walk away, leave the room without stopping him, without asking him to stay just a little bit longer, to hold her even for a moment. She'd pull herself together before long; she could manage, carry on as she always had, with Sara, the two of them, alone together — but sometimes she needed just a little love … just a few drops of tenderness, a little company.

'What is love? Nothing. A transient feeling. Something we think we possess but never really belongs to us.'

Mr Who stared at the computer screen, contemplating what he'd just written. It was five o'clock in the morning and he couldn't sleep. He'd tried, but his bed was like a shroud and he a corpse staring out at the darkness, eyes open. Tired, scattered, sleepless, he got out of bed and looked through the slats in the blinds. The neighbourhood was deserted, illuminated by a streetlight on the roundabout, which was ringed with old olive trees some local government official had decided to plant there, in a little plaza surrounded by concrete. The parked cars had frost on their windshields — it was cold out. He sat at the desk in his underwear and rifled through drawers until he found the Chinese cigarettes, with the unpronounceable name and strong harsh taste that he had started smoking when Chang had told him that *that* was the brand that *real* Chinese people smoked. And Mr Who had decided to become *truly* Chinese, whatever it took.

'Ultimately, this is already inside you, you simply need to awaken it after such a long period of oblivion,' Chang lectured. Chang was the one in charge of supervising his progress, so smoking harsh Chinese cigarettes and giving up the light American blonde tobacco he had been smoking was far from the worst that could have happened.

Who massaged his forehead and then cracked his neck like a wrestler, twisting it left and right. He turned back to the screen and, for a few seconds, held his fingers suspended over the keys, as though he were pianist about to begin his recital. Then he deleted what he'd written — intended as a poem for Mei. In the end he'd deemed it too naive, too childish. Sighing deeply he logged into his secret email account, the one Maribel knew nothing about and couldn't snoop through. She swore up and down that she never invaded his privacy, that she wouldn't dare — but Mr Who had set invisible traps for her, and had discovered that she'd been keeping tabs on the web pages he visited, had been going through his emails, reading his texts. The secret account had been Chang's idea — that was where the restaurant owner sent him the addresses of new clients.

He had a new message, ten minutes old — it seemed Who was not the only one with insomnia: a hotel near Calle Montera. After jotting down the directions, he deleted his browser history.

Mr Who shuffled down to the kitchen, dragging his slippered feet, and sat down with a can of Coke in his hand, staring fixedly at the steel clock on the wall. He downed his soda, feeling the gut-churning bubbles hit his empty stomach, and, flicking the ash of his cigarette into the can, listened to it hiss. Then he tossed the butt into the can, and the can into the garbage, making sure to close the plastic container fully — and, finally, aired out the kitchen, opening the door and window. Maribel couldn't stand the smell of smoke in the house — and though she must have realised Who had taken up the habit, he kept trying to pretend he didn't smoke, at least in front of her, out of respect. Still, despite his precautions, he soon heard the parquet creak and the mechanical whir of her wheelchair in the living room, approaching the kitchen.

'I'm sorry, I didn't mean to wake you; I just wanted something to drink.'

'And to smoke one of those stinky cigarettes …' Maribel said, from the doorway, fanning the air. She was wearing a fake silk robe with a gaudy floral motif, a kimono she only wore because Mr Who had given it to her for her sixtieth birthday. Pushing the little lever on her chair, she wheeled over to the counter. Mr Who got there first, filling the kettle.

'How long did you sleep, a couple hours? I heard you come in — it was very late,' Maribel said, one hand in her lap. Beneath the red kimono, he could make out her shrunken, atrophied thighs; she had a svelte, well-formed trunk but there was total dysfunction below the waist — her legs were useless. To one side of the chair he saw her drainage bag, with a small quantity of urine in it. Maribel saw him looking and demurely covered it with the kimono.

'More or less,' Who said, turning to watch the kettle boil. 'Mr Chang is really busy at the restaurant, and he doesn't have time to teach us until we finish cleaning the kitchen, after closing.'

The truth was, he'd been at the house of a *special* client and had dawdled too long, missing his bus connection back to Madrid. He'd ended up having to hitchhike and then walk several kilometres, but it had been worth it. The rich are always worth it.

'It's quite admirable, the interest your boss shows in teaching you to write Mandarin,' Maribel replied pointedly, her sarcasm ill-concealed.

'Chang is a patriot, he doesn't deny his roots,' Mr Who retorted, 'and he doesn't want me to forget mine.'

Mr Who poured the steaming tea into two porcelain cups, added a teaspoon of sugar to his mother's cup; he took his black, blowing at the edge of his cup. Instinctively, Maribel reached out and tucked his hair back.

'Around here they call Chang other things besides "patriot" — which by the way is a word I'm not thrilled with. The majority of crooks and cadgers seem to wrap themselves up in one flag or another.'

Mr Who smiled tenderly and his eyes shone, giving him the innocent boyish look he seemed to have lost so long ago — especially since he decided to become *Mr Who*, start smoking Chinese cigarettes, and dress in black.

'You don't want to lose your roots either, your connection to your parents and grandparents … And I wouldn't say you look like a crook or a cadger.'

'I'm from Murcia, and I've been here in Getafe so long I'm part of the scenery now, so you can't pull that on me,' Maribel retorted, annoyed. 'I know Chang a lot better than you do. Your father set up his coin collector's shop here, and this is where I opened my classical dance studio. Chang bought the ground floor of the building at the same time, and opened his restaurant. He was, you might say, more pragmatic than we were. He always had a head for business, and did so well we were forced to sell both the school and shop. For the past thirty years he's done nothing but prosper — yet he was never willing to give me back my studio.'

'Mr Chang has the utmost respect for you; he says so all the time. You shouldn't be so hostile toward him.'

Maribel traced the edge of her cup with one finger. Speaking about the past and attempting to connect it to the present was sometimes as exhausting as trying to make your way through a maze, one you can only see part of. As far as trying to convince her son to be careful around Chang, that was a wasted effort. What made her uneasy was the sudden change in his clothes and behaviour: dressing all in black, wearing eyeliner, painting his fingernails, filling his body with piercings and rings and other nonsense, tattoos even. He was twenty-two, so of course he was going through some sort of metamorphosis, and she could accept that — his using his body to explore the kind of character he wanted to invent for himself — but this sudden insistence on what he called 'discovering his roots' was worrisome.

They'd never hidden from him the fact that he was adopted — besides, it was obvious — and she and Teo had agreed that one day, if he wanted to know, he should be told who his biological parents were and know

where he came from. Maribel had always known that s‍o‌‍‍
moment — the questioning — would arrive, and she w‍‍
face some sort of calm transition, but her son wanted to cr‍
too quickly. Ever since he'd started spending time with the o‍
become taciturn, reserved. He hardly spoke to her anymore,‍‍‍‍
he did, Maribel could tell he wasn't really present. He was spen‍ding a lot
of nights away from home, and sometimes when he returned, it was as if
something vital to his existence had been lost out there on the streets — a
heartbreaking emptiness was reflected in his eyes. It took forever for his
old smile to return. Teo would have known how to handle the situation,
but Teo wasn't there, and she felt overwhelmed.

Mr Who looked down into the bottom of his green teacup and his
eyes softened.

'I went to the cemetery today. To visit *papá*,' he said, the conversation
taking a sudden turn.

Maribel eyed her son uneasily. Mr Who rarely brought up Teo, and
visited his grave even less.

'I suppose that's good.'

He raised his chin, lacing his fingers, their nails painted black, behind
his head.

'Sometimes I can hear you crying through the bedroom door.'

Maribel exhaled with displeasure and tucked a strand of grey hair
behind her ear.

'He was the man I loved, the one I chose to spend my life with, and we
had twenty good years. You don't just forget something like that.'

'I, on the other hand, can hardly remember him. To me he's just a
closed bedroom door, the one you won't let me open.' It wasn't a reproach
but a statement of fact. Mr Who wasn't allowed in Maribel's bedroom.

'My pain is mine alone. It's not something I want to share, nor do I
have any desire to. It's all I have left of your father.'

'But I *should* be able to remember him. I try, but I can't do it. Over the
years he's become just a blur, something that gets further and further
away, as if he never was.'

Maribel shook her head sadly and finished her tea. She left the glass in
the sink and wheeled herself to her son's side.

'I suppose your going through this is inevitable — your changes, your

..tions, your doubts. But honestly, I wish it could be avoided.'

Mr Who stood up and crossed his arms.

'What would you do if you could go back in time? Would you adopt me all over again? Would you take that trip to get me?'

Maribel stared at her son, incredulous.

'Why are you asking me this? What sense does it make? Of course I would; you're my son, I love you, I'm proud of the man you're becoming — it's just that you're changing so quickly it scares me.'

Mr Who blushed slightly and looked away, visibly uncomfortable. He snuck a peek at the clock.

'I'm sorry, forgive me. I have to go someplace,' he said, walking out of the kitchen.

Though the streetlights were still on, it was starting to get light. A garbage truck lifted a bin. A few yards away a woman was walking her Yorkie — dragging it more like — on a dainty chain. At a taxi rank, two men argued in hushed tones, exchanging cigarettes, and a newspaper seller to the right of Puerta del Sol was just cutting the seals off his bundles of papers and magazines. Mr Who didn't have to walk too far up the street before he hit number 123. A cheap hotel. He buzzed the intercom and within a few seconds a voice told him to come right up to the top floor. The elevator was the old birdcage style, and the building had a porter's lodge, though it was still closed.

As the elevator rattled its way up, floor by floor, he tried to imagine what kind of rendezvous this might be. Experience had told him that attempting to figure it out in advance was a waste of time, but feeling a certain anxiousness was inevitable, the closer he got. Normally, clients who wanted more aggressive, kinkier experiences went to Chang's secret location behind the restaurant — it was more discreet. No one wanted to risk having the screams alert a well-intentioned neighbour, who might call the police. The fact that this guy had chosen a central hotel calmed his nerves, at least a bit. Maybe it would be a bourgeois type, or a professional, or freelancer — a doctor, lawyer, writer, musician. Dealing with them was always relatively easy, and in a way could almost even be pleasant. They tended to be far more conventional in their sexual proclivities than you might expect from people in their broad-minded professions.

He had experience with a certain well-known singer whose reputation as a wild-child and zealous practitioner of every vice imaginable was part and parcel of his image on his records, on his tours; and yet in private, he turned out to be a tame little kitty cat, just a guy who needed the cuddly affection that his status as an enfant terrible made impossible for him if it wasn't clandestine. Mr Who felt real affection for the man, who played him quiet ballads on his Spanish guitar rather than the raucous, hard-core numbers he was famous for — though before he paid, he'd make him promise to spread the word that he was the nastiest, most degenerate party-boy in all Madrid.

Hoping for something along those lines, he slid back the metal grate of the elevator when it stopped at the top floor. The door to the room was ajar, but Who rapped on it with his knuckles anyway.

'I'm out here, on the balcony,' said a female voice from the back.

So it was a woman, Who thought. Well, it wasn't so unusual for women to request his services, and when it came down to it, it wasn't that different from what he did with men, either.

He went from the light outside to the darkness inside in the blink of an eye. The smell of fresh coffee and bath soap floated in the air. In contrast with the derelict facade of the hotel, the room was quite nice — a bit minimalist, which led Who to find it cold: bare white walls, cheap furniture. The television was tuned to a classical station, and the violinist Vanessa Mae was playing a Vangelis arrangement.

The woman was leaning over the railing of the small balcony, staring out at the grey horizon of Madrid and the anarchic forest of pointy antennas.

'Beautiful view of the city,' Mr Who said, by way of greeting.

She didn't turn right away and simply nodded, stroking her bare arms. Then she slowly turned her head, revealing a face puffy with sleep, hair falling untidily onto her forehead. She wore a crimson spaghetti-strap nightie, tight enough to reveal a body that had begun to sag a bit. And she was barefoot, her right foot resting on the instep of her left. Mr Who noticed that each of her toenails was painted a different colour. She seemed somewhat eccentric, and he liked that.

'You look older in the photos,' she said crossly. She examined Who with a mix of sadness and determination. 'How old are you?'

'Twenty-four,' he lied, without batting an eyelid. He knew it was an intermediate age that would fend off any prejudices, and he could fake it with no problem. 'But I can leave if you want,' he added, with just a hint of spite.

She shot him an ambiguous look, which morphed into a forgiving smile. Reaching out, she pulled the young man's body to her. In person he was really much more attractive than the online photos had led her to believe. Stroking his androgynous face, she felt a momentary stab of regret, of weariness, but she left that behind when he took her by the waist and kissed her neck slowly.

'I want you to kiss me on the mouth. Is that included in your fee?' she asked, the cruelty in her voice restrained, like a dog biting its own tail.

Mr Who gazed into her eyes, which were half-hidden by deep bags, and shrugged.

'French kissing is very personal, almost as personal as saying your name out loud to a stranger.'

'My name is Rocío. Satisfied?'

Mr Who rested his fingertips on the woman's crotch by way of reply. Then he kissed her on the lips and felt her kiss back impatiently.

Some lovers love with gestures full of veiled rage, secretly blaming themselves for that moment of pleasure they concede, tormented by fears and reproaches. That was how the woman on the sofa of that hotel room surrendered herself. She wouldn't even let him take off her nightgown, refusing to grant any part of herself — anything intimate — to the stranger, who very quickly stripped her bare with the insolence of his moves, his expression.

Mr Who observed her closely. She was no longer young, and didn't wear her age well; she'd probably grown used to the comfort of these transactions, the nonchalant denial of feelings and the ease of not giving anything she didn't want to give, while still able to demand anything she wanted in return. Paying for sex gave her certain rights, and that excited her — the certainty of knowing she was an object, an obstacle standing in the way of her contractual lover's goal: the cash awaiting him on the table. Desire was therefore purely carnal; sex was practical, her skin became excited but her heart was protected, safe from wounds new and old.

'Everything okay?' asked Who. He knew that abstract feeling, that stiffness of the hips, the type of kissing that was more like biting, the indifference to his caresses. It saddened him to note that no matter how much effort he put in, he'd never break through the ice that must have frozen her heart long ago. So all he could do was apply himself, mechanically, conscientious of technique and skill. An orgasm, maybe two, and that was it. That was all that was being asked of him that morning.

'I'm fine,' the woman said, pulling off her panties. 'Now, could we stop talking and fuck?'

Mr Who closed in on himself, like a conch snail retracting, in order to become invulnerable. He hardly even undressed: she ripped a few buttons off his shirt, exposing part of his tattooed torso, and freed his cock — but wouldn't let him take off his pants or boots. When they were finished, she pulled away, her face tense. If she'd enjoyed the encounter at all, she certainly didn't show it.

'Can I use the bathroom?' Who asked. The woman gestured indifferently toward a door at the end of the hall.

Mr Who locked himself in and gazed into the mirror, contemplating himself with a sombre expression. After doing it, he felt supremely lost and empty for a few minutes, as if blood was being drained from his body. Then, little by little, it began circulating through his veins once more, and the colour returned to his skin. *Sooner or later,* he thought, *I've got to stop working for Chang.* But he had several thousand euros to go before he'd have saved up all the money he needed. And Mei needed him.

He went back to the bedroom. The woman was smoking, sitting cross-legged on the mattress. One of her nightgown straps had fallen from her shoulder, exposing part of her breasts. The cash was folded on the bedspread. Who walked over and picked the bills up without counting them.

'I'll leave you a card, in case you need me.'

The woman nodded very slowly, not looking up at him. Then Who realised she was crying.

'Are you alright?'

She tilted her head and gazed intently at him. Then, very slowly, she lowered the other strap and let her nightgown fall to her waist, exposing

71

one sagging pink-nippled breast, and a scar where the other should have been.

'My name isn't really Rocío. It's Graciela.'

Mr Who walked back out onto the street, flooded with relief. The sidewalk had just been hosed down, and two hookers were offering their services in tight red dresses covered in stains, and cheap patent-leather thigh-highs with dizzyingly high heels.

We are all alone. Utterly alone, he thought.

5

The housekeeper greeted him with a smile of recognition and led Eduardo straight to a room he'd never been in before. Debussy's *Clair de Lune* was playing, but the grand piano presiding over the room stood silent, producing a strangely magical effect. Atop a very thin layer of dust on the fallboard covering the keys were the imprints of four hands. He could imagine that piece was being played by a duet of ghosts, their invisible fingers betrayed by the dust. Gloria was leaning against a bookshelf reading something. Seeing Eduardo she forced a smile and placed the paper inside a roll-top desk.

'I thought you wouldn't come back, that you left here convinced I was completely out of my mind.'

'I've decided to take on your commission,' Eduardo replied, quashing her fear.

'I'm glad to hear that. Smoke?' Gloria held out a pack of Hungarian cigarettes — she had them shipped from Budapest specially — and sat sideways on the edge of a chair that looked fairly uncomfortable. It was not a good posture for confidences. Gloria had scratches on her neck and a bruise below her ear. Her arms, too, bore marks, as though someone had held her forcefully.

'Did you have an accident? Have I come at a bad time?'

'There's never a bad time to get what you expect, Eduardo,' she replied cryptically.

Eduardo cleared his throat and put all his weight on his good knee. She hadn't asked him to sit. Instead, she eyed him from a distance, somewhat aloof. He had no idea what had changed since his first visit, but he attempted to forgive her: people are predisposed to overlook other's offenses when they're attracted to the offender. And he was deeply attracted to the woman, though he wasn't exactly sure why.

'I can't promise you anything, Gloria. Perhaps it would be best to not expect of me more than I can offer. But I'll try.'

Gloria looked at him as if he were prey to be shot on a hunt, an insignificant animal in the forest, frightened and frantic at the barking of the dogs, the sounds of the chase.

'If you're going to work for me, I suggest we stop speaking to each other formally,' she said, inviting him to use the familiar *tú* form.

For the next three weeks, Eduardo visited the house almost daily. Gloria generally received him in a good mood, sometimes in her office or another room, others — when the changeable February weather permitted — out on the desolate grounds surrounding the house, which extended along a narrow path into a grove with a stream, and a stone bridge in poor repair. Sometimes they talked about art, painting, music, and film, other times they got lost in everyday anecdotes, current events they feigned interest in. But in one way or another, they were always circling around their anguish — sores that appeared on the skin like bends in a stream.

Gloria found it difficult to talk about what was killing her — the pain of losing her son Ian. But more than that, she couldn't find the words for the other, deeper pain festering inside her, the one Eduardo glimpsed in her silences. There are people who spend their whole lives suffering without realising it, who die without discovering the cause of the heaviness that weighs down their days, the vague uneasiness that makes them sullen and sometimes mean, and always unhappy. People who live in the dark, never learning the cause of their private, personal pain, so routine that they accept it as normal, like a migraine or a backache. But sometimes something happens — maybe too late to fix it — that suddenly gives them the key to understanding that pain, if not the time to repair it.

Early one morning they went out to the backyard and walked to a bandstand that must not have been used for quite some time. Its wooden stairs were full of cracks and its domed roof was full of large holes. Gloria held onto Eduardo's forearm without resting her weight on him, more a gesture of complicity than a sign of weakness. That woman might be many things — nostalgic, sad perhaps — but she certainly was not helpless. Quite simply, women occasionally feign weakness so that men won't feel threatened.

Eduardo let himself be led, docile, to a bench under an evergreen oak with a gnarled, desiccated trunk. He felt the urge to stroke Gloria's beautiful face, so like and yet so unlike Elena's, but cowardice

74

hammered his fingers all the way down into his jacket pockets. For a few seconds they both stared straight ahead, very close, without saying a word. Eduardo listened to their hearts beating out of time, the different rhythms of their breathing.

'Sometimes I come here to say my son's name out loud,' Gloria said suddenly. 'As if by doing that I could invoke his presence — it's crazy, I know. But without his name to repeat there would be no trace of his time on earth. When I call him, his face comes to me among the trees, or in a room, or sometimes sitting in the first few rows at a concert. I see his face in my mind, his little boy face, the unruly curls that were impossible to tame; I stroke his velvety eyelids and let myself be rocked by his voice and I feel like he's still here with me, ready to take on the world, to chase his dreams.'

She could still feel the way he moved around in her belly, how uncomfortable he had been in the womb, how anxious to come out into the world that scorching hot, dry day in 1984, in the mountains of Cáceres. Gloria and her husband Ian had gone to the patron saint festival in her grandmother's town, Aldea del Cano. The evergreen oak the town kids had chosen for the festival that year was astonishing — the largest Christmas tree in living memory. They dragged it in using two carts, tied together with thick ropes, that were pulled by two mule trains, and headed for the Plaza del Ayuntamiento, in the centre of town. There it would remain, surrounded by kindling, until New Year's Eve day, when they'd set it alight.

Ian was riding up on one of the carts, perched atop a bunch of dry roots, filming it all on a movie camera — totally absorbed, all worked up — waving like a government minister. He was radiant. Gloria waved back with a smile that took everything she had, holding her swollen belly. The baby would not stop kicking. Gloria was due, and the closer her labour got, the stronger the pains, the shortness of breath and dizziness, but she was trying to hide it so she wouldn't ruin the moment for her husband.

From the corner of her eye she searched among the crowd in the plaza, trying to find the sign for the medical dispensary she'd glimpsed earlier, in case her son decided to come out right there on the dry red earth of the square, in a small town in the sierra, over a hundred kilometres from any city that might have a decent hospital that could treat her, in case of emergency. At first she'd thought she could hold out until night, till they got back to the city where there were real hospitals. But she was no longer so sure. Hiding from Ian the pains she'd started feeling that morning had been reckless; they were stronger than usual — maybe not quite contractions yet, but they certainly felt like them.

'I knew it was a boy. No one had told me — I wouldn't let the gynaecologist reveal the baby's sex, compelled by a sort of family superstition: my grandfather always said the only thing you should hope for is what you get. But I knew; I was carrying a healthy, beautiful boy and he was going to be a musician, like all the men in my family, like me. I hadn't said anything to Ian because he always wanted a girl and I didn't want to disappoint him unnecessarily. It wasn't a conscious secret, at least not at first, just one of those things you keep quiet because you can't find the right time to bring them up.'

Eduardo nodded, despite not being sure he understood what Gloria was trying to say. Between him and Elena, there had never been secrets.

'What mattered was that my son was going to be born, was going to live a long life. That's what I was praying for to the Virgen de los Remedios, the town's patron saint, when Ian approached, his hair sweaty and dishevelled, his shirt unbuttoned. He was holding a plastic cup of cheap wine. Rarely had I seen him look so happy. He told me what a great idea it had been to come up to this remote village, said he was getting fantastic material, and he was convinced he could sell it to the BBC. Then suddenly he looked at me and realised something was wrong. "Are you feeling okay? You look tired." I said yes, I was fine — I didn't want to rain on his parade — but when I tried to smile, my face contorted.'

She had barely managed to reach out and grab the arm her frightened husband held out to her.

There was no time for ambulances or hospitals. Her labour was long, painful, agonising.

All the while, Ian waited on the other side of the door that separated the examination room from the rest of the clinic. When the nurse came out, Gloria could see him through the gap in the curtain. He was anxiously scratching the chair's upholstery with his fingernail, attempting to tune out the screams coming from the other side of the curtain.

After over an hour the midwife came out, still dressed in her festival clothes, shirtsleeves rolled up above her elbows, an oilcloth bib splattered with dark droplets. Ian stood to one side, adopting a composed, serene appearance, aware of the woman's accusatory, suspicious eyes.

'How's it going?' he asked neutrally, as if asking what the weather would be like tomorrow.

The midwife shoved him aside brusquely, strode to a glass cabinet and pulled out a pack of sterile gauze. 'Not well, it's not going well,' she said crossly, and then fell silent a moment, staring at the back of the room, measuring her words carefully in order to express precisely what she wanted to say. 'Do you mind telling me what on earth you were thinking? Putting a woman in that state on a hellish road, full of curves and potholes. Can't you see she's about to give birth and here we are in the Godforsaken middle of nowhere?'

Ian blushed. The midwife lowered her head like a ram about to charge. She'd have loved to slap him around the head, the stupid jerk, not a drop of common sense.

She went back to the birthing room, but before walking in, she tilted her head at him. 'The ambulance is on the way, but it will be another half an hour until it gets here. If her situation gets any more complicated, I don't know how this is going to end. If you believe in miracles, start praying.'

Now, Gloria let out a cynical laugh.

'Ian, pray? Impossible. A godless Anglican — a subject of Her Majesty the Queen with St George's Cross; an arrogant, unpredictable man kneeling before Christ in a remote town in the mountains. That would never have happened. But neither of us died that morning. I suppose we were too excited about life, about finally meeting one another.'

When he was born, her son, also named Ian, barely weighed more than a sparrow, his little body fragile and discoloured. He hardly even cried. Seeing him close up, Gloria felt a crack in her throat.

'I realised right away that something wasn't right; the doctor took him from my arms immediately, alarmed. He was the colour of just-burned ash, with that light look around his neck and the back of his head. Later, when they ran tests on him in Madrid, they told me that I had held him in too long during labour, causing his blood supply to be cut off for a short time.'

Gloria interrupted herself and stared pointedly into Eduardo's eyes. Her expression was impenetrable.

'I cut off my own son's blood supply, I got scared at the possibility of dying with him. In those brief moments of panic I'd have given his life for mine, I wanted to survive at all costs. And now I'd give my life just to have him here a little while longer. They told me that the trauma of that childbirth would affect my son, would result in consequences difficult to predict. Can you believe that? *Consequences difficult to predict.*'

Her voice trembled.

'I loved my son beyond anything imaginable, loved him more than anything. But there's one thing that horrifies me. I'm starting to forget what he really looked like, what he smelled like, what he felt like, his voice. That's oblivion, don't you think? That's true death.'

It was a few seconds before she looked up. Her eyes pulled Eduardo in, peeking out from beneath tortoise-shell glasses that gave her the air of an intellectual — an intelligent, fiery woman. Eduardo couldn't help but think that she looked beautiful with that expression on her face, like Michelangelo's *Madonna*. That was the first time he got the irrepressible urge to kiss her, the first erotic desire he'd had in fourteen years for any woman other than Elena. He had never cheated on his wife, never even been tempted to, even though sometimes Elena would punish him for any little thing with the words 'don't touch me'. *What about Elena?* he wondered. Had she ever cheated on him? Had she felt the temptation, the desire to cheat? Did she fantasise about other men when she was with him?

Unaware of the swirling thoughts she had awakened in Eduardo — or perhaps simply feigning ignorance — Gloria walked to the desk and took out the paper she'd been reading when he walked in.

'This is a letter from the man who killed my son. The mailman delivered it.'

Gloria (it's stupid, but I don't know how to address you, if I should put Señora before your name, or Dearest — though clearly not that — if I should keep my distance by addressing you formally, or use the informal *tú* ...).

By this time, you may know that the Council of Ministers has signed off on my pardon. These are my last few hours, the final minutes in this cell, and I'm spending them writing you this letter before the sun rises, as my cellmate snores in the bunk above me and the searchlight on the prison yard wall is all I can use to guide my lines on this paper. In the distance I can hear a dog barking, furious at something — maybe the huge moon, which looks full of holes — behind the wall. I can also hear coughing, the quiet murmuring of restless conversations; the walls of a cell are not nearly as thick as they lead you to believe. And I want to write to you here, now, while I'm having all the same feelings I've had these past three years, in the same place, because I am certain that the second I walk out the prison gate it will all start to be forgotten, as soon as I take my first step of freedom. Soon the imprint left by this experience will seem ephemeral, a black hole in my memory, one I'll dredge back up over and over again until it has been completely deformed, until it becomes fictional — an anecdote to tell people who know nothing about what goes on here.

I know you hate me. It couldn't be any other way. I understand that you fought to the end, first to have the harshest sentence possible imposed and then against my pardon. It's the least you could do, the least I would have done so if I were you. So I accept the possibility that the minute you receive this letter you'll see who it's from and tear it up without reading it; but I trust that in the end your curiosity, the very revulsion and contempt you feel for me, will compel you to read these hasty lines. I would have liked to be able to tell you this face to face, but I gave up long ago on the hope that you would ever come visit me in prison, as I asked you to several times during my first year, and my lawyers have made very clear that I am absolutely forbidden from going anywhere near you or contacting you from the moment I gain my freedom, so this is my only recourse.

There are so many things I'd like to tell you, but words turn vicious when forced out by anger. And you have suffered enough; you'll suffer for the rest of your life. As do I. I am sorry, Gloria, sorry for you, and for me, for us. I wanted you to know that in my freedom lies my penance. The bars that imprison me are not made of steel, and there is no jailer who can open this door for me. Perhaps that will console you.

Rimbaud wrote:

What do we care, my heart, for streaming sheets
of blood, hot coals, and countless murders, the long screams
Of rage, every weeping hell upsetting
All order; the north wind still scouring the debris

Erase me from your heart, Gloria — today, now, sooner rather than later, before my deadly venom poisons you.

Yours,

ARTHUR FERNÁNDEZ

Gloria slowly took the letter from Eduardo's hands and then stared at it for a long time. She wasn't reading it, just staring at it, as though trying to imagine Arthur leaning over the windowsill, writing by the light of the perimeter wall searchlight.

'He's being released ... and this is all he has to say to me.'

Eduardo contemplated her expression for quite some time. It was empty, like a gigantic rock blocking out the light. And then calmly and serenely, Gloria tore the sheet of paper in two, and then again, and again, until it was nothing but tiny scraps she held in her fist. She raised it and opened her hand, and the pieces fluttered down chaotically.

What are words that go unheard? Anvils, sledgehammers that keep pain from ever dying.

Gloria was wrong. True death is not oblivion but constant memory, the inability to escape a fateful moment that, by sheer force of repetition, becomes unreal, invented, like a movie whose ending you know because you've seen it a hundred times and so add something each time, some new pinprick to help keep the suffering alive. Eduardo didn't want to think of Elena's lips as she spoke, didn't want to think of her perfect teeth ...

He couldn't even forget her teeth. For a very long time, he'd kept her toothbrush in the holder, and he'd see it there each morning, its white bristles and ergonomic handle beside the mouthwash and the dental floss. He thought it would always be there, her toothbrush, a fallen swan in a glass cup, nestling his.

Death meant imprisoning the day your wife and daughter died in a red circle on the calendar; it was the agonising countdown, the minutes bringing you closer and closer to that moment, the tick-tock of the clock, as if counting time were the only thing you could do between one anniversary and the next. For fourteen years.

Summer, late August, 1991. They had made love in tangled sheets, slowly. Eduardo ejaculated onto Elena's stomach and collapsed by her side, breathing fast. She gave him time to recover, they smoked a couple of cigarettes and then did it again, her way this time, passionately, almost violently, excessively, like a fight in which kissing vies with biting, tenderness with roughness; an animalistic game in which the seam that joined their souls tighter than any other bond was revealed through moaning and talking dirty.

'We could just stay here like this, forever,' Eduardo said afterwards, when they should have been getting dressed, because Tania would be back soon; and yet there they were, lying in bed, letting their stuck-together skin slowly pull away in its own unhurried time. Eduardo reached out a hand and placed it on the curve of Elena's hip. His fingers dropped down over the valley of her belly and came to rest between her legs. And he left them there, almost motionless, his fingertips just barely grazing the lips of her vagina, feeling the heat it gave off.

'Sure, why not?' Elena giggled, biting one of his pink nipples.

They laughed together, complicit, and then fell silent, breathing in time, she with her head on his belly, he absently stroking her freckled shoulder. Lying there in bed, just looking at her, Eduardo could see everything about his wife's nature, all in one glance. His eyes were the only thing capable of expressing what he felt for her; words could only distort it, ruin the totality of moments like those. That was the reason he loved to gaze at her as they made love — sometimes slowly, their rhythm quivering and contained, sometimes wildly, her fingernails clawing his hips. He needed to look at her so that he could penetrate her eyes, too; needed her to look at him with her eyes wide open, like they were both part of the same hallucination. He needed it in order to reach ecstasy, in order to stop thinking and disappear, and simply feel.

It wasn't just physical attraction, wasn't just a primitive, visceral desire that Elena aroused in him. It was much more than that. After being married so many years, nothing, in essence, had really changed. If anything, the rough edges of their madness had softened, the sharp corners had been filed down and now rested on a more stable plane; the wild exploration of his first few years, his desire to conquer her territory by hacking his way with a machete, had been replaced by a conscientious study of the lay of the land, a methodology of maps, valleys and rivers that he analysed, taking notes in his mind like a topographer. Surprises were no longer abrupt and disconcerting but a gentle discovery of different things, like the tiny streams of water that sometimes gurgle up from underground when the earth's surface has been mined. He no longer had to force his way; he walked calmly and the way was revealed to him. And Elena was his way.

'We could stay like this forever,' she said, repeating Eduardo's words, her body folded over his legs. Her violet dress was floating in the window, hung out on the line with two pegs. The wind played with the dress, fluttering it up and dropping it down, fluttering up, dropping down, briefly revealing glimpses of the harsh landscape, the rocks, the beach, the little boats in their slips, staked to the shore. Time and space were marvellously ungraspable, the sounds drifting in from outside bathed in a soft, beautiful afternoon light.

Eduardo sat up to reach for a glass of water on the nightstand. He took a long sip and sighed, staring at the ceiling. A fan spun lazily, its long blades revolving slowly, circulating the hot air in the room.

'We should really take a shower and get dressed. Tania must be about to walk in. By the way, I haven't seen her all day.'

'She must be in town with her friends. There's a going-away party today. Let her enjoy her last few hours on vacation.'

Eduardo frowned. To him, Tania was still that tiny body he had to crouch down to if he wanted to say something, and he took refuge in his own vague obliviousness, in opting not to know too much when his daughter reacted to something in a way that told him she was slipping through his fingers and he couldn't do a thing about it. For Elena, though, their daughter had become a compendium of dilemmas large and small, which had to be dealt with ad hoc. Sometimes it was an irritating, gruelling job, and other times her relationship with her daughter was full of secret satisfactions, confessions, shared fears; it was a means of returning to the crossroads of her own adolescence.

'She's almost fourteen; believe me, she knows more than her sweet little face lets on.'

By the time Tania got back it was late at night, but that wasn't what really infuriated Eduardo, who was just finishing packing his books into a travel bag as Elena put the kitchen chairs on top of the table.

'You reek of booze and cigarettes. Do you mind telling me what kind of parties your friends throw?'

Tania's character was too bossy for her father's liking. Sassy and foul-mouthed, she didn't shy from conflict, using any excuse to test the waters, unconsciously measuring her strength, seeing the world as but a stage on which to act out her desires. But that night she misjudged her father's reaction. The transition from the festive air of the party — her friends, music, a joint or two, a little gin — to the paternal domicile had been too brusque, and she hadn't had enough time to adjust, to adapt her expression, put on the proper disguise.

'Leave me alone! I'm not a little girl anymore, I don't have to put up with sermons from a boring old fart.'

'Don't talk to me that way! I want an explanation.'

'Well, how do you expect me to talk to you? In sign language? Because you're acting like a deaf-mute.'

The slap came out of nowhere, slicing through the air like a whistle, taking her off-guard as it landed across her mouth. Tania took two steps back, more out of shock than the force of the blow. A sorrowful silence descended on all three of them, as though nobody — least of all Eduardo — had expected that to happen. He looked down at his hand like a foreign body that had suddenly, for a fraction of a second, possessed its own free will. Elena stood in silence, her jaw set, tense, and Tania sobbed something her father didn't want to hear, but which was perfectly clear: 'You son of a bitch,' and then she ran to her room and slammed the door so hard the house shook.

'I don't know what came over me,' Eduardo murmured, looking to Elena.

It was the first time he'd ever laid a finger on his daughter. And yet the worst thing was not that he'd done it, or whether or not she deserved it, or his instantaneous regret. If he could turn the clock back one minute, there was no doubt he'd undo what he'd done. But what he wasn't willing to confess, not even to himself, was that as he slapped his daughter's face, he'd felt a complete and total sense of release.

Elena simply stared at him, something hanging there on her lips, words struggling to come out that she tried to hold back with her teeth.

'Don't you ever touch my daughter again,' she finally uttered coldly, cuttingly, without the slightest hint of compassion.

Eduardo felt that the perfect circle they had formed was now distorted, its poles flattened and shamed, felt that their loyalties were not as absolute as he'd thought.

They had left Cadaqués early, before dawn. The first hour was tense, Eduardo at the wheel, brooding, seemingly concentrating on the traffic, but really immersed in a tangled swirl of feelings he would have liked to put voice to. Elena stared out the window, her forehead to the glass, her expression revealing nothing about what she was thinking. In the back seat, Tania dozed fitfully, on and off, from time to time waking fully to shoot daggers at her father in the rearview mirror.

At the halfway point, they came to a rest area with a gas station and a wooden cabin-like structure that was a restaurant and café. They were close to a small town on the Toledo highway and could have skipped stopping, but Eduardo needed to rest. It smelled like fresh-cut grass, and there was a grove of trees where the ground was covered in leaves. It was very pretty, totally unexpected.

'Why don't we all take a photo together?' Elena asked, her voice too festive, unnatural. Tania was sitting across from her at a picnic table, picking at a bit of dry wood that had begun to splinter away from one of the table's planks. Eduardo had gone to the café's self-service area to buy them all sandwiches.

'What are we celebrating?' she asked dryly. 'The fact that my father is a stupid jerk?'

'We could celebrate the fact that I have an irresponsible daughter who doesn't understand or value the freedom she's been given, or how much her father loves her; or maybe we should celebrate how stupid your mother is for having believed you were mature enough to understand that we all make mistakes. You're just a girl, after all.'

'He slapped my face!' Tania protested.

'Yes, he did. And he shouldn't have. But guess what? Every time you talk back, or give us the silent treatment, or show contempt, that's a slap in the face, too. How many slaps do you think we put up with from you every day? And we take it, because you're our daughter, and that's life, and we understand that you need to feel like you're in control ...'

Tania adopted a bored look.

'Enough lecturing, *mamá*.'

This time it was Elena who raised her voice.

'No, it's not enough lecturing; I'll lecture you as long as I have to, and you'll shut your mouth and listen. You think you have the right to judge your father, but you know nothing about him and you don't care. I met that man long before I'd ever even contemplated your existence and it hurts me to see him suffer because of you and your selfishness. I know it's hard, I know you feel like you need to break things to find your place, but you could go a little easier on him — that's all I'm asking. I don't want you constantly putting me between a rock and a hard place, Tania; you can't keep making me choose between the two of you. It's not fair. You've got your whole life ahead of you — why are you in such a rush to challenge him now?'

Just then, Eduardo appeared with a tray full of sandwiches and soft drinks. Seeing him approach, mother and daughter fell silent. He hesitated, not knowing what to do with the tray, where to sit. Elena scooted over to make space for him, and then stroked his leg under the table. That gesture, for him, was all he needed, the best thing he could have hoped for.

'I think your daughter wants to say something.'

Tania glared at her mother, affronted, but Elena compelled her with a harsh look.

'I'm sorry, *papá*. I shouldn't have talked back to you like that. It's just that sometimes you make me so mad ...'

Eduardo smiled, pushing up the bridge of his glasses on his nose. The worst had passed.

85

'I think I've heard the same thing from your mother's mouth a couple million times.'

The peace achieved after a fight is never total, the calm is not the same; there are always things left unsaid, rough edges beneath the surface that prick like thorns, but if you try to avoid them, things can go smoothly enough. A tacit agreement allowed them to eat in relative contentment, recalling anecdotes from the trip that, although it hadn't yet even ended, they evoked with premature nostalgia. Elena insisted that they take a picture in the grove, it would be the perfect culmination to a vacation that, in time, they'd look back on with affection — provided they overlooked that last final incident.

'Let's take that picture.' Eduardo found a rock they could balance the camera on, and then set the timer, and the three of them tried to determine exactly where to stand so as to be framed perfectly. They laughed and posed this way and that, jostling and joking like they always did. But no matter how they laughed, Eduardo couldn't shake the strange feeling he'd gotten when he slapped his daughter, the first violent act of his life — the surprise on discovering that he was capable of causing harm to those he loved most.

They got back on the road. Eduardo drove slowly, the window lowered slightly so the air rushing in would keep him alert, while part of his mind drifted to the inevitable series of things he had to do to re-establish their routine when they got back — trivial but necessary things like turning the gas and electricity meters back on, telling the building association president to turn their water main on, doing laundry, putting away the suitcases, washing the car. Elena and Tania were asleep in the back seat, curled up around one another under a travel blanket. He contemplated them in the rearview mirror — so different, so the same, now that they couldn't hide behind any masks, unaware they were being observed, at the mercy of their emotions.

And suddenly, all his thoughts vaporised, proving how pointless they were.

The car was struck violently from behind, and he felt as though the car flew up off the ground; that his arms were being ripped off by the extraordinary centrifugal force, making it impossible to keep his hands on the wheel or his feet on the pedals. At the same time — or perhaps it was afterwards, but the sense of immediacy made it all blur — came a terrific jerking movement, right to left and top to bottom, that slammed him into the roof of the car, into the suitcases, into the hydraulic jack, and into something soft that could only be the body of his wife or daughter, who'd been hurled forward.

An idea slowly crept into his head, like fire licking at his dazed bewilderment. An accident, he was part of an accident, like a rag doll whipped this way and that by the impact. It was really happening.

He felt a horrific pain in his knee, a pain so intense he'd have never thought it possible. There was more jerking, and at some point the front windshield shattered into a thousand pieces. Then the car slid down an embankment, upside down, flattening everything in its path. And finally it came to a standstill, in silence.

The stillness and silence were surreal.

His face was wet: the stream. Water was coming in through the broken windshield. Blindly he managed to undo his seatbelt, but he couldn't move. He was face-down, his head buzzing like a blender, and nothing was where it should have been; his eyes not seeing, his hands not feeling. He tried to get up, but something made him cry out in agony. A chunk of metal, sharp and pointy as a spearhead, had skewered his knee, pinning him to the twisted wreckage of the car. He could hardly see through the smoke and blood clouding his vision. He groped around and touched something with his fingers. Hair. Wet hair, a motionless head, Elena's broken neck. A few inches from his face, she stared at him, lifeless, with almost embarrassed modesty. Eduardo tried to get up, to move her, but it was utterly impossible. He let her head fall back and thought of Tania. He couldn't see her among the heaps of metal and plastic, glass, clothing and smoke. He tried to call out to her but a spurt of bloody bubbles was all that came from his mouth. His daughter wasn't in the car.

And then he saw her, dragging herself like an inchworm cut in two, on the other side of the stream, a trail of blood in her wake. She was crawling very slowly, her dress in tatters. She stopped moving, her head and body out of the water, her legs floating in the stream. Eduardo tried to reach her, but his leg was impaled by iron, and nearly every bone in his body broken. He watched her move again, crawl a bit, and then fall still. Her eyes open. She convulsed and vomited blood, and after that she moved no more. Eduardo could only lie there, contemplating her agony, his face reflecting no emotion.

The three weeks after the accident Eduardo spent in an induced coma. The doctors said it was the only way a body so battered could withstand the pain. The list of broken bones and affected organs was astonishing. After several operations they managed to salvage the mobility of most of his joints, with the exception of his right knee, which was totally beyond hope and was going to be substituted with a complex prosthesis. After a few days, his spleen and renal function were stabilised, and although he still had a catheter and there was blood in both his urine and faeces, he was at least able to begin ingesting liquids fairly quickly. The bruises on his face had left him a swollen shapeless mass; he had cuts on his right retina; he'd lost several teeth, and his left earlobe had to be sewn back on; but miraculously he would have no visible scars, except for a few deep gashes on the back of his skull which, in time, would be easy to hide. He would never again walk comfortably, the screws and metal plates used to reconstruct his knee would cause him pain for the rest of his life. But that wasn't the worst of it.

The worst thing was that he was alive. Little by little, he stopped hearing doctors' and nurses' voices, focusing instead on the movement of their lips, on the food stuck in their teeth, tiny spit bubbles — things of that nature. His tuning out of reality, and immersing himself into a deeper layer of all that surrounded him became more intense and more frequent, gaining space and breadth, and was increasingly difficult to keep under control. Slowly he sank into a deep well, a black hole that no one and nothing could pull him out of.

When he was transferred from the ICU to a regular ward, they put him in a private room under twenty-four-hour surveillance, with a camera that the ward's security guard watched at all times from behind a counter. He received regular visits from a hospital psychologist, sometimes accompanied by a member of the Association of Victims of Traffic Accidents. The medical team feared he would try to commit suicide.

They administered high doses of tranquillisers and antidepressants every day, which plunged him into a state of lethargy he had no desire to emerge from. He hardly walked, and proved unwilling to do the physical therapy exercises he'd been assigned; he didn't eat, either, and tried to sleep as much as possible. He couldn't even be bothered to ask for help when he felt his urinary tract function return, the bag full and the sheets already stained. He just slept and, when he was awake, allowed himself to be moved this way and that, hearing the doctor's questions — 'Does this hurt? What about this?' — and answering them by moving his head vaguely, in a way that meant neither one thing nor the other. He accepted with indifference the encouraging pats offered by acquaintances who came to visit, wishing they would simply go away and leave him in peace.

Eduardo recalled the last visit he'd had from the police officer in charge of his case. It was a Sunday afternoon and the ward was nearly empty.

The officer stood, dressed in a wrinkled suit, and matching vest and tie. He was jiggling his legs a bit, as if on the verge of losing his patience. His cologne mixed with the other smells in the room and the result was unpleasant, overwhelming. He told Eduardo that the accident had been caused by a vehicle, travelling at high speed, slamming into them from behind. Traffic Unit tests had indicated that it was most likely an SUV.

The police were working from the hypothesis that the driver had run a stop sign before hitting Eduardo's car. Perhaps he'd stopped at first to help, but when he saw how serious the accident was, had gotten scared and taken off. They'd studied the scratch marks on the bodywork in an attempt to narrow down the make of the other vehicle, but water damage had made any recent traces of paint unusable. All they had to go on was a piece of headlight cover and some tyre tracks. Not much at all, he admitted. Most likely they'd never find the guy, unless someone came forward with the exact licence-plate number or turned out to have seen the accident, both of which were highly unlikely in such a desolate area. Regardless, the officer said encouragingly, they'd notified both the press and any police stations in the vicinity.

'Something might crop up, lead us to the guilty party. But you should keep one thing in mind, Eduardo: even if we find him, if the guy's had time to get his car fixed, it will be your word against his, and he'll get off. *In dubio pro reo*, that's the law. But don't worry, I'm not the type to give up. I can't fucking stand impunity.'

Eduardo was hardly paying attention.

Another day, some court officials came to pay him a visit. They had some of his wife's and daughter's belongings in an envelope, and a pile of papers for him to sign. Eduardo gave them a quick glance. At the time, he had a nasty conjunctival haemorrhage, and his eye was full of blood. He looked away, disgusted, and clung to his pillow. The mere act of producing simple words, asking for a glass of water, getting up to go to the bathroom, wore him out completely.

Then came a whole series of procedures required for the burial. Elena had no family, and they had no insurance for anything like this — she had been too full of life to have even contemplated the possibility of death, so it had been a small, discreet civil service. The bodies were cremated and given to Eduardo in an urn. The expenses ate up his meagre savings, but he didn't care in the slightest; his father had to be the one to take care of preparations, informing their friends and accepting their condolences, ordering the flowers and dealing with cumbersome paperwork at the civil registry. Eduardo, meanwhile, spent his days prostrate, staring out the hospital window at the world outside, seeing nothing.

Four months later, he was released, his loved ones' belongings in one hand and their ashes in the other. The everyday sounds of the street bounced off him like rays of sun, but Eduardo heard nothing. The voices of passers-by, buses honking, people chatting at sidewalk cafés — all of it came to him muffled, as though he were underwater in a swimming pool, and could only make out a dull reverberation that gave everything a surreal quality. His father was waiting for him on the other side of the street, by the open door of a taxi. Eduardo ignored him and headed down the block, dragging his suitcase and feeling like a dead man walking through the land of the living.

Afterwards, he stopped painting, working, going outside, bathing. Sometimes he would experience things he later found out were auditory hallucinations, things he was unable to separate from everyday sounds. They were real, with sounds and subsounds, and he heard them both. For instance, he might be listening to the complex arrangement of a Dexter Gordon piece, focusing on the music's vibrations, and at the same time part of his brain heard the flutter of a dragonfly's wings as it buzzed around his ear — except that the dragonfly wasn't there, despite Eduardo being utterly aware of its beating wings. That was how he began to let go of the one thing that didn't help him understand — his mind. His head became a locked room, a dark place where he lived among nameless shadows. Shadows that brushed up against him, startled him, and made him leap from the bed covered in sweat in the middle of the night, screaming.

The things around him — people he saw in the elevator, at the supermarket, on the street, conversations he overheard or tried to have — were pieces of a puzzle that didn't fit, shades of colours, shapes that didn't add up to a sufficiently credible reality. He spent weeks contemplating portraits by Lucien Freud he'd once so admired. The paintings had the same intense magnetic attraction as before, but now the spell they cast seemed evil. He tried to find himself in the canvases that had so inspired him to become a painter of souls, a man who depicted the shadows inhabited by his models, but their cold eyes and merciless expressions now hurled him into a world of profound desperation. The subjects' eyes bore into him, piercing him, mocking him. He felt like the self-portrait of Freud, hanging in his studio, was no longer an inspiring brother but his executioner.

It must have been then that he began contemplating the best way to put an end to the stinging that the blood circulating through his veins produced. Life, in his body, in his skin, disturbed him; he found it offensive.

6

Arthur strode through the office building's sizeable vestibule, a visitor's badge on his lapel. It seemed everyone was very busy; on seeing him, some gave a fake wave, others pretended not to realise he was there, but the majority simply ignored his presence without giving it a second thought. Though he was still the firm's majority shareholder, almost nobody thought he'd have the gall to show his face there again after being released from prison. To the employees of his own company, Arthur was an outcast.

Standing there among the cubicles, in the way, ill at ease, not knowing what to do, he finally saw the enormous silhouette of Nadia Rueda. His old director waved emphatically, one arm aloft. Was she happy to see him back there? It was hard to tell, but Arthur smiled, relieved as a shipwrecked sailor finding a buoy in the middle of the ocean.

'Nice suit,' Nadia said, not really paying attention, shaking his hand vigorously and planting a noisy kiss on his cheek. Rueda was, in every sense, a most energetic woman.

They rode the elevator to the top floor together. As if he were a guest, Rueda ushered him into his old office and kicked the door closed behind her. Arthur looked at what had once been his desk. She was now using it to stack dossiers.

'Since you left, no one's been as good as you; sounds like the lyrics to a fucking bolero, but it's true. I thought you'd take a few months sabbatical — we all did, around here.'

'Well, it is still eighty per cent my company, after all, isn't it?' Arthur replied. 'I wanted to see how things have been going in my absence.'

Rueda motioned for him to take a seat on a new Swedish-designed armchair, which as well as expensive looked to be exceedingly uncomfortable. Arthur would have preferred to sit in his creaky, old wood-backed, suede armchair, frail but accustomed to his weight. His chair, however, was gone, no doubt hidden in the back of some storage room.

Rueda brought him up to speed.

'I've arranged for a meeting with the minority shareholders this afternoon and have prepared a summary of the books so you can go over them with the financial advisor. You'll see things have gone fairly well ...' She pulled out a drawer, took out a piece of paper and laid it on the table, tapping emphatically with a fingernail. The sharp rap of polished nails on paper was, to Arthur, like a bee rubbing its feet together.

'You've done a good job here, Nadia.'

Rueda leaned against the edge of the table with her fingers interlaced over her thighs, like a priestess about to deliver bad news; she looked up at the clock behind them, then turned her eyes back to Arthur and stared at him pointedly.

'Actually, I've done very little. When you got locked up, you granted full power to Diana. Now the US office runs your business, and my hands are tied. All I can do is swallow whatever she bites off for us.'

'I did what I thought best, but that doesn't mean I pushed you aside; you're still very important to me,' Arthur said, exasperatingly well-mannered and unconvincing.

Rueda let out a wounded laugh.

'You don't have to be polite. Fat old ladies just get in the way, in every sense. Ageing sucks, doesn't it? You think it's never going to happen to you and then — bam! — suddenly a gorgeous, siliconed panther appears, speaking Spanglish, and your name's off the list. I'm not dead yet though, dammit ...'

'Nobody said you were,' Arthur responded.

Rueda swallowed hard.

'I suppose you feel betrayed, and I can't blame you. I so nearly went to visit you in jail, several times, but in the end I didn't have the guts to do it. The pictures of that six-year-old girl, that boy crushed under the car, and you in cuffs, drunk. Fuck, Arthur, the whole thing, what you did ... We all ended up thinking you'd become a real bastard.'

Arthur listened without batting an eye. He betrayed no emotion whatsoever. He knew what Nadia thought, what they all thought. Even the best, most loyal and honest people, like her, wondered how he could have fallen so low. Maybe they'd done some thinking, made some calculations and realised — horrified — that it could have been them.

A spell of bad luck, one desperate move, and everything was lost: job, friends, relationships, sanity.

'... But it was an accident, and I shouldn't have judged you — me of all people should not have stooped to that — after having known you since you first started this company.'

'It's all in the past now; I'm over it,' said Arthur, forcing a smile that he hoped looked friendly.

Rueda nodded, unconvinced. He was in pain, he felt betrayed. She could see it in his cloudy expression.

'Really? Around here, people are saying you're going to pull out a scythe, that heads will roll. When they heard you were out of jail, a lot of folks started packing their bags. I'm half-packed myself.'

Arthur looked away, gazed out the window. The quality of the light reminded him of being at university, those anodyne days when his eyes would drift out to watch the winter weather, unable to concentrate on the Greek professor shouting about the importance of Plato's discourses in the development of modern-day dialectics. 'So, you don't find what I'm saying of any interest, Monsieur Fernández?' the professor's voice railed, trembling at his impotence, his inability to pique the interest of an easily distracted young man, a young man who showed undeniable talent. His director's voice, too, fell like rain, a voice that lulled him, dozing as he waited for the storm to pass.

'I need to get back into the swing of things slowly. Then I'll decide what to do. But for now I need you to do something for me, right away, and it doesn't exactly fall under your job description.'

'If you're going to ask me for sex, I'm warning you now, I haven't waxed in awhile,' Nadia retorted without missing a beat.

They both laughed, and their laughter seemed to put things in place.

'In prison, my cellmate was a man named Ibrahim. He saved my life, and I promised him I was going to try to take care of his legal proceedings. I want to know what the options are as far as getting him out. I'd like to have him close by.'

'What crime did your friend commit?'

Arthur shrugged.

'I don't care what he's done, Nadia.'

'You don't owe that man anything. You're not a jailbird; you run a company that generates millions of euros in investments; send him a box of chocolates with a thank-you card, but don't get mixed up with that kind of person.'

Arthur recalled the words his mother used to say when he was a boy, a *pied-noir* son of a lieutenant jailed in France for being a terrorist, but a military man, nonetheless. The children of Europeans were not allowed to go down to the Kasbah, not allowed to run around by the walls of Djemaa el-Kebir mosque with the native-born Algerian kids. He, his mother and his siblings lived off of whatever they could sell at Triad market: spools of thread, batteries, household furniture, even clothes; they barely had enough to eat and there was no electricity or telephone at home, but it didn't matter.

In the miserable little apartment where they had lived hung a painting by General Sagan himself: flowers, signed and bearing the inscription *Semper fidelis*. His mother kept his father's best suits in the closet, along with his military uniforms, polished boots, leather belts as shiny as their buckles, and an endless array of medals he'd earned for service in the Algerian War ... They had no food on the table, but *France loves her children even if they're led astray*, his mother would say, every time a cheque arrived from the State, which still sent a few francs each month, although no one knew how long they'd keep coming. And that was why they had to remain faithful to Lieutenant Fernández's ideology: they weren't rabble, they were different — better — and they couldn't mix with the low-lifes down at the port who hung off supply trucks trying to steal an apple or a bar of soap, while flying the FLN flag and singing the ridiculous hymn of the new Algeria.

All of that had been a long time ago, very long. But not long enough, it seemed.

Arthur eyed Rueda with hostility, blaming her for something she was not to blame for, simply because she was there. He was no longer a boy, willing to take well-intended, worthless advice. The old lady didn't know a thing, she was just like the people who'd stared at him contemptuously when he'd walked in. They had no idea of the bonds that were formed in prison.

'Take care of it, and do it now if you want to keep your job. Oh, and cancel this afternoon's meeting with the shareholders. Send all of the information to me at my hotel. We'll meet after I've gone over the books. I don't like walking into a game without knowing everyone's hand … And one more thing: when I return, I want to see my old chair here; get rid of this Nordic piece of shit.'

Rueda stood and anxiously removed her glasses, which hung around her neck on a little fuchsia-coloured cord. She started to say something, but Arthur held up a hand, cutting her off.

'I'd like to be alone now, if you don't mind.'

He picked up the phone and dialled.

It was very late in Chicago, but Diana would still be in the office, getting the most out of her poor interns, bleeding them dry with her unyielding insistence, as she bent over ever-changing charts and graphs on a screen, watching as the international markets closed in Tokyo, Sydney, Hong Kong and London. It was less than two minutes before he heard her soft voice, the American accent she'd never been able to get rid of, despite having lived in Madrid for several years.

'Arthur, you're free.'

Arthur felt a tickle in his throat, an old familiar warmth like the memory of a fire burning in a fireplace that's no longer alight. He thought briefly of one of the many nights he'd spent with Diana, the beautiful summer moons they shared on the Côte d'Azur. He pictured her, face to the shore, smoking, gazing absently out at the water, her long-lashed almond eyes; and behind her, he, encircling her waist, stroking her glimmering black skin, soft and smooth, caressing her with his eyes, thinking how lucky he was to be wanted (loved was too much to ask) by a woman like Diana. Their affair, for years, had been just that: glances, smiles, few words, much touching. Furtive encounters when she came to Madrid to take care of some business or other, or when he travelled to the US for some equally nebulous reason.

'Yes, I'm out. Thank you for taking care of everything.'

'Any problem with the paperwork?'

Diana's voice, more than her manner, came off as a bit critical — she was a pragmatic American after all; she sounded busy. Perhaps she had a client in the office, one not so important that she'd ignore Arthur's call but not so insignificant that she could keep him waiting as she chatted on the phone. It wasn't the same — her voice no longer trembled like that of a nervous schoolgirl.

'The lawyer you put on the case was very efficient. I congratulate you on that.'

'Don't: you're the one paying his fees. And I warn you, they won't be cheap.'

It was strange, disheartening, for him to be wasting his first conversation with his one-time lover on an exchange of painful trivialities.

'Not one visit in three years is a pretty harsh punishment, don't you think?'

Silence. Deep silence. On the end of the line he could hear Diana's heavy breathing, flustered — she breathed that way after an orgasm and during heated arguments.

'I wasn't prepared for what happened, Arthur. I'm still not.'

He heard a click. Diana was lighting a cigarette. So she'd gone back to smoking. It upset him, knowing that his ex-lover had been able to re-establish the course of her everyday life in his absence. For him, things were not so easy. Starting over, relearning his old routines, was not going to be a simple task.

He looked at himself in the mirrored glass of the door. He looked like shit — up until that moment he hadn't realised just how far downhill he'd gone.

'I've changed, Diana. We all have.'

'I've got work to do here; I can't talk right now,' she replied. Her voice sounded distant, hollow.

Arthur was wounded. He paused, and then spoke again, his voice loud and confident now — the commanding tone of a boss who expects efficiency.

'That's fine. So how's that job I gave you? Where do things stand?'

'I'm on it. But remember I warned you when we last spoke: Guzmán is not a door that can be easily closed if you decide to open it.'

'Leave that to me. And send this Guzmán to Madrid as soon as possible.'

There was still one more thing that Diana needed to know.

'Are you going to see Andrea?'

Arthur considered his reply. It was a question he expected, an obvious one, but he didn't know how to face it.

'I don't know yet,' he lied. Of course he knew.

When he hung up he felt absolutely exhausted. Had anyone walked into the office at that moment, they'd have found a man who, though not old, was certainly no longer young, splayed awkwardly in an uncomfortably designed armchair — a king on a throne of mud. And if that unwitting witness had seen the expression on his face, he would probably have tiptoed back out, stricken, closing the door very softly behind him. Arthur's sadness was not resigned, not melancholy, or nostalgic. It was a fist swinging through the air, not knowing who or what to pummel.

He ordered a taxi and showed the driver the address, written on a shiny folded pamphlet that he pulled from his inside jacket pocket.

'That's more than seventy kilometres from here,' the driver protested.

Arthur loosened his tie and gazed at the building's glass front. Behind the windows, he pictured his employees, observing him furtively. The firm's corporate name was emblazoned across the entire first-floor facade: 'Incsa' — it was one of the biggest investment-fund management firms in the eurozone. It belonged to him, he was majority shareholder, but he'd never felt like it was his.

'I don't care if it's seven hundred. Drive — and turn up the volume. I like this song.'

Nobody listened to Charles Aznavour anymore. 'Mourir d'aimer'. He remembered his mother sitting at the record player, curtains drawn, clutching a wrinkled handkerchief.

How bizarre, Aznavour, an Armenian.

His mother missed Lieutenant Fernández, cried for him like a schoolgirl, and it didn't matter to her at all that he'd been overly fond of the strap, using it on her and the children alike, didn't matter that the eldest had lost an eye to a poorly aimed lash that ruptured his eyeball when it was struck by the buckle. He was that record, spinning in the dark, that music, that voice.

It didn't matter that at dinnertime, when he sat down, he did so with a loaded pistol within reach, just to the right of his silverware, the barrel pointed at his children, looking out the window like a dog trapped in a corner.

His mother crying as the record spun, warped, beneath the needle.

She knew one day they'd let him out, and she'd be waiting for him, in the red-checked dress with straps, her hair pulled back the way he liked. She'd be waiting for him with his uniform freshly ironed, the braids on his cuffs, his medals and awards all laid out.

But instead what arrived was a telegram. Two short sentences. Terse. Definitive. In 1969. Aznavour was playing, and from the gangways on the port arose the fetid stench of a cargo ship flying the Egyptian flag. Kids were acting like kids, down on the street — playing ball games, rolling hoops, hitting each other, pretending to be FLN patriots and skydivers. Not Arthur. He was sitting across from his mother, noting the way she used the door handle to support herself, in order not to faint. Arthur picked the telegram up off the floor. The lieutenant was not in jail, they'd freed him months ago, but rather than return to his children, he'd opted to run to his putative father, going into exile with General Salan, to Málaga, where the dregs of the OAS — the Secret Army Organization — were hiding out. There he'd been found by some Armenian mercenaries, hired by the secret service. They didn't even waste a bullet on him. They took him to the beach, in shackles, and bashed his skull in with a shovel. Then they had tossed him into the sea. Maybe the tides would bring him back to Algeria.

Two weeks after receiving that news came a notice from the military command. His widow would have to pay burial expenses if she wanted to repatriate the body. In addition, she was officially no longer eligible for any State aid. But his mother was no longer the woman in that room, she no longer heard anything, no longer hoped for anything. Except that record, that song, that voice.

He contemplated the near-empty parking lot beyond the ivy wall. This was not a wall to impede entry or exit, simply a discreet line separating two realities — inside and outside, here and there — and the vines and hedges just invited you to one side or the other. A gentle breeze stirred the fallen leaves of plane trees this way and that. On the other side of the wall surrounding the premises was a street lined left to right with identical terraced houses, each with the same red-tile roof and the same little stone wall topped with a well-manicured hedge. Exactly the same as the picture on the promotional brochure published by the residential community, as if the photo had been taken from the same spot, at the exact same time of day. 'Paradise Community': an idyllic residence, as good a place as any to die without getting in the way.

The afternoon sun flooded the room, bathing it in a warm pale glow that detached the objects inside it from reality, making them seem somehow less solid: Andrea's clothes on the bed, the brush on the dresser with its bristles full of hair, a pair of plastic clogs lined up demurely by the step leading out to the terrace. Still, it disconcerted him to note the crucifix above the headboard of her bed and a small bible on the nightstand. There was also a glass of water and a tube of blue pills. A shadow of doubt hung over Arthur's expression. Yes, everyone had changed in that time, as he'd said to Diana just a few hours earlier. Andrea, too, no doubt. He breathed in the scent of a shirt draped across the back of a chair. His wife's scent, at least, was one thing that hadn't changed during those three years.

Andrea was out in a little garden, tending to some tomato plants. She seemed content with a small plot of earth where she could sink her hands into the moist soil, pinch off yellowed leaves, water and fertilise, feel the roots, contemplate a tiny worm crawling up a stalk. Movement. Appreciating the flow of something that was alive. That's what her life had been reduced to. She was lucky.

A girl wearing the residence's light-blue uniform appeared and asked him, with a fake smile, if everything was all right.

'Everything is fine, thank you,' Arthur nodded, heavy-hearted. All prisons are alike, no matter what colour they paint the cell walls.

The girl looked out the window and adopted an informative tone.

'Your wife is very happy here with us, there's no need to worry. She's taken up horticulture, and she's actually a very good gardener.'

'That's good to know,' he replied, concentrating on Andrea's figure, which was now hunched over, attaching stalks to a pole staked into the ground.

'She's improving, she really is. Her nightmares have abated and she almost never cries out at night. We spend a lot of time talking,' the girl added with secret pride, as if a good part of Andrea's improvement were thanks to her efforts. Arthur stared at her with rancour: who was this girl, to be taking his place in Andrea's life?

'Would you mind leaving me alone?'

He opened the sliding window and leaned out, resting his body on the sill. The cold air blowing in from the sierra whipped against his face. Arthur lit a cigarette, pretending not to know that smoking was strictly forbidden throughout the building. Who was going to care if for once the rules weren't followed? The world was full of idiotic rules.

'Andrea ...'

She looked at Arthur as if seeing him for the first time. 'You're as pretty as ever,' he added, gazing at her with mixed love and sadness.

He was lying. It was a farce he could find convincing enough not to feel guilty about only if he avoided looking at her dirty pyjamas; if he refused to notice that her hair was longer than she liked to wear it and had been hacked off unevenly; if he looked away so as not to see her broken, bitten fingernails; and did not glance at her lifeless eyes. The spectre before him was nothing but the ellipsis at the end of the memory of another woman, one who no longer existed despite sharing a few lingering traits with her former self. There was nothing left of the young bride from the photo, of the trip they'd taken to Algiers where they shared sweet childhood memories and roamed the same streets. Long gone were those nights in the desert, smoking pot on the fine sand by the light of a bonfire, that didn't go completely out until dawn, when they were both exhausted and satisfied after making love, shielded by the dunes.

'I missed you.'

She spurned his attempt to touch her. He could tell she made an effort to look at him with contempt, but she couldn't quite manage it. Perhaps she was thinking that Arthur looked thinner, sadder, older. But she didn't say a word.

'Honestly. I thought about you every single day.'

Andrea tried to come up with something hurtful to say, an insult: *Well, I didn't miss you, you son of a bitch*. But she said nothing. Sometimes when she wanted to speak, she kept quiet instead. She couldn't find the right words, the right tone, the right timing. Perhaps she kept quiet because, in her silence, everything was implicit, because she'd grown used to watching her own life like she was a spectator made of stone. Speaking was a waste of time; breathing was inevitable — but words she could hold in. What she truly wanted was for someone to get her out of there — not her room, or the garden, or the clinic. Out of her head. For someone to tear her from her head, her body, her guts, and carry her off someplace where there was no Andrea, because she no longer had the desire nor the energy to keep being who she was, but also lacked the energy to stop.

Eat, rise, sleep, yawn ... she cared nothing about hygiene; if her caregiver took too long on the phone to her Puerto Rican boyfriend, or sat mesmerised watching a soap opera on television, she'd simply defecate on herself. She wouldn't say anything even if she was covered in shit, didn't bat an eye until that horrible stench roused the caregiver, who changed her diapers angrily, and insulted her — *you disgusting pig* — and sometimes even slapped her, if no one was around; and still Andrea hardly blinked.

And all of that neglect was absolutely voluntary. It was the penance Andrea had imposed on herself. Sometimes she burst into tears for no apparent reason, in the clinic's common area where the other patients were playing games, reading the paper or watching television. She'd sit in her chair staring out the window until her eyes turned red and then the tears flowed, gently sliding down her face, down her nose to her neck, falling onto her folded hands. Despite her silence, the doctors could tell when her will to live had ebbed dangerously: it was when she shivered, despite the room being kept at a comfortable temperature, or stubbornly pursed her lips, refusing to ingest the soup they tried to feed her. At times like that it became necessary to sedate her even further or, if things had reached an extreme, to lock her in her room, after ensuring there was nothing in reach that she could use to harm herself.

In light of what the pain had done to Andrea — eaten her alive — it was almost impossible to recall her as she once was: sitting in an armchair in her office at the University of Paris, her back straight, correcting exams in red pencil, circling students' errors and omissions, a resolute look on her face. 'These kids don't get it; Rimbaud's poetry can't be understood by the mind alone. It can only be captured by leaving your preconceptions behind. For the love of God, what is wrong with young people today? Are they scared to open their minds and think for themselves?' She always voiced her thoughts passionately, even when they were taking long walks from Rue Saint-Sulpice to Notre Dame, always winding up at some sidewalk café along the Seine. There they'd spend hours, as if time were theirs alone, smoking gracefully, bundled up in heavy jackets and hats and scarves, Andrea talking about her true love, Rimbaud's poetry, and his life.

Arthur's role in those routines was to be eager, attentive, hanging on her every gesture should she need another *demi* of beer or a pack of cigarettes, that he'd rush off to buy at the nearest newsstand. 'Sometimes I think you only married me for my name,' Arthur would joke. And Andrea would gaze at him in a sort of mystic trance, before stroking his cheek somewhat condescendingly. 'And because you're French, and a poet,' she'd add, laughing. It was a laughter that paved the way to every desire, every form of paradise a man could imagine.

When they met, he was twenty and had just enrolled in honours courses at the faculty of letters; she was an adjunct to Professor Cochard at the Sorbonne. She was thirty years old. But back then it hadn't gotten in the way of his falling madly in love with her. He knew, the moment he saw her, that she too was a child of Algiers. No woman could be that beautiful — her brown skin, her long hair flecked with snow, her wide mouth so fond of laughter and poetry — without the influence of the glimmering white backdrop of his beloved city.

Snow was falling elegantly over Paris the first time he laid eyes on her. To him, snow had always been a mysterious dance of flakes that whirled this way and that as if following a secret rhythm, and it left the streets looking like the set of a nostalgic movie, one involving trysts — though the people he saw on the street now were struggling to protect themselves with clumsy-looking ear muffs and woollen caps, unmoved by a landscape that, to them, was simply everyday, a nuisance. At the quays along the Seine, pleasure boats void of tourists sat bobbing in the water, and waiters at bistros shooed snowflakes like flies. That was when he saw her, in a long overcoat and beret set at an angle, watching in delight as a dog jumped up, trying to bite the snowflakes falling around his snout. She was in her own world, sitting on a platform almost motionless — soon she, too, would be a statue covered in snow. For a long while, Arthur simply watched, until finally she saw him, too.

If he could erase the here and now, he would enjoy looking back on the nights that city gave them — clandestine music clubs; the smell of their smiling bodies sweating as they danced among prostitutes who were happy and sad at the same time; their late-night strolls through the

Trocadero as a trumpeter played Miles Davis, marking the rhythm with the tip of his worn shoe against a sidewalk littered with smouldering cigarette butts. Each corner was a tale of oil and water; and the two of them kissed and made love in fire-escape stairwells.

Where had that Andrea gone? Who was this bag of bones, this frail old woman, this soulless pile of muscle and skin who'd replaced her?

'I want to take you home, to *our* home. Let's go back to Algiers together.'

She turned to him nervously, almost a twitch. Her eyes, once shiny, now flitted back and forth, erratic, empty. It was chilly and she pressed her arms to her belly, hiding her hands in the sleeves of the little knit jacket she wore over her pyjamas. In profile, her eyelashes drooped like the branches of a tree heavy with fruit — pretty eyelashes, eyes that were dead.

Arthur took a step forward and tried to stroke her shoulder, but Andrea pulled away, frightened. Arthur's hand lingered in the emptiness, trembling. After a few seconds' hesitation he took Andrea's hand, holding it tightly.

'I know it was my fault, Andrea. If I'd been here, with the two of you, if I'd realised what was happening right before my eyes, I could have avoided it. But I haven't lost hope. Things are different now. I'll get Aroha back, she'll come back to us.'

Andrea studied her husband's fingers, imprisoning her there, holding her like claws. She felt an irrepressible urge to slap him, bite him, beat him with her fists.

There are certain parts of truth that cannot be measured or calculated, and there's no way to know exactly how much of a lie resides within. It becomes confusing to look at the person speaking, because the contrast between their expression and their moving lips overwhelms — the pieces, quite simply, do not fit. She knew that Arthur was lying, yet again. Covering the hole Aroha had left with something else, with anything, a house, a yacht, a car, jewels, a stupid book, pretending nothing had happened.

'Let me go.'

Arthur didn't obey. In fact, quite the opposite, he squeezed her wrist tighter, as though trying to leave the marks of his lost presence on her skin.

'I can't change the past. But I'll fight to get our family back, to go back to the beginning, a new start.'

Andrea looked at him without seeing. Arthur's shape, reflected in her pupils, was no different from the tomatoes in her garden. Slowly she loosened his vice grip, finger by finger, as though it were a dead body that had entered rigor mortis. Without a word, she turned her gaze to a capsized flowerpot and ignored Arthur as if he weren't even there. She made a tremendous effort not to let him see her cry.

The last thing in the world she wanted was to be consoled by that man, a man she'd once loved with the same intensity with which she now detested him.

The telephone in Arthur's room rang several times before he picked it up.

'What took you so long to answer?' fired an unfamiliar voice, skipping the preliminaries. It was a man's voice.

'Who's this?'

'Is this Arthur Fernández?'

Arthur confirmed that it was. The man on the line had a commanding tone, his Spanish slightly accented, though Arthur couldn't place it.

'I need you to go to Casa de la Panadería. You know where that is?'

'Of course I do, but if you don't tell me who this is I'm going to hang up.'

'Diana sent me. Name's Guzmán. I'll be waiting in twenty minutes. Be on time or I'll be gone.'

'What's so urgent?'

'You ought to know. You've been waiting for me.'

'Why don't you come to the hotel?'

The only response was the harsh grainy sound of a dial tone on the other end. The man had hung up.

Arthur held the phone for a moment without moving, perplexed.

He had to take a detour to get to the Plaza Mayor. There were a lot of streets under construction. Madrid is in a constant state of reinvention, as though the city were never finished. To make matters worse he ran into a noisy crowd of protesters, holding signs and making their way to the Community of Madrid headquarters, chanting things he couldn't understand. It had started to rain, but that didn't scare off the marchers, who took refuge under plastic ponchos and coloured umbrellas. To one side of the crowd the riot police, looking ominous, studied the flood of people.

He might have been five minutes late, maybe ten. The plaza was almost empty. The outdoor cafés had their chairs all stacked up under the balconies that lined the square. A few idlers stood smoking, watching the rain and looking melancholy. Normally the place was full of life, the bustling cafés full of customers, and there was a weekend flea market where people bought and sold stamps, books and coins; it had a nostalgic air, as though trapped in the Italianate days of its magnificent buildings. Arthur's eyes scanned the place popularly known as Casa de la Panadería — The Bakery House — despite it now being a municipal building. It was on the north side of the plaza and had old balconies from which the Bourbon monarchy had once looked out, to watch both plays and executions.

He waited a little while, prowling up and down, but no one paid any attention to him. He saw a couple of pedestrians — a woman with an enormous umbrella taking up the entire space with the vast expanse of its tines; and a Japanese man who stared up at the sky, looking cheated; plus a wet, dirty dog, and a couple of kids splashing around in puddles. Beneath the arcades were small commercial establishments, some bricked over, a few still in business. In the olden days, those vaulted-ceilings had contained artisans' workshops, gold and silversmiths' shops, gambling dens and brothels, even cells during the Spanish Inquisition. Arthur wandered into a few places — a trinket shop and a Bolivian mini-mart. In neither of them did anyone seem to notice him. Furious, he left the arcade.

And then someone approached. A guy of medium build, nothing remarkable about him, a guy like any other — with one exception: the hand holding his enormous black umbrella was horrifically burned, and his pinky finger was missing its top phalanx.

'I was about to leave. You're late.'

Arthur felt an immediate revulsion for this stranger. His deep voice sounded as though he were speaking from inside a vault; it didn't match his harmless appearance in the slightest. And that's what was so disconcerting, so unpleasant. Or maybe it was his breath.

Guzmán was chewing mint-flavoured gum and smoking a black tobacco cigarette.

'Let's go someplace we can talk quietly.'

They walked to a place a few blocks from the plaza. There were very few customers at that hour. It seemed to be a pub that, in the mornings, attracted office workers and students avoiding their studies. But a smell leftover from wild nights lingered, permeating the walls and the barstools' mustard-coloured upholstery. Guzmán leaned on the bar looking annoyed, and shook out his hair like a dog. He left the dripping umbrella between his legs and rubbed his hands together.

'Shitty weather. I thought the sun was always shining here,' he complained.

The waiter smiled when he saw them, and Guzmán called him over. He was a man used to giving orders, and used to having them obeyed, pronto.

Arthur ordered an espresso. Guzmán glanced at him out of the corner of his eye, smiled mockingly, and ordered a gin — double, with two ice cubes.

The waiter was back in under a minute with their order.

'A little early to start drinking.'

Guzmán nodded, swirling his highball glass and observing the iridescent effect of the bar's light on his ice.

'It's a little late for coffee, and I have trouble sleeping if I have too much caffeine. Jet lag doesn't suit me,' he said, flashing a cynical smile.

Guzmán, if that was his real name, looked like the kind of guy you see lurking drowsily in a corner, eating pistachios and boozing, his eyes never leaving the glass until the second he collapses onto the bar. He pulled out a pack of Chilean cigarettes and offered Arthur one.

'They're shit, but that's all there was in my last city.'

Arthur declined the invitation, and warned him that smoking was prohibited. Guzmán looked around and feigned disgust. He lit the cigarette and exhaled a puff of smoke, jutting his lower lip out like a springboard. His teeth were stained and his gum flitted back and forth on his tongue.

'This country is pathetic. People think anything goes, think it's all party-party-party and sangria,' he went on. 'But things are going from bad to worse, it's like the worst days of Prohibition.' He said it like he was some 1920s Chicago mobster.

Without his umbrella as a shield, Arthur could study him carefully. Were his eyes hazel now, or was that just light from the bar, reflected in his irises, giving him a different expression? Arthur made a mental note that he'd have to ask Diana where she'd found this guy. He couldn't have read more than a dozen books in his life but he was certainly shrewd, he had the shrewdness of a survivor. He was one of those men whose ugliness was somehow attractive, a guy whose appearance was carefully dishevelled, the knot on his tie loosened. Guzmán kept his right hand in his pocket and Arthur heard the raspy sound of paper between his fingers. He got the feeling that the guy had been waiting to show him something, but at the same time maliciously holding back, delaying one minute after another. He seemed unaware of the passage of time. Reality, for him, was found in contemplating the liquid in his glass.

Staring at the mutilated hand holding the highball, Arthur considered what Diana had told him about the man.

'Diana told me about the … methods you use.'

Guzmán flashed a sort of half-smile.

'Reputations are bullshit. All legends lie, and mine is no exception. We all invent whatever truth best suits our needs. I'm not the monster you've heard about, but it works for me; it's useful to have others think I am. In my line of work, nobody thinks you're anybody if you haven't eviscerated your best friend. Which, by the way, I have. But anyway, what do you care about the methods I use? I was asked to come, and here I am.'

'Did Diana tell you what I want you to do?'

Guzmán blew a long puff of smoke up at the ceiling and began flicking his lighter with his thumbnail, sparking the flint.

'You want me to find your daughter.'

'You think you can do it?'

Guzmán shot him a condescending look. Rich guys like Arthur might be able to *buy* him, but they couldn't *fool* him. He'd done his homework before accepting Diana's proposition. *Human beings are unpredictable,* he thought. *They'll cling to anything — a hope, a memory, an object — and protect it with their lives if that's what enables them to hold onto a shred of sanity amid the madness.* He pulled an envelope from his pocket and slid it across the bar until it touched Arthur's coffee cup.

'The police report on your daughter's disappearance. Bunch of amateurs, as was to be expected. According to what it says here, she disappeared about four years ago. She was a minor at the time, but she must be twenty-one by now, which means that, if I do find her, she could decide of her own free will that she wants nothing to do with her filthy rich parents. Still, it's certainly true that the police didn't exactly knuckle down in their search. When you want to find someone, you find them. But your daughter had run away before, isn't that right? With a student from London she met at Heathrow, to Wales — that lasted three weeks; then at sixteen she escaped from the boarding school where you'd sent her to detox and went missing for four months, until her expense account ran dry; at seventeen she broke her riding instructor's nose and disappeared for two months — off someplace in Portugal ... et cetera. With a record like that, I'm not surprised the police didn't have her down as a top priority.'

Arthur straightened on his stool and eyed Guzmán severely. He placed his coffee cup in its saucer atop a dried ring of spilled coffee.

'That's why you're here, to find her and bring her home, bring her back to me.'

Guzmán glanced around for an ashtray. Not finding one, he dropped his butt into his glass and raised a finger, ordering another.

'I'm good, my friend, but I'm not the Wizard of Oz. It's been four years.'

'Then what are you doing here?'

Guzmán barked out a short laugh like he'd just heard a private joke.

'Looking for a white rabbit?'

The waiter returned with a fresh drink. He looked uneasy, cleared his throat and informed Guzmán that smoking was prohibited. Guzmán nodded very slowly, his eyes boring into the waiter until the man blinked, stammered an apology and departed.

'I can find her, but I'm expensive — very expensive. And first I need to know how far you're willing to go. I don't like leaving things unfinished.'

'As far as necessary. I don't care if you have to go to hell and back to find her,' he replied vehemently, staring at Guzmán's butchered hand.

Guzmán adopted a skeptical expression. He could imagine the idiots that this desperate father had wasted a fortune on: manipulators, unscrupulous smartasses, schemers, peddling smoke and mirrors, spurred on by their own greed. But he wasn't like that. He didn't stop — at anything — until he achieved what he'd set out to do.

'That might be very far, my friend. You'd be surprised how many people out there demand an answer, and when you give it to them, they can't handle it. See, people's blood runs cold fast, and I need to know that's not going to happen in this case; otherwise, I'll go back to where I came from. It's important for us all to be rowing in the same direction, and even better if we do it with equal effort.'

'I want my daughter back. There's nothing else to be said.'

Guzmán paused briefly to take a sip. He smacked his lips and nodded decisively. They had an agreement, then.

'We could start with you: I heard you had quite an ugly accident. Killed a boy and a little girl.'

Diana's words echoed in his head once more. Guzmán was a door he couldn't close whenever he felt like it, once that door was open. He shook the voice from his head.

'That's totally unrelated, and besides, it's none of your business.'

Guzmán shook his head slowly back and forth.

'Everything is related, we're all connected — butterfly effect and all that shit, haven't you heard? Besides, from here on out, until I find your little girl, everything that affects you is my business. So: give me your version of what happened.'

Arthur remained pensive. Then he raised a hand and ordered a beer.

'I think I'll have one of your cigarettes after all.'

Guzmán held one out to him.

'… By the way, isn't Tagger a Jewish name?'

7

'El Español' was a one-of-a-kind instrument, a Stradivarius built between 1682 and 1687. It had been in the Tagger family for over a hundred years, if you added up the different periods in which the violin had been in their possession. At the end of the Second World War it had been lost, and remained so until Gloria A. Tagger managed to recover it, restoring it to the family estate almost by coincidence. And now, suddenly, she was relinquishing it, in exchange for an unknown sum of money, to the Palacio Real's royal Stradivarius collection. Gloria didn't need the money, so no one could understand why she had made the decision to never again play the amazing, unique instrument, a violin that her grandfather, her father, and she herself had spent large chunks of their lives attempting to locate.

National Heritage specialists opened the case with great care, their hands gloved. Despite various certificates of authenticity and documentation that had already been analysed by experts, they had to conduct additional certification assessments. A Stradivarius was an almost liturgical object — more, in fact, it was almost alchemical, and that was how they treated it. The quality of sound it produced was considered unique, although x-rays and tests conducted on the varnishes covering its surface revealed it had not always been treated with the same loving care. The violin had undergone great alterations and modifications since its manufacture: at different points in time, the neck, frets and strings had been changed, and it had been periodically revarnished. The only thing that remained intact — though scarred, as tests revealed — was its maplewood body. In a way, that violin, soon to be taken off in an armoured car to a display case in the Palacio Real, was like a map charting the most tumultuous decades of the ever-mysterious and little-known Tagger family, which had produced no less than three great soloists.

As the experts worked — under the attentive gaze of both a notary and a lawyer for the state's insurance company — Gloria's eyes drifted to an old framed photo of a young man in a German interwar uniform. He looked Prussian, humourless; his face was serious, he probably smelled of pipe tobacco, and he had straight white teeth — quite a luxury at the time. Gyula A. Tagger was her great-grandfather.

'Not many people know this, but I've got Balkan blood — Jewish, to boot. And the funniest thing is, Hungarian Jews are largely descended from Spain's Jews, the Sephardi, who were expelled by Queen Isabel in the fifteenth century.'

'It's very odd that your great-grandfather served in the German army,' said Eduardo, who was with her that morning. Gloria had wanted him there to witness the transfer, and though he didn't understand why, he knew it was important to her and so agreed without demanding an explanation.

Gloria seemed to hesitate before continuing.

'It is, yes. He denied his ancestry, like the Marranos in medieval Spain under the Catholic Monarchs, and like all converts was the harshest of executioners when it came to his own people. He changed his first and last name, invented a new background to explain his past — and had he been able to, I bet he would have changed his blood, too. Legally, the violin belonged to him, and I can only imagine he'd be twisting his Prussian whiskers right now to see what's being done to it.

'The Taggers hail from Lake Balaton in Hungary's Transdanubia. By the time I was born, in 1968, the story of my great-grandfather and El Español was already hazy. Like my father, I was born in Madrid, and it wasn't until I turned twenty, and the Hungarian government invited us to the Budapest Orchestra's centenary commemoration, that I learned the details of my Hungarian, Jewish, and Nazi past.'

That association seemed to amuse her, but the truth was that it did not. Gloria stepped back from the table where workers were poring over violin parts like forensics experts.

'The first thing my father did when we landed in Budapest was take me to visit my grandfather's grave. I remember it was late afternoon, near the lake; the spa with medicinal waters there was closed, the pier empty. Families who had come from Budapest to bathe were returning to the various guesthouses dotted throughout the surrounding vineyards, in the shade of the majestic Bakony Mountains. There was a gentle breeze blowing, rocking the little boats tied there. At the time, my father had just turned forty-five. I remember him sitting at the wharf, gazing out at the reddish clouds reflected in the lake's surface, seeming unaware of the passage of time. He was on the pier's wet wooden planks, swinging his bare feet back and forth. You could see the north shore — with swampy areas where tall reeds and cane grew — and the roofs of the village houses, mostly thatch. "This is where it all began," he said, giving me a strange look. I think that was the day, there on Lake Balaton, when he first told me the story of my great-grandfather Gyula, his son — my grandfather — and *our* violin.'

Gloria walked over to the display cabinet, where all that was left was the Stradivarius' cushioned rack. She smiled as she recalled that afternoon, sitting on a deserted pier with her father, listening — entranced — as he told the story of her ancestors. It was, for many reasons, an unforgettable trip.

'In the early forties the Hungarian army, allied with Hitler, suffered a large number of casualties on the Russian front, and since the balance was slowly tipping in favour of the Allies, the Hungarian government entered conversations to negotiate a separate peace. Despite the fact that negotiations were secret, everyone knew about them, and the German presence was increasingly aggressive. It was only a matter of time before they formally invaded the country, so most people's anti-German sentiments were on the rise. My great-grandfather Gyula, however, ordered my grandfather and great aunts to minister to wounded German soldiers at their home. It wasn't unusual to see Germans at their house, convalescing or on leave. Some had incredibly disfigured faces, others were covered in burns or missing limbs. My grandfather, influenced by his own father's ideals, couldn't help but feel sorry for those young blond men who at one time, not long before, had been living happily in their German cities with their wives, their girlfriends, their kids.'

Eduardo nodded, intrigued by the story Gloria told.

'The war was hard on everyone,' he said, recalling his own grandfather, who had fought to defend the Alcázar of Toledo during the Spanish Civil War while his very own brother fought to attack it.

Gloria gave a little smile.

'But even in wartime, young people have a great will to live. In 1943, my grandfather was a promising young man, a brilliant cellist with the first Orchestra of Budapest. His father — my great-grandfather — had previously been one of Chancellor Bismarck's musicians and played El Español for the Nazi high command, including Göring and Himmler in Berlin, before the war. No one had a clue that his impeccable musical and military records hid a distant Jewish past; he'd taken every precaution to ensure that all traces were erased, and they only came to light far later. Because of that, his son was exempt from joining the ranks and enjoyed special privileges as a musician.'

Gloria went to the window and, with two fingers, pulled the curtain back slightly to peek out. The throng of journalists was still out there, armed with tripods, cameras and mikes, awaiting the Secretary of Culture who was set to give a joint press conference. The handing over of the violin to National Heritage was newsworthy enough for politicians to make the drive out to the house to be photographed.

'Tell me something, Eduardo. Have you ever wondered what it would be like to have had different parents? To have been born in Tripoli, say, rather than Madrid? Your whole life, everything you are, might have been different, just by virtue of your father or grandfather having chosen a different life partner. That single decision marks every generation thereafter, don't you think?'

Eduardo had never even considered such a thing. Coming out of the blue like that, the question was just too complex to be answered with a pat response. In any event, Gloria wasn't expecting him to answer. She was thinking out loud.

'As I said, on that trip, my father took me to visit my grandfather's grave. But he also took me there to show me something else: beside his grave was not, as you might imagine, my grandmother's grave. My grandfather was widowed many years before he died, and though I never met my grandmother I knew her name. Carmen de los Desmayos was her name, and she was born in Aldea del Campo, Cáceres, in 1920, where she was buried in the church cemetery when she died. But the gravestone my father showed me next to my grandfather's belonged to a woman named Álek W.T., who was born in Budapest in 1924 and died in an undetermined location on the Romanian border in 1944. My father crouched down and stroked the moss on the ground that had grown in the space between their graves, close enough for them to hold hands underground.'

114

The housekeeper walked in, wiping her hands on her apron. She stood for a moment, focusing on the workers' progress, failing to see why they felt the need to wrap the violin in a chamois, as if it were a baby that might catch cold. Then she approached Gloria and whispered something — something Eduardo overheard, although he wished he hadn't. Someone named Guzmán was on the phone, wanting to speak to her. He claimed to be a Chilean reporter, hoping to interview her before his return to Santiago. Gloria considered for a moment. Then she told the housekeeper to get his number and set up a time for them to meet the following day.

'What were we talking about?'

'Your grandfather and his mysterious graveside companion.'

Gloria picked up where she'd left off.

'Alejandra — Álek — was the great love of my grandfather's life until he met my grandmother. And judging by his decision to be posthumously laid out beside her, I'd say for the rest his life. My father knew, at some point my grandfather must have come clean to him — perhaps after my grandmother died, maybe because he was an only child and therefore the only one who could ensure that his wish to be buried with her be carried out. Apparently she was a very pretty girl, joyful and carefree. Time stood still for her; she lived in her own world, a world with no wars, schedules, obligations or conventions. Maybe that's why my grandfather loved her so much, because she was like a bird that flew wherever her little wings wanted to take her. A celestial soul.'

A celestial soul, she repeated silently to herself, shaking her head. That was what Ian, her husband, had called her the first time they made love. Exactly the same thing. 'I love you because you're so free, a bird who flies wherever its wings desire.' And she'd believed him when he swore that trying to change her would be like stripping her of precisely that which had made him fall in love with her to begin with. But that was exactly what he'd tried to do. Change her. Why was it that the men who seemed the most confident were often really the ones who were the weakest and most afraid?

'Alejandra was even more at risk because she, too, was Jewish, but unlike my great-grandfather's family, hers had not renounced their customs, although they'd agreed to take precautions. Like my grandfather, she was a musician, a clarinetist. In fact, they'd fallen in love while rehearsing one of Bach's allegros. But, by then, the orchestra she

115

played in had disbanded — many of its members were dead and others fled so as not to be recruited into the ranks of the Soviet front. Those who were left were begging in the streets and cafés of Budapest, playing Bach, Mozart, Beethoven and Wagner — more to the Germans' liking. Álek detested the Germans, and showed equal contempt for the traitor Gyula A. Tagger, who of course vehemently refused to allow his son to keep courting her. Her hatred made her rash, arrogant to the point of provocation, particularly when talking about my grandfather's father, or when she went to Budapest to play in the cafés where German soldiers gathered. She'd sing old Magyar ballads that the foreigners couldn't understand, slipping jibes into the lyrics, insulting the Nazis, the Führer, President Horthy and his fascist-loving minions.

'People had seen her on the streets of the capital openly fraternising with gypsies and Jews marked with the Star of David; she'd politely step aside to let them pass on the street, and give them food. She herself refused to sew the obligatory Jewish badge onto her clothes — a crime that could be severely punished. My grandfather argued with Álek a lot, he'd even threatened to break off their secret engagement — which, year after year, had been postponed because of the war. Of course his threats were in vain; he loved Álek more than anything, despite her flaws, and would have married her under any circumstances. But it was the only weapon he could use in an attempt to shake her steadfast determination not to hide from the Nazis. Only when my grandfather threatened to leave, never to return to the lake, did he see her grey eyes cloud over with doubt; but then she'd smile deviously, hold him in her frail arms and kiss him. "No you won't; you can't live without me." And it was true, my grandfather couldn't live without her, and the fear of losing her drove him to distraction.'

Gloria paused. One of the civil servants examining the violin's surface under a special light gestured timidly. Gloria approached. There was a tiny fracture, fairly recent — and by recent he meant at some point in the past sixty-two years — at the base of the neck. It was invisible to the naked eye and in no way affected the quality of sound or the violin's ability to be played, but the technician would have to make a note of it in his report. Slowly he raised the instrument up to eye level, and his pupils shone in the reflection of the reddish wood's fading light. For a moment,

Gloria's face, too, was captured in that light. Eduardo held his breath, afraid to break the spell by brushing against her.

'It wasn't long before the Nazis in the cafés of Budapest began to understand the lyrics to the songs Álek composed in their honour. Without intending to, she'd become something of a legend. In late 1943, one of her Jewish friends was arrested by the Hungarian security forces. It was only a matter of time before he betrayed her. They hardly even had to torture him, a couple of broken fingers and a chipped tooth were all it took before he told them where to find her. He even informed the agents, in writing, that Álek was a sworn Jew who systematically flouted the laws of racial segregation. His betrayal didn't save him, though; the man was executed on the spot. They tossed him from a fifth-floor window and his body smashed into the hard cobblestones of a deserted street one random night without so much as a whimper.

'A small unit of Hungarian guards arrived in the village, late one night. There was no time to put up resistance or attempt to flee. But despite the fact that no one resisted, Álek's oldest uncle, a music teacher at the Hungarian Academy, was beaten to death with a shovel by the soldiers, who were clearly drunk. The uncle's only crime had been to request that he be allowed to pack a bag of books before he was taken in. The entire family witnessed his murder, unable to lift a finger, paralysed by the horror of its gratuitous violence. Álek's father, by that time quite old, covered his eyes with his gnarled fingers, unable to watch his brother being beaten, but they forced him. The poor man watched until his eyes burned.

'The squad was under the command of a German officer who seemed almost uninvolved, watching impassively from a convertible where he sat smoking and looking bored; he'd give an order in German to a subaltern, which the man then translated into Magyar for the guards, who then carried it out immediately. He was just a boy — a blond, square-jawed boy, with eyes as blue and cold as the lake.

'They searched every shack in the village looking for Álek. When my grandfather heard the commotion he went to see what was going on, hoping she'd been able to run into the forest. He protested vehemently to the German officer, mentioning his father's — my great-grandfather's — rank and relationship with the Reich's authorities. He put forth that theirs was a peaceful village that collaborated with authorities, and explained that dozens of German soldiers were in fact convalescing at his home. But the officer wouldn't listen to reason, and they were prepared to massacre the entire family. He was convinced that torturing the weakest would loosen the men's tongues. And for one never-ending hour, cries rang out all across the lakeshore.'

Gloria was floating, drifting, suspended between the waters of nostalgia and sadness. She'd no doubt researched her father's story, uncovered all the details. She knew it so well now that it had become part of her, like a second skin.

'My grandfather watched it all, clenching his teeth, trying to escape the madness, recalling the walks he used to take, hand in hand with Álek along the Danube, the plans they made before the war, the house they'd planned to build near the lake's resort. But the screaming went on and on. No one betrayed Álek, but they all looked to him — son of the traitorous Jew, son of the Nazi — imploring him with their eyes to put an end to it. And he did. "I'll tell you where she is. I know the hiding place," he shouted. And then he collapsed onto the floor, sobbing like a little boy. At that point the German officer finally stepped out of the car and issued an order. The soldiers withdrew, as ferocious as dogs restrained before their prey. My grandfather led the soldiers to an old abandoned mine where he and Álek used to meet for their trysts. He begged them not to hurt her. The officer looked at him with a bemused smile, an evil glint in his blue eyes, and ordered the hunt to begin. It didn't take long for them to find her, and although she put up no resistance, the guards leapt on her and beat her to the ground.'

Gloria glided to the sofa to the right of the window and stroked the engraved silver frame with her great-grandfather's portrait. But Eduardo got the feeling that really her fingers wanted to scratch it.

'The last thing my grandfather saw of Álek was her tiny, fragile birdlike body being dragged along the ground to the officer's car. Her face was swollen and she was bleeding like a lifeless lump. But she managed to smile. A smile that infuriated the guards and made them beat her even more violently. Still, she forced herself to raise her head from the ground to give my grandfather another one of her mischievous smiles. They never saw each other again. My grandfather made it to Spain, where he met my grandmother — whom he never told about Álek — and they married. In 1948, they had their only child, my father. And when he was just twenty, he and my mother, a student at the Madrid Conservatory, who at the time was eighteen, had me.'

'So what happened to your great-grandfather?'

Gloria clucked her tongue and traced a question mark in the air with one finger.

'You didn't ask me how it was that the Gestapo managed to find the boy who betrayed Álek, or how they knew she was the one who'd written the songs offensive to the Reich, songs whose lyrics had been printed and were being circulated on the streets. It was him.' She pointed to the photo. 'He denounced her, perhaps out of fear that my grandfather and his siblings might be involved in something that could jeopardise his plans for self-preservation, or maybe it was just out of his visceral hatred of Álek and her family. It didn't take long for my grandfather to find out, and when he did there was a terrible, violent scene. My great-grandfather was at home, alone, playing a Schubert piece on El Español, which he sometimes did to exercise his fingers, and ensure the wood would not forget his touch.

'My grandfather burst in — livid, out of control. He shouted, they hurled insults at one another and even came to blows. In a fit of rage, my grandfather tore the Stradivarius from his father's hands and hurled it to the ground, breaking its neck. Then he left, and they never saw each other again. My great-grandfather died a few months later — a heart attack, while he was strolling along the edge of the lake. They say people saw it happen, saw him collapse and beg for help as he lay there struggling, but no one was willing to lend a hand. Now he's buried in a plot in the village cemetery, far from Álek and my grandfather.'

From behind the windows came the sounds of reporters murmuring, and a car approaching. The Secretary of Culture had arrived and the National Heritage conservators were finishing up their report. It was time for Gloria to go outside for the joint press conference.

After everything she'd just told Eduardo it was hard to believe she could simply recover her poise, adopting the radiant smile she now wore.

'What about the violin?' Eduardo asked, as she was already making her way to the door.

Gloria stroked the case they'd carefully laid it in for the photo shoot.

'My grandfather enjoyed playing it, but by the time I managed to recover it, his fingers were all gnarled, stiff as claws, unable to grasp so much as a spoon.'

'But why get rid of it now? It's the violin of your ancestors.' It was easy to think the instrument was somehow the embodiment of the Tagger soul.

Gloria massaged a temple with one hand. *How had she ended up talking about all of this?*

'Well, you see, a concert violin like this is quite long. It's not easy for a novice to handle. Normally someone just learning to play would use a smaller violin, perhaps three-quarters the size. They make even smaller ones for children. But my son managed perfectly. We'd actually played together right here, in this room — a Strauss operetta that my father loved, *Die Fledermaus*. It almost always gave us trouble when we played it together, but that day was special. It was as if rather than fighting the notes he let himself glide over them, through the violin — it was magical. You've got to understand — a violin is like a horse, a living being, proud and rebellious, and it will refuse to be tamed by a stranger, only giving its best when it senses its master's touch. And that's exactly what happened when my son played my great-grandfather's Stradivarius: the strings, the wood, the sound box all recognised in his fingers that he was one of us, a Tagger. It was as though the link that had been broken for decades was being soldered back together. But two hours after that miracle, Arthur Fernández killed him, ran him over on a Madrid street … And now the strings shriek, as if screaming in pain, and their shrieking is driving me mad … I didn't tell you this before, but tomorrow is my farewell concert. I don't ever want to play again.'

The National Auditorium of Music symphony hall was packed, the rows for the chorus and those around the stage a tumult of people searching for their seats. The orchestra had yet to appear but the sheet music and instruments were all laid out and ready. Enormous twinkling chandeliers were gradually being dimmed over the auditorium. That night they were playing Mahler's 'Songs on the Death of Children', performed by the National Orchestra of Spain. Guzmán took a seat. Before him was the stage, on which hung the spectacular windpipes of a colossal organ. To the right, a lone chair, placed apart from the cluster where the orchestra would sit. This was Gloria's spot, and across from her was where the soloist would be. On a rack by her music stand sat the beautiful Stradivarius, giving off its own special light.

'How can you claim you don't like something when you've never even seen it live?' Someone — a woman — had asked him that question fifteen years earlier, as he helped her on with her bra, careful not to brush against the scratch marks he'd left on her back. Classical music, at the time, was something he found boring. He smiled, imagining what she'd say if she could see him now.

The lights went out and the auditorium plunged into darkness. Gloria appeared, together with the conductor and soloist, holding hands. They waved, and the rest of the orchestra emerged. Gloria wore an elegant black strapless dress that served to heighten the contrast with her white skin. A light dab of earth-tone lipstick and a bit of eye shadow was the only makeup she wore. Her hair, up in a high bun, accentuated her bare neck and the tiny pearl studs she wore in her ears. From the stage, she shot a quick glance out over the audience, obscured in the same darkness as the rest of the auditorium.

The woman — almost a girl — was named Candela, Guzmán recalled, rubbing his singed hand. *That must have been the mid-80s,* he thought. Candela was Basque, a music teacher at an *ikastola*, a school where children were taught primarily in the Basque language. A music teacher, and an ETA militant who had travelled to Chile to purchase machine guns on the black market. She could tell stories about the lives of Chopin, Mozart and Tchaikovsky as easily as she could pull apart and then reassemble a FARA 83 Argentine assault rife.

The soloist, an alto tenor in a dark suit and bowtie, came in on the orchestra's first notes:

Now the sun will rise as brightly
as if no misfortune had occurred in the night …
You must not keep the night inside you;
you must immerse it in eternal light

Guzmán was focused solely on Gloria. He didn't care about what was going on around her — the orchestra's music, the soloist's voice.

121

Just her face, so concentrated, almost frozen, as her body moved gently. She swayed to the sound of the notes she produced, as if ushering them from the violin, into the air, and then gathering them back up, over and over again.

The Basque woman, too, had worn that expression, navigating the waters of melancholy. Perhaps that was why he had fallen in love with her. She had no fears, no hopes. Just her music and her own determination. It was a beautiful thing, to watch all that energy squandered on a single object, a single aim, as if nothing were more important than that very instant — and in truth, nothing was. She once confessed to him that playing music was the only way she could escape her demons. It created an invisible shield that nothing but the music itself could permeate. Not the clamps applied to her nipples, not the wet towels used to lash her stomach, not any number of threats. Absolute concentration closed the doors to all other emotion.

During the intermission, Guzmán went outside for a smoke. Calle Príncipe de Vergara was glimmering in the lights of the auditorium and the streetlamps. On the opposite side of the street, a long line of taxis waited patiently for the concert to finish. Guzmán would have liked to leave; Mahler was too much for him. Though he might admire Gloria's mastery, the soloist's voice, the orchestra's clarity, and the skilled conductor, the truth was that the music simply didn't evoke in him any deep emotions. *That's because you need to train your ear. True pleasures are not to be scarfed down like hamburgers*, Candela would have said, her fingers toying with his curls.

There were no stars in the Madrid sky. Where was Capricorn?

Which one is Capricorn? Candela had asked him the afternoon of the ambush — they would arrest her in the planetarium; that was the plan — and Guzmán, who was to be the bait, had scratched his unshaven cheek. After hesitating slightly, he pointed to a cluster of stars in one corner of the sky that was painted onto the domed ceiling. *There you have it*, he'd said, as if he himself had discovered the constellation and were now presenting it to her, magnanimously. Candela smelled like the twenty-something she was, ready to tackle the world. Guzmán felt her chest resting against his elbow. Having her that close, in the darkness of the planetarium, pained him in a way that was difficult to explain. She

122

picked up on it, sensed his remorse at the downward spiral that was about become something monstrous, wicked. And she accepted it benevolently, not knowing what awaited her. She made no move to shrink from his contact, to remove her body from his, and Guzmán was grateful for that. If she'd pulled away, it would have hurled him into a deep, depraved abyss. Sometimes people turn something natural into something dirty simply by reacting disproportionately. She seemed to sense this, and simply passed him the popcorn, allowing their bodies to remain touching.

It was beautiful to imagine not having been born, living in a far-off jumble of stars, waiting for all eternity. To think that he existed in some part of the universe, somewhere in outer space — the great beyond — before his mother and father brought him into the world, was somehow mysterious, almost magical. Guzmán would have stayed there like that forever, sitting beside her, his elbow resting against the edge of her nipple, beneath the mythical light of Jupiter; but then that transgression would have eventually become routine, would have lost all significance. For guys like him, it was better to want than to have. With no expectations, there can be no disappointment. So he had removed his elbow, regretfully, and put his Star pistol to her back. *National Intelligence Directorate. You're under arrest, young lady.*

A chime announced the end of the intermission. Guzmán returned to his seat. The music had left him in a daze. Gloria seemed tired; she had to be, she was really giving it everything. He gazed at her red fingertips, her fingers still flitting about, all by themselves, as though they had trouble keeping still after the performance.

He had no trouble making it to her dressing room after the concert. Flowers open more doors than picklocks. Guzmán knew Gloria liked calla lilies. She'd worn them on her wedding day twenty years ago, and the day she had signed the divorce papers, several months after her son's death. But the fake credentials claiming he was a reporter with *Allegro* magazine conferred an advantage that would vanish the moment she realised he knew nothing about music. Unaware of exactly what he was looking for, Guzmán sensed that this was very much like making his way blindly through a minefield, trusting that luck would keep him from stepping on one. And despite what the scars on his body suggested, he was a lucky guy.

Gloria was smoothing her hair, and greeted him without much enthusiasm.

After introductions, they chatted for a bit, and following the inevitable questions and clichés, Guzmán began to narrow the conversation, in ever-shrinking concentric circles, toward Gloria's personal life. Why was she retiring now? Was it over the death of her son three-and-a-half years ago? And so on. The woman was slippery, Guzmán thought. Didn't pull a face, didn't fluster in the slightest, but also didn't give anything away. He'd have liked interrogating her in the basement of La Moneda palace a few years ago.

'What's your view of Arthur Fernández?'

Gloria eyed him coldly.

'What would *your* view of the man who killed your son be?'

'But from what I understand, it was an accident. An unfortunate coincidence.'

'A coincidence that took my son's life.'

Guzmán apologised. He was about to end that first gentle foray, before his insistence made her suspicious, when there came a knock on the door.

A man appeared, a man looking like a sour civil servant, more doughy than fat. Though he tried to hide it, straightening up as tall as he could, Guzmán realised that he had a slight limp on the right side. He had brought flowers, a bouquet of orchids. *You slipped up, my friend,* Guzmán thought. Gloria hated orchids. But to his surprise she complimented the flowers and gave him an affectionate peck on the cheek.

'Let me introduce my good friend, Eduardo. He's a great painter — he was very successful in the past, and I have no doubt he will be again.'

Guzmán shook Eduardo's limp hand — the man's name rang no bells. His interest in painting was as non-existent as it was in music. Still, the conversation immediately took an interesting turn. Eduardo mentioned he'd seen a couple of government officials loading up the violin Gloria had played during the concert. He said it with sorrow.

'They must have paid quite a hefty sum, for you to get rid of it,' Guzmán said, hazarding a guess.

'No more than it cost me to get it back, I can assure you.'

'And how did you come to get it back?'

'That's one of those stories filled with coincidences. Funnily enough, it was a friend of my husband's who came across it at an auction in Vienna five years ago. It was in very poor shape, as though out of our care it had been treated like a common, everyday object. The violin's neck, which my grandfather broke, had been repaired, but it wasn't the same; it was just some soulless everyday object. Through that friend of my husband's, I got in touch with one of the best luthiers in Madrid and had him undertake a complete restoration.'

'That's a lot of effort to only play it for five years.'

Gloria and Eduardo exchanged a knowing glance.

'Regardless, it's part of the national patrimony now, and that's a good thing. It's late and I'm tired, Señor Guzmán. I'm grateful for your attention but I think that's enough for today.'

'Seems like an interesting story for an article. *The Trajectory of El Español: from the fields of Hungary to the display case of Madrid's Palacio Real.*'

This time, Eduardo was the one to offer a weary comment, saying that it struck him as a rather pompous title. Guzmán shot him a look that suggested he was nothing but a bird dropping that had landed on his shoulder. He seriously did not like that sack of shit.

'Maybe so, but it's a worthwhile story.' He turned to Gloria. 'I won't take up any more of your time. Just one more thing — would it be possible for me to speak to your husband,' he asked intentionally, knowing that Gloria was divorced, 'and his friend, the one who found the violin in Vienna?'

'My husband is in Australia directing a film, and I don't think he'll be back for at least six months.'

'Strange for him not to have attended your farewell concert,' Guzmán noted, feigning ignorance.

Gloria touched her knee nervously.

'You don't know the Welsh.'

'What about his friend? Do you know his name?'

Gloria nodded.

'I can give you his name, but I don't think it'll do you much good: Magnus Olsen. From what I understand, he committed suicide a few years ago.'

Guzmán shot her a look of surprise.

'The head of GRETR investment group? I read about his racket and subsequent prosecution in the press. The tsunami his firm's bankruptcy unleashed hit Chilean companies, too. Though it's hard to believe someone would kill themselves over a few million euros that weren't even theirs.'

'What makes you say that?' Eduardo asked. 'Maybe remorse got the better of him. He brought entire families, thousands of them, to ruin.'

Eduardo noted the way Guzmán's lips turned dark and glassy as he let out a growl that was supposed to be a snigger.

'This is the twenty-first century, and we're not in Japan, my friend,' Guzmán said, flashing him a look like the blade of a knife. 'Executives here don't commit suicide when they lead their companies to disaster — they take the money and run, move to a tax haven and let everyone else take the hit. There's no such thing as dignity in the business world; results are all that matters. Regardless, he took his secrets to the grave — or to hell, which is where I imagine all speculators end up.'

He turned to Gloria.

'Your husband is Ian Mackenzie, the film director. What would he be doing with a friend like Olsen, a speculator?'

'You'll have to ask him that when he gets back from Australia,' Gloria replied, not batting an eye.

'I'll do that. Thanks again for your time.'

Guzmán walked in silence, passing a homeless man writing something on the wall: SIT TIBI TERRA LEVIS — 'may the earth rest lightly on you'. What a tragic sentence, a sort of condemnation to unhappiness. Guzmán had once believed that the world expected something of him. A stroke of genius that might bring him closer to the kind of immortality aspired to by painters, musicians, and film directors who got to spend their time working in Australia. Now he knew that was not the case. No one expected anything of him at all. He was common, everyday, like any other guy, a fraud hiding behind a name, a face that would go through life unnoticed. The only thing the world expected of him was a definitive downfall.

And so he thought of Candela. She was his last train to dignity.

'Come on, Paco. Don't be a dumbfuck. Come clean. This could go on all night.'

Bosco was losing patience. 'Bosco' was his boss's nickname at DINA, the national intelligence directorate — he'd gotten it because his hellish

126

view of the world brought to mind the Dutch painter Bosch's canvases, which he had a soft spot for. He had liked Guzmán, they'd worked together for years. But at night, the Atacama desert got so cold it put them all in a foul mood, and Bosco and his men just wanted to go home.

'Where's the girl?' As he repeated the question yet again, he delivered a swift kick to his ribs, hard yet restrained. Guzmán could barely move, his hands and feet staked to the ground. He knew Bosco could kick a lot harder than that. He was a good guy, despite it all. He had to prove before his men that there's nothing worse than a traitor, but at the same time he didn't want to make it more painful than necessary.

Guzmán wasn't going to talk. He knew it, Bosco knew it, and his men knew it, too. But they had to follow protocol. Cruelty and violence need to follow an established course in order to achieve results. At the officers' school they'd been taught how important it was not to let your instincts guide you. *We're not animals, we're professionals*, the interrogation instructor would often repeat, before explaining how much voltage a man can take to the testicles, or a woman can tolerate from an electrode in the anus.

Formalities were important to Bosco. He didn't see himself as a butcher, didn't even remove the suede jacket he always wore, or loosen his tie like a two-bit goon. He barely even mussed his hair when beating the living daylights out of whomever he had to; he even offered his victims a bit of clemency, speaking in a soft slow voice, making them think mercy was possible — sometimes their vain hope provided the final push, lurching them into terror, loosening their tongues. Bosco was the hatchet man with the most confessions under his belt.

Guzmán had been his right-hand man — who now found himself tied and staked to the ground by his old colleagues, as his boss approached with the blowtorch they always kept in the trunk of the old blue Chevrolet with Santiago plates. Guzmán knew what came next; two days earlier some other poor wretch — some poor guy who was now six feet under a mound of red earth — had felt its flame on his skin. And Guzmán himself had been the one who slowly burned his face.

Screaming in the desert is demoralising. There's no echo. Your voice has no obstacles to bounce off, and so is simply lost in the night. There's no one around to help you, and even if there were, they certainly wouldn't dare approach the circle of light cast by the Chevy's headlights.

'A Spaniard? Some skinny bitch with no tits? That's who you're going through this for?' Bosco's voice was wriggling into his brain like a snake. It was a pomade that soothed his burning hand, the singed hair giving off a smell like fried pork skins, nails hanging off his fingers. The bastard was good, Guzmán had to grant him that. You almost felt sorry for him, almost believed that the whole thing disgusted him, the way he covered his mouth with a handkerchief, feigning a well-rehearsed look of horror. Bosco could have just taken out his Beretta and shot him. But Guzmán wasn't going to get off that easily. That would come later, at the end, and it might not even be necessary. Maybe they'd beat and burn him to death first.

There could be no dissent among the ranks of DINA. No one would have batted an eye at his going down to the basement every night to interrogate the Basque woman that they'd nabbed at the planetarium. The victim's cries, the grunting of a tormentor raping her, those were normal, despite the guards' disgust with her body — a bag of bones, no tits. And that was precisely what put them on alert. The silence. When Guzmán went down to the basement there was no *music*.

'How could you be such an idiot? Falling in love with a prisoner! That kind of shit happens in soap operas, not in real life — and not to one of my best fucking men, God dammit!'

Candela must have been long gone by then, following the trails crisscrossing the desert that everyone said was uncrossable. But nothing is impossible when you've got an iron will to live. She was safe in the hands of some bootleggers who brought in drugs and weapons, taking routes that only they knew. At that time of night, beneath that same sky, she must be nearing salvation, foot by foot, minute by minute. All under the same starry sky. *Follow Capricorn, the goat*, he'd told her. And she'd looked at him with her extraordinary eyes, such a tiny thing, terrified, all eyes. *Where's Capricorn?* she'd asked. *Up there, east of Sagittarius.* It was easy to see, they were in early August and all you had to do was draw a straight line over from Vega, crossing the Milky Way until you got to Algedi and Dabih, the horns of the goat.

And there he was, gazing south of the equator. There is no place on earth more beautiful than the Atacama desert, and no place like its night sky to make you feel both connected to and apart from the universe. Even the horrific pain of a knife slicing through your foreskin can seem like it will come to an end. But in order to endure the pain, you have to keep from fainting, keep your tears from blurring the hundreds of thousands of stars twinkling in the sky above your twitching face. It doesn't matter if you shout; no one is going to hear you, even up there. But unlike the silence of the agony down below, the indifference of the heavens is a promise of peace. Soon it will end, and it will all disappear.

'Got to cauterise that, we don't want you to bleed to death like a little piggy. Come on, man, don't be an arsehole. If I don't get that bitch back I'll be demoted for having trusted you. And we can't have that, my friend. My family's got to eat, my kids go to that fucking English school that costs an arm and a leg.'

Guzmán listened to Bosco — the man actually sounded miserable, the blade in his hand, his hands bleeding. He'd put on rubber gloves and rolled up his sleeves for this. He could have had the others do it but he didn't want things to get out of hand, didn't want them to slip up as they cut. Lacerating a penis is like peeling an apple, you have to do it all in one piece, without letting it fall off. Guzmán knew that — he personally had helped increase the ranks of secret eunuchs crowding the universities and secret meeting halls throughout half of Latin America and Spain. He was almost glad Bosco had taken the reins.

Look up at the sky, he told himself. *Don't listen to your screams. It doesn't matter if they rip off your finger.* The smell of burning flesh at his crotch, blood evaporating in the blowtorch's heat. *Don't die, look up, look up at the sky. Is that one Orion? Is that one ...?*

He wished he could have found Capricorn.

He wished he hadn't betrayed Candela to save his own life, at the cost of his penis, an amputated finger and a horrifically burned hand.

Guzmán clucked his tongue, scornful. He was getting old, thinking too much about the past — and that was the sign of a small future.

It was time to get to work.

He didn't have much trouble finding Mía Börjn, despite the fact that she'd changed her name to Irena Wlörking in an attempt to be less identifiable. In a half-empty Costa Dorada town, it wasn't often you came across women over six-feet tall, looking like Nordic models. *The blonde* — that was what they called her when he'd gone into a bar to ask; she lived in 'the ghost town'. No one knew she was Magnus Olsen's widow, and they'd probably never even heard her husband's name anyway. People live in ignorance — and that made things easier for guys like Guzmán.

You didn't have to be a genius to figure out how that part of the planned community had gotten its nickname. A collection of half-built homes perched on a hill far from the town's centre. Abandoned cranes swayed lazily against their counterweights like colossal weathervanes, and everywhere were piles of debris, construction materials, chain-link fencing and rusted promotional signs featuring a virtual re-creation of what was supposed to have been paradise on earth: streets paved with blacktop, parks full of palms and exotic trees, water features with spouting fountains, swimming pools and Mediterranean gardens, rosy-cheeked children, smiling mothers, well-trained dogs, and fathers who looked proud and satisfied beside their enormous all-terrain vehicles. All that remained of that dream was the air of a nuclear holocaust, the crusty neglect of all that would soon be completely taken over by overgrown brush and garbage. Although Phase One of the construction had been completed, there couldn't have been more than a dozen villas, which had clearly been eked out just before the real estate collapse.

Mía — or Irena, as she now called herself — lived in the house closest to the scenic Mediterranean overlook. Despite the fact that the house looked luxurious, it wasn't, not at all. The front gate was rusted and didn't close properly, and Guzmán could see that where the intercom should have been was nothing but a gaping hole — the device had never been hooked up — so he simply pushed open the gate, which yielded with a creak. The front yard was unfinished, a wasteland of unpruned shrubs, overgrown plants and a prairie of tall weedy grass. In one corner lay a bicycle and a few toys strewn around. Behind the house, he heard children's voices and let himself be guided by them, making his way to the back. Beside the pool stood a statuesque woman fishing leaves from the bottom of the pool with a long pole.

'Mrs Olsen?'

The woman looked up. Why on earth they'd called her *the blonde* he had no idea. Her skin was dark as a Tuareg and she had jet-black hair, short with long bangs, though it could have been dyed.

'Who are you?' she asked, her voice hostile. Her expression was less than friendly. The woman had a perfect face, taut skin; she'd certainly had work done. It was clear that she was far older than she appeared at first glance. Still, she must have been pretty — very pretty, in fact — when she was young; and she still could have been, had she been willing to age naturally over time, rather than fight it with the scalpel. But that was what rich businessmen who bought women like her valued: high cheekbones, wrinkle-free necks, enormous erect breasts, thighs and hips free of flab. Homogeneity, in short — uniformity, and the recognition of their superiority over mere mortals. Guzmán imagined that this woman had been little more than a possession, an expensive piece in Olsen's collection of exotic objects. The two children running around nearby — blond, almost albino, staring at him with the budding animosity they'd learned at elitist private schools — had been her insurance, her guarantee that he couldn't simply kick her out of paradise when he got bored and decided to exchange her for a newer and more exiting model, like he did with his sports cars.

'I'd like to have a word with you about your deceased husband.'

Mía, or Irena, whichever she was at that moment, glanced over at her kids and dropped the pole.

'Not here. Let's go inside.'

Guzmán nodded and followed her into the house. He noticed a framed portrait of Olsen on the wall, posing with his kids, who looked a couple of years younger than they were now. Oddly, she was not represented in this family picture. Olsen looked like an orderly sort of person, a meticulous, legalistic guy in his straight-cut suit, impeccable tie, buttoned vest and pinstriped handkerchief poking out of the jacket pocket. His little eyes were hard, his eyelids so narrow they looked to be entirely lashless.

The widow glanced at Guzmán — who stood there, hands in his pockets — out of the corner of her eye.

'So, are you here on behalf of the police, the creditors, or are you a homeowner who feels swindled?' she asked, her weary expression charged with sarcasm. She was wearing jeans, cut off above the knee. Her calves were hard and toned, no doubt from the step machine in the corner by the large window overlooking the yard and pool and, beyond the unpruned hedgerow, the peaceful surface of the distant Med.

'I could just be a friend,' Guzmán replied flatly.

'Don't be ridiculous. My husband had no friends. No one who works in finance does. In the past few years, everyone who's stopped by has come because they had some unresolved business with my dead husband.'

Guzmán decided to forget about beating around the bush.

'I work for Arthur Fernández, if you want the truth.' Guzmán pronounced the name intentionally, slowly, watching for any sort of reaction. But all she did was stare up at the ceiling looking bored.

'I have no idea who that is. You'd be surprised, but all sorts of people come around claiming to have had business dealings with my husband. I know nothing about his business deals; they never interested me and he never wanted them to. So whatever this is about, don't waste your time with me. There's a law firm in Barcelona in charge of asset stripping, debts and bankruptcy. You'll have to speak to them.'

Guzmán glanced around. There was nothing of any great value. A few antiques, a couple of Chinese vases, a sculpture of questionable taste, furniture that looked old but not especially valuable. The place was either half-empty or half-full, but it was hard to say if they were settling in or getting ready to move out. He nosed around the living room with no particular aim in mind. Sometimes you had to stop searching in order to find what you wanted. He'd learned that over the course of his professional life. Most things are in plain sight, waiting to be discovered if you simply take your time observing them. He noted that the only books on the shelves of the small library were on film — Mark Cousins' *The Story of Film*, Étienne-Jules Marey's *Camera Obscura*, Emile Reynaud's *Théâtre Optique* — and tomes that looked very old.

Out in the yard, the little albinos were really letting each other have it. A dog, possibly a dachshund, leaped around between them, barking and wagging its tail excitedly, not realising that it wasn't a game. When humans fight, it never is.

'I'm not here about money.'

'Are you a cop, then? A detective? A journalist?'

Guzmán shook his head and smiled.

'I told you, I'm working for someone. I'm not here to stir up any trouble, I assure you.'

The widow eyed him warily.

'So what do you want?'

'It's my understanding that your husband helped track down a very valuable violin belonging to the Tagger family. I'm interested in Mr Olsen's relationship to that family.'

She took down a volume of an encyclopaedia on the evolution of cinematography in post-war Europe. From between the pages on Vittorio de Sica's *The Bicycle Thief* she pulled a medium-sized photograph in which a posh-looking Olsen appeared with a very tall, well-built individual smiling uncomfortably, the Swede's arm thrown over his shoulder. It was signed, at the bottom, in marker:

To my friend Magnus. Ian Mackenzie, Berlin, 01/03/1999

'He absolutely loved film,' she muttered with a smirk of irritation. 'He spent a fortune on his toys — old movies, books, autographs, objects that had belonged to famous actors. He would pay outrageous sums to anyone who could get him originals. That's how he met the director Ian Mackenzie.'

Guzmán examined the photo carefully. Gloria Tagger's husband was certainly a good-looking guy, as had been her son.

'Magnus met him at the Berlin Festival, the year his most famous film came out.' She waited for Guzmán to realise what she was talking about, but the guy had no idea, so she finally spelled it out, exasperated. '*Everyone Lies*? It was a milestone in cinematography, despite receiving poor reviews at first. Magnus guarded that picture like one of his greatest treasures.'

'So the connection between the Taggers and Magnus came not so much from music as from your husband's interest in film?'

'That's right. I think at first Magnus didn't even realise that Ian was married to the violinist. He found out later, after they became friends. I remember Gloria A. Tagger, we met at a dinner, at their home in the Madrid suburbs. That was where she told us the story of the violin that had been in her family for decades, and her unsuccessful attempts to get it back. At the time, Magnus had contacts in every arena that involved big money, and as you can imagine the world of antiques and auction houses moves quite a bit of money. I don't think I'm revealing any big secret if I say that auction houses and galleries, on more than one occasion, have been used as giant money laundering machines, whitewashing black-market cash. My husband was so taken with Ian and his wife that he moved heaven and earth to win them over. A few months after that dinner he found the violin at a Vienna auction house and the Taggers got their instrument back at an exorbitantly high price. And with that, Magnus rose in his friend's esteem, and his wife's.'

'What kind of friendship did they have?'

'Magnus belonged to a very select film club. So select, in fact, that sometimes I thought they were more like a secret Masonic society or a sect or something. As far as I know, they met at an antique dealer's place close to our apartment in Madrid a couple of times a month to exchange rare films, books, findings, photographs. My husband showed off his signed pictures with Ian and even got the man to come give a talk once. He'd paraded him around like his own wild game animal.'

'Just out of curiosity, what was your impression of Mrs Tagger?'

Judging by the face she made, it couldn't have been very good.

'I'd say that by that time she and her husband were going through something more than a marital crisis. They argued a lot at dinner, which was quite awkward for us as their guests. Later, I learned that these arguments were normal, and they didn't care about attracting attention in public. She drank a lot, and it was clear she had a caustic tongue. Actually, I felt sorry for her husband. He spent the whole time trying to appease her, but she refused to cut him any slack.'

'What were they fighting about?'

'They talked a lot about their son, Ian junior — who, by the way, I only saw once or twice, but he seemed like a great kid. Quiet, a bit reserved, but very handsome, with the sort of elegance that can't be taught, it was just something in his bearing; he was sensitive and cultured. I think his parents couldn't agree about his upbringing. They referred vaguely to health problems, the boy had some sort of disease — though honestly he never seemed sick to me. His father was in favour of sending him to some kind of boarding school somewhere in the Austrian Alps, an elite private sanatorium. Gloria steadfastly refused to be away from her son and accused her husband of inventing the illness as a way to keep the boy away from her. She swore he was fine and that he could be treated in Madrid or Barcelona without being locked up at that institute. I read in the papers that he died a few years ago, in a terrible accident, and that a few months later his parents divorced.'

Guzmán nodded. By his calculations, that happened more or less a year after Mrs Tagger got her violin back, thanks to the efforts of Magnus, and then the Olsens and the Taggers became friends. But none of that got him any closer to Arthur's daughter, the circumstances surrounding her disappearance, or her possible whereabouts.

'You've been very kind. I won't take up any more of your time. All I ask is that you give me the address of the antique dealer's where your husband and his film-buff friends met.'

Mía — Irena — averted her eyes, looking out the window to where her kids were still beating the crap out of each other. She must have seen what was going on, and yet seemed to not notice, as if she weren't even there. Then she looked Guzmán over, head to toe, as though she'd only just noticed his presence. She hesitated. For the first time in the conversation she seemed unsure of what to say or do.

'I assume you know that Magnus committed suicide.'

Guzmán did know, as did anyone even tangentially related to the world of finance.

'Me and the boys found him, hanging, one day when we came back from shopping. It was horrific. The son of a bitch killed himself knowing the boys would see him hanging there, knowing I'd see him.'

This time it was Guzmán who hesitated before making his next comment. The widow seemed sincere in her distress, as though her husband's limbs were still there now, swaying before the children's terrified faces.

'That must have been awful. I'm sorry.'

She did something strange with her mouth, a sort of clucking of her lips that seemed to sum up how tired she was of it all, of everything that had happened.

'Magnus was always a coward, and he remained one until the end. When his house of cards began to crumble, he simply removed himself from the equation and left me with the kids, and all his debts and problems. You should hear the messages I get on the answering machine — insults, death threats, people harassing me and the children constantly. No one's going to pity me and my situation … What I'm trying to say is, in the past few years all I've done is flee, run constantly from one place to another, always hiding from something I'm not responsible for. This is my last refuge, no more aces up my sleeve. If any of my husband's enemies find out I'm here, my life will be impossible.'

Guzmán told her not to worry, promised he wouldn't say anything. For some reason, he liked this woman. Maybe it was because he liked survivors. But if he'd managed to find her without any trouble, then others would too. Hiding out in a deserted, half-built planned community that Magnus Olsen himself had developed was not the world's cleverest decision. But still, that wasn't his problem. He picked up the paper she'd written the address on and said a friendly goodbye, promising not to bother her again.

8

Eduardo and Olga's on-again-off-again friendship meant that it had all the quirks to be expected from such an unlikely relationship. They might argue, go weeks without seeing each other, and suddenly one day, one of them — normally Olga — would pick up the phone and call the other as if nothing had happened. The strange thing about this time was the place she'd asked him to meet her: inside a church, the Iglesia de San Sebastián.

Eduardo dropped onto a pew in the last row, from which he could see the altar lit by a candelabra full of votive candles all burning at different heights. An altar boy prepared the Book of the Gospels on the lectern, opened a silver tabernacle lying at the feet of a painted plaster Jesus, and placed the chalice and Eucharist on the altar. Mass would begin in a few minutes and Eduardo didn't want to be there. His knee hurt like hell, but that was nothing compared to the pain of his anticlerical genes.

It didn't take long for Olga to appear, making her way down a dark side-passage, the sound of her heels ringing out on the sacred stone floor. When she sat down next to Eduardo, the candlelight illuminated her face.

'What are we doing here?' Eduardo asked her.

Olga's head was covered with a lovely, natural silk headscarf. No one covered their heads when they entered church anymore, but Eduardo found that it gave her face a beautiful symmetry.

'I come from time to time. It helps me think and be at peace with myself. Some people get that feeling on top of a mountain, or by the sea, or in cemeteries. To me, this is the place to clear my thoughts,' she replied, settling beside him on the pew. It was odd to see the way she pressed her knees modestly together, tugging down the hem of her skirt. Eduardo looked at her, perplexed.

'I'd never have pictured you in a place like this.'

Olga gave him an understanding smile.

'Madrid is full of people lost at sea, don't you think? The waves of its invisible ocean hurl hundreds of desperate souls to its shores every day;

137

they're everywhere. This is like Noah's ark to me. Besides, we all have something we need to be forgiven for, and here, that's possible.'

Eduardo glanced at the pews. They were nearly empty, just a few people scattered here and there, almost all well-over sixty. Maybe there really were thousands of souls out there lost at sea, but most of them were finding other rafts to cling to. Meanwhile, up at the altar a little drama was unfolding: the altar boy was shuffling from one side to the other with the as-yet unconsecrated wine in a sort of carafe, trying to make room so he wouldn't collide with the priest, who was smoothing the white linen atop the altar, but instead he stumbled. Eduardo saw the whole thing happen in slow motion — the boy's look of horror, the carafe falling to the floor, shattering, the wine splattering all over the altar. It lasted only a few seconds and almost no one even realised that it had happened, but Eduardo could read the priest's lips and it looked to him as though the man had cursed the boy in Aramaic. Eduardo felt sorry for the boy, awkwardly endeavouring to clean up the shards of glass as quickly as he could.

He glanced at Olga with a look somewhere between alarm and resignation.

'I suppose I owe you an apology.'

'What for?'

'My stupid, cantankerous comment the other day — about you not being able to have kids. I was being a jerk. I know it's a touchy subject for you.'

Olga nodded openly. She inhaled and gave him a wide grin.

'How's the portrait going?'

This change of subject implied forgiveness, and Eduardo accepted it.

'I found the hotel where Arthur is staying, and I've jotted down a few things from a distance. Today, I'm going to try to get closer, make a sketch. I'll keep you up to date.'

Olga kept quiet for a few seconds, trying to confirm the vague feeling she had that everything was changing between them because of that damned portrait.

'Honestly, I regret having gotten you involved in this. I suppose if I asked you to forget about it, you wouldn't listen, would you?'

Eduardo regarded her with open curiosity. What was the matter with her? She was the one acting like a different person. In a way, he liked the change, it laid bare something clean, something authentic, but at the same time he wasn't sure that that particular kind of purity was a good thing. He'd seen the same sort of poise and apparent serenity in people whose insides were being eaten away by worms.

'Why do you keep going back to that?'

Olga opened her handbag and placed a padded envelope on the bench between them.

'I have a friend in the police who told me a few things about Arthur.'

'Since when do you have friends on the police force? I thought you hated cops.'

'I hate cauliflower, too, but I eat it from time to time. The guy you're planning to paint is not your average man. In fact, Arthur Fernández is a rather shady figure. He's amassed one of the greatest fortunes in Europe, and everybody knows he's a speculator, a man involved in high finance and the stock market. But how he managed to create that empire is still rather murky. They say he started out in drug trafficking, human trafficking, anything that sounds illegal. He was involved in several court cases but they've never been able to prove his involvement in the crimes beyond a reasonable doubt.'

Eduardo had opened the envelope. In it, he found photocopied dossiers, documents about the man's companies, photos of Arthur in the company of some unsavoury-looking characters apparently involved in high crime. He didn't even recognise their names.

'If they couldn't find any proof against him, that means he's innocent in the eyes of the law.'

'Innocence often depends too much on the lawyer's fees, and he's got the best. Did you know he was forced to flee from France when he was young? It seems he had a promising future as a poet and even published a well-received collection of poems. But one day, out of the blue, he beat up his mentor at the university — almost killed him, in fact — and then he disappeared, only to re-emerge as the successful impresario he is today. It's an incredibly strange trajectory, don't you think? Still, that's not what worries me most.'

Olga told him to look at the last page of the report.

'I didn't know he had a daughter.'

'She disappeared a few months before the accident Arthur caused near Oriente that killed our client's son. Arthur tested positive for drugs and alcohol in the police report. Although it wasn't the first time he'd been in that kind of trouble — he'd had his licence revoked several times for speeding, reckless driving and traffic safety violations — I bet his lawyers used the extenuating circumstances in his favour, the anguish and depression Arthur has been suffering since his daughter vanished into thin air.'

Olga's opinion of Arthur did not seem exactly compassionate. Her voice was full of exasperation, almost contempt.

'I don't like you getting mixed up with that kind of person, Eduardo. You should let him and Gloria deal with their misery on their own.'

The priest rang the bell. Mass was about to begin. Eduardo glanced at the altar boy. He was as pale and stiff as a Vatican sculpture. The sight of the downcast little boy saddened him. They exchanged a quick look and Eduardo gave him a smile. Don't worry; some things just don't always work out, he attempted to communicate.

'I think I can handle it on my own.'

They walked out of the church, and there beneath the ceramic figure of Lope de Vega, Olga lit a cigarette and snatched off her headscarf with a nervous gesture. With that one move, the calm that had enshrouded her inside the sanctuary vanished. She was once more the same tense woman as always, the one who held her cigarette too tightly between her fingers, and constantly frowned as though upset or on the verge of hurling an insult.

'You said in there that you come here because we all have something to be forgiven for. So what is it you need to be forgiven for?'

Olga exhaled smoke, angrily.

'Did I say that? I must have been high from all the incense in there.'

Eduardo recalled the first time he saw her.

It was a few weeks after he was released from the hospital and he was still recovering from the accident. He'd started drinking heavily during that time, and had stopped taking care of himself. His father came to visit every once in a while, bringing clean clothes that he bought at the flea market and which often didn't fit since Eduardo was losing an alarming amount of weight — he wasn't eating and hardly slept at all. All he did was drink and smoke, smoke and drink.

It must have been about that time that his father told him he'd been diagnosed with oesphageal cancer. Eduardo couldn't remember, now, whether his father had been afraid, had said it calmly, or simply mentioned it in passing. He hadn't wanted to add to his son's sorrow and anguish over the deaths of Elena and Tania. He also couldn't recall if the surgeon who operated on his father had mentioned that it wasn't really worth doing, that the cancer had metastasised and spread very quickly to his liver and lungs. Perhaps he whispered that the man had maybe three months to live and the best thing would be to offer palliative care, administering morphine. No chemo. He robotically accompanied his father to his blood tests and biopsies. He'd wait for the nurse to call them, go in with him to the doctor's office, and listen to what they were told without taking it in. Then he'd go home. He didn't call his father, didn't ask him how he was doing. He didn't even know if he cared. Most likely, he now understood, he simply didn't have room for any more pain. So he had blocked it out.

The day Olga had showed up at his door, Eduardo was weeping. Actually, by the time she'd knocked, he'd stopped and was simply sniffling like a kid who'd worn himself out crying. One by one, he had flipped through the records and dust jackets of his father's jazz collection. Twenty minutes earlier his father had brought the whole collection over. *I want you to have them*, he'd said. All of them: Mildred Bailey, Barbara Lea, George Benson, Louis Armstrong, Dexter Gordon, Miles Davis ... all his treasures. He'd left them in a cardboard box on the kitchen table, kissed his son, and departed. That was when Eduardo could no longer keep pretending that he didn't know what he knew. Charlie Parker's 'All the Things You Are' was on the record player when the doorbell rang. At first Eduardo thought the girl on the other side of the door wasn't real, that she was a hallucination, just another mirage. He wanted her to leave, wanted to get rid of her and keep losing himself in the sax and piano, sinking into that dark sea of bubbles where everything is hopeless. But the young woman rang insistently, so he finally opened the door.

Olga was, at that time, very young — practically still a minor. She turned up in mud-caked hiking boots and a soaking wet khaki-coloured duffel coat. Her hair was bright orange and her eyelashes matted with a thick layer of mascara, the water dripping down her cheeks, leaving jet-black trails. Her breasts were small, like little potatoes, and she was anxiously rubbing her palms together the way heroin addicts do when they've gone too long without a fix. But Olga wasn't a junkie looking for spare change, and she wasn't asking him to show solidarity to some pretend cause, by signing up for something, so she could bankroll a vice. She introduced herself quickly and said she'd heard his story on the radio, heard about Elena and Tania dying four months earlier. She said she lived very close to the place where the accident had occurred and she'd seen something, something that she had to tell him about.

Eduardo asked her in. Olga looked shiftily around the apartment, the records strewn across the table. She accepted the coffee Eduardo offered her but didn't touch it; instead she spent the whole time smoking and tapping her ash onto the saucer. At first she had trouble speaking, and took her time getting around to it, instead mentioning that she'd seen some of Eduardo's canvases in a gallery that she neglected to name. Disturbing but deep, those were her words. Perhaps what she should have said was that they were deep because they were disturbing. She also asked him why his portrait subjects were anonymous. Because that's what they were, anonymous, he replied. No one knows their names. Names are excuses, inventions we use to hide behind. She said she understood. Eduardo didn't believe her. She was too young, and besides, she wasn't there to talk about his paintings. She also said she was studying art history and that she was planning to go into the art business, into selling paintings. He didn't believe that, either.

She sighed, taking her time: sometimes she liked to go down to the stream to swim. In the summer it was a pleasant place to be, far from the eyes of nosy neighbours. 'In small towns,' she explained, 'people frown on the idea of women swimming in the nude.' She was obviously one of 'the women' in that comment, and it made Eduardo uncomfortable, and struck him as unnecessary. He was about to say as much, but she spoke first, returning to what had brought her to his door to begin with. And all the while Charlie Parker floated through the apartment, though neither of them paid any attention.

Olga told him that, a few minutes before the accident, she saw a dark-coloured SUV go by. It stuck with her because it was driving too fast, as if the driver either knew the road to the stream well, or was crazy. But she didn't really think about it until two minutes later, when she heard a tremendous crash. There was a really sharp curve there and if you didn't know about it, it would be easy to drive off the road.

When she got to the stream she saw Eduardo's car, overturned, the wheels spinning up in the air and, a few metres away, a girl's body. She looked, then, at the SUV, stopped atop the embankment with the driver's door open. The driver rushed down the slope to the girl's side and leaned over her. He shouted something, running around her body in circles a few times as if he didn't know what to do. And that was when Olga realised what was about to happen. She could tell it because suddenly the man stopped holding his head and moaning. He stood very still, looking toward the overturned car, and then looked around, making sure nobody had seen him. After climbing back up the embankment he picked something up — she couldn't see what but she imagined it was car parts or bits of broken glass — and sped off.

'I was the one who called the ambulance.'

In addition to that, she'd done something else, too, she explained, taking out a wrinkled sheet of paper that had been ripped out of a spiral notebook: she'd written down the SUV's licence plate.

Eduardo paled. He didn't know what time it was but suddenly the temperature dropped. He looked down at the paper as though it contained a secret formula, and then asked her why she'd decided to come to tell him something like that four months after the fact. Olga responded that at first she thought it best not to get mixed up in the whole thing. She didn't like cops and had no intention of testifying in court or doing any of the things she imagined were required of a witness.

'I told the police I didn't see anything, but I can't keep hiding what I know. Whatever you decide to do about it, that's up to you. I've cleared my conscience, but if you tell the cops I told you, I'll deny it. I don't want any trouble.'

And just like that, a life changes. Suddenly someone appears out of nowhere and rips it apart. And nothing can ever be the same as it was a minute prior. When Olga entered his life, Eduardo was like a meteorite speeding toward the void — and when he collided with her, his course altered and he began heading toward a different sort of abyss. Her revelation didn't solve anything. All it did was push him a little further into the darkness, toward a deeper, blacker state.

Perhaps he himself should have gone to the police the moment she left. Maybe that would have changed something; maybe it would have changed everything. But he didn't.

'Sometimes I feel bad for having told you,' Olga said, staring at the sidewalk of Calle Atocha.

They'd taken a leisurely stroll and were now standing in front of the Centro Ruso, the Russian centre of science and culture. A thuggish-looking guy was leaning against its metal gate, hands in his grey overcoat, watching the passers-by. He didn't exactly look like a museum guide.

'You were only trying to help me,' Eduardo consoled her. That had happened thirteen years ago; it was absurd to try to rationalise it now, to seek solace. And yet there Olga was, determined to justify herself.

'The road to hell is paved with good intentions ... Would you at least seriously consider forgetting about the damned portrait? I can get you a better gig, I'm sure.'

They went to say goodbye and Eduardo offered his cheek, but Olga instead kissed him full on the lips. She didn't know why, it was just an impulse. It wasn't a real kiss, but on feeling the contact of her lips, Eduardo's lips went as hard as the mouth of a cave.

That night, lying in bed in the dark, Olga felt ridiculous. Conjuring the image of herself swooping in to give Eduardo a kiss was so embarrassing that she cringed, and recalling what she'd said to him irked her. She'd told Eduardo too much. Luckily, it was clear that he had no idea the number of different lives Olga had lived, all accumulated inside herself. He was too blind, too navel-gazing and focused on his own pain to notice anything around him. Maybe it was better that way, she said to herself, stroking the scar on her inner thigh beneath her pyjamas. The reminder of an old tattoo, one that it had cost her dearly to get rid of.

That scar was the path that once led her to a cobblestone street at midnight. The address scribbled on a scrap of paper turned out to be a basement. The place was sordid, dark, tense. She was a scrawny girl, accustomed to bearing the heavy load of her life without so much as a sigh, but she was only sixteen, and she was terrified.

The woman who took her coat seemed high, smiling with a mouth

144

that drooped grotesquely, as though her makeup had melted down her face.

'Fun nights, but sad mornings, eh?' She led her to a small room. In the centre was a cot on wheels, and a gooseneck lamp that cast a harsh, intense light. On a cart with Formica shelves was a selection of surgical tools, all lined up. The woman tried to comfort her, stroking her shoulder, but the touch of her hand only increased Olga's trembling. The woman told her to take off her dress and panties. It was all going to be quick and painless. She promised.

'OK, young lady, let's *get that out of you*, and then you can go back to your life as though nothing happened.' But the whole procedure was horrific, long, solemn and very painful. There were complications from the start — she said she was only going to aspirate; Olga was only three months' along, after all. But the woman tore her insides up. She could have died there, and sometimes Olga thought maybe it would have been better if she had. She refused to look at the thing the woman showed her before tossing it into the bin.

'You're going to be fine. But you need to get to a hospital — a real one.'

She didn't. She left, feeling with each step as though she was dying. She had trouble keeping her balance and only managed to get back by leaning on the alley wall for support.

She couldn't say a word at home. Her mother would never have believed that one of *her* boyfriends had seduced her daughter and gotten her pregnant. That couldn't happen to *her*.

Olga's father had died when she was three. A civil servant who worked in the prisons, he spent his weekends worrying about the lottery — perhaps fretting about money, which they never seemed to have enough of — and about his sudden headaches, which the social services doctor could not explain and which altered his moods, making him more and more bitter. He didn't make Olga's mother miserable — but nor did he make her happy. He was simply a shadow, slipping through her fingers without leaving any physical trace.

From the time she was a little girl, Olga learned to make do with an outward appearance of normalcy, with the life everyone else truly had and her family could not renounce. But in private her father was withdrawn, living in his own secluded little corner, emerging only from time to time in pyjamas and robe, dragging his slippers, a glass of water in one hand, sitting down to watch the news and falling asleep within ten minutes. And her mother watched from a distance, a look of repulsion on her face. She could hardly remember hearing any stories about what her father had been like, what they used to do, or how her parents had met, and her mother had never said a single word that shed light on what her own feelings for the man might have been.

Her mother never spoke about her feelings in public; the only chinks in her armour that allowed a glimpse into her inner life came out when she was drunk or — after her father died — when she brought home a new boyfriend. Her mother was pretty, far prettier than the men she brought home deserved. But it was so easy to fall into despondency, as though hers were a life not intended to prosper, as though the effort that growing older required was one that responded not to a concrete objective but to mere coincidence and the submission of its protagonist. Some people are like that. They find no purpose in life, they don't ask anything of anyone, except to keep eking out their petty existence with no major upsets.

The last boyfriend was a guy whose train had left the station. He was about fifty — perhaps younger but that was how old he looked. He'd turn up at her mother's door in a wrinkled twill suit, his shirts sometimes missing a button at his stomach, as though the fabric couldn't take the onslaught of his belly. He had long curly sideburns and a little Hitler moustache that covered his top lip, which drooped down on the right as though he were paralysed. In his right hand he held a box of Lola cigarettes, with a lit one between his yellow-stained, ragged-nailed index and middle fingers. His clothes were messy and his black boots caked with mud. In the beginning, he looked at Olga indifferently, like an inevitable presence not worth bothering to contemplate. He seldom smiled and when he did, it seemed like someone was trying to force him but he couldn't quite manage it.

But, in time, his look evolved, without her mother noticing.

Though she couldn't recall the month, she knew it was a Wednesday. Wednesday was the day the supermarket delivered their weekly groceries. Olga remembered the shiny handlebars of the bicycle leaning against the door, its worn brown seat, and the boy unloading wicker baskets filled to the brim. Her mother's boyfriend was sitting across from her, staring at her intently. The room was in semi-darkness and the cool air contrasted with the suffocating, maddening, white heat coming in from outside. Slowly, he stood and approached Olga; he pulled her to his mouth by the neck, firmly but not violently.

That was the first time, but then came others, many others. Strictly speaking, you couldn't say he forced her, not violently at least. The truth was, Olga allowed herself to be taken, as if in a narcotic dream in which nothing mattered because she had no free will, no power to change anything or stop anything, as if with each kiss the man were injecting her with poison from his tongue, paralysing her.

And without realising it, she fell in love. A married man, thirty years older, who was also her mother's lover. She was so stupid that she actually got his name tattooed on her inner thigh, and she would have done far more than tattoo a pathetic symbol on her skin for that man. For months, she shared him with her mother without her mother suspecting. She found excuses to phone him, even though it wasn't always him who answered; sometimes it was his wife or a little boy. She put up with humiliations, came running like a little dog in heat to any fleapit he wanted to meet her at for a quick fuck, and dug her nails into her own flesh whenever she heard her mother orgasm with him inside her on the other side of the wall.

And then that hallucinogenic trip abruptly ended. One morning, he'd arranged to meet her at some rundown rooming house, off the road to Villaverde.

Olga had decided she'd give him the news after making love, as they smoked a cigarette in bed. But *she*, the man's real wife, burst into the room — and it was as if with that invasion her whole fantasy world came crashing down in a thousand pieces, like an airplane cabin suddenly losing pressure. They shouted. But no one can shout and actually communicate at the same time — it all just descends into chaos.

For a few minutes, Olga had truly believed that her youth would win out, that she'd win the fight, he'd stand up to his wife, tell her the same things he'd whispered to her dozens of times between the sheets. But he caved. In fact, he didn't even put up a fight. He simply left Olga, just like that, flicked her off as though she were a disgusting bug clinging to his marital bliss.

'We're going to have a baby!' Olga cried.

It shouldn't have come out like that, she was expecting to be met with the same warmth and rhythm that accompanied them at night, hip to hip, so she could say: 'Leave your wife, leave my mother. We're a family now,' as if that baby were a bond that now made them inseparable. But her cry — desperate, animal-like — was the only thing she had left, the only hope she had of holding on to him.

He looked at her with the horror of a rotten old man. And in that look, in that tenth of a second, Olga realised her tremendous error. She realised that capital-L Love does not exist, that men are selfish and weak. She realised that she would deplore the man whose name was tattooed on her skin as passionately as she'd loved him a minute earlier.

He left them, her and her mother, just like that, shooed them out of his life the way you do an annoying insect interrupting your siesta, with a wave of the hand. And that was the end of romantic weekends, of uncomfortable but exciting lovemaking in the back of a car, of promises, poems, gifts, and phone calls at midnight; that was the end of tattoos and complicit glances.

And when her mother, drunk and lost, called out to him at night, sniffling, not understanding why he'd suddenly abandoned her, Olga glared at her and hated the world.

No, there was no way Eduardo suspected anything like that. He always looked at her with the impatience of a man obliged to explain the obvious. And the obvious was that Olga was frightened.

She half-closed her eyes and pictured a naked defenceless body, dead, there on the dirty floor of her room. Her adolescence, butchered.

How absurd, how pathetic a dead, naked human can seem. How useless, how futile that sort of redemption turns out to be.

9

According to custom, *salat* — Muslim ritual prayers — must be performed five times a day, every day. The most important is that of the mid-afternoon, and that was the one Ibrahim performed most devotedly.

There was a time when he led prayers among the congregation, an act Sunni Islam allowed members well-versed in the Koran, which he was — as was his father, a man beyond all reproach. Now, however, Ibrahim made do with finding a relatively clean surface on which to rest his forehead before an east-facing wall, an imaginary *mihrab* pointing to Mecca. In his cell there was no imam or religious officiate to motivate him to pray. Allah cannot allow any man to speak to Him directly, which is why prophets and angels exist. But in there, there was neither one nor the other. What he had to say was between him and God. Though God didn't seem to want to listen.

He couldn't blame him. It wasn't enough to wash his face, hands, armpits and feet to feel purified, nor to kneel on a mat to find paradise. It wasn't enough to beg forgiveness in order to deserve it, and he wasn't even sure he wanted it. From the time he was a child he'd been taught to spiritually distance himself from pleasures, taught that his only objective in this life was the annihilation of the self through Allah, that all human beings are born with two souls, the human and the divine, and that life is a struggle, a road to perfection whereby the human must be extinguished in favour of the divine. But Ibrahim knew, after a life of strife within himself, that his faith was shaky and his behaviour inconsistent. No, God no longer had faith in him. And he no longer had faith in His kindness. Still, he solemnly adopted the position of *qiyam*, head bowed and hands folded before his chest, bowed, and then knelt, legs behind him and forehead on the ground.

One of Ibrahim's favourite *suras* was number eighteen, which discussed Iblis, the fallen angel, the only one to disobey Allah. As he whispered it, he couldn't help but think of his own childhood. About what was expected of him. 'And then we told the angels, "Bow down before Adam." And they prostrated, except Iblis. He became a jinn, for he disobeyed the order of His Lord.' How many lords had he himself disobeyed, how many precepts had he infringed? He had not honoured the memory of his parents, had filled his mother's life with nothing but tears, had not been able to follow the example of his older brother, martyr of martyrs in Algeria. He was a murderer, an arms trafficker, a mercenary. A fake.

He poked his head down to the empty cot of his cellmate Arthur and reached a hand to the mark left on his headboard by the photo taken on his honeymoon. Ibrahim had no children, no wife, no family to cry for him when he died, no one to intercede on his behalf when Allah decided that his time had come and sent him the Angel of Death. He'd given everything up for a chimera. Suddenly, he'd found he was nearing old age and had no idea how it had happened. He had no inner peace, he never had, but nor was there war — not anymore. Just loss, blood spilled for no reason, regret, voices and faces lost inside him. The dreams he once had, as a boy, had turned into a nightmare.

He turned to the cell door and saw Ordóñez, the warden, leaning against the bars.

'I don't know what you did or how you did it, but you're getting out of here,' he said, brandishing the order for his release.

Ibrahim looked at the bare wall and, in his mind, evoked the photo from Arthur's headboard: Algeria, Andrea …

Perhaps Allah was not as harsh and silent a father as his own, after all. It seemed The Merciful had a sense of humour, a dark sense of humour.

Arthur was seated at a table in the back, by a window with lace curtains that allowed him to see the trees out on Paseo del Prado. A warm glow bathed his surroundings, and it was as though blocking the light from the window somehow revealed two versions of him, of the same man: his brawny silhouette, and the luminous sparkle he emitted. He ordered breakfast from the waiter and immediately focused on a small notebook. Whatever it was he was reading required all of his attention; the waiter was forced to clear his throat a couple of times before Arthur noticed his presence and made space for him to place down the tray containing his breakfast: a cup of coffee, one hardboiled egg, a piece of fruit, and two slices of toast with jam.

Skimpy breakfast for someone with such an impressive physique, Eduardo thought. From the chaise longue in the lobby he had a privileged view of the dining room in general, and Arthur in particular, which allowed him to observe the man, study his movements, analyse the symmetry of his features and overall appearance with no interference.

The first thing he found incongruous was his name: Arthur. He'd come across few people whose looks seemed to go with their names — sometimes their appearances were too grandiose for their names, other times their names were too overbearing for their appearances. In a wild association of ideas, he condensed all the Arthurs of the world into one; he pictured men with friendly features, men who had some slightly ostentatious illness — a respiratory condition, say, or chronic headaches, or a heart murmur. It was easy to imagine a blond Arthur, one with wispy hair, with dainty hands. Particularly if that Arthur were a poet, or had tried to be, as Eduardo knew this one had. He'd been expecting a man with a shifty expression — not cowardly but sort of elusive, probing, hypersensitive to the most trivial of details, a man no doubt on the brink of insanity.

But this man was nothing like that, at least not physically or in his demeanour. The expensive clothes he wore — a bespoke Italian suit in earth tones, matching silk tie, titanium wristwatch — did little to soften the brutish look of a body that seemed too strong, his muscles poised to fight and force, imprisoned beneath his shirt. He picked up his egg and peeled it in a way that seemed chiselled; his hand didn't hesitate when raising the coffee cup to his lips. And yet what most divorced Arthur from his name was his expression, the way he had of reading that notebook and then turning his body to the light outside the window with a contemplative air. His reflection seemed not to be fruit of anything beautiful — a few verses or an idea jotted down in a moment of inspiration — but nor did his eyes shine with melancholy or nostalgia. No, what was behind that look, that tense expression, was more like cold calculation, a weighing up of pros and cons, possible alternatives to something he was turning over in his hard, inscrutable head.

And then suddenly Arthur's expression shifted; it was fascinating. An almost triangular smile lit up his face on seeing another man approach, a man who immediately captured the attention of all those present.

151

The new arrival wore a *djellaba* like those used by Muslims during holidays, with gold trim and vegetal motifs on the V-neck and sleeves. The *djellaba* covered his arms and legs, but visible beneath it were western-style trousers and leather shoes. His face was horrifically mutilated by zigzagging scars, giving him a terrifying appearance. Nevertheless, the way he windmilled his hands to gather the wide sleeves — bending forward slightly and bringing his right hand to his heart — was so elegant, and almost ethereal, that he seemed more like a dancer than a Muslim terrorist about to blow the place to kingdom come — which was no doubt what the nearby customers feared. He radiated an undeniable magnetism, not solely because of the scars on his face but also the graceful constraint he showed when handling objects, and the sincere consideration he gave anything that caught his attention. There seemed to be a sort of tacit understanding between two opposing forces: repulsion for his disfigured face balanced out the admiration for his innate elegance.

For a second, his glance met Eduardo's. Eduardo felt himself openly examined and then, as though having dismissed a possible threat, the man turned back to chat animatedly with Arthur. The pair rose and exited the hotel together.

Eduardo followed at a distance.

For a good part of the morning they walked the streets of Madrid, wandering into bookstores, buying clothes, and stopping at a sidewalk café in the late morning for a drink in Madrid's Barrio de las Letras, the literary quarter. Plaza Santa Ana was bustling with cafés, men selling cans of beer and soda from coolers, and people wandering around with no apparent destination. A group of South American musicians was playing by the marquee of the Teatro Español, and nearby Russian tourists stood listening to a young tour guide who was pointing out the names inscribed on the theatre's facade. A police car cruised by at a prudent distance, slow as a bolero; an African kid passed out fliers for a tapas joint; and a couple of gypsy women in mourning made their way through café tables, proffering the ever-present branches of rosemary, touting the luck it would bring. All of this with apparent harmony. A simple backdrop, and one that allowed Eduardo to stick fairly close to Arthur and his friend without being seen. Luckily, they didn't seem to be in any hurry, and

Eduardo was thankful for that — his knee was killing him after walking all morning.

Arthur stopped at the base of a sculpture of Lorca and suddenly looked up, his eyes happening to meet Eduardo's. Eduardo barely had time to avert his gaze. It was unlikely that he'd recognised him or suspected he was being followed. But when Eduardo turned back, Arthur was heading out of the plaza striding toward the eastern side as though he were suddenly in a hurry. His friend was nowhere to be seen.

Eduardo sped up in an effort to not lose sight of him in the crowded square, momentarily forgetting the searing pain in his knee.

After attempting a short jog, he reached a side street that Arthur had turned down. It was a narrow alley full of popular tapas bars, too crowded to make his way down quickly.

'Dammit. Fucking cripple,' he cursed himself, slapping his damaged leg, when he realised he'd lost his target.

Nadia Rueda had told Arthur that Ibrahim was now free. And indeed, there he was before him.

He liked having his former cellmate near: he felt safer, and he felt they shared something real and tangible in the world — a world he'd suddenly returned to, and one that disconcerted him. But Ibrahim, too, seemed to have changed, outside the grey environs of prison. He seemed more radiant, and his embroidered cotton robe lent him an air both extravagant and captivating. His innate wariness, however, was still very much intact.

'Don't look, but there's a pasty looking guy at the back of the room who can't take his eyes off you.'

Arthur didn't look.

'One of the Armenian's men?'

Ibrahim made a show of examining the man, and discarded the notion. He was just a weirdo, not a likely threat. Suspicion was a survival instinct in him, that was all. He expected the worst of people, and that way he was always prepared. There was a delicate balance to remaining permanently alert without becoming cynical. In his opinion, there was no such thing as good or bad people, good or bad things; that kind of black-and-white thinking was the stuff of novels. He, on the other hand, saw only grey — a dance of shadows — and tried to keep one foot on either side.

Arthur admired his composure, and in a way he also feared it. Even when he was being friendly, Ibrahim's eyes could bore straight through you, and others felt defenceless against his gaze. Nothing is more dangerous than a man who knows who he is and what he wants. And Ibrahim knew. He spoke little, but when he did he seemed to weigh the value of each word; each syllable had a precise purpose.

The two of them talked about their time in jail and about how difficult it was trying to reinsert themselves into the world, but it was Arthur who started and finished all of the sentences. Ibrahim revealed very little of what he really thought. He was present, listening attentively, sometimes even smiling and showing his horrible teeth, but he never stopped being the one on the other side of the conversation, a patient observer.

Later, they walked around Madrid, evoking the streets of Algeria: the Hai el Badr neighbourhood, the questionable areas surrounding the port at Agha, places around Rue Didouche Mourad, the botanical garden of Hamma, the cable cars that ran from Palais de Culture and Notre Dame d'Afrique. And when they'd finished their stroll down memory lane, Ibrahim pushed the topic of conversation back to Arthur, to his present.

'How is your wife? Have you gone to visit her?'

Outside of their cell, the question sounded odd.

'Why do you ask?'

Ibrahim quickly realised his mistake, and tried to explain.

'Well, when we were locked up you were always saying the first thing you'd do when you got out was go to your wife, get her out of Madrid.'

'Andrea doesn't want to see me, she blames me for Aroha's disappearance — and in a way, she's right.'

Ibrahim knew the story; Arthur had told it ad nauseam. He also knew the devastating effect that his daughter's disappearance had had on both of them.

'I haven't exactly proven to be an exceptional father. You think you know your kids and that it's your responsibility to keep them safe, make sure all their needs are met … but clearly I failed at that.'

'Some people get a second chance in life. Perhaps you are one of the fortunate ones. You can get your daughter and your wife back, and you'll do things better this time.'

Arthur gave him a curious look.

'How can you be so sure?'

Ibrahim looked away.

'It is not I who should be sure, but you.'

'If I could only convince Andrea, ask her for another chance.'

'Do it.'

Arthur shook his head.

'I told you, she doesn't want to see me. You don't know my wife. I'm afraid she's sinking deeper and deeper into a void, and when the time comes and I find our daughter, it'll be too late to get her back … If you'd met her when she was young — she was so happy and strong!'

Ibrahim smiled and nodded. Something inside him glowed with a radiance that reached all the way to his dark eyes, like a bonfire burning inside a mountain cave in the dead of night. He, too, had memories.

'Why are you smiling so strangely?' Arthur asked.

Life has a curious way of experimenting on human beings, Ibrahim thought, wiping the smile from his face. Allah played games with a man's destiny, scattering the pieces of a puzzle that somehow always managed to fit back together, one way or another. Some people called it causality, maybe it was predestination, who could say? Perhaps the desire to be free, to control our own lives, was nothing more than an unattainable fancy, human folly in the face of the evidence.

From time to time, though, impassable doors were opened, inviting you to walk through.

'I could speak to her, if you like.' He said it without thinking, urged on by his own instincts.

Arthur was surprised by the offer. He contemplated his friend doubtfully. *Why not?* Ibrahim was special. In prison his loyalty had been unerring, even though Arthur always got the feeling that the man's intentions were not completely transparent. On one or two occasions he'd found him gazing at the photo of him and Andrea in Algeria, thinking God knows what; and one night he'd actually caught his cellmate staring at him as he slept in his cot. For some reason Arthur had been afraid — that was the only time he had been truly scared of Ibrahim, and he pretended to sleep, feeling Ibrahim's breath on his face and sensing his deep, heartless eyes. Still, it was thanks to him that Arthur was alive, and he considered the man a friend. Besides, Ibrahim was thankful to Arthur for having gotten him out of jail. He was Algerian like Andrea, they'd been raised in the same neighbourhood. Unlike Arthur, Andrea had never felt French; she loved Algeria as much as Ibrahim, so if anyone could act as the bond that rekindled his connection to his wife, it was him.

'Sure, why not? Go see her, speak to her.'

Ibrahim nodded, rock-like, displaying no emotion whatsoever. He looked away, to avoid Arthur's gaze, and then something more urgent caught his attention.

'The guy from the hotel is over on the other side of the plaza. It can't be a coincidence that he's here again.'

Eduardo felt tired. After traipsing through half of Madrid playing spy, he was sweating profusely and his knee was on fire. He limped down the street, wondering what idiotic impulse had led him to follow a stranger all over town for no apparent reason.

Suddenly the door to a building opened just as he passed by. From the corner of his eye, he only just had time to catch sight of the fist that flew at his face. Instinct made him turn his head, but he only partially managed to dodge the blow. Most of it landed between his jaw and neck, leaving him dazed. His glasses went flying and before he could recover, a second fist slammed into the pit of his stomach, winding him. It was a confident blow, like that of a pro who knew exactly where to aim. Two powerful hands grabbed him by the shoulders and shoved him inside the doorway like a sack of potatoes. It all happened in less than five seconds, and no one saw a thing.

The building's lobby was dark, but not so dark that Eduardo couldn't see his attacker's face. It was the guy in the *djellaba*. He tried to say something, but his words were stopped by another blow, hard and clean, to the mouth. Ibrahim had struck him with something metallic — a ring, or keys maybe. Eduardo felt all his teeth shift, and a second later the taste of blood filled his mouth. Next came a knee to the solar plexus, and Eduardo collapsed in a heap. Crumpled on the floor, he felt Ibrahim's forearm holding his head down as his other hand felt around, moved beneath his shirt, finally found his wallet, and yanked it out. Eduardo's wallet in one hand, Ibrahim stood up. He was panting slightly and his hair was out of place, but he could easily have kept dishing it out for some time before tiring himself out.

'You work for the Armenian?' he asked Eduardo, pointing his national ID card at him, which he'd just extracted from Eduardo's wallet.

From the floor, Eduardo raised a hand to request a truce. He had to answer fast or the guy might kill him on the spot.

'I don't know what Armenian you're talking about. My name is Eduardo Quintana, and I'm a portrait artist — a painter.'

His reply took Ibrahim off-guard. He crouched down to look closer at Eduardo; his face was swelling quickly. He certainly didn't look like one of the Armenian's goons. Ibrahim nodded toward the still-dark space beneath the stairs. Eduardo's anguished face followed his glance. Arthur Fernández's silhouette emerged from among the shadows.

'Who the fuck are you?' His voice was commanding, but imminent threat no longer filled the air. Eduardo would have to improvise. He certainly couldn't tell the truth. That would ruin everything. His brain rattled inside his skull like an off-balance washing machine.

'I'm a portrait artist. That's how I earn my living. I just wanted to use some of your features, make a sketch without you realising.' With this, Eduardo bought a few precious seconds, and managed to lean his back against the wall and struggle up, with great difficulty.

Arthur examined Eduardo, from head to toe, as though he couldn't believe what he'd just heard. He shook his head a few times and then looked back at him.

'Are you kidding me?'

At that moment, the lights came on in the hallway. A few seconds later, an elderly woman appeared in a robe, shuffling along in house slippers. Seeing the blood on Eduardo's face she let out a tiny rat-like cry and rushed back the way she'd come.

'We better get out of here. It won't be long before that old lady calls the cops. I think it would be best if they don't find you here, given the circumstances — and it wouldn't look good for me, either,' Ibrahim said calmly, massaging the hand he'd used to hit Eduardo.

Arthur hesitated for an instant. He knew his friend was right.

'You shouldn't be out spying on people like a psycho,' he warned Eduardo, clearly too late to do him any good. Eduardo nodded sluggishly.

His whole body ached. He felt like he might vomit.

Ibrahim handed his wallet back.

'I know who you are now,' he said, smiling darkly, pocketing Eduardo's ID. 'It's good to know things about other people. You never know when you might need to use them. If I were you, I'd wait for the cops and request an ambulance. You might have a broken bone, and that lip doesn't look good.' He stood on the threshold for a moment, doorknob in his hand, scanning the street outside like a hunter, and after insuring there was no threat, the two of them left.

The police arrived minutes later. Eduardo, too, would have preferred not to be there when they arrived, but as soon as he tried to make it to the door he realised he wasn't going to get very far. His knee was swollen, and every time he took a breath he felt a sharp pain in his right side. He thought he probably had a broken rib, so all he could do was sit on a step and wait for the cops, and then the ambulance, to get there. He didn't tell the police the truth, or at least not the whole truth: he gave an accurate account of what happened, but rather than describe Ibrahim and Arthur he provided a much more generic and unidentifiable description.

Nor did he tell Graciela the truth when he called and asked her to come pick him up at the emergency room — where an X-ray had shown that his rib was cracked but not broken. Aside from his bruises, there was nothing a few days' rest wouldn't fix. So with a prescription for painkillers and three staples in his lip, he sat down to wait for his landlady to arrive.

'He was just a regular guy, what can I say? He took me by surprise and forced me into the doorway. I presume he wanted to steal my watch and wallet.'

Graciela shot him a dubious look.

'Your watch is on your wrist, and your wallet's in your hand.'

Eduardo stroked his swollen cheek. Ibrahim could really hit like a jackhammer.

'A woman came out of her apartment when she heard them beating me up. I assume they got scared and ran off.'

'And they did all this just to try to get your watch and wallet?'

Eduardo recalled Ibrahim's ironic expression, the veiled threat his words contained.

'The world is full of evil people … Would you mind taking me home? I need a spare pair of glasses.'

'What you need is a good dinner and a little company. Lately you're spending too much time alone and I think the solitude is consuming you,' Graciela said blatantly.

Eduardo didn't have the energy to protest.

Sara was bent over a round formica table. Like all left-handed people, she set her notebook at an angle to draw, and her forearm was stained with ink, smearing the page. She wore pyjamas with green elephants holding coloured balloons — children's pyjamas that any other girl her age would have flat-out refused to wear. But Sara wasn't like other girls. On a bookcase close to her hand, sat her lucky cat.

'Hello there, Sara.'

The girl glanced up and broke into a smile when she recognised Eduardo. She got up and squeezed his belly with her strong arms. Her hair rubbed his chin; she smelled of lemony shampoo.

'How are you feeling today?'

'The doctor monitoring her case says she's improving for now; we're convinced that if we're really disciplined with her meds she'll get better really soon, aren't we, sweetheart?' Graciela replied for her, using an exaggeratedly optimistic tone.

Sara nodded energetically, as though trying to physically shake off the unmistakable doubt showing in her eyes. It would take other children of the same age far longer to realise that things were not as they'd been told — and with those lies would their innocence be lost — but Sara had learned to lie to herself, and learned it a long time ago.

'The doctor says I think a lot; she says there are some thoughts I can't process right because I'm still too young. And I try not to think, but the thoughts think for me and I don't know how to stop them.'

Eduardo stroked her forehead. Sara was from another world, lived in a place all her own; only when the meds knocked her out sufficiently could her brain slow down and visit this other reality, temporarily leaving behind her own promised land. She was like a ghost, a soul divided, and only a quarter of her was accessible to others.

'But doctors don't know everything, do they?'

The girl laughed complicitly.

'No, they don't. The things I tell Maneki, nobody else can know. But you I can tell, if you stay for dinner.' Maneki was her lucky cat.

'That's a tempting offer, so I don't see how I could turn it down,' he granted.

It was a pleasant evening. Plenty of wine, and Sara — sitting beside him — as well as Graciela, who was funny and casual, kept Eduardo from thinking for a few hours about the pummelling Ibrahim had given him. He told stories about his childhood, about his father and his records, the trips he'd take up north, to where his roots were. He wasn't trying to impress Graciela — or at least not consciously — but judging by the way her eyes shone and the way she hung on his words — enthralled, elbow on the table and cheek in her palm — she was anyway.

Suddenly, Sara got up and went to a dresser full of drawers.

'Where do you have the old pictures, *mamá*?' Sara rummaged around in a cupboard until finally emerging with the family album.

Graciela would have preferred she hadn't found it, preferred that her daughter hadn't sat at the table, with a triumphal air, and opened it up, with Eduardo looking on curiously. But there was no way to stop her.

'Look, this is my mother when she was a girl, in her hometown.'

The portrait was of a girl teetering on the precipice of a modern invention called adolescence. Despite her bushy unwaxed brows, her ratty, torn black shirt and big, dirty skirt, she looked ready to make the leap. Graciela's hesitant smile — not quite daring to be happy — was testament to a time gone by. She looked shocked by the sudden glare of the flash, nervous and uncomfortable at the photographer ordering her to pose by an old farmhouse with its zinc roof, the barn door ajar. A girl whose expression had not yet lost its glow, not earned the right to show weakness.

'I was only ten then. My God, the rain that's fallen since that time,' Graciela nodded, taking the photo carefully, as though afraid she might tear it. Her words were really intended for Eduardo. While showing him photos, she conveniently brushed against his forearm, let herself get worked up by the intoxicating heat caused by the touch of his body.

Eduardo sat stiffly, his smile increasingly fake. Sometimes from his apartment he could hear Graciela singing Luis Miguel boleros. It was nice, Graciela had a good voice. The songs told stories of romantic trysts, star-crossed lovers, overflowing passion. But life was no bolero. There was nothing else he wanted to know about Graciela, he had no desire to get close to her; he didn't want to walk through that door, the one that she and her daughter had opened and were now trying to push him through — gently, amicably, but a push nonetheless.

'That doesn't even look like you.'

'Pictures just reflect an image — and over time, that image dies,' she murmured.

Eduardo watched Graciela like a dog watching the moon: it was something far off, something that glowed, true, but something he knew nothing about, had no curiosity about.

She gazed at him, her eyes glimmering in a way that foreshadowed tears. Yet they continued looking at photos. Sara was in charge of turning the pages, hardly giving them time to see the pictures at all, much less note any details. Life went by as quickly from snapshot to snapshot as it did in her feverishly bubbling head. Graciela and Eduardo let her, smiling in weary resignation. Sara was her own little whirlwind, capable of draining anyone's energy. She rushed on, announcing what they were going to see in each picture before showing it. Sometimes she made up stories about the photos, things she invented based on a single captured instant. For instance, that she and her mother had travelled through Africa all the way to the Lower Nile, where a direct descendant of Cleopatra had personally given Sara the solid-gold bracelet she was wearing in the picture taken at the 2000 Carnaval celebrations. And to make sure that Eduardo believed her, she raced off to her room and returned with the bracelet so he could hold it in his own hand.

'Solid gold, it sure is,' he declared feigning curiosity.

Sara continued her dizzying tour through the pages until, on one of them, something attracted Eduardo's attention.

'Who's that girl?'

Graciela stroked the profile of a pregnant young woman, her belly huge beneath a strappy indigo-coloured dress with a full billowy skirt. She took a sip of wine, leaving a scarlet lipstick imprint on the rim. Then she held the glass, spinning it between her fingers, staring lovingly down at the photo.

'My mother. Her name was Esperanza. When she was in a good

161

mood, I remember, she'd sing me children's songs. Sometimes, as night fell, we'd sit, tired but happy, on a bench in the plaza outside our little apartment in Leganés. Then she'd tell me about all the things she'd seen as a girl, at the movie theatre in her hometown, in the summertime: the enormous buildings of a city projected onto the screen; the sound of convertible Fords, their horns honking; teeming streetcars. Her eyes shining, she'd describe the actresses' dresses, their hairdos and make-up, their long legs and slender waists, the elegant way they moved, and spoke, and smoked. Once she even told me, trying to hide her wistfulness beneath a smile, about a famous photographer who wanted to take her picture as if she were a world-famous starlet. But her father — my grandfather — said no.'

They'd run out of cigarettes and the wine was gone. Sara was dozing in the armchair with a blanket draped over her, arms around the lucky cat that was now her inseparable companion. Graciela closed the photo album slowly and put it back in the cupboard. She bent over Sara and brushed her bangs from her eyes. The girl squirmed fitfully.

'She's obsessed with that animal. Sometimes, outside, she'll look at real cats, trying to find one like this, and then declare proudly that none of them look like hers. She thinks Maneki understands what she tells him.'

'Your daughter has an extraordinary imagination,' Eduardo said quietly.

Graciela nodded. The condition she'd been diagnosed with was irreversible and she knew it, but she couldn't help getting her hopes up whenever the symptoms abated and she seemed — for a time — capable of carrying on with a normal life. But then it would all get worse again.

'I ask myself over and over, why it is that some people get to have a little happiness and then waste it, while others never even get a taste.'

Eduardo looked away, at what was left of dinner, still on the table. He wasn't the right person to answer that question.

'I'll clear the table,' he offered.

Graciela let him, and stood watching. She knew what Eduardo was thinking, she always knew what the men she fell in love with were thinking, but there were some defeats she wasn't willing to accept. She went to him and stroked his hair as if he were a little boy. Then she leaned in and kissed him on the lips. Her lips were cracked and cold. Eduardo's recoiled from her contact. Graciela stepped back, a little ashamed.

'I wasn't trying to make you uncomfortable.'

'You didn't, don't worry,' he whispered, mollifying her.

Graciela regarded him with an exhausted expression.

'I know almost nothing about you, only the part you've been willing to show, and I don't know if that's a lot or a little. But for me, it's enough, Eduardo. You have a way forward with us, if you want. A new start. I'm not foolish enough to think you love me. Not yet. And that doesn't matter, I can wait.'

Eduardo had rolled up his shirtsleeves and was rinsing a glass. For a split second he stopped, the soap bubbles dripping off the glass and onto the counter. Instinctively, he turned his head to the right. Sara was still sleeping.

'I don't think you and your daughter deserve to be saddled with a corpse like me.'

'Don't talk like that. You're not dead. Even if you want to be, the fact is that you're still here. You must have some hope. Besides, neither my daughter nor I are going to replace your family; we're not going to cover up a hole, Eduardo. What I'm offering you is an opportunity, for all three of us.'

Eduardo found a clean cloth and dried a plate patiently, spinning it like a steering wheel.

Would Graciela know the real meaning of the French word *charme*? Elena had it. It's not something you can acquire, or even learn. It's a talent, an air that certain things have, certain people have, from the time they're born. It's something that makes them different, regardless of what they do; it's in the way they behave, walk, look at you, breathe, hold out a hand or sing a song. They're immortal; little stray angels who lost their wings in the original Fall, who now wander among humans looking for a way back home. If any of them had ever crossed her path, deigned to rest their gaze upon Graciela and smile, she might understand; if not, anything he might tell her about Elena would be in vain.

'It's late. Thank you for dinner, and for the company, but I've got to be up early tomorrow. I should go.'

'Yes, I guess that's probably for the best,' Graciela accepted stiffly, like a mannequin being removed from a shop window. Without realising, she'd smeared her lipstick, wiping the back of her hand across her mouth.

Eduardo went to the door. Graciela didn't move from her place at the table, where she sat smoking, with a lost look, gazing vacantly at an empty wineglass. Eduardo turned the doorknob and opened the door, but held it there and looked back over his shoulder.

'I killed a man, Graciela. Shot him in the head. And his wife. And I would have killed his son, too, if I hadn't been stopped. That's the person you say you want to have sleeping in your bed at night, curled up against your back.'

He walked out without waiting to see his landlady's reaction.

The afternoon smelled of mimosas. A heartbreaking afternoon, too beautiful to be real — a foretaste of nostalgia, of a perfect moment that could be ruined at any second.

'You've got a visitor.'

Andrea frowned slightly, displeased at the nurse's interruption.

'I don't want to see anyone,' she murmured.

'It's not your husband,' the nurse replied, guessing at her thoughts.

Wooden benches were strategically placed around the edge of the large pond, inviting visitors to gaze at its green, slimy bottom, at the blue and red fish that appeared from time to time, circling slowly, begging for breadcrumbs. At one time, the pond had been surrounded by green, but now it was nothing but a patch of dried yellow grass.

Ibrahim gazed at the water, leaning against a tree. Arthur had prepared him for the worst, warning him that what he'd find was someone resembling a coma patient. 'Talking to her is frustrating,' he'd said, 'sometimes even absurd. She doesn't seem to listen, or see, or hear.'

The sound of a leaf crackling woke him from his trance.

Andrea approached with hesitant steps. Her haircut was clumsy and boyish, flat on the sides, and her eyes had an erratic look; her arms and hands hung listlessly at her sides, and her shoulders drooped lethargically.

And still, he felt his heart race.

Though wasted away, Andrea wasn't dead — at least not completely. The girl he once knew was still there, somewhere, hiding behind those eyelashes and that receding chin, behind those sunken cheekbones and drooping mouth. Her skin was wrinkled and age spots could be seen among the folds; her muscles were no longer firm and toned; her triceps were flabby, and her hips sagged. But it was her — he was as sure as he had been when he'd first seen the wedding postcard on Arthur's headboard.

Almost forty years had passed — they were on the verge of old age, and defeat. But there they were, face to face.

'Hello, Andrea.'

Andrea was surprised at his voice, so unexpectedly soft. Its warmth stirred a memory of something that had happened long ago. In some part of her mind, she felt she recognised it.

'Do we know each other?'

So you do remember me. You don't know when or where or what part of your memories I fit into, but something deep inside you remembers me, Ibrahim thought with a strange elation. And yet, he couldn't say 'yes'.

'I'm afraid not — although, like you, I was born and raised in Algeria.'

The mention of this shared place from their past made Andrea's face light up briefly.

'My name is Ibrahim; I'm a friend of your husband's.'

It was a short-lived illusion. Ibrahim had pictured distrust, rancour, perhaps even some sort of unpleasant scene. He could have handled that; in fact it would have been desirable. Anything. But he wasn't prepared for her stony look.

'He knows you don't want to see him, that's why he sent me. He wants you to know that he's doing everything possible to find your daughter, and that he put me in charge of making sure she's alright — that it will all be okay.'

Andrea tilted her head imperceptibly toward the pond. Somewhere, fallen leaves were rustling on the ground, stirred up by a gust of wind that seemed to have come out of nowhere. It was going to rain, she thought. And that one idea eclipsed all else — rain, round fat drops, as heavy as transparent mercury; rain, flooding everything, the drumbeat of it falling on dead leaves, on rooftops; ripples forming in the pond, little birds flapping wildly in search of refuge, clouds that looked almost pleated coming down from the sierra.

'It's going to rain,' she said. 'The rain here doesn't weigh much; it's light.'

'Do you understand what I said, Andrea?'

'The rain here isn't sticky,' she went on, eyes beseeching him from the bottom of her pupils, two dark tunnels.

Ibrahim understood. He couldn't stop himself from reaching out a hand — a hand with so much death on it — to stroke Andrea's face, as broken as his own.

'You're right,' he murmured, 'it's going to rain. But the rain here isn't like in Algeria, is it? There, the wet ground gets so steamy it steals the air from your lungs.'

And then he recalled an afternoon from that summer when they had run to catch the bus after spending the day at the beach, she with her sandals in one hand, he with a wet shirt tied around his waist; wet, black hair plastered to his face; then both of them dripping, holding the steel handrail on the bus, staring at each other from up close as the storm whipped across the metallic roof of the bus, and the sea salt on their skin mixed with the smell of diesel as they headed back to the city.

Andrea sniffed the fingers touching her face, her nose trembling ever so slightly. The faintly acidic smell brought to mind an image: where from? When? Old busses, a scrap heap. She thought of inland roads that ran past fences and great bales of hay covered with big black tarps to protect them from the frost. Horses and Berber labourers in straw hats peeking out from above the top. From time to time, a dog running crazily, sending a cloud of partridges flapping. The reapers sang Mohamed El Anka songs on their way to the harvest, riding in carts pulled by lazy mules. On her way by, Andrea would smile at them and they — especially the younger ones — would straighten up proudly and sing a little louder, waving their straw hats at her. The sun was slow, following the curve of the Algerian sky. Those were wonderful days, those harvest days. They were good times, indeed; the past people invent is always better than the present.

Ibrahim pulled back gently, his fingertips feeling an electric current that flowed from his flustered heart to that stony face. Those memories — partly invented, partly disguised, partly lived — had given him the courage to accept Arthur's assignment, to put aside his anger and see Andrea. But now he felt unsure. Perhaps he'd been foolishly hoping she would recognise him, hoping she'd throw herself into his arms as she did when they were little more than children — and then everything would have been alright, would have made sense, and this uncomfortable feeling, this painful beating of his heart wouldn't have begun. But none of that was going to happen, he knew that now.

Andrea hugged herself weakly and turned away, walking back down the same shrub-lined path she'd just walked up. Then she stopped and straightened her shoulders, almost imperceptibly. She smoothed her hair down, pointlessly, and turned back.

Where had she seen that face before, without the scar now disfiguring it? Where had she heard that voice that made her insides stir?

That night, Andrea opened the top drawer of her desk and pulled out a crude ceramic ashtray. The bottom of it was engraved: *To the best mother, on Mother's Day*. It had been the last, naive gift her daughter had given her, just a few months before she'd started pulling away, before she'd lost her trust and innocence. She'd given it to her just as she was on the verge of that painful phase when children discover the power of lies, and how they could take control by manipulating their parents' fears; when they turn their parents from heroes into monsters who exist for the sole purpose of making them unhappy and forbidding everything: no piercings, no clubs, no make-up and certainly no talking about sex at home. That blackened, baked-clay ashtray, a project from her manual arts class at school, was the last thing left of Aroha's innocence.

She went to the window and opened the slat a few inches, just enough so that she could smoke and blow the evidence outside. She lit the cigarette, which she'd bought off a security guard for the price of gold, and gazed at the crescent moon above. Andrea thought about the stranger, his rough hand stroking her skin, a gesture that hadn't seemed odd, hadn't frightened her — quite the opposite, in fact: it had calmed her, as if her skin already knew his. Why had she felt, looking at him, that his dark eyes were like home, felt as if they took her to a place that knew no misery?

His hand in the air turned back the pages of her life with the same shocking ease that the decades sped past — friends, births and deaths, holidays, trips, and thoughts that were increasingly trivial, that were less and less her, becoming more and more simply habit. Arthur's lovers, his lies, his shady business dealings, and his excessive urge to accumulate power, money, influence. And she had grown ever smaller, ever farther from what she'd dreamed she would one day become. The years had worn her down — her husband's bouts of depression and his fears, always tormented by the past, a past in which the shadow of an invisible father dressed for battle hung in the air like a malignant presence.

Two or three times, Andrea had tried to get away, tried to divorce him, start again someplace else, alone, without the need to justify her life with the presence of a man. She'd had one lover, an engineer from Madrid the same age as Arthur, twelve years younger than her. Age, back then, was already a burden between them, just one more part of life that pulled them inexorably further apart. It hadn't worked. Andrea had never loved anyone but Arthur — and sex and phony passion were nothing but placebos that she'd found unsatisfying. She only did it to get back at him. How stupid that had been: he'd never even found out, or else had pretended not to.

What horror she'd felt on discovering she was pregnant, and over forty. In a strange city like Madrid, no family, no man who would love her above his own ambitions. The nights spent lying awake, watching her belly grow, the fights and arguments, Arthur's absences, her first attempt to abort with an overdose of pills. She never told Aroha about it — her daughter would have claimed it as the reason for all that ailed her.

'Do you mind telling me what you're doing? You know that smoking in the bedrooms is strictly forbidden.'

The security guard's voice startled her, coming from the other side of the window. The woman had been standing right there in front of her the whole time and Andrea hadn't even noticed. She put her cigarette out in the ashtray and closed the window. 'Strictly forbidden,' the guard had barked. She wanted to laugh. To prohibit something *strictly* was moronic; did anyone prohibit leniently? It was redundant emphasis.

Her world was like that these days, full of useless emphasis.

Aroha was — had been since the day she was born — Andrea's beginning and her end, her heaven and her hell. Her daughter had brought about the miracle, or curse, of giving her what she'd lost so many years ago with Arthur, a reason to live. Without her — without the daily dose of pain that her daughter inflicted, as well as the hope that only her daughter could breathe into her — her days had turned into never-ending darkness.

Andrea placed her hands in her lap as if she could still cradle Aroha to her chest; as a baby, she had been so tiny that even holding her had been frightening; it was as if she were made of glass, so fragile, so little hair, always sleeping. The only thing that would wake her was her mouth, moving when she wanted to be fed, though never too much, just a little, and Andrea had to pat her bottom to keep her from falling asleep with a nipple in her mouth.

How had she turned into that quarrelsome child — so angry with herself, with everything around her, especially Andrea and Arthur? It wasn't something that could have happened overnight. It must have been a gradual process, a metamorphosis that Andrea hadn't managed to see, blinded by unconditional love, until it was too late. That was what upset her the most, not having realised that her daughter was sinking below the surface, into the depths of arrogance and anger, becoming a spoiled, capricious rich girl whose whims Arthur indulged constantly. Aroha had become ravenous at a very young age, cruel and demanding, filling her life with things, things that could be bought with money — and then had disappeared, just like that, leaving nothing behind.

What are those marks? she asked her the day she walked into the bathroom and saw the spots on her ankles, her neck. They weren't overly shocking — finger marks, and a few dots that looked like fleabites. Aroha reacted by covering herself with a towel and screaming her head off, saying she had no right to walk in without knocking, that it was *her* bathroom, and that whatever she decided to do or not do with *her* life didn't concern her. Andrea had shouted back, filled with rage, insulting her daughter in both French and Arabic, as if to draw a line between her past and her daughter, *the fucking stuck-up rich bitch from Serrano* who didn't appreciate how lucky she was to have been born with a silver spoon in her mouth.

The pair of them had screamed their heads off. And then Andrea had caught a glimpse of her twisted face in the steam-covered mirror and had felt ashamed — because the rage she was feeling was not toward her daughter but toward Arthur, who'd now been in the US for weeks, fucking that beautiful black woman who worked for him. She was shouting at

169

her daughter because she felt old, abandoned, and exhausted; because she needed to lash out at someone to keep her head from exploding.

'I'm sorry,' she whispered, sitting on the bed in the solitude of her bedroom, the ceramic ashtray in her lap, staring at the bare wall as if it were a window back to the past, back to that bathroom. Aroha standing in the tub, gripping the towel as though strangling it, wet hair falling over eyes — eyes that glared at her in hatred and anguish. Eyes that were crying out for help. But she had been blind, so full of her own frustration, that she'd refused to listen to what her daughter's eyes were telling her, what they were imploring. She refused to see that she was not in fact shouting in hatred or anger, but in fear — that she was terrified, lost. She'd been reaching out her hand, and Andrea had let it go.

She should never have let Arthur check Aroha into that institute in Geneva. She'd come back a different person. Andrea had known then that she'd lost her. She began hanging out with a group of kids older than her, though not by much. Aroha never wanted to bring her new friends to the house; didn't want to *contaminate them* with the bitterness in the air at home, was what she said.

The last time she saw her, she was getting into a car with one of them. The car had roared off, raising a cloud of dust. And when the dust had settled, the car was gone. And so was her daughter.

That was four years and five months ago. And Andrea was still looking at that cloud of dust, hoping her beloved daughter would come back to her.

It took her several minutes to realise that she was crying, a stream of furious, uncontrollable tears, her mouth opening and closing in a silent scream, snot running down her nose and between her lips, into her mouth.

Outside, it was beginning to rain.

10

The antique shop was hard to find — it was as if the owners didn't want any passers-by to happen upon it without first undertaking a painstaking search. It was a small place close to Calle León, with no signage on the door or facade. Nor was there a doorbell, and the opaque glass louvers at the entrance made it impossible to see anything inside. The wooden door had two grooves, each forming a half-arch and was studded with thick Roman nails; there was also an iron mailbox that bore no name but was crammed full of junk mail and bank notices. The place looked abandoned.

Guzmán knocked twice, waiting several minutes each time, but nobody came to open the door. He was about to leave when someone buzzed him in from inside, and the door mechanically clicked open.

The air was heavy and the place smelled of wood and mildew. A monastic silence reigned, and a floor lamp with glazed shade was the only — and insufficient — form of light in the long, cavernous room crammed with paintings, sculptures, books, furniture, and even clothes. No one came out to greet him despite the noise the door had made closing behind him. In the back — amid tables of various styles, baroque chairs and suits of armour, and behind a high wooden counter — an old man sat examining old coins with a magnifying glass. Beside him were an ashtray overflowing with butts and several rags, stained with dye. He was enveloped in a dense cloud of smoke.

'Good afternoon,' Guzmán called.

The old man barely looked up to give him an obligatory wave, and then went back to ignoring him. He looked like he'd just stepped out of the nineteenth century, as did the rest of the shop. The man's little, round, frameless glasses were perched atop his pointy ears, and he had almost invisible sideburns. He was wearing a loose high-collared smock like the kind once worn by weavers.

Guzmán flipped through a few books piled on a little table — a collection of Kipling stories from the thirties. The rough yellowed paper and tiny, cramped print brought back childhood memories. Not good memories. He left the books and walked over to a chalice with a silver base and marble inlay, a heavy goblet that bore the inscription *Sanctus Christi* and a cross in bas-relief.

'Would you mind putting that down?' the old man inquired from his place at the back of the room. 'That chalice is not for you.'

Guzmán obeyed, feeling awkward, as if he were a pickpocket, or a kid who'd been caught red-handed doing something naughty.

'Sorry, I was just curious. These things fascinate me. I can't help wondering about their original owners, what their story was.'

Now the old man looked at him more carefully. He'd taken off his glasses and was using his smock to clean the lenses mechanically. Finally, as if he weighed much more than his tiny frame suggested, he emerged from behind the counter and ambled over. Stroking the chalice that Guzmán had handled, he gently wiped the rim with a cloth.

'That's a good thing, that curiosity. Objects are important, you know? Even the most insignificant object in this place deserves the respect of ending up in the hands of someone who will know how to appreciate it. We've got everything from silver thimbles belonging to Queen Victoria Eugenie's seamstresses to the construction certificate of the Hispano-Suiza driven by King Alfonso XIII on his wild nights out in Madrid. There are Hussars squadron uniforms, 18th-century pistols, and exquisite altarpieces; I've even got a beautiful set of Bohemian crystal glasses that belonged to Emperor Franz Josef I. But I've also got a modest gouge left to me by my great-grandfather — a carpenter — that won't be sold until I find the person who will care for it with the devotion it deserves.'

'Quite an impressive variety of antiques.'

The old man smiled scornfully.

'That's what you'd expect from an antique shop. Time stopped ticking long ago, and that's the way it will stay as long as Dámaso Berenguer is in charge. Dámaso, that's me,' the dealer clarified, casting an eye around the place quickly, as though to make sure nothing had gotten up and moved.

'The fact is, I'm not here to buy anything,' Guzmán responded.

The antiquarian squinted at him.

'You don't look like a policeman or a detective,' he said suspiciously, staring at Guzmán's mangled hand, albeit not with disgust but outright — and slightly malicious — curiosity, as if drawn to deformity. 'You also don't look like a city council inspector or taxman, but you never can tell. Are you here to look over my books, see how much more the government can skim off? Everything is in order. They've already stolen everything that can be stolen.'

'I'm none of those things,' Guzmán said, attempting to calm him.

'Then what *are* you, exactly? We're all *something*, to the degree that whatever it is we do defines us, don't you think?'

Guzmán found the old man's observation amusing. By his definition, Guzmán should reply that he was a fallen angel, a demon, a sort of monster disguised as a human.

'I'm a businessman, and I've been told you can help me. I'm looking for Magnus Olsen. I have in my possession a roll of pictures shown on Émile Reynaud's praxinoscope, in 1877. It's my understanding that Mr Olsen pays a hefty sum for original filmography.'

The antique dealer could barely contain himself, almost shouting out loud. Immediately, though, his surprise gave way to distrust. The old man eyed Guzmán with something bordering both curiosity and uneasiness.

'And if this Magnus Olsen is such a special collector, why come in search of him here?'

'I've been to several antique dealers in Madrid. And they've all sent me here — they say you sold him some real works of art, and that you also run a very select film club that Olsen belongs to.'

The old man pursed his lips as if he'd been about to whistle but had then thought better of it, after all, and waggled his fingers with a look of confusion.

'I certainly don't remember Magnus Olsen very well, that I can tell you. Maybe he came here once or twice, but it's been a long time since he's come around.' The old man's face twisted, and he smoothed his hair. He didn't appear comfortable talking about this. He turned a couple of times, picking up scapulars and placing them back down, repositioning a classic fountain pen with gold nib. 'As far as any film club goes,' he continued, 'I don't know who could have told you anything like that. There's never been one, at least not here. The only films I'm interested in are the ones Juanito Valderrama starred in, and that was ages ago. I'm afraid I can't help you.'

Guzmán shrugged and forced a gullible smile.

'Well, that's a shame.'

The old man nodded slowly, running a whitish tongue over his top lip.

'But I could take a look at that roll of pictures, if you're interested. I might not know much about film, but I can always appreciate a good antique.'

Guzmán weighed up the proposal. A single false step, an out-of-place comment, and the deceitful house of cards he'd built would come crashing down.

'Actually, I was hoping to show it to Olsen. And I was hoping he'd tell me about the film club, too. From what I understand it's full of real experts. I imagine they'd be capable of properly assessing a piece like the one I'm looking to sell.'

'Yes, yes, of course. You see that?' Guzmán turned to look in the direction that the old man's bony finger pointed. There stood a pile of cardboard boxes labelled with marker, waiting to be unpacked. 'That's the entire contents of someone's inheritance, sold for a song. The dead couple's children didn't want to know anything about the estate their parents had accumulated over the decades. It's more common than you'd think. Greedy offspring who don't care about an object's history or its memory; all they're interested in is getting all the *junk* off the property. That's what young people think of old people's lives; they just see it all as a tedious, unnecessary accumulation of stuff — souvenirs and experiences that are all useless. So unfair. The objects of art, the vintage books and some of the Napoleonic furniture, will bring in a considerable sum; the rest of it I just stock to get rid of, sell it for peanuts. Some people think antique shops are like junkyards, you see. They confuse *old* with *antique*, which is like confusing something's worth with its price. In order for an object to become an antique it needs to do more than stand the test of time; objects don't increase in value with each passing year, they're not like wine. A piece of shit is still a piece of shit even if it's so dried out it no longer smells.' The old man underscored his joke with a wry smile, forced. Guzmán didn't laugh along with him.

'And what does that have to do with Olsen?'

The old man was surprised at the stranger's blunt question. He felt a twinge of disappointment, although his disappointments were like very small aftershocks — he'd been through so many that he hardly even

174

noticed anymore. It upset him that someone might show more interest in an economic transaction than in the intrinsic value of what he was trying to sell.

'Among the things discarded by those heirs is a precious Lumière box camera, first displayed at the Paris Expo in 1867. It's absolutely priceless, but the owners couldn't tell, and in order to get that I had to buy all this crap as well. Look, honestly, I don't think that Olsen guy or anyone else who isn't a professional antique dealer is going to know how to appraise what you've got to offer.'

'Still, I'm going to try to find him. Thank you anyway, though.'

Guzmán held out a hand. The old man scratched his earlobe, visibly anxious.

'You see, the thing is, I seriously doubt you'll be able to find him unless you're some sort of medium. From what I understand he was in trouble with the tax collector and the law, back in his home country, and he ended up killing himself, in a rather tragicomic way, if I may say.'

Guzmán forced himself to look both surprised and disappointed.

'For a man you couldn't even remember, you sure have a lot of details on him.'

'Your Reynaud has refreshed my memory. Listen, Magnus Olsen was a good collector, and he paid whatever price he was quoted, like all eccentric millionaires; but the truth is he was an amateur, and that doesn't even matter because it's impossible now for you to make a deal with him. I, on the other hand, would be able to appraise the fair value, tell you what your article is really worth, and give you a firm offer on it.'

Guzmán pretended to think it over, as if he were a bit disconcerted. Of course, the roll of pictures didn't even exist. So he improvised.

'You're right. I'll bring the roll in, maybe we can come to an agreement. After all, I really do need the money.'

This was more than the old man could have hoped for. The guy's got a priceless artifact he was willing to sell that fucking Swedish amateur, and he makes a blunder like that — admitting he seriously needs the cash — and now, the perspective of a profitable deal predisposed him in Guzmán's favour.

'Come back anytime,' he said, walking him to the door. 'Hermits like me end up realising how nice it is to have company when the noise inside

175

our heads no longer fills the loneliness. Old age is comprised of silence, you see. A silence that's not very pleasant, too much like an empty room. We value all the things life has to offer when they're almost gone — intelligent company, going for walks, a good shit in the morning, a song we've heard a thousand times without ever really listening ...'

Guzmán nodded. He already had one foot out the door when something he seemed to have forgotten, soothing minor, made him retrace his steps.

'Listen, Dámaso, one more thing: do you know a man named Ian Mackenzie? He may have come in with Olsen at some point.'

'Who is he?'

'A Welshman, film director. You may have seen one of his movies — though I'm afraid Juanito Valderrama didn't star in any of them.' He said all this slowly, staring at the old man. He took pleasure in noting the way the muscles on his old, indifferent face contracted ever so slightly. Bosco had taught him that: make them feel the knife entering their flesh before you've even shown it to them, let them imagine the horror you're on the verge of inflicting, let them fear you before you've even lifted a finger.

'I ... I don't think so. No, I'm sure I don't,' he declared with a sudden finality that slipped too quickly from his lips.

Guzmán feigned frustration.

'Doesn't matter, I was just curious. You've been a great help; I really appreciate it. I'll be back with those Reynaud pictures.'

As he walked down the street, he didn't need to look back to know that the old man was watching him from behind the opaque louvers of his shop. Guzmán felt an almost instinctual, animalistic glee, like a hound who picks up the scent of blood — a weak, uncertain trail — and will not let up until it leads him to the pray. No one breaks immediately, that much he knew from experience. But the old man had committed enough blunders to make him suspicious. He had no reason to lie about Olsen and yet he had, only to backpedal pathetically as soon as he thought he might lose out on a lucrative deal — one that would never come off. Guzmán didn't have — nor had he ever had — pictures of anything but his own graduation, from when he became an officer in the Chilean navy. Plus, the man had lied when he said he didn't know or remember Ian Mackenzie. The dried spittle in the corner of his mouth had given him away. But what excited Guzmán's bloodhound instinct most was that he'd denied all knowledge of something as apparently harmless as a private film club.

The years had taught him to be patient and to observe. In the cells at La Moneda, he'd often take a stool and place it just outside the door to observe the detainees before he interrogated them. He could spend hours sitting there, cigarette butts piling up at his feet, searching for any sign of weakness, any tiny weakness he could pounce on and exploit later. Others preferred using brute force to break a prisoner's will — fists, electric shock, beatings, knives, rats — whatever it took. Guzmán wasn't one of those, he wasn't a sadist, wasn't deranged. He kept his goal in sight, and his goal was to penetrate the mind of the detainee, to find out what he or she knew. Violence, of course, was a necessary part of that. Sometimes after a long torture session even death became routine, predictable, desirable, if there was nothing more to be learned from the person being interrogated. But that was always after a long and painstaking plan, an assault on the prisoner's very soul.

Only idiots and lunatics lied for no reason. And that old man was neither. In other circumstances, simply squeezing his armpits with pliers a few times would have done it — he'd have given up what he knew that easily. But these weren't the eighties in Chile, and Spain was certainly not the same place he remembered from his days working with Carrero Blanco's anti-terrorist forces.

There are no coincidences, there are only different ways of making sense of things — a code to be cracked, he thought.

He was thirsty. It was late afternoon in Madrid, and the streets — lively, joyful, boisterous — offered new opportunities on every corner. An opportunity to forget who he was. He wondered what Olsen's widow was doing right now. Maybe drinking alone.

Guzmán wasn't sure why that woman reminded him so much of Candela.

The pub had a large, pleasant barroom, with small, grey stone vases, each with a few fresh-cut flowers, decorating every table. The walls had been painted surreal colours and were heavily lacquered. The bar lined one wall, with mirrored glass cabinets behind it, and a buzzer that, when rung, ding-donged like a doorbell. A few metres from the bar sat a group of throwbacks — pseudo-bohemians in faded leather jackets and moccasins, smoking machine-rolled joints that were systematically perfect and uniform in appearance. They discussed art and politics as if the two topics naturally flowed back and forth, while hookers sauntered around, far more tormented than their laughter and primping would seem to indicate. You could sense the overwhelming failure that already inhabited them.

Some of the other customers looked sad and defeated. There were businessmen in cheap suits and ties, their briefcases full of useless samples, and truck drivers with languid eyes who sat quietly, downing their beers — men who washed their faces and heads at rest stops to make themselves minimally presentable. There was a piano in one corner, its top open, keys as yellow as an old man's teeth. The pianist played with no brio whatsoever, a potpourri of songs that punctuated the gulps he took from a tall glass of gin, which he made sure was never empty. Each time he raised the glass in the air, an attentive waitress came to fill it up again. In a couple of years he'd be dead, his fingers perhaps atrophied from arthritis, unable to play or even clutch a highball glass between his gnarled digits, and unable to beckon the cocktail waitress.

'Thinking of an old song?'

Seated at a table, Guzmán startled, like a jellyfish floating in the water. An inert body reacting only when something bothered him.

A woman with a drawn-on mole smiled at him, leaning back indolently, staring out at the world through fake eyelashes and wearing a smile prone to both ridicule and pride that did her no favours.

'Not exactly,' Guzmán replied, wrenching the words slowly from the depths of his soul.

'Mind if I sit with you?' She already had, so Guzmán simply shrugged. *People should take more care around carnivorous plants*, he thought. *They have the brightest colours, and on the surface they seem harmless.* The woman must not have been able to tell.

She told him her name, but he immediately forgot it.

'Here we are, at the "ineluctable limit of the diaphanous",' she said.

His tongue thick, Guzmán asked her what that was supposed to mean. She smiled, revealing a mouth full of teeth so crooked that flashing them even momentarily seemed too much.

'I don't know. I heard it on the radio when I was driving. I liked it, so I wrote it down so I wouldn't forget. That's what I do with odd words and sentences I find interesting. I write them down so I don't forget.' She didn't say she did it to learn them, or to understand them, or to be able to use them later. No — it was so she wouldn't forget.

Guzmán smiled, moved by an almost perverse curiosity at the defective behaviour of human beings.

'Great. Tell me your life story.'

'There's not a lot to tell. When I was fourteen a friend of my father's took my virginity before I'd even had my first kiss, and it's all been downhill from there,' she said, giggling. She was drunk. Or pretending to be.

What was he doing when he was fourteen? He was just a kid with short eyelashes and bushy brows, riding the octopus at the local fair. But he couldn't recall who his first kiss had been.

The woman kept drinking. She'd run up a long list of boyfriends, exes, husbands and lovers by that point — relationships long and short, each with the common denominator of having been complicated.

'Men don't know how to give me what I want.'

'Well, do you know how to ask them for it?'

'What I need is for men to eat me up with their eyes, to bite my legs and neck and tits in their minds. I want to feel wanted, not admired like some sculpture in the gardens of Venice. I need to be touched by impatient hands, *lubricious* hands — I read that word in an ad for vaginal cream this morning — to get me wet.'

There's a place for every freak at this carnival, Guzmán thought. People want to lead different lives, lives they'd conjured up in their minds, but few of them have the courage to actually do it. She didn't care if he was listening to her or not. She just needed to vent. She'd drunk too much and, in all honesty, didn't find him attractive in the slightest; still, she would end up asking him to go to bed, just to keep from being alone.

The woman pulled out some coke, tapping it into a line on her compact mirror. Then she cut the little worm in two and they each snorted their little insect eagerly. Once it was inside, closer to sorrow, coke turned into truth. Suddenly she kissed him. *This is like drinking cyanide*, Guzmán thought, feeling his tongue inside her mouth. He closed his eyes and downed his hemlock.

He let himself be led to the top floor. The room was pretty. It had cathedral ceilings with thick cedar beams. The whitewashed walls weren't flat but had the bulges of a crumbling building, like the fatty cysts that spring up on old people's faces. The carpet was red, and gold-leaf mirrors reflected every part of the room's anatomy.

Guzmán sat down on the bed — wide, morgue-like, covered in a white crochet bedspread with a lifeless, antiseptic-clean smell. The bed was sad, like everything else about poor people trying to emulate wealth. It wasn't the bed of a princess, it was the bed of a hooker, but it had a nice canopy and mirrors on the ceiling that made it easy to explore the precise geography of a naked body.

'You okay?' she asked, washing herself in the bidet.

Guzmán eyed her with profound sorrow. *From the old ever springs the new*, he thought. He repeated this in silence, trying to make the maxim true, but he couldn't pull it off. He looked away. She slithered over to the bed and gave him a sideways smile. He could feel, in his fingertips, the beating of his own heart: *boom, boom, boom*, the steps of a giant trapped in a cage.

'I can make the screaming in your head stop for awhile.'

'You got a stake to drive into my heart?' He could hear someone screaming through the walls, a truck starting up in the parking lot, and the distant laughter of other prostitutes in the hallway, the sounds mingling as if he were at the bottom of a pool. Sometimes he was drawn closer to being certain that life was nothing at all, nothing but a fantasy that would vanish if you just opened your eyes.

'You want me to suck you off?' she asked.

Guzmán smiled cruelly.

He sat very quiet, staring into darkness, penetrating it as if trying to see into a dense forest full of mist. He thought of Candela's voice, the headlights of Bosco's car illuminating grains of sand floating in the air, the sound of the blowtorch being lit, the spittle on the lips of the thugs, laughing as they held him down. Then he closed his eyes and felt another type of darkness — deeper, with no tones. He watched the woman undo his zipper and stroke him through his pants. Guzmán squeezed his eyelids shut, recreating the Basque music teacher's fingers, the touch of her warm fingertips on his glistening foreskin, the taste of her tongue slowly licking him from the base of his testicles up, tracing the length of his erect member.

The woman had gone quiet. She was staring at his singed skin as though she'd accidentally opened the door to hell. His lacerated penis and scorched, empty scrotum were a truth too intense and horrific to face.

'What? You don't want to suck me off? Use your imagination. It used to be there,' Guzmán said with a sorrowful laugh.

People think they know what true horror really is, they feel cursed. But they always end up looking away when faced with a greater horror than their own, he thought. *That's how fragile the human condition is.*

Guzmán stood and suddenly felt too drunk and high to keep his balance; he tripped and took down the lamp on the nightstand, breaking the shade and cutting his hand. He dragged himself to the bathroom, trailing drops of blood that exploded as they landed, like little red bombs hitting the floor in slow motion.

Above the toilet bowl was a paper valance decorated with a little blue-and-yellow winged bird; its brown eyes gazed out in profound silence. Guzmán traced the bird's outline with one finger. He pulled up his pants and washed his hands, contemplating the tiny rivers of blood washing down the drain with the water.

When he walked out of the room he saw the woman sitting there on the bed.

He closed the door quietly, leaving her to cry in peace.

11

Mr Who took a small step back and glanced down toward the basement. He didn't like being there: it was like walking through the narrow, claustrophobic passageway of a submarine, and enclosed spaces made him uneasy. The room was occupied by a long table filled with endless scraps of cloth. Two dozen women, some very young — almost girls — all of them Asian, sat along either side, working in silence beneath the enormous fluorescent lights that hung on chains from the waste pipes and plumbing of the restaurant above their heads. In some places the pipes leaked, rank water puddling on the table. The stench was pervasive, a mix of human sweat, kitchen grease and industrial oil.

At the end of the hall was a screen made of thick plastic panels through which the silhouettes on the other side could just be made out. Judging by the hum of machines, it was an illegal sweatshop. Mr Who fought the desire to go through that door. He knew Mei was in there, somewhere in that labyrinthine hell. He'd heard terrible things about what went on in those places, the working conditions, but he couldn't think about that — contemplating what Mei might be going through made him weak, and she needed him to be strong enough for the both of them. Otherwise he'd never be able to get her out of there.

On the stairs, Chang was saying goodbye to a customer, shaking hands. When Who was a kid and Chang saw him on the street, he'd bring him to the back of the restaurant and invite him to drink tea and smoke, something Maribel and Teo would never have let him do. Chang knew how to make him feel important, older. 'You're one of mine,' he'd say, stroking his head. And to Who, that seemed like the greatest praise he could possibly receive. Chang was garrulous and told him things about his past in Dalian, an important coastal town in China. He fantasised about moving back one day and setting up a real emporium.

Chang was the first one to see the potential of Who's androgynous physique, the bonus it might bring to his business. He was the first to offer him money in exchange for sex. Mr Who, at the time, was fifteen.

That first time, right after Chang ejaculated into his mouth, Mr Who ran to the bathroom trying not to gag, and vomited. The old man looked on coldly, displaying no emotion — not even anger or amusement. When he'd emptied his stomach, he made Who rinse his mouth and then ordered him to start all over again.

As a result of his new life, for Mr Who, the line between good and evil stopped being so clear and became, instead, a blurry place, a no man's land he roamed as if he were from a world where people didn't breathe or eat or drink, a world with no personal needs. In the end it was a matter of keeping still and letting his mind go blank. He stopped feeling uncomfortable, wanted to work more and more in order to forget the previous job; the limitations of his own modesty, first, and repulsion, later, fell by the wayside, to the point where he ended up an indifferent spectator of his own actions. Guilt and morality, scruples — they all fell by the wayside. His thoughts about anything outside of those rented rooms slowly languished, until they became nothing more than a bothersome, sticky mess he tried to remain detached from.

Once he'd overcome the torment, in time — over the years — he became a magnificent, attentive lover. Now he felt a sense of absolute control over his clients, a domination that was sometimes sadistic and other times comforting, depending on what they asked of him. He could fill their needs without his clients even having to express them. Each gesture, each detail conveyed information, and that unspoken language taught him what the men and women who bought his services wanted — things that often they themselves were not aware of. He pleased them all, he was bold and intrepid in his dedication, capable of penetrating any defences they attempted to put up. That's why he could charge so much, that's why he was so valuable to Chang; and that's also why the old man would kill both him and Mei if he found out Mr Who was saving up all his money to run away.

Chang had invited him to lunch that day. He wanted to see how he was progressing with his Mandarin — or at least that's what he claimed. But as soon as they went up to the private quarters the old man kept on the top floor of the building — the very place that had once been his father's coin-collector's shop and his mother's ballet school — he realised that Chang wanted something else. The old man sprinkled dried petals into a cedar bowl and within a few seconds a vegetal aroma filled the room. He took off his shoes to enter a room with floor mats and, with a benevolent gesture, took out a small metal box and opened it.

'It's early to be getting high; I have to work in a few hours.'

Chang smiled like a rat, showing his teeth. He liked that boy, really liked him. He'd turned him into what was often called 'a high-class professional escort'. Mr Who had self-restraint, he could control his facial expressions and body language. A single expression, a disagreeable look or a sneer could give him away far more easily than a lie. And despite his youth, Who was a great lover — the best. Nothing about him gave his thoughts or intentions away. But he couldn't fool Chang.

'We've got time. Come, sit down here with old Chang and let's have a chat, father to son, grandfather to grandson, whatever,' he said, offering him a joint from the metal box. Chang's voice never raised above a few decibels, and that little trick ensured listeners paid the utmost attention to everything he said.

There was a painting on the wall — a lush green meadow leading to a distant waterfall. Asian-faced peasants in conical straw hats were bent over rice paddies. For some reason, that was the landscape all Westerners seemed to think of when they thought of China. Mr Who was from a border area between Mongolia and China, and his town had belonged to both, given the vicissitudes of history, but he could never recall having seen fields anything like those, and certainly no waterfalls like the one in the painting. The land he'd known before coming to Spain when he was nine — when his birth parents died — was dry and arid, smelled like camel dung, and was whipped day and night by terrible winds, with no hills to block it for thousands and thousands of kilometres.

Mr Who lit one of the opium joints with a slender reed from the box. Chang nodded, pleased when he took a long hit, closing his eyes and then slowly letting out a thick cloud of smoke. The old man lit a second joint for himself and leaned back on a pillow, and the smoking room soon filled with a smell somewhere between rose-scented soap and lemon. Chang took advantage of their position, brushing against Who's hand. The younger man flinched almost involuntarily, and Chang smiled secretly at his mortification.

'I've heard things. People are saying you're quite taken with one of my workers.'

Mr Who didn't bat an eye.

'Your workers stink like sweat. And I'm getting more than enough sex as it is.'

'That's good, I feel better hearing that. You're my lucky boy, and you must keep being lucky. By the way, do you still have my little gift?'

'I lost it.'

'You lost it.'

'I accidentally left the lucky cat on the metro. I'm sorry.'

Chang leaned back against the pillows and idly watched the beautiful spiral of smoke curling up from his lips.

'So, you're the kind of boy who can afford to leave his luck around town. You're very fortunate. But fortune can be wayward — sometimes it comes and sometimes it goes. Tell me something. What is it that you're so worried about? You work so much, much more than you used to, and you earn a lot of money. You learn quickly, master everything I teach you. You're more and more a man of the world, and yet you're unfocused, on edge. Something's worrying you. You can't fool old Chang. You have no expensive habits, as far as I know your mother is well cared for, and yet you work and work — your drive is destructive. It's as though you were trying to run away from something, to keep from thinking. I don't understand why you do it, why you're in such a hurry.'

'There's nothing to understand. I just do it.'

'Do you expect me to believe it's for the love of the art?'

Mr Who thought of Mei, imagined her in the basement of that very same building, and his body trembled in sadness and rage. Luckily, he was able to keep the sorrow from showing.

'I like what I do. We all have a talent — to each his own. Mine is loving and hating in equal parts. I'm like an alchemist.'

Chang shot Who a mocking glance.

'So, what do you have for me?' He opened his robe and spread his legs, showing the boy his penis and shaved testicles. 'You think your life should be different, that you're special; you think the world owes you something, that life has treated you unfairly, that you have to tip the scales — because you saw your adopted father die for no reason, and spent your whole life with your mother paralysed in a wheelchair — am I right? But you're not special, boy. There is no other plan for you but the one I offer. There is nothing romantic about what you do. Do you see that? Only destruction. And right now, this is what I want — to see your pretty little face splattered with an old man's semen.'

Mr Who stared fixedly at the shadow cast by Chang's penis.

'You want me to do it now?'

Chang barked out a bitter laugh, one that sounded like a walnut cracking.

'Why else would I ask you to come?'

The woman slid her middle finger across Who's heaving chest. After having been alone so long, she felt strange beside a man's body. She looked up, resting her chin on Who's torso, and gazed at his hard profile.

'What do you think about, after making love with a stranger for money?'

Mr Who slipped out of the sheets, firmly pushing the woman's body aside, and glanced at the light from the window. It was starting to get dark.

'I don't think about anything,' Who replied. And he was only partly lying. 'We should talk about money.'

The woman rubbed her hands. She should have prepared for this moment. Sex with a gigolo was not like it had been in her fantasies. This, here — what had just occurred a few minutes ago — had been nothing but a sad, convulsive stand-in. Now she felt irked by the presence of this stranger, by having allowed herself to be attracted to his body, which was nothing but a mirage.

'Of course, I'll get it right now.'

'Good. If you don't mind, I'm going to use your bathroom to rinse off.'

'Sure, make yourself at home.'

The paths to heaven and hell are narrow indeed. You have one foot on one side, and the next minute you're on the other. And you don't know how you got there, Who thought, recalling Chang's veiled threats, his suspicions about him and Mei. He stared at the stool on which the woman's dress and underwear lay — her tiny lace panties, stockings and bra. Expensive, sexy lingerie. And in that instant he realised he couldn't do it anymore.

He walked out of the bathroom already dressed, his hair wet. The woman gave him a look devoid of all intensity.

'Wait here. I'll get your money.'

Mr Who waited, glancing at the framed diploma on the wall.

So the woman was a shrink. Shrinks are supposed to guide us, help us find our way, act as beacons in the night so we can find light in the darkness — Ariadne's thread leading us out of our own labyrinths. But that woman didn't seem sure of anything at all. People can't be explained by what they do; professions are nothing but a mask.

He walked around the room. The small apartment was big enough to cost more than anything your average worker could afford, but it was cold — there was very little furniture, all in minimalist greys and whites, steel and glass. There were no personal photos, no paintings. The only frames he saw, in fact, still held the place-holder photos they came with — cherubic children, men and women with perfect fake smiles. Maybe, Who thought, that explained more about his client than the diploma on her wall.

On top of the glass table he saw an open file folder. He glanced at it with disinterest, simply to distract himself while he awaited her return. But then something caught his eye. Among a thick pile of papers, there was an official-looking photocopy sticking out, replete with check-marked boxes, personal details and notes. Stapled to the upper corner was a passport-style photo. Mr Who pulled the page out and stared at it, astounded.

When Martina returned with the carefully folded bills in her hand, she found the room empty. The boy had left without his money.

Dumbstruck, she glanced around, unable to figure out what could have happened. Everything looked the same — except for the file folder she'd been consulting a few hours earlier and had forgotten to put back in the cabinet. It was in exactly the same position. But she remembered having left it open. And now it was closed.

She opened the file and saw that the pages were out of order. After a quick count, she realised that the patient-intake form of one of her patients was missing — Eduardo Quintana's.

'You don't look too good, Eduardo.'

He didn't. He'd shaved fast and poorly, nicking his cheek several times and missing spots, where grey stubble sprouted on his pale skin. He'd managed to find a decent shirt somewhere, but hadn't noticed that it was missing a button and the collar was stained. His tie, with its fat, poorly tied knot, didn't help matters. Was it already Thursday? It had to be. He couldn't recall the last time he'd gotten out of bed. His head was throbbing, about to explode.

He gave Martina a deranged look. One eyelid drooped lower than the other. He twisted his head, as though trying to find another perspective from which to see her.

'You're not exactly fresh as a daisy yourself this morning, Doctor.'

Martina blushed. She automatically brought her hand to her hair and straightened her spine until she felt the back of the chair against her shoulders.

'How are things going with your meds?'

I'm constipated, vomiting, can't get a hard-on, and I've got a mouth as dry as the sole of a shoe. Why did she ask him questions she already knew the answer to?

'I feel fine, thank you.'

'What about your nightmares?'

'I haven't had any more. I assure you I'm sleeping like a log.'

Martina didn't buy it.

She carefully laid her pen down on the pages of her notebook and folded her hands on the desk. She'd hardly taken a single note. That Thursday, she didn't have it in her to fight Eduardo. And yet still, after massaging her temples, she managed a smile.

'Let's talk about what happened. And then maybe I'll give you your prescription.'

'You already know what happened, you've got my records.'

Martina nodded.

'I'm not asking you about the accident, Eduardo. I want to hear what you have to say about what happened on Calle Montera five months later. I want you to talk to me about the last thirteen years, which you spent locked up.'

Eduardo just wanted to forget about it, but how could anyone forget *anything* when you were forced to dredge it up all the time?

'There's nothing to talk about, Doctor.'

'You killed a man, Eduardo. Shot him in cold blood. And there's nothing to talk about?'

Eduardo stared at her, hard. For a few seconds, Martina thought he was going to get up and walk out. She thought she'd gone too far, that she'd lost him. But ploddingly, like a train struggling to gain speed, his words slowly began to flow, almost in a whisper.

'We all have something we need to be forgiven for,' he stated. Wasn't that what Olga had said at the church of San Sebastián?

'You can't look at things that way, with such detachment.'

'Flesh rots and decomposes, and so do memories. That's all I know. Elena died, and so did my daughter. And I should have died with them, but I didn't. And I'll never know why. Maybe it's just a coin toss, a game of chance, and you never know which side luck will fall on.'

'Life is much more than chance. It's the result of our actions, Eduardo. You can't keep using that as an excuse to avoid accountability.'

'Do you think if we all knew life was just an accident, and there was nothing else after, we'd give up? No. We'd still drink it all down to the last drop. And then beg for more. There's always some reason — doesn't matter what it is — to keep going. But that doesn't make things any better, Doctor. Things happen, and no one knows why.'

'So you don't believe in anything? There's nothing that makes you question whether what you did served any purpose? It must have affected you somehow, left some kind of mark.'

Eduardo didn't know what he believed in. People? God? Eternity? Everyone believes in something, or at least that's what they say. But he had no credo whatsoever. He felt no commitment to himself, and there was no one else they could take from him. Live, die. It hadn't seemed particularly transcendent until a few months ago. Then the appearance of Gloria, the possibility of that painting, had given him an excuse to keep going a little longer.

'Could I have some water?' He would have preferred vodka, whisky — even poison — but all he could expect the psychiatrist to give him was a little water.

Martina got up and went to the mini-fridge in her office. When she opened it, Eduardo got a glimpse of her gastronomical world: yoghurt, fruit, a lone tomato, and one beer that disappeared like a mirage when she returned with a pitcher of cold water and a disposable plastic cup.

The doctor softened her gaze as she handed him the cup. She was trying to feign affection. *We're getting somewhere*, her look said. Eduardo pretended to believe it. He drank slowly and handed her back the glass.

Martina filled it again, clumsily. A few little drops formed bubbles on the varnished table. Eduardo took the glass but didn't drink, holding it with both hands as if trying to warm his fingertips.

'Killing someone doesn't make me a killer,' he said with a lack of conviction. He didn't even believe his own words, but the idea of talking about it turned his stomach.

Martina examined his face carefully and realised that, even when he was being sincere, it was only partway.

'Then why do you still feel guilty?'

Eduardo stared at her. His expression — cold, vacant horror — made her uneasy.

'Just give me my prescription and leave me alone.'

As he walked through the cemetery gate, Eduardo was enveloped in a pervasive silence. It was late afternoon, twenty minutes before closing, and the caretaker looked annoyed. He made a show of looking at his watch but Eduardo paid no attention. He liked that dusky time of day when the cemetery was almost empty and the shadows were long, the darkness they cast almost hiding the individual graves and family tombs. It had rained and there was a smell of cut grass. If he stood still and closed his eyes, he could hear the almost imperceptible sounds of dry leaves stirring, of rain dripping onto the grassy expanse where the gravestones poked out like stalks. Eduardo felt the squishy, waterlogged ground beneath his feet. He was comfortable here in the quiet, surrounded by graves — some with plastic flowers, others with real bouquets languishing in waterless vases.

He didn't know what he was supposed to feel. His shrink had waited in vain for some sort of explosion — suppressed regret, the confirmation that he'd shot that man out of vengeance. But it wasn't true. And she didn't understand. The only thing that was true was that, aside from an emptiness that resembled calm, he felt nothing at all. Death didn't make any sense to him, it wasn't something he wanted to think about.

He looked around and thought of his father's funeral. There had been several adults present, plus Eduardo, his cousins, aunts and uncles, and siblings; all around him, kids were pinching and kicking each other as the workers unsealed the family tomb from atop a mechanical elevator. On the elevator's platform had lain the coffin, with two floral wreaths. The adults were composed and proper, their formality clashing with the behaviour of children playing as they tried in vain to keep them quiet. The workers swung picks at the rotted cement and then pulled out the headstone. One of the employees used a rake to pull out a tangle of rotted wood that crumbled upon touch. Moving quickly, he shoved everything into an industrial garbage bag, attempting to be discreet, but accidentally missing one round, grey bone. That had been his mother. They slid the gold-trimmed, cedar coffin adorned with a cross inside, and then, before sealing the tomb back up, placed the bag of remains they'd just collected on top.

That was death.

The grave he was searching for now was in a fairly new wall niche, at the end of an unpaved lane, which ended at a rotunda adorned with a somewhat crude plaster archangel that presided over its quiet domain from atop a dark granite column, wings open like a bird in mid-flight. The angel wore a dazed expression, eyes cast heavenward, bare muscular arms extended toward the graves like a farmer scattering seed. The tomb was the third from the left, and on the wall of niches his was the third one up, out of seven. Someone had left a freshly cut bouquet of rhododendrons on the iron ring hanging from one end of his gravestone.

Teodoro López Egea. Motril, 1946 – Madrid, 1991

That was the life he'd cut short. Teodoro López Egea had been the driver of the black SUV with the licence plate Olga had given him. The man who'd caused the death of his wife and then fled like a coward as Eduardo's daughter Tania lay dying, bleeding out beside the stream.

Eduardo stroked the niche's dust-covered ledge and looked down at his hand. And that was all it took for his mind to hurl downhill once more: the memory of his father leading him through an abandoned quarry, the plaster dust that covered his shoes and stung his eyes.

Hold it properly, by the grip. Do you feel that? It's awkward and steely, but you'll get used to it in time. Now look through the sight and aim, gently.

Eduardo had never liked the Astra revolver his father had taught him to shoot with. It was light but inhospitable, cold. The Astra kills before death; by the time you hear the sound of the shot being fired, it's over before it's even begun and there's nothing that can be done to stop it.

Eduardo extended his arm and aimed at the shadow cast by the memory of a father and son doing target practice in a quarry that echoed with every shot. What would it be like to kill the dark, remorseless part of you that — though it is you — lives outside of you, hounding you insistently. The feel of a weapon in the hand of a boy is no different than it is for a man. *The apathetic are guilty*, he murmured, squeezing the imaginary trigger. It echoed in the emptiness of his mind. He could recall every step, every second, every sensation surrounding the death of Teodoro López Egea, taken down by an Astra that had begun to mark its final destiny many years before, in the hands of a boy being taught by his father.

It was winter, cold and grey, you could see it on the pedestrians' faces. Eduardo was hiding behind a dumpster and pulled out the revolver, gripping it with both hands. He felt nothing, and all he could see was people walking up and down the street, not paying him any attention. But at the same time, he felt everything — the touch of the revolver hidden beneath his clothes, the weight of his coat, growing heavy in the rain, his own ragged breath, the beating of his heart, the voice pounding in his head like a drum: *do it, do it, do it.*

Amid a sea of bobbing umbrellas he managed to discern Teodoro López Egea. He could just make out part of his face beneath an enormous black umbrella with trickles of water running down its sides, happy and smiling. He was walking along, speaking excitedly to a little boy whose hand he held, a boy bundled up in a slicker, his nose almost the only thing exposed; on his other side walked a slim, muscular woman with her own dark umbrella, and she was holding his arm. They were happy, everything was fine, they were all together: father, mother, child. A family in the rain, an ordinary day. There was no reason for anything to go wrong, anything unforeseen to occur. Especially not death. The scene, far from pacifying Eduardo enough to reconsider his lunatic plan, filled him with such rage he could hardly breathe. Was that the portrait of regret? Did they even feel guilty?

He couldn't have been more than twenty-five metres away. He curled up behind the dumpster as if to summon his courage, squeezed the revolver tightly in both hands, counted to three and took a deep breath. As soon as they got close, he stepped out quickly and cut them off.

Teodoro López Egea stared into the barrel of the revolver, eyes filled with incredulity, and for a second he stood there with his mouth open, not saying a word. Then he shook his head, as if to convince himself that he hadn't seen what he'd seen, and immediately his expression became so panicked that his lifeless face was ridiculous, an embarrassment to his wife and son. The man tried to run, taking cover behind his wife's body. *Coward*, thought Eduardo. A coward who lets people die, runs away, who takes cover behind the very people he's supposed to love. Whimpering, *please, please*. Eduardo shut him up, forcing the gun violently into his mouth, breaking several teeth. He'd never fired a gun at a human being before, and didn't know what it would feel like — how loud it would be, penetrating flesh, the unalterable nanosecond after which you can't undo pulling the trigger, not once you've pulled it.

It's just a dream, he told himself. *Do it and the dream will disappear. Kill him.*

He fired the gun and felt certain it wasn't real. The sound was so faint, the flash hardly more intense than a match being lit. He didn't even feel any kickback. But the bullet that blew his head apart was very real. Teodoro fell sideways, as though someone had just severed the invisible threads that had been holding him up.

Then Eduardo turned to the little boy, who was now screaming, his eyes popping out of his head. *Shut up, shut up.* The only way to shut him up was to shoot him. But his mother threw herself between the bullet and the screaming little kid. It entered through her back, and for a minute Eduardo thought she had stopped the bullet. The woman pulled the boy down to the ground, as though her final urge was to get him out of the street; she stumbled, tripped, and fell flat on her face in the street. Eduardo saw a thin stream of blood start to flow from the hole in her back.

It was over in seconds. The umbrellas were twisted between their bodies, rain bouncing off them indifferently, and the blood became quickly diluted. Someone hit him on the head, hard, from behind.

Then it was quiet. The last thing he saw was the body of Teodoro. He was staring up at the sky, eyes open, palms down, focused on himself. And in his left hand he held a few bills, bloodstained, and soggy from the rain.

And at that first moment of utter horror, of total assimilation of what he'd done, Eduardo's mind began burying the evidence under a heavy cloak of silence and detachment.

12

Graciela examined the man standing before her closely. Despite the scar disfiguring his face, he must have been quite handsome in his day. He looked hard, as though every source of joy in his life had been lain waste to. And yet his deep eyes, boring into her, filled her with a fatalistic sort of tranquillity, an understanding that when nature's fury was unleashed there was nothing to do but stop and admire the beauty of its destruction.

'It's important, señora. If it weren't I wouldn't be bothering you. I need to know where Eduardo is.'

'Leave me your phone number. If he shows up I'll tell him you were here.'

They were standing by the door, at the entrance to the living room. Ibrahim filled almost the entire doorframe and Graciela was blocking his way with her body. It struck her as a meagre defence, should he try to force his way in, but in fact Ibrahim seemed to be perfectly amiable, as though his character compensated for his threatening appearance.

Sara appeared from the back of the room, still in pyjamas and barefoot, glittery stars on her toenails, which she'd painted herself. She'd had a bad night, and had deep bags under her eyes, and dishevelled hair; she was clutching the Chinese lucky cat Eduardo had given her in one hand. Lately, it was her constant companion. She was surprised to see Ibrahim, but not intimidated. Her eyes focused on him as though she was attempting to hypnotise the man.

Ibrahim smiled at her.

'I like your cat.'

'I like your scar. It must have hurt a lot. Did you deserve it?' Sara asked.

Graciela was about to intervene, but a glance from Ibrahim stopped her.

'Actually, yes, it did. It hurt a lot, and it still hurts; you know, scars are like subterranean rivers, like the lava flowing beneath volcanoes — they never die down. And as to whether or not I deserved it, let's just say it no longer matters. The fact is, whether I deserved it or not, I got it and I have to live with it. So, what can you tell me about your cat?'

Sara half-closed her eyes and then opened them slowly, not taking her eyes off Ibrahim. Although she liked that he'd treated her like an adult, she didn't trust him.

'He's not really Chinese. He's Japanese. His name is Maneki. I like that name for a cat. Different coloured lucky cats are for different things: money, happiness, health. But this one is really special. When he looks at me, I can keep my *this*' — and with that Sara put her index finger to her forehead — 'quiet for a while.'

'I could use one of those.'

'Do you like cats?'

Ibrahim nodded. In Meco — the prison — he'd looked after a black-and-brown kitten for a time, feeding it milk and letting it sleep on his clothes. But then, he explained, the cat had grown and started to show more interest in the sparrows Ibrahim fed from his cell's barred windows, tossing them crumbs. One day he'd found the kitten tearing off the head of a little bird, so he'd had to get rid of it — but decided not to explain to the little girl how he'd done so.

'Are you going to hurt Eduardo?'

'Should I?'

'No. He has a scar, too, but he didn't deserve it. Like *mamá*.' Graciela turned so red she was scarlet, but Sara didn't seem to notice. 'Everyone has scars. But not everyone deserves them.'

Ibrahim nodded.

'That's true.'

His serious face must have convinced her. Suddenly, Sara flashed a beautiful, unexpected smile. That was her real strength; her moods, anarchic and changeable, were infectious.

Graciela went to her and placed a soothing hand on her daughter's shoulder, imploring Ibrahim with her eyes to understand.

'I'll tell Eduardo you were here, when he comes back.'

Ibrahim handed her a card with a phone number.

'Tell him that Señor Arthur wants to speak to him, urgently.'

Then he held out his hand to Sara. She eyed his heavily calloused palms and, before shaking his hand, asked him very seriously:

'Have you killed a lot of cats?'

He held his hands up, making light of it; Sara had actually been quite a

195

pleasant surprise. When she grew up, she'd be a magnificent fighter.

'Only the ones that eat my birds. As long as your Maneki doesn't eat sparrows, you can rest easy.'

'I'll keep my cat away from your sparrows. And you don't make any scars on Eduardo.'

Ibrahim let out a sincere laugh. But Sara remained straight-faced.

'Agreed,' he conceded sombrely. 'A deal is a deal.'

Sara shook his hand firmly. They'd just entered into a pact, two serious adults.

Arthur Fernández had a magnificent office overlooking Paseo de Recoletos. Eduardo admired his books, nestled elegantly in a solid mahogany bookshelf where a complete collection of French poetry held pride of place: everything from Baudelaire, Rimbaud and Verlaine to Mallarmé.

Arthur was standing when Eduardo walked in. In one corner, Ibrahim paced like a tamed panther. He seemed totally harmless, his attitude both solicitous and friendly. Eduardo couldn't help but clench his stomach, remembering the painful beating the man had given him without so much as blinking.

'I see your bruises have healed nicely,' Arthur said by way of greeting, pointing to Eduardo's face.

'It could have been worse,' Eduardo agreed. Ibrahim cocked his head. Had he been a dog or a bat he'd have tilted his ears at Eduardo, but instead he simply shot him a brief look, nodded, and blinked delicately.

Arthur asked him to take a seat, and although there was certainly more than enough space to avoid contact, the man leaned forward, invading his space. Eduardo felt uncomfortable — perhaps that was what Arthur was aiming for.

'So, you want to paint my portrait. Isn't that what you said? Are you still interested, despite our *accidental* first encounter?'

'Of course.'

Arthur folded his powerful hands and placed his elbows on his thighs, resting his chin on his knuckles. For one long minute, Eduardo bore the man's scrutiny without moving a single muscle on his face. Meanwhile, Ibrahim's sweetish cologne wafted, reaching him each time the man paced behind him, a latent presence.

'I'm sure you'll agree if I tell you it strikes me as a somewhat odd proposal. You don't know me, you know nothing about me. And the method you chose to introduce yourself — following me around Madrid — was a bit unorthodox. So I can only imagine you have a compelling reason, something to convince me.'

Eduardo had practised his reply. But for some reason his words reordered themselves, coming out different than he'd intended.

'I'm an artist; I spend my time doing portraits of people who for some reason emanate something different, people who have a spark unlike others, who have faces that aren't true or false, black or white, but are an amalgam of greys. Your face, if I may, is like steel. Light bounces off it, but doesn't go through it or warm it, doesn't shape it. It simply reflects it. I've read a few things about you in the press. You're a rich man, famous. But the experience of causing the deaths of that boy and girl in the accident in January 2001 must have transformed you. I'd like to know who it is you became after three years in prison.'

There followed a tense silence. If Eduardo's comments had bothered Arthur, he certainly didn't show it. After a few seconds, he got up to have a private word with Ibrahim. They spoke in hushed tones, in French. Then Ibrahim left the office. Arthur went back to his armchair, but didn't sit. He stroked its leather back roughly, as though his fingers were unaccustomed to anything delicate.

'I hope you won't mind my using the informal *tú* with you … You want to find out who I am through a painting? Come on, you can't be serious. You, better than anyone, should know that art is not truth: it's nothing but "a lie that makes us realise truth. … The artist must know the manner whereby to convince others of the truthfulness of his lies." Do you know who made that incredible statement? A buddy of yours.'

Eduardo knew: it was Pablo Picasso. And in essence, he agreed. But the truth he was searching for was not a simple metaphor, an image. He examined Arthur's profile with a critical eye, already unconsciously sketching him. The Greeks would have no doubt called him a beautiful man, but at the same time he seemed to transcend any such frivolity, to possess something much deeper. Something that a stranger to his life would never pick up on. The man was intriguing and captivating in equal measures.

'Art is the thing that brings us closest to the human psyche. We can't lie to art.'

Arthur smiled, as if not taking Eduardo's words very seriously.

'I remember having those sorts of ideals. I had them too myself, once. Beauty, truth. The distillation of the human soul into one astonishing sentence, one magisterial brushstroke, one magical note ... But I no longer believe in art's capacity for redemption.'

'Then why did you ask me to come?' Eduardo asked, his voice coming out hoarse.

Arthur approached and sat on the arm of the chair, his arms crossed. He inspected Eduardo as though he were a little animal.

'Logically, I, too, did a little research on you. I know everything: that you lost your family, that you killed the man who caused the accident, that you spent thirteen years locked up, and that you've tried to kill yourself half-a-dozen times ... So my question is: is there an element of the artist in his own work? Are you going to paint me, or are you attempting some sort of self-portrait, Eduardo? What's the link between us? Loss? Guilt? Remorse?'

Eduardo felt like an idiot.

'I don't know. I honestly don't know.'

Arthur remained pensive.

'I also found out that the idea of doing my portrait didn't come from you. You work for Gloria A. Tagger, the mother of the boy who died in the accident.'

Eduardo felt the back of his neck grow hot. He went to say something, but Arthur cut him off.

'Did you know that Mallarmé had a son, Anatole, who died when he was eight years old? Mallarmé wrote hundreds of fragments and notes for a funeral poem he never managed to finish. The poet wanted to bring his son back through his genius, give him back the life that Death had snatched away. He never managed to finish it — he, who could do anything with words. He never could cover the emptiness left by "the wind of nothingness / that breathes ... and a wave / that carries you away". He didn't even dare to write that his son was dead, because doing so would have required admitting that it was true: "no I will not / tell it to you — for then you / would disappear — and I would be alone / weeping

198

for you, me, / mingled". I can picture his quiet, candlelit hours, pen in the air. And then his desperation, the inability of words to truly unleash and express his pain, night after night.'

He regarded Eduardo as though he'd already gotten from him what he wanted and had no need to ask anything else.

'What that woman is trying to do is not forget her child, by means of the hatred she ascribes me.'

'Maybe not,' Eduardo ventured. 'It may be that our mutual losses are something we all have in common.'

Arthur let out a sneering laugh. 'You don't know much about Gloria A. Tagger, do you?'

He's going to say no, Eduardo thought, distressed.

But Arthur spread his hands and nodded. 'Where would you like me to pose?'

That meant he was saying yes; it took a few seconds for the confirmation to reach Eduardo's brain.

'I, I haven't thought about it yet,' he stammered. 'At my place, or any other place. At first, all I'll need is a few sketches. Then we can figure it out.'

'We can start tomorrow, early.'

'Alright,' Eduardo agreed, still in shock.

Arthur held out a hand, and he shook it firmly.

'You can paint my portrait on one condition. You tell me everything Gloria does or says. Quid pro quo.'

Their meeting was over.

Ibrahim was there waiting on the other side of the door. From his intent expression, it was clear he'd been listening in on a good part of the conversation. He offered to accompany Eduardo to the exit.

'Are you familiar with Sufi music and poetry? It's almost metaphysical; it uses algorithms to explain the essence of the human soul, and it does it through verses, numbers, metre … But even we fail in the attempt to create a true voice of authenticity. The most we can aspire to is harmony — balance, if you will. But what you're aiming to do, friend, is to convey something unconveyable. You're trying to map out a man's inner soul.'

Eduardo observed the scars on Ibrahim's face, fascinated. *Two men full of scars*, he thought. Though in essence they were quite different. His own were the scars of surrender; Ibrahim's were the scars of struggle.

'Ugliness reveals more about a person than beauty, don't you think?' Ibrahim asked, as though he'd read his mind. 'Sometimes we're drawn to that which we most condemn, that which we find most hateful, but in time we manage to accept what we found so repulsive. That's the way humans are — complicated, changeable. But I have learned one thing: what we feel in the deepest part of our souls never perishes, it just awaits the right time to emerge ... Be careful, painter. You might end up creating the portrait of your own personal hell. Think about that when you pick up your brush.'

Ibrahim patted his shoulder and walked back toward the office.

Eduardo heard him let out a laugh so soft it was hardly distinguishable from air hissing quietly through his teeth.

Despite their agreement, Eduardo hardly progressed on his work at all in the weeks that followed.

Arthur was not your typical model. It was impossible to know if he was going to turn up at the agreed time, or whenever he felt like it; sometimes he didn't show up at all and didn't bother to let Eduardo know, leaving him there with his canvases set up and brushes ready to go. And when he did show, he had a hard time sitting still for more than twenty minutes. Arthur couldn't stand motionlessness and fidgeted, and his face hardened when he felt himself being watched. The further he got, the more Eduardo doubted he'd ever be able to capture what Gloria had commissioned him to do.

That's what he was thinking on the flight to Barcelona. Gloria had gone to Barcelona to finalise details for a foundation that was to bear her son's name, and despite Eduardo's reluctance, she'd insisted on seeing his early sketches. The window seat allowed him to daydream, gazing absently at clouds and patches of clear sky. The flight attendant took his empty whisky glass from the tray table and replaced it with a full one. Eduardo preferred vodka, but they didn't have any on board. He couldn't smoke either, and it was impossible to escape the sickening cologne of the guy sitting next to him. He wanted to land at Barcelona's airport, El Prat, as soon as possible and get good and sozzled. Drunk, he could better accept the utter absurdity of his life; sober, it was so unbearable he almost couldn't breathe.

'She's very pretty. You've got such a skilled hand,' said the man seated beside him, examining the sketches of Gloria he'd been doing to pass the time. Eduardo noted a twinge of jealousy in the man's tone. But what he envied was a ghost, an inexistent perfection, one unchanged by time, something invented by the mind.

When the door is open, people don't knock, they just walk right in — so Eduardo closed his sketchbook and stared out the window as the pilot announced their initial descent into Barcelona. He could see the foam on the waves breaking below, the narrow strip of beach, and the luxurious housing developments in Gavà, with their identical houses, lawns and pools. To the right lay the city, trapped between the sea and mountains. From above, it looked perfect. Like everything when seen from a distance.

His hotel was economical but clean. In exchange for the narrow room and inevitable carpeting, he got a balcony with magnificent views of the Barrio Gótico and narrow alleys of the Jewish quarter. Rooftop terraces were joined together in a seeming labyrinth of antennas, washing hung out to dry, birdcages and chimneystacks. He had just enough time to unpack his weekend bag and down a small bottle of vodka, with lemon, from the minibar.

Gloria was meeting him in twenty minutes. He had the restaurant's address and asked for directions at reception; it wasn't far. He decided to walk. Strolling through Barcelona was a magnificent experience if you were not prone to falling in love. Like all lovers, the city's defects began to surface as soon as you got to know her.

Gloria saw him arrive and raised a hand to wave from the other side of the street. That woman seemed to continuously reinvent herself, Eduardo marvelled. Maybe it was the effects of the Mediterranean, or the crisp morning light — so phosphorescent — or her informal attire, but whatever it was she looked ten years younger than the last time he'd seen her, at her house in the outskirts of Madrid. Her eyes were hidden beneath enormous sunglasses, like a diva, and her hair fell loose around her shoulders. The wind coming in off the port blew it back and forth across her face, and she did nothing to stop it.

They greeted one another affectionately — Gloria even stroked his cheek for a moment, which gave a sense of familiarity he found irresistible. They walked among the bobbing masts of pleasure boats, along a wooden gangway where water lapped at the sides. It could have been Monaco, or Cannes, or Casablanca, with the two of them sidestepping rigging and pails of fish destined for the market, bringing each other up to date like two old friends who've been longing to see each other for ages. Eduardo sensed that it wasn't all quite true, that it was too perfectly staged, but somehow he didn't care; he simply let himself be led along by Gloria's cordial laughter, by the sea air, by his own self-deceit. What was he playing at? Who cared? All he had to do was let himself be led along, and believe whatever she wanted him to believe.

The restaurant was exclusive: only half-a-dozen or so empty tables. The owner greeted them, congratulating himself on his luck; he recognised Gloria and claimed to be a fervent admirer, lavishing her with excessive praise and leading them to a pretty corner by a large picture window looking out over the pier and breakwater. The walls were decorated in nautical motifs, old nets and fishing tackle. After a few minutes, melodious music began playing softly in the background. Sitting there opposite one another, their faces were barely illuminated by a small lamp that cast everything else in shadows, evoking a sadness that didn't fully materialise.

They chatted for a few minutes about trivial things: trips, projects, everyday nuisances. Eduardo got the feeling Gloria was avoiding the subject that had brought them together, that she was putting off — perhaps out of fear — the moment to bring up Arthur. He wasn't in a rush either, but out of sheer nervousness he'd have liked to pull out the drafts and first sketches the moment he'd sat down. He wanted to please her, to see a look of admiration in her eyes.

Maybe Olga was right, why deny it? He was falling in love with a fantasy.

It was upon finishing their main courses, waiting for the coffee to be served — neither of them wanted dessert — that Gloria asked him directly.

'Can I see it?'

Eduardo gave her an imploring look, wanting to ensure her support.

'They're just early sketches.'

Gloria responded with poorly disguised impatience. Eduardo pushed the plates aside to make room and took the drawings out of his portfolio bag — half-a-dozen sketches that he spread across the table like a hand of cards. They could be seen as a sequence that unravelled the passing weeks, days, hours, even minutes. In each one, though the image was the same, the nuances of Arthur's frame of mind could be sensed, as could the time of day he'd been drawn, by the light — or an increasing lack of it — emanating from the model. In some he was wearing a black open-necked shirt and the detail was so precise as to include the wrinkles on his loosely tied necktie, the thread coming off a button, the creases in the cigarette he held — you could almost hear the tobacco crackling as it burned, the smoke being exhaled through the unseen hairs of his nostrils. And yet despite the detail, there was nothing trivial or anecdotal. Everything served to explain something about him, to highlight some nuance of his body.

In another image he appeared lying on his side, on a sofa, looking scornful, exuding an affected carelessness that faded as the sessions went on, each one slightly less forced and less forceful than the last, each one slightly closer to expressing the metaphysical essence that Eduardo aspired to, as though by sheer force of repetition Arthur's face and body would eventually throw in the towel, lower their guard and simply be. Eduardo showed undeniable talent in the way he handled his subject, always searching for the exact light and backlight to make his skin, eyes, red hair and parted lips seem transparent, like an x-ray; you could almost hear the way he spoke, hear his voice, hear what he was saying at the precise moment he'd been captured by the brush. His deep voice seemed to murmur a few words of mistrust, discomfort on realising he was being possessed, dissected rather than painted.

'I have to say, I am totally caught up in this project,' Eduardo murmured, fascinated with his own prints.

Gloria examined Eduardo's work as if contemplating a chilling, empty landscape. But deep in her eyes was a glimmer of increasing curiosity.

'What's he like up close?' she asked, almost embarrassed.

Eduardo remained pensive. He gestured, making no sound whatsoever, as if stirring his thoughts into some sort of order so they might be expressed.

'He comes to my studio; we sit, chat, fall silent, and then he poses for me, though not for long — he's fidgety and gets tired. I'm trying to capture his essence, but it might be early still for that. If I'm honest, I think the chances of really getting to know him through painting are very remote.'

'But that's what this is all about, that's why I contracted you.'

Eduardo squirmed in his chair.

'Nothing about him seems entirely true or false. His expression makes me uneasy. It's like a knife scraping at the useless top layers of skin, removing dead scales. He's always watching you, at every moment. And it's only when he realises that the intensity of his expression is going to suffocate me that he pretends to be distracted by something else. But even then, I can hear the sound of thoughts swirling in his head.'

Gloria brought her glass to her lips and drank slowly, as though buying time in order to rectify her mask — distant and dispassionate. There was a visible tension there, a struggle to see who would take control inside her. And from that tension arose the true Gloria, the perfect image.

'Why did he abandon his promising career so rashly? He could have been a great poet.'

Eduardo was surprised by the confidential tone to Gloria's question. As though she felt some affection — an affectionate sorrow, if that's possible — for the man she was supposed to hate.

'Something terrible happened with the professor who was his adviser. He had to leave France quickly.'

Gloria seemed to already know this. In fact, Eduardo was beginning to suspect that she knew everything there was to be known about Arthur Fernández. And he got the same uncomfortable feeling that she also knew much more about him than she'd let on the first time they met.

'Did he tell you that?'

Eduardo nodded. Dreams can so quickly turn into nightmares. It only takes one move, one second, a single impulsive decision, for one horizon to disappear and another to emerge.

At just twenty years old, Arthur had been a student that Cochard — his advisor and mentor — saw as one of the most promising; saw him as a sort of experiment in which Arthur played the role of noble savage, and the eminent professor that of generous, intellectual father and teacher.

One afternoon at the Sorbonne, there were very few students wandering through the cloister — it was late, it was Friday, and classes were almost over for the trimester. Old Cochard was awaiting his most talented student in the gloom of his office, in the west wing. Sitting atop the professor's desk was a framed photo of himself shaking hands with Pope Pius XI, signed by His Holiness. On the wall above it hung a heavy, ornate cross.

The professor, with an air of ceremony, invited Arthur to sit. He was normally distant and haughty with his students but felt a special predilection for the young *pied-noir* — a diamond in the rough, and one he intended to polish with care and patience, for the greater glory of the Republic's letters. Cochard spoke incessantly, moistening his hot lips — cracked and austere — with his tongue, his breath smelling of English tobacco. As he spoke, he gestured frequently, his hands furtively touching Arthur's forearm, shoulder, biceps. The young man pulled back carefully, but the old man kept on as though nothing was the matter, pretending not to realise, amused, condescending and paternal. Paternal.

'"*Lost little boat of mine, rocking broken among the rocks, wakeful in the wake, so lonely in the surf. Where are you off to, lost one? To where do you set sail? There can be no sound desires, with hopes that are so wild.*" That's Lope de Vega. Your father was Spanish; did he never speak to you of Lope?'

'My father was French, although he was born in Spain. He could barely even read or write his name in Spanish,' Arthur replied.

The professor gave him an odd look.

'A poet can be many things, but one thing he cannot be is a coward. Experiencing the unknown should be the mechanism that drives you. Come, Arthur, tell me, you who so admires Rimbaud: what would have become of him without the protection of Verlaine? And what harm did it do him, to be led by the experiences of his venerable mentor?'

With no warning, Cochard's clawlike fingers gripped his face. The old man leaned his bony cheek in and gave Arthur a sickening wet kiss.

'Don't do that, professor. Don't.'

'Does ardour between men upset you?' he asked with a half-smile, his voice heavy with sarcasm.

Arthur's eyes darkened. He was back in Algeria, the dim light of dawn slowly illuminating the space, his eyes fixed on the grainy stucco of his bedroom wall. He could hear the voice of Fabien, his father's cousin who'd come from the continent to take charge of the family's repatriation. A rich cousin — that's what he'd said, and they had all believed him. A filthy, lying pederast who set his sights on Arthur's arse the second he saw him — the smooth, hairless, white backside of a little boy. His mother pretended not to hear, when he screamed — Fabien was her ticket back to France after her husband's death. Arthur could once again hear that pig buckling his belt after having made his anus bleed, could hear the creaking of bed springs, the quiet moan of the door on opening, could hear him grunting. He'd dreamed of biting the man's penis clean off, bashing in his head and splattering his brains around the room, watching them drip down the wall. But he was paralysed by fear, and by his mother's eyes, and the papers bearing the seal of the new Republic, which his rapist kept in his wallet.

The old professor brought his lips to Arthur's once more and tried to kiss him, wearing an expression somewhere between lascivious and bemused. Arthur was filled with rage. He pushed the old man, making him trip and fall back into his divan.

'Don't you dare touch me!' he shouted, furious, threatening him with a fist.

The professor's expression altered then, brimming with indignation and surprise — perhaps feigned, perhaps calculating the weight of the tremendous error he'd just made, and weighing the consequences his rash act might have on his reputation among university faculty. He had to react quickly, before he had an angry little troublemaker telling everyone what had happened.

'You'll never publish another one of your ridiculous poems in this country. If you breathe a word of this, I will personally see to it that you're sent back to that African pig sty you should never have been let out of. Fucking Algerian monkeys, with your Spanish blood.'

Arthur, who was striding out of the room, stopped. He clenched his fists and turned back, confronting the old man. Before him was a large gold-framed mirror, and in it he could see the crucifix, the bookshelves, the table, and Cochard himself. He looked ridiculous, half-collapsed there atop the sofa, his grey hair falling messily over his face, his brown eyes reflecting fear and hatred. But that wasn't what Arthur saw; what he saw were images from his childhood, the tiny steps Fabien took — little nun-like steps — the pain that seared through his backside when the old pervert penetrated him, first with his fingernails and then with his filthy penis. It was the impotence, the humiliation of dragging himself to the latrine in the back yard so that no one could see him taking off his blood-stained underwear to apply iodine; it was the contempt he felt for himself for not having dared, all those nights, to kill his rapist; his submission in the face of terror. *Scum*, he thought, *scum who think they have the right to take whatever they want from others, scum who traffic in the dreams of dreamers. Unscrupulous, soulless bastards.*

At that moment, he still could have walked out; he could have forgotten about everything, spat away the saliva the old man had left on his lips with his revolting kiss. But he didn't. That kiss had violated his mouth — and it consumed him, outraged him, as did the old man's rancour and his fear, and his crazed despotic threats. Without looking, he snatched the first tome off the shelf: Rimbaud's *Pagan Book*, and with it he struck Cochard in the face. Again and again until the pages fell from the spine and the covers were spattered with blood.

His career as a poet was over, forever.

'He broke both his cheekbones, several teeth, and took out one of his eyes. No one would have bought his lousy version of events over the gravely injured professor's. No one would have let such a scandal come to light. Arthur had to leave — and not just the university. If the police caught him in France, a jury would have taken no pity, would have given him an incredibly harsh sentence, admitting no extenuating circumstances.'

Gloria felt a little disappointed. Eduardo's distant tone and bovine expression hurt her, though she now understood that they were just a defence mechanism.

'It sounds like you really pity him.'

Eduardo glanced at Gloria, not understanding her flip tone.

'Sometimes something happens, and it awakens a monster.'

'How many *things* did it take to turn Arthur Fernández into what he is?'

Eduardo looked away, upset.

'I don't know what you're talking about. I can't hate that man, Gloria. He didn't do anything to me.'

207

Gloria made no reply. Not with words. A slight breeze rattled the shutters. She tilted her head back and massaged the back of her neck, as though her thoughts had been interrupted by a ghost kissing her there. Slowly she turned Eduardo's hands over, placing them palm up. She pulled back his cuff and examined the scars on his wrists. She must have seen them dozens of times, but it was as though this were the first time she really noticed, as if every other time his wounds had gone undetected. She did it without softening her face or showing a hint of generosity, or apology. She didn't care how upset he might feel; she cared only about her mission.

'You've been a victim, you've been an executioner, and now you're just a witness — is that what you think?'

It's called denial, Eduardo thought. That's why Martina wrote his prescriptions one Thursday per month.

Gloria shrugged with a look of disenchantment, boredom even, which mortified Eduardo.

'*This* is not the man that killed my son. This face is just a dead image. We both know that.'

Eduardo brought his vodka tonic to his lips. But before taking a sip, he stopped for a moment to contemplate the effervescent liquid. On its surface, floating in the bubbles, was an insect. *Not the right time of year for flying ants*, he thought, as though nothing had just been said, plucking the bug out with his fingers. Sometimes the mind finds curious ways to escape.

'Maybe you should find someone else. I'll tell Olga to return your deposit. I'm not sure I can do this; right now, I'm not sure of anything, quite frankly.'

Gloria scowled. She slid her fingers across the table and stroked the raised veins on the back of Eduardo's hand. He felt an electric shock that excited him, in spite of himself.

'I know there's a monster inside that man. I know it, and I need to see it come to the surface. You're the only one that can do that.'

Eduardo shook his head. It wasn't a convincing refusal, more a gesture of disbelief. Don't we all have monsters inside us, just waiting for the right moment to burst through the skin? Arthur, Gloria, himself.

'You should take the advice Arthur sent you from jail: erase him from your life, forget about him, or he'll end up taking the very last thing you have left of your son — the pain of having lost him. And then you'll have nothing. Absolutely nothing.'

Gloria placed her napkin on the table. She picked up one of the sketches of Arthur and contemplated it for one long minute. Then tore it carefully in half.

'What good is pain if you can't share it with the person who inflicts it on you? I'm no good at forgiveness, Eduardo. I need to understand, and I need to hate.'

They began walking down the middle of the street in silence, not looking at one another. Both had their reasons for going through life ignoring the rest of the world.

Gloria seemed to trust no one. She was alone, and sometimes her loneliness was like lead, dragging her down to the bottom of a dark pit, where she could neither see nor breathe. All she had were her thoughts, her addled and indiscriminate rage, her insane desire to understand the man who'd killed her son. To understand him and then watch him die, slowly and before her eyes, contemplating his agony, perceiving every scintilla of suffering on his face. As long as she harboured that hope, she could keep her son alive, through his connection to Arthur. Using him. And the only thing she had, to get her wish, was this broken, bumbling man. Eduardo walked beside Gloria, looking at her with so much disappointment that she knew his admiration for her had been shattered into a thousand pieces, an admiration she'd spent so long patiently cultivating.

'Will you come back with me to my hotel? I don't want to be alone tonight.'

Eduardo looked away, uncomfortable, as she undressed and then walked to the bed, silently inviting him to join her.

They made love. Of course, that's an exaggeration, a perversion of the term. Gloria draped her naked body weakly atop the sheet like a brushstroke, a pale blue watercolour. Eduardo contemplated her curves, her large sagging breasts, her pubic hair, feeling not desire but need. Gloria held out a hand and drew him to her without so much as touching him; invisible strings on her fingertips were all it took for him to let himself be pulled him in. Everything written on the skin — everything.

He was silent, pitiful at times, as he attempted to penetrate her, unable to muster a real erection. He cursed the Risperdal, blamed it on the booze, but the truth of the matter was that he kept seeing Elena's face, watching him from the armchair where their clothes were piled.

Gloria thought of nothing. In order to withstand the nauseating performance — the moving forward, stopping, going back, seeking something even she could not identify in Eduardo's body, his flaccid member — she had to force herself, remove herself from the scene, picture it from the outside to gain perspective, to see why she was subjecting herself to such horror. She had no interest in Eduardo as a man; the only man she'd ever been interested in sexually was her husband Ian, and since the divorce she'd felt no desire, no need or urge for any other sexual relations. Although Eduardo was in love with her, he would probably never have asked her to make that sacrifice. He'd have made do with whatever scraps she fed him. But those were just tedious observations she had to cast aside if she wanted to keep him on her side. If she could get past the revulsion she felt at prostituting herself that way, she could convince him. Sex was more revealing than other activities. When people's senses and instincts are unleashed, they become less cautious, they make mistakes. They become malleable. It's a story as old as all humankind.

Less than an hour later, Eduardo sat on the unmade bed, gazing at the Hopper painting on the wall, with nothing concrete to think about. He felt tired — not sleepy, but worn down, like a knife that's become so dull that it's useless. He was like a sailboat whose sails have been torn in a storm — anything could toss him around, vary his course, even sink him with very little effort. He smelled his hands, the skin on his face, his chin. He smelled of her, of her vagina. He couldn't help but feel that everything that had taken place was pitiful — the way it had all gone down. He could hear her in the bathroom, scrubbing herself with a bar of soap, using the shower gel repeatedly to remove Eduardo's scent, and realising that hurt him. There was no doubt that she would never belong to him, not even one tiny part of her.

210

He lunged for the minibar and walked out onto the balcony with the last mini bottle of booze.

A minute later he sensed Gloria's presence behind him. He turned to her sadly and gazed at her damp body, wrapped in a bath towel. For a fleeting moment, the image of Graciela's amputated breast flashed into his mind.

'There's something else about Arthur that I didn't tell you at the restaurant. He knows you commissioned the portrait. And he only agreed to pose for it on the condition that I tell him everything about you. But really there's not much I can tell. I don't know who you are. I don't know you at all.'

Gloria's face hardened, resembling a smooth impenetrable stone.

'Poor Eduardo, so lost, so blind. What is it you think you know about *him*, that man you're starting to admire?'

13

Back in Madrid.

Eduardo opened his eyes slowly. He'd have preferred not to have to wake up, preferred to stay in bed, just waiting for the minutes to tick by, stalking the shadows that the passage of time would project onto his apartment walls. But whoever had been banging on his door for the past ten minutes didn't seem inclined to leave him in peace. He dragged himself out of bed, his mouth thick, bones aching. He smelled sour and, for a minute — when he stood up and realised he was woozy — he cursed himself for so readily seeking solace in a bottle of vodka. The last track of a record he'd forgotten to take off crackled on the turntable: Miles Davis' *Kind of Blue*. Looking through the peephole, all he could see was a blue shirt, buttons undone.

'Open up, I know you're standing right there.' The commanding, omnipresent voice of Ibrahim.

Eduardo massaged his temples; his head was about to explode. He had no idea what time it was, what day it was. And his growling stomach and weak muscles made him realise that he had no idea when he'd last eaten anything solid. He opened the door without removing the chain, just enough to see Ibrahim's disfigured face appear in the crack.

'What do you want? I'm feeling under the weather.'

On the other side of the door, Ibrahim wrinkled his nose.

'Judging by the stench, I'd say that's obvious. You smell like you're decomposing. Open the door or I'll kick it down. We need to talk.'

Eduardo opened the door reluctantly, allowing Ibrahim entry. The man gave him a severe look and then glanced with displeasure around the filthy, untidy apartment.

'There's more methane in here than at a nuclear power plant. We better open the window or the whole place is going to blow.' He drew back the curtains and opened the window. It must have been late: the raucous sounds of children on their way home from school were filtering in from the park, and a grainy light seeped through the curtains. Ibrahim snatched up one of the open pill bottles on the table and read the label, and then nosed through the fridge, which was nearly empty.

'What are you doing here?' Eduardo asked, struggling to articulate his words; it was as though a wasp had stung his tongue, making it swell up.

Ibrahim stroked his hair mechanically. Before replying he stationed himself at the window and gazed across the street.

'Arthur hasn't heard a word from you for over a week, and neither have I,' he said, once he'd gotten his fill of whatever it was he was watching outside.

So it had been a week, Eduardo calculated, since he'd returned from Barcelona. Thinking about that revived the heartache he'd felt.

He went to the tap to drink a glass of water, and the chlorine aftertaste made him spit it into the sink. He began searching for his cigarettes but couldn't find them, so he stuck a wrinkled butt into his mouth and lit that instead, squinting. After days spent lost in a drunken stupor, his eyes felt different, distorted, as if they belonged to someone else.

'I went to Olga's and asked about you; she told me you hadn't shown up for days and weren't answering your phone, so I came here. Graciela is worried about you and Sara's spent two whole nights like a puppy dog stationed by your door. I couldn't convince her that you're not worth that kind of loyalty. You should show a little concern for that girl. She might be the only person who actually thinks highly of you.'

So this stranger was on familiar terms with his acquaintances, had become a household presence, Eduardo realised. It bothered him to the point of real vexation, that invasion of his privacy, his realm. Maybe it was just a nebulous, childish, perverse form of jealousy.

'Thanks for the tip, I'll keep it in mind, especially coming from someone like you, who must have a very rich social life,' he replied sarcastically.

'Get dressed. We're going out. You need some fresh air and so do I. Someone is going to have to come disinfect this place.'

Eduardo obeyed. He didn't feel like arguing. And Ibrahim's attitude made it clear that he wasn't about to take no for an answer.

They went out and walked to the plaza outside the Reina Sofía Museum. It was a nice day, and the steps leading to the entrance had been taken over by skaters, and performers with flea-ridden dogs and questionable juggling skills. The outdoor tables at the surrounding bars and cafés were quickly filling up with tourists. Behind Atocha train station, the horizon was alive with intense colours. Life was flowing by, and Eduardo felt out-of-place there in the middle of it all.

Ibrahim traversed the plaza in a few long, determined strides and used his hefty presence to occupy a table that had just been vacated, causing a group of hovering Japanese tourists to withdraw, intimidated. He ordered an espresso. Eduardo asked for vodka — a double, neat. As the waiter was about to walk away, Ibrahim stopped him.

'Make it a sandwich, and forget the vodka.' The waiter glanced at Eduardo questioningly and he gave a resigned nod. Ibrahim didn't ask, didn't make requests. He simply forced whatever he said to be accepted, just like that.

'Why are you looking at me like that? Do you find me pitiful?' The way Ibrahim was examining him annoyed Eduardo. They weren't friends, he had no right to feel sorry for him.

'I like you,' was all Ibrahim said after the waiter had served them. He ripped the sugar packet open with his horrible teeth and stirred it into his coffee. The way he said it, almost in passing, was simply offhand; it wasn't intended to mean anything. He'd killed men he was a lot fonder of than Eduardo. As he stirred the sugar, spoon tinkling against his cup, he glanced over Eduardo's shoulder, eyeing the plaza and its surroundings.

'Kill someone? You're so tense you look like a cat about to pounce,' Eduardo spat, irritated. His chorizo sandwich sat untouched on its plate. Each time he looked at it, he felt a wave of nausea.

Ibrahim shot him a furtive glance and for the first time gave a little smile, flashing his gnarled teeth.

'Stupid question, don't you think?'

Indeed, it was.

Eduardo examined Ibrahim's pupils. The man's expression, he now realised, was mournful, always; the emptiness was something Eduardo himself knew, too. He'd experienced it; it had taken root inside him. It was a look that bore no pity, nor condescension, nor even a hint of phony friendship. All it revealed was a truism that they both recognised: people sometimes betray one another. It's part of being human, something to be accepted. But nothing hurts more than malice on the part of those we took to be on our side unconditionally.

'Have you killed many people?'

Ibrahim listened with his eyes, lips pursed and fingers gripping the table tightly.

'What kind of question is that?'

'I was just wondering if the dead weigh on you, that's all.'

Ibrahim looked away and murmured something in Arabic. He was recalling the voice of an imam reverberating through his adolescent heart, standing before the deep dark grave that held his father's enshrouded body. Recalling the words spoken by the man of God — the virulence and hatred of his fatwa against the French and their descendants — as other men nodded and whispered verses of mercy and piety, their heads lowered, weapons hidden in their clothes. They weren't killers, they were patriots, holy men, the imam told them, spewing vitriol as he spoke, his saliva landing on Ibrahim's not-yet disfigured face. *Killing does not make us killers*, the holy man repeated, his ire contained in a trembling hand. *Not when it's for Algeria, for the FLN, for God.* Recalling those words, Ibrahim gazed at his own hands, now old, the blood of the men he'd killed still staining them like a tattoo, mixing with his own in an invisible flow that bound him to his victims forever. One death is no different from another; they all weigh upon you the same when night falls.

'I know killers who've never laid a hand on anyone, who live among us, who are fathers and mothers, siblings and children; people who seem kind, good people who go to work, are respected, loved, and even admired. But I can tell a jackal when I see one, hiding in their eyes; all it takes is the right time, place, and circumstance to unleash their instincts.'

'I'm a killer,' Eduardo said, his voice hoarse.

Ibrahim gave him a look of commiseration. A poor dog licking his pitiful wounds.

'You, friend, are nothing but a gravedigger. Killing a man doesn't make you a killer.'

Just a week ago he'd used the same argument at his psychologist's office in his own defence. But now he wasn't so sure.

Without realising it, he'd pushed the barely touched sandwich to one side and was gazing absently at the crumbs on the table.

'So what about Arthur, then? You know him better than I do; you're his friend. Would you say *he's* a killer?'

Ibrahim was unperturbed by Eduardo's sarcastic dig. It didn't even ruffle his feathers. But he saw that the little man with his tatty old shirt had his own kind of dignity, one that he himself lacked. He stood and dropped a twenty on the table.

'Ask him yourself. You've still got a portrait to paint. Make good on your promise, and then you can go back to your hole and lick your wounds. You might even cure them.'

Eduardo observed Ibrahim carefully. There was something there that didn't quite fit, but he couldn't put a finger on it.

'It seems strange to me that a man like you is so loyal to someone like Arthur.'

Ibrahim shot him a murderous look.

'The only loyalty I have is to myself.'

'But you protect him.'

Ibrahim let out a chilling little laugh.

'You're pretty blind for an artist, friend. What is it you think you know? Appearances are but obstacles, there to fool the fools ... Now, run back to your hole, little mouse.'

Eduardo watched him amble off, leaving the plaza at the far end, until his shirt and cheap trousers could no longer be seen among the throng of people wandering up and down.

'Want me to cast a spell on you, handsome?' A gypsy in mourning, a branch of rosemary in one hand and fake gold teeth, addressed him. There were three of them, combing the tables like a military squadron on combat orders. Eduardo didn't even bother to be polite. The woman's sweet talk made him sick. He got up angrily.

'There's no magic spell that can save me,' he murmured, pushing her brusquely out of his way.

'I'll put the evil eye on you, you wretch! You'll be a wretched man for the rest of your life, I swear upon my dead!'

Eduardo couldn't suppress an irate cackle that made passers-by turn and stare, as if he were insane.

The café where Arthur had arranged to meet him was at the bottom of Calle Fuencarral. Just on the other side of Gran Vía, two prostitutes stood by a photo booth smoking, offering themselves. One winked a lifeless eye at him, her heavy fake lashes like the rise and fall of a tragic theatre curtain. Eduardo picked up the pace. Sometimes something as simple as a crosswalk acts as an invisible border. You get to the other side and think you're safe, in a world somehow more tolerable.

He saw Arthur sitting in a corner, talking to someone. Eduardo recognised the guy. It was the journalist from *Allegro* he'd seen in Gloria's dressing room a few weeks earlier. What was he doing talking to Arthur? Eduardo got a bad feeling.

Arthur was listening to Guzmán, engrossed, deep in silence. He was staring at the wall as though something only he could see were behind it, something horrible judging by the way he was involuntarily tensing every muscle in his face.

'Are you absolutely sure?'

'Positive. It was him. The painter. He was with her in Barcelona; they had dinner in a restaurant. I waited for them to leave before going in. On top of the table was a sheet of paper, ripped in half. Guess whose face was on it when I put them together? That's right; yours. Then they went up to Gloria's room. I can't say for certain what they were doing for an hour and a half, but I can guess.' He said it with a mix of interest and disgust, as though he'd witnessed something that went against nature, something that should never have happened. It was clear that even for someone like Guzmán, Eduardo didn't deserve the attentions of a woman like Gloria.

Arthur dug his fingers into his hair and clasped his forehead, trying to make sense of this unexpected turn of events. Eduardo and Gloria? It made no sense. Suddenly, he shot Guzmán a look of mistrust.

'What were you doing in Barcelona?'

Guzmán stroked the rough ridges of his singed hand and smiled. He pulled out an envelope and laid it on the table.

'What's this?'

'From what I understand, in the winter of 1990 you had Aroha enrolled in a special boarding school in Geneva, isn't that so?'

Arthur nodded.

'This is the clinical file on Gloria Tagger's son. Curiously, when your daughter was admitted, this kid was there too. So it's more than likely they knew each other.' Guzmán scrutinised Arthur's face. 'Were you unaware of that?'

Arthur skimmed through the file quickly. It was just a page but more than enough to make him go pale. When he finished, he raised his head and saw the mockery in Guzmán's eyes, as he sat blowing smoke rings at the ceiling. Arthur remembered Diana's warning: *Guzmán is not a door that can be easily closed once you decide to open it.* Arthur could no longer stop what he himself had set in motion; he realised that when he saw the man's hard little brown eyes glinting like a predator.

'I had no idea. Must be a coincidence.'

Guzmán stood and straightened his jacket. He was looking at the door, and on seeing Eduardo, he smiled.

'Let's just say that there's something about this whole story of your daughter's disappearance that doesn't add up: a rebellious girl who runs away a lot, a violinist with a backstory out of a novel and a son you accidentally ran over, an antique dealer, a financial shark ... Well, maybe coincidences do exist, but when they're this close together they stop being coincidences and become patterns, don't you think? One door leads to another. And my job is to walk through them all.'

Guzmán passed Eduardo at the door and gave the painter a military salute.

Seeing Eduardo, Arthur leapt up from the sofa, grabbed his jacket and gave him a cloudy, absent look.

'I need to go for a walk. I'm suffocating in here. Let's go.'

'I know that man,' Eduardo said as they stepped out onto the street.

Arthur gazed up at the heavens, as though aware of how far they were from the ground.

'There are some people it's better not to know,' was all he said in reply.

Arthur was taking quick anxious steps, heading for the Malasaña quarter, and Eduardo was having a hard time keeping up.

'Where have you been all this time? I thought we had a portrait to do, you and me.'

Eduardo felt a stabbing pain in his bad knee. He couldn't keep Arthur's pace, and what's more, he sensed that something terrible had happened. He leaned against the corner of a building and massaged his knee.

'I'm calling it quits, Arthur. Actually, I think it was a bad idea from the start.'

Arthur stopped short and gave him a *sinister* look. That was the word.

The man's face became sinister whenever something seemed to make him uncomfortable. It was his way of drawing an invisible line that was not to be crossed.

'Señora Tagger no longer requires your services?'

So that was it. He knew.

'So, she's your lover. Why didn't you tell me?'

Eduardo faltered, averting his gaze, eyes darting from one side of the street to the other like a cornered animal. Ibrahim had called him a little mouse, and that's exactly what he was.

'I'm not her lover; just a tool.'

In an alleyway off Calle Espíritu Santo, one beggar was cursing another, squawking like a crow and shuffling around the other, gesticulating anxiously. They were fighting over the rotten fruit in a dumpster. Their argument grew louder as they became more riled.

Arthur couldn't take his eyes off them.

'Poor Gloria, the devastated mother … I'm sure it wasn't hard for her to seduce a poor fool like you. I bet you're in love with her. All men fall in love with Gloria A. Tagger.'

The skirmish between the two beggars was escalating. They were now embroiled in a slow-motion, clumsy, vicious brawl, reminiscent of Goya's *Duel with Cudgels*. Two tattered men bludgeoning one another in some godforsaken place, up to their knees in muck. No honour at all, just brute strength, biting, scratching, vicious kicks aimed at testicles. They were literally killing each other over a rotten apple and a carton of sour milk. And neither of them would stop until they had achieved their objective. But the object itself — food — was lost in the fray. The scraps on the ground no longer mattered. What drove them to beat one another so savagely was welled-up rage, a hatred so intense and so profound there was no way to shout it out. They wanted to kill each other, kill themselves, their life stories, their past, their demons, wanted to murder their present and seal their future. Perhaps they were secretly hoping someone would come and intercede, call off the fight, declare it a tie. But no one did.

Eduardo looked on absently.

Arthur and Gloria, Gloria and Arthur. They thought they could do anything they wanted, toy with anyone at will, maybe keep hurting the

219

other, poison their miserable lives as though their venom were the blood that no longer coursed through their veins.

'You lost a daughter and you're looking for her. Gloria lost a son and, in some sense, she's still looking for him, too. And I feel trapped in a downward spiral, tossed from side to side with no will of my own. Enough — I've had it.'

Arthur contemplated Eduardo coldly, without a hint of sorrow, or understanding, or affection.

'You feel like the victim in all this. But you're not innocent, that's for sure. Your hands are as dirty as ours. What about the man you killed? And his wife, who you left crippled in a wheelchair ... Do you think she's been able to just let it go? You think she doesn't hate you with all her might?'

The arabesque was perfect, displayed in a sequence of four positions on the wall, one after the other, just above the mannequin draped with tulle and gauze from her old outfits and a pair of slippers whose reinforced toes were completely worn out. From her wheelchair, Maribel extended her right arm gracefully, until its shadow projected on the wall as a perfectly straight line, fingers together, index finger raised slightly, pinky slightly down, like a soft waterfall. In a flawlessly choreographed move, she next bent her torso sideways and did exactly the same with her left arm. Gazing at the shadows, you could easily picture a pair of wings flapping gently. With her eyes resting shut, concentrating on her breathing, on getting just the right intake of air, she pretended her wheelchair didn't exist. Executing the move properly required the body's weight to rest on one leg, *demi-plié* over and over, again and again, until the thigh no longer felt the body's pressure, the other leg fully extended from the hip like an elegant tail. Arm and leg created one long stylised line. It was the closest thing to flying that a human could aspire to without wings, and Maribel had felt that freedom, that impossible combination of gravity-defying lines and contours, hundreds if not thousands of times.

She opened her eyes slowly and once more felt the heavy sombreness of the room, her catheter and urine bag, the rough feel of the plastic, the atrophy of her leg muscles, useless now after having supported her for so many years. She gazed at the sequence of exercises immortalised in the four framed photos. They were taken during a demonstration by the dance school, on tour in Barcelona. Standing before her three best students, Maribel executed the moves, wearing a very tight, very black outfit that left only her shoulders, arms, and the tips of her pointe shoes exposed. The real challenge, however, had been that she was executing the moves on a beach, a damp irregular surface, the shore seen in the distance. It must have been very painful in those circumstances, must have required incredible balance, poise, strength and obstinacy. Yet Maribel's face, like that of her students, betrayed not the slightest doubt. Tall, with straight black hair down to her chest, she gazed confidently into space as though somewhere there were an invisible barre holding her up. She radiated determination.

As she nearly always did when looking at those photos, hung in a place that made it impossible not to see them when she went into her old bedroom, Maribel stroked her skin. The images forced her to remember what she'd never again be: young, light, ethereal, beautiful and free.

At sixty, she shouldn't feel old; women her age still took care of themselves, used all sorts of creams, often had no compunction about getting a little plastic surgery if that meant they could keep living a virtual youth that even they themselves knew, deep in their hearts, no longer went with their bodies. But Maribel felt ancient. Her skin had become scaly for lack of fresh air, her bones frail from lack of exercise, and her muscles were so wasted they had practically turned to mush, held together by a sack of skin. She wondered what Teo, her husband, would think if he could see her in such a sorry state of neglect. He'd worked long and hard to conquer her and she hadn't made it easy, teasing him over and over before finally giving herself to him, feigning indifference to his love and complete dedication to her one true passion — dance.

Teo had been a patient man, not much of a talker, and could even appear cold and distant, but he had had the perseverance befitting his stubborn meticulous character; it made him a great coin collector and dealer. Those two qualities — patience and perseverance — finally created a chink in Maribel's armour, and once he'd achieved that, he eventually made it all the way, through sheer determination. She'd always assumed that they would grow old together, that their mutual decline would be gradual — he with his coins and she with her books on dance technique, using theory to keep teaching what exhaustion and the laws of gravity meant she could no longer demonstrate herself.

Sometimes, when she entered her bedroom, she still thought it might be possible. She was afraid that she'd lose his smells if she let in any contaminated outside air. Not even her son was allowed to enter. It was her sanctuary, the one place she could still be the woman she'd been before that degenerate took away the two things that meant the most to her — her ability to fly, and the only man she'd ever loved.

She opened the armoire where Teo's shirts and suits hung. Every so often she would take them to the same drycleaners she had always used, and they'd return them freshly pressed. When his smell started to fade, she would bring out the aftershave Teo had used and lightly sprinkle the collars, cuffs, and sleeves so that when she opened the armoire it was as if her husband were coming out to greet her. She'd inhale the smell of his shirts and then exhale slowly, and her heart was thankful for that dance of the senses. Though never an elegant man, Teo was always meticulous and austere, almost English in his dress and footwear. He kept each pair of Italian loafers with its corresponding brush and polish.

She still had a watch case with a few of his watches — none of them valuable or aesthetically striking — that matched his plain ties, scarves and handkerchiefs. It was all kept in perfect order — folded, unfolded and refolded. Maribel could while away many hours each morning absorbed in the task, but she didn't mind. She had nothing to do but remember, fold and unfold, and pine.

In the back of the armoire was a dark plastic bag that Maribel rarely dared to pull out, despite being unable to make herself get rid of its contents. It held the clothes her husband had been wearing the day his soulless killer had blown his brains out. The police had handed it over after the autopsy, and she'd refused to burn it or throw it away, unlike the coat she herself had been wearing that morning, which ended up with a hole shot through it and a black trail of gunpowder, but almost no blood. In the bag, she kept the pale blue shirt that he'd liked to wear on Sundays, when he went to the numismatic association. The collar was a bit thin, worn with use, and they'd often argued because it drove her to distraction to see him put it on. But Teo never wanted to get rid of it because ever since he acquired an *aureus* of Emperor Alejandro Severo coined in 223AD, it had become his lucky shirt. Embedded in it, like scars in the weave, were blood spatters, shards of his skull, particles of scalp and brain matter that had exploded with devastating violence when the shot was fired into his head.

She'd also kept his corduroy jacket, its elbows worn thin, and his dark chinos. His clothes hadn't even matched, the day that lunatic killed him. And that absurd thought had festered in Maribel's brain, all those years. Like a stuck cog, her brain obsessed over it every time she decided, for whatever reason, to get out the bag and spread its contents on the bed.

You didn't even match, but you refused to listen to me. You'd become so irritable and distracted by your coins and things that you wouldn't even let me pick out your clothes.

Nearly fourteen years later, she still didn't understand why some so-called happy people are punished in such unexpected, horrific ways. Who decided their destiny? God? Fate? And why her? Why her and not some other woman? She'd struggled all her life; she understood that life was a question of sacrifice, dedication, effort and tenacity, that it was rife with failures. Classical dance had made her suitably disciplined, but it had also taught her to expect some reward for all that discipline. And she'd hardly had time to enjoy it, just a few short years — 'the most beautiful years', said her romantic, optimist friends; 'the most unrealistic years', said those not carried away by facile emotion. They couldn't even have the child that she had so yearned for, and Teo also dreamed of. In the end, they'd adopted their son, and although Maribel had thrown herself body and soul into loving him, deep down it hurt her to know that her husband had never felt the boy was fully his.

'I wish you could see him. He's become a handsome young man, hardworking, smart, and so sensitive, but now he needs a father to help him through this confusing time.'

Maribel didn't feel she had the strength to battle the inevitable. Children grow up, they learn things about themselves, some of them erroneous, and then they leave — whether physically or not, they stop belonging to their parents. Children are temporary, they're given only on loan, and sooner or later they have to be returned, given back to life itself. Lately, when Mr Who looked at her, she felt a strange trepidation, as though her son were hoping for something from her, a sign, as though he wanted to tell her something but didn't know how. And when she asked him, he'd put on a mask, act like the angel he'd always been, kiss her on the forehead and then leave, burdened by his sadness and his demons.

It took her a moment to hear the doorbell. When she finally did, she looked at the time, surprised. It was too early for her son to be coming home, and besides, he had his own keys and never rang the bell. Maybe it was those two old ladies again, the Jehovah's Witnesses who came to see her every afternoon, with their pamphlets and their proselytising spirit, commendable but hopeless in her case. She pushed her wheelchair down the hall to the door, trying to think up an excuse that wouldn't be offensive, so as to get them out of her hair as soon as possible.

But when she opened the door she saw not the old ladies with their pious faces, not her son. The sorrowful man who stood looking at her from the hall was a ghost from the past. The face that had filled her nightmares for the past fourteen years.

'Good morning, Señora. I'm Eduardo Quintana.'

Soon it would be spring; you could feel it in the night air and see it the treetops, where early buds, still too weak to survive a late frost, were beginning to bloom. They were like Mei, a new bud that might not be able to bear another frost, thought Mr Who.

In the alley that led to the back of the building where he lived, a prostitute was working a john. She was one of Chang's girls. They exchanged a look of recognition. Neither merited the other's sympathy; each of them simply trafficked in other people's sorrows, made them easier to bear, and carried on their way. That was the sort of people they were, he and the hooker. Lusterless shadows. The john was frantically groping her buttocks, shoving his tongue in her ear. The girl was still looking at Who. *Come now*, she seemed to be saying, *don't get sentimental. You've got your tragedy and I've got mine. It's not like we're in love*. There are those who say hookers are just after easy money. *Fools. They have no idea what they're talking about*, he thought. Imagining that *that* was the destiny Chang had written for Mei was driving him out of his mind.

He walked into the house and took off his shoes in order not to make any noise. He saw the light on in Maribel's room and went to see if she needed anything, but stopped halfway there, hearing her crying. Maribel always cried alone, and never in the dark. Mr Who had grown up with that sadness since the time he was a child. He'd also learned that it was better to leave her alone.

So he retraced his steps and went to his room.

He took off his jacket and left it on the unmade bed. Then he sat down at the computer and opened the folder with the scanned photos he'd compiled of the one and only vacation the three of them had taken together — a surprise trip in the summer of 1991; he, Maribel and Teo had gone to Menorca. He'd planned to use the pictures to make a slideshow and set it to music. Maribel would be touched by his thoughtfulness.

The trip had been unexpected. Teo never wanted to leave Madrid; at most he'd occasionally go to Toledo or Cáceres, never any farther than that. And yet he was the one who turned up one morning with the plane tickets.

He remembered a ferry that had brought them to some of the island's coves only accessible by sea. In the photos, his father's glasses went over his eyebrows. He was half-smiling, twirling his moustache like a matinee idol. Maribel stood beside him. Between them, pressing up against their legs, a boy whose face was pale from the rocking of the boat. The sea frightened him. Leaning against the rail on the observation deck, he watched flocks of seagulls soaring over the frenzied crests of waves that kept crashing in the distance with a dull roar, one after the other.

He must have been happy that summer, although that wasn't exactly what he remembered. What he did remember were the days when he'd hear them arguing and catch them in the kitchen, composing their expressions with the speed of those trained to conceal shortcomings.

Four months later, Teo was dead and Maribel lay in the hospital with a broken spinal column.

Mr Who let his gaze drift, but suddenly his eyes froze on a spot behind the computer. Behind the wood-panelled wall was where Who kept his secrets hidden. And someone had moved a slat.

Maribel was in her wheelchair beside the bed, stroking one of her tulle dance outfits — the last one she'd worn before her vertebrae had been broken. She stared at Who and her eyes were like glass, unbearably certain. She straightened in her wheelchair and, with a casual gesture, dropped the sheet from Eduardo's file onto the bed, the one Who had stolen from Martina. On it was the photograph of his father's killer, the man who had destroyed their lives for no reason.

'How could you hide something like this from me?'

Mr Who tried to calm her, but Maribel rebuffed his attempts to take her hand, as though he were a leper. Her lips were trembling, and although she seemed to implore him with her gaze, her expression was hard.

'I didn't want to reopen old wounds.'

'How long have you had this?'

'The first time I saw him was by chance, in Parque de El Retiro. He was sketching a woman. I recognised him by the photos you keep, the newspaper clippings from what happened. But I wasn't sure, so I went back the next day, hoping I'd find him again so I could be positive. He was sitting on the same bench, like he was waiting for someone who never came. For weeks I went back to the same place and followed him. I watched him, tried to imagine what kind of man he was. There was no reason to do it, I didn't have a plan, didn't know what I'd do when the time came to confront him. One day I approached him in the metro. I sat beside him on the platform, watched him from up close, saw the scars on his wrists, the wrinkles on his skin, the grey in his hair. I smelled his body and heard his voice. I spoke to him, goaded him — provoked him, really. I wanted to see if he remembered me, if he remembered us, but he didn't react. I'd pictured the scene so many times before — what I'd do, what I'd say. When the train came, I thought I'd shove him, push him under the tracks, and watch the wheels crush him. But the train pulled in and I stopped; I couldn't do it. A few weeks later, I happened to meet a person. By chance, I found that piece of paper from his file: it explains everything.'

Maribel threw her head back, as though an invisible hand were pulling her hair, and let out an unbearable wail.

'Why?' she managed to ask, gazing at Who with a mixture of incredulity and shock.

Mr Who sat down on the foot of the bed.

'Because I need to understand the man who killed us.'

He used 'us' because that's how he felt it. Teo was not the only one who died that day; he might even have been the luckiest of the three because he'd died on the spot. But the two of them had had to keep dying

226

a little more each day. From the time he was nine, there was no playing in the house, no laughter, no fresh air. Maribel withdrew from him; she did it gently, slowly, in the same way she withdrew from everything, turning her whole life into darkness — the same permanent darkness she kept in her bedroom. Love, true love, had ended before it began. Mr Who had learned to take care of her in his own way. He smiled, and his smile was different from hers, because when his mother smiled it was nothing but a painted-on expression, while his was a smile of yearning. He longed to win her back, to regain her affection, the devotion he'd hardly had time to experience. But he never again felt her warmth, and little by little he'd descended into his own quiet world, tiptoeing around the house so as not to disturb her. Mr Who stopped being a child, a teenager, lost his youth and became his invalid mother's shadow.

Maribel lifted his chin with her finger, forcing him to look into her eyes. Mr Who averted his gaze, didn't want to connect to the reality of that inquisitive look.

'He was here. This morning.'

Mr Who's face contorted completely.

He wasn't expecting that. He felt his throat go dry, the rage boiling up in his stomach. He pictured his mother for a moment, defenceless in her wheelchair, powerless in the presence of that man.

'*Here*?' he asked, as if it would have made a difference had she met him in the supermarket, or turning a corner. 'What happened?'

'Nothing. He told me his name. We looked at each other for a while, and I closed the door on him. He didn't knock again, but I know he stood there on the other side of the door for a long time. I could hear him. Then he left.'

Maribel gazed around her bedroom. The bed, the armoire, the dresser, the display case with Teo's coins, the calm air, the pretence that nothing had changed.

'I want you to put an end to this, son. I don't want to know that that man is still breathing the same air as us. I don't want to know that he might come near me.'

Mr Who stood.

'He won't. I promise you.'

14

On the wooden countertop lay a newspaper whose front-page headlines told of a tragic fire in a nearby building. The doorwoman stopped reading when Guzmán walked in. She was middle-aged, and clearly hadn't waxed her moustache in quite some time. After greeting Guzmán, she leaned on her broom with a cigarette hanging out of her mouth, the filter stained with lipstick.

'The antique dealer's next door — do you know if they're closed? No one's answering the bell,' he said.

'Dámaso closes up shop before five o'clock. He won't be back until Monday.' She exhaled smoke through the gaps in her teeth as she spoke.

Guzmán feigned annoyance.

'That's too bad. I've got something he's really interested in. You couldn't tell me where he lives, could you?'

She glanced at him with mistrust. Instinctively, she straightened her shoulders, clamped her teeth down on the cigarette, and then — sounding affronted — began enumerating her many chores and responsibilities: sweeping the staircase, taking out the garbage, seeing to the gas men who were coming to do an inspection. How did he expect her to keep track of where every shop owner on the street lived? And even if she did know, why should she tell him? People might think doorwomen talked too much, but *she* — and with a thumb, she jabbed her own chest emphatically — was not the type to sit at her desk all day reading *Hello!* or *Lecturas*. She spent her days working.

Guzmán smiled. And behind the smile, he pondered how easy it would be to wring her little chicken neck with one hand.

'I understand. I'll come back on Monday when he opens.'

He walked out onto the street with a sense of relief and sat down at an outdoor café, choosing a table where he could keep an eye on the lobby of the building and the antique dealer's connected to it. Now all he had to do was wait.

When he'd yet to touch his coffee, the doorwoman left the building and walked down the street, leaving a trail of cigarette smoke in her wake. Guzmán walked back to the building and pushed open the front door. The reception area was empty, inhabited only by the heavy sweetish smell of burning tobacco and the voices that carried through the elevator shaft. Music came from somewhere, a Chilean bolero that Guzmán recognised, by Lucho Gatica: 'Contigo en la distancia', it was called.

There's not a moment of the day
I can stand to be far from you

The music put him at rights with the world for a moment.

The half-door to the woman's cubicle was open. The newspaper no longer lay on the desk; now, instead, there was a note, scrawled in boxy, childlike letters: 'Back in five minutes.' She'd left her broom to stand guard, leaning up against the wall. Guzmán slipped his hand behind the little door and undid the latch. Hanging from a corkboard on the wall were master keys to every unit. To make matters even easier, each one was labelled. He grabbed the one that said *Dámaso's place*.

A door beside the elevator led down to the antique shop. Once he'd gone through, Guzmán felt around for the light switch and turned on a fluorescent bulb. To the right stood the door into the shop. To the left, a partial staircase leading down to another closed door. Guzmán decided to investigate.

The storeroom was sizable; everywhere were paintings, boxes of books, dressers, chairs, clocks, tapestries and other assorted items waiting to be catalogued.

For a good while, Guzmán hunted around with no clear idea of what he was searching for. He knew from experience that people lie for one of two reasons: to hide something, or to invent something. In Dámaso's case, it was clear that he was hiding something. It was just a matter of finding out what that was.

Nothing he came across seemed particularly interesting. Stuff. Just silent stuff, that couldn't answer his questions. Disappointed, Guzmán sat down on an old trunk with a floral pattern and antique metalwork; he took a slow look around. Sometimes it's only when you stop looking that you actually see, when you stop searching and open yourself up to coincidence. In one corner was a collection of furniture whose arrangement caught his eye. Although at first glance the storeroom seemed chaotic, in fact it was not. The pieces were grouped by commonalities, whether period, or style, or function.

In one area were the oldest pieces, Napoleonic-style furniture; in another were more baroque objects; in front of those, pieces from the seventies and eighties. But right in front of him, amid rows of paintings and coat stands, mirrors and a few hunting scenes, was an enormous travertine table, on top of a fake tiger-skin rug that was wrinkled around its legs — as though the table had been moved and had dragged the rug with it.

Guzmán shifted objects out of his way to clear a path. Beneath the rug, he discovered a trap door. It took him several attempts and almost all his strength to move the table. Whatever it was underneath there, Dámaso had no way of getting to it without help; the table was far too heavy for someone his age to move alone. And judging by the cobwebs that stretched like chewing gum when he pulled up the hatch, he hadn't used it in quite some time.

The opening was no more than a metre and a half squared, give or take. It was very dark, and he couldn't see the bottom or sides; all he saw was the top of a ladder hanging down. It looked like the entrance to an underground bunker. Perhaps it was another storeroom that Dámaso had stopped using years ago.

Feeling his way through the dark like a blind man, using his lighter, Guzmán finally found a light switch. He flipped it and heard an electric buzzing.

Guzmán let out a low, admiring whistle.

It wasn't a storeroom, garage or tool shed. The walls were insulated with natural fiber, and from the ceiling hung small gooseneck halogen lamps. In the centre of the room were two dozen red, comfortable-looking theatre seats with cushioned backs, and in front of them a huge screen with an overhead projector and DVD player. This was a screening room, a private movie theatre. So the old man had lied, and this was where his lie began: it must have been the meeting place for the film club Olsen's wife had told him about.

In a display case stood a near-identical copy of the first projector to be manufactured by the Lumière factory in 1895. Beside it was a metal box with several of the films first shown in Lyon the same year, shorts that lasted no more than ten minutes: *Le jardinière, L'Arroseur arrosé, La Sortie de l'usine Lumière de Lyon*. They must have been worth a small fortune. Maybe the old man was naturally distrustful and wanted to keep it a secret so he wouldn't be robbed. The people who met there must have been a very select group of collectors, *bon vivants* who delighted in being able to enjoy their marvels in private. It wasn't unusual for the rich to pay astronomical prices to be able to enjoy works of art privately. Often they were anonymous, people who sent employees to auctions to bid for them, so they wouldn't have to show their faces. There had even been cases, much discussed in the media, of very important people who'd bought art stolen from museums or other places, just so they could have the exclusive privilege of owning whatever they wanted. Maybe that's what got those freaks off, Guzmán thought, scanning the room slowly — having what no one else could have. Maybe.

But there was something that still didn't add up. He didn't know what it was, but it was there, in plain sight, challenging him, waiting for him to put the pieces together.

Bosco had always advised him to have patience when he started a 'file'. That was what they called them at the National Intelligence Directorate, rather than cases or investigations. By the time the 'files' reached his hands it was never a matter of discovering some hidden truth. They didn't need proof, didn't have to follow clues or pretend to be cops, detectives you read about in novels. They weren't there to waste time. They were there to crack their 'files': get confessions, names, dates and addresses. Signed statements, admissions of guilt. As far as DINA — the directorate — was concerned, no one was ever innocent. Ever. They were all guilty of whatever they'd been accused of, even when they hadn't formally been accused of anything. They didn't go into the basement cells of La Moneda palace in the hopes of a fair trial or some improbable absolution. Anyone who fell into the hands of Bosco and his team of interrogators (they didn't like to use the words 'torturers' or 'executioners'; that reduced the importance of their work) was going to confess their guilt. Their 'file' was going to be closed and sent to the archives. And still they had to be patient: ponder the use of force; set the stage of terror; decide whether to play it nice or be hard; find a crack in the prisoner's resistance; spend day and night searching, for days, weeks, months (no one had ever held out more than three months) until they found it.

The weakness could be a childhood fear (he himself had been afraid of dogs ever since the time, as a boy, he'd seen his brother ripped apart by a wild pack, while they were combing through the debris at the dump south of Santiago); it could be a son or daughter, a husband or wife, a father or mother. It could be wounded pride, vanity, fear of betrayal or being denounced by colleagues. It could be sexual humiliation, lack of affection, anything. And when they discovered it, when they got a whiff of the weakness, that was it. That was when they pounced, merciless until they'd reached all the way to the bottom of the prisoners' very souls. Then they got everything, hollowed them out and then delivered their bodies to the grim reaper — and a common grave.

'What are you hiding, you old bastard? What are you keeping from me?'

The time had come to change tactics, Guzmán decided. Spain might not be Chile in the days of the Pinochet junta, might not even be the Spain of the GAL — the so-called Antiterrorist Liberation Groups, which were really death squads fighting the forces of the separatist ETA. But men were still men, and they still reacted to the same stimuli. And he still had contacts, people who owed him favours, feared him, and just a few who actually held him in some regard. He might not be an orthodox cop, or even a typical private investigator. He wasn't Mr Clean or Dirty Harry. He hated those clichés. Guzmán was something else. Something they'd never seen in Spain. And the feeling that he didn't have everything under control annoyed and frustrated him. So he was going to fix that.

On the second visit — unlike his first — Guzmán got the impression that Olsen's widow's house was rather ordinary, that the sea was too far away and the sun blazing down on the limestone facade just foreshadowed the wasteland that the entire planned community was no doubt destined to become. There was no sign of the two attractive, rosy-cheeked, IKEA kids or the hysterical yapping Yorkie. It was all quiet.

Guzmán walked into the backyard. He could see Olsen's widow lying on the sofa, flipping through a fashion magazine. He got her attention by rapping on a window with his knuckles.

She looked up, and on seeing him her whole face tensed. Visibly displeased, she got up and opened the sliding door.

'What do you want now?' Her expression made it clear that she thought she never should have let him in the first time.

She had beautiful eyes, Guzmán thought.

Maybe her eyes were what Magnus Olsen had first fallen for, at one of those exclusive parties thrown at some embassy where those who make it past the red cord know they belong to a select group. Maybe the widow had been practising that look in the mirror for years, waiting for the right moment to use it, the chance to escape the Stockholm slum where her beauty fetched nothing but obscene remarks from Turkish and Armenian louts, who watched her walk by like some sort of extra-terrestrial, a diamond in a pigsty.

'I thought we should finish our conversation.'

She looked away in irritation, her face seeming to say that no one is ever satisfied with what they've got, that everyone always wants more.

She looked lovely in her designer top and tight pants. Maybe she'd had to borrow money to buy her first dress; who knows what it cost her to finance that very first outfit. She must have managed, though, and maybe managed to hide the fact that her heart was racing when she found herself in some Versailles-style palace with frescoes on the walls and ceilings, surrounded by crystal chandeliers that reflected the light off her fake jewels. No doubt she'd had to force her hand not to tremble when the waiter offered her a champagne flute, had to force herself to sip it slowly, as though she'd been doing it all her life, attending these parties where upmarket hookers dressed in style, on the hunt for a golden retirement plan.

'You're just not going to leave me alone, are you?'

She glared at Guzmán but the disdain she felt was for herself — a life of swallowing humiliations, like a trained monkey on a leash that might be jerked by the master at any moment, a trophy to be flaunted before friends and enemies, an exchangeable good. 'Wear the low-cut dress; the minister likes your tits', 'Smile at the bank manager; he wants you to suck him off in the back seat of his Mercedes and we need him to approve a loan for millions.'

Eyes like hers — eyes devoid of dreams — had tried many times, in many places, and with little luck, to touch Guzmán's heart.

'The day your husband committed suicide — what happened?'

'What kind of question is that?' she asked. Her lassitude had morphed into an expression of disgust.

'The kind that's got an answer. I can pay for that answer, or I can make a few calls so that all those friends, the ones who are tearing what's left of Olsen's estate to pieces, find out that this house is in his widow's name. Times are tough in real estate, but I reckon they could still get a few thousand euros if they evicted you. And believe me, banks aren't a whole lot more compassionate than your husband was, so the sight of those little blonde angels of yours won't do much to melt their hearts. So: a cheque with a few zeros on it, or an eviction notice — your choice.'

Olsen's widow made no attempt to suppress her disgust and scorn for Guzmán. He accepted her look stoically, waiting until she realised that expressions of pride are useless when you're in no position to make demands. She stroked the wrinkle creasing her forehead with an index finger and then rummaged in her purse for a pack of cigarettes. Guzmán thought he saw something metallic; it looked like a pistol. Maybe she had opened her purse in search of a smoke, but he couldn't discard the possibility that she'd done it as a warning, so he would see her weapon, the implication being that she knew how to defend herself and was prepared to do so. Guzmán was unimpressed. In order to intimidate someone, a threat is not enough.

'Lately we'd hardly seen each other. Everyone assumed we took off, went to Stockholm — but I can't go back there. My husband's company used me as a front for some of their deals and the police would arrest me the second I set foot in any territory of the Swedish crown. That's just one of the reasons I hate him. We were hardly sleeping together anymore, and I spent much more time here than at our Madrid apartment.'

'But the night he committed suicide you were all in Madrid together.'

'He'd called me the day before. Said he wanted to see me and the kids, but didn't say why. He never gave explanations, just expected his orders to be carried out, immediately and without question. So I took the kids to the apartment in Serrano. The problems had already begun with his firm in Sweden — tax inspections, accusations of fraud and embezzlement — and I'd gotten used to the way he'd aged and become taciturn, irascible. He was quickly destroying himself, the man who was always so proud of having made it out of the gutter by his own wits, having tripled his fortune in a few short years. It was all slipping out of his grasp. And he couldn't stand it. But that day he opened the door and greeted us, and he was like a new man. Maybe not the one I'd first met, but at least a faint reflection of him. He was euphoric, confident, had the same ravenous expression he used to have. He told me he'd found a way out of his legal and financial troubles. "A trump card just fell into my hands," that was what he said. He promised me everything would go back to the way it had been, in the good old days. Even though we could never return to Sweden, we'd start again here, then Tarragona, then Málaga, and then Murcia ... He'd build another empire from nothing. And I believed him,' she concluded bitterly. 'I had no choice but to believe him.'

'That *trump card*, did he tell you what it was?'

She looked as though she'd just been caught in a crossfire in no-man's land, no barricade to hide behind.

'No, he didn't tell me. He never told me anything, and I didn't need — or want — to know about his schemes.'

Her reply was as obvious as it was disheartening. But Guzmán hadn't come to ask questions he knew wouldn't be answered. He'd just been feeling her out. The real reason he was there was to clear up another kind of doubt.

'When your husband hung himself, what was the first thing you saw?' He stared at her, wondering how much sincerity he could expect. She must have read his mind, because she smiled maliciously.

'His body swinging from a crossbeam in the living room and a pile of shit on the floor. It was still dripping from his pants. Excrement, falling from his feet. I don't know why but he was barefoot. He'd taken off his socks and shoes, but not the rest of his clothes — except for his belt, which is what he used to hang himself.'

Guzmán remained pensive for a moment. He wished he could have seen Olsen's body before the police and medical examiners had gotten there and taken him down. Most people think committing suicide is easy, but they're wrong. If they knew how hard it was, lots of people wouldn't try to go all the way; they'd give up first. Hanging, in particular, is a process that seems simple, but it's not. If you're lucky, you break your neck. That's quick and you almost don't feel the pain; there's just a snapping that you have no time to process. But if you don't calculate all the variables properly — the weight, the noose, the height you're jumping from — and something goes wrong, then you just suffocate, and it takes entire minutes of sheer agony before you die.

He'd seen a 'file' hang himself in a cell once. The man had used a sheet, but didn't tie the knot in exactly the right place. For minutes the guy was flailing, kicking and swinging his arms in the air, just a few centimetres off the ground. Guzmán stood there, watching, dodging his desperate attempts to grab hold of him, begging with his eyes for help. Guzmán refused to give it. He could have lifted him up by the knees — the prisoner hardly weighed anything at all — but stepping in would only have made matters worse. That man had decided to put an end to his life, and he had no right to stop him. The poor wretch would have regretted it later, once his initial panicked fear passed, as soon as the unbearable torture and interrogations started back up. All he had to do was overcome that fear, the instant of absolute terror in the face of death. And then let go. As far as Guzmán was concerned, interfering with nature's destiny is wrong.

'Your husband weighed, what — a hundred, hundred and ten kilos? That must have been a really strong belt to take his weight. And it must have been very well tied to the beam. I can only imagine he'd have struggled desperately to get it off when he couldn't breathe.'

'What are you insinuating?'

'That maybe he didn't commit suicide.'

'That's what the police report says. You should consult it before launching into that kind of speculation.'

'I have. From the time you found him until the time you made the call, over thirty minutes went by. The report also states that the apartment was neat and tidy and there were no signs of robbery or struggle, but the cleaning woman who came three times a week said in *her* statement that she found the drawers and the clothes in his closet jumbled and put back different from the way he kept his things organised.'

Olsen's widow looked away. Those beautiful, dead eyes. *Shame*, he thought. For a second they'd reminded him of Candela's eyes, the first time she asked him if he was going to kill her.

'I straightened up — drawers, dressers, the whole apartment — before I called the police.'

The memory of Candela vanished.

'Why?'

'My husband always kept a large amount of money stashed in the house, cash and jewels. That money and those jewels went to a whole slew of little whores. He liked girls, the younger the better, and kept a reserve fund so he could satisfy his urges. I wasn't about to let the lawyers hand those funds over to the creditors after the properties had been searched, so I looked everywhere until I found the money. It was a substantial sum, substantial enough for me to start fresh somewhere else. I don't know, it was all so fast, and I was thinking a thousand things at once — that I'd tampered with evidence, that my fingerprints would be all over everything, that if they found me with the money they'd make me give it back or, worse, I'd be considered a suspect or an accomplice to murder.'

'Can you remember anything else?'

She looked pensive, as though debating something. Then she gave him a distrustful look.

'You said before you were willing to pay for my answers. About that cheque ... how much are we talking?'

Guzmán looked around with resignation.

'I imagine it'll be enough to throw a couple coats of paint on the walls and buy the lamps this place needs. It'll be less than a defence attorney's fees, true, but at least I might decide not to report you to the police for giving false testimony and absconding with frozen assets.' Guzmán had no idea how to say 'son of a bitch' in Swedish, but guessed that that was exactly what she was saying under her breath.

'While I was searching the apartment, someone phoned. I didn't pick up, I let the answering machine get it. It was a man. He sounded very old. And very pissed off. He mentioned a recording and insisted that Magnus hand it over.'

Guzmán's eyes flashed like a flame being reflected on a dark surface. He could guess whose voice it had been.

'That's not in the police report either. Doesn't it strike you as relevant?'

'I told you, I never wanted to know anything about his business transactions and I still don't. I erased the message. Are we done?'

'Just one more thing. This will be the last one. The first time we saw each other, I mentioned that I worked for a man named Arthur

Fernández. You said you'd never heard of him, and you almost convinced me. I admit you're good at hiding your reactions; I suppose you've had a lot of experience. But you were lying. A tiny blink gave you away — you know, like when you open the window and a gust of wind rushes in.'

Olsen's widow stood up, decisively. She looked at Guzmán with an expression that said she was the kind of woman who made her own decisions and faced up to the consequences.

'I don't know who the hell you are or what you're looking for. But we're done. Pay me for what I've told you if you want, or turn me in; the truth is I don't care anymore. I want you to leave and never set foot in this house again.'

Guzmán weighed up her determination with an expert eye. He saw Candela in the interrogation room that first time, standing before him, hands tied behind her back. *You can break my back if you want. You'll never get what I have inside.* Guzmán didn't know it at the time, but that was the start of his only failure and only triumph in life. What she had inside — her hopes and dreams and will to live — he never got.

Before leaving, he handed Olsen's widow a cheque far more generous than necessary. After all, Arthur was the one paying his expenses, and being generous with other people's money was something that made him feel especially good.

'Why so much?' she asked in wonder.

Guzmán gave her an appreciative glance. He liked survivors. He liked *her*, no point in denying it.

'Because I hope the money will encourage you to take a long trip to another part of the world. Maybe you can make a fresh start someplace where nobody will treat you like a bimbo.'

Four days later, Guzmán was feeling like the outside world was somewhat indifferent, like it was keeping a prudent distance, one that varied according to the speed at which people moved. It occurred to him that he was but one tiny part of a greater whole, and that someone somewhere was watching his tiny insignificant life. Reality was a set of Russian nesting dolls — it could go on forever.

Guzmán stopped to listen to a street musician playing Spanish guitar. He was a languid-looking young man, and played extraordinarily well.

His guitar case lay open at his feet, a few coins and some CDs he'd recorded lay inside it. He could have been a consummate virtuoso who earned millions playing concerts in prestigious auditoriums all over the world, but people just kept walking by, no time to stop and listen.

'Art can't change a boorish soul, because humans are deaf, blind boors with no soul left to lose,' he murmured, dropping a few coins into the case. It wasn't his line. It was Candela's.

In the distance stood the imposing granite and limestone Palacio de Oriente. Tourists were taking pictures at the fence surrounding the courtyard while the ceremonious changing of the Royal Guard was performed. Behind the palace were the winter gardens known as Campo del Moro, which had excellent views of the palace and the Manzanares River. Tree-lined walkways prophesied the inevitable arrival of spring. That morning the sun was shining, warm but not yet suffocating. Peacocks spread their feathers like rainbows in the fields, undisturbed by the passers-by, some of whom stopped to snap photos.

But not Dámaso. Nor did he stop to feed the pigeons drinking from the Conchas fountain, despite the fact that in his hand he clutched a bag of breadcrumbs he'd purchased at the little kiosk by the east entrance.

Guzmán followed at a distance. Were it not for his constant turning to look behind him, Dámaso would have looked like what his appearance suggested — a retiree out taking a stroll on a Sunday morning, nothing to do but lose himself in nostalgia. Even his clothes seemed to confirm his harmlessness: light-coloured shirt buttoned to the neck, knitted cardigan, grey trousers belted tightly and worn too high, rubber-soled shoes, eyeglasses hanging from a string around his neck, thin white hair slicked back, straight sideburns, closely shaved chin. The picture of a venerable grandfather — maybe a slightly unsociable one, but harmless at any rate.

Seeing him walk into the public restrooms close to Caverna, an onlooker might think that maybe the man had prostate trouble, imagining that he went to the bathroom four, five, six times an hour, unable to squeeze out more than a few reddish drops with a grunt. A well-intentioned individual might have recommended he smoke less. He wheezed climbing the stairs to the restroom, his lungs like broken, leaky bellows. People on the steps who stood back to let him pass (Sunday mornings, people always try harder to be nice) might also have thought that the boy following him — no more than fifteen, covered in acne, wearing cartoonish glasses — was his grandson. Had anyone thought to compare them, they'd have realised that, quite obviously, any blood relation was improbable. The kid was too dark, his hair too curly, and his nose diametrically opposed to Dámaso's. But people don't think about these things when they see strangers. They don't picture their lives, don't ask questions about them. They have no reason to.

Guzmán, however, was asking a lot of questions. One after the other, and he didn't let them go. People in general didn't interest him. But the subject of one of his investigations did.

It hadn't been hard to verify a few things about the antiquarian. People aren't very careful with their past, especially if they think they're safe. All he'd had to do was phone a few old colleagues, people he knew from another time, another country — a country very different from the one he was in now. His old comrades from the Spanish police force, who'd had no qualms about coming to him when they wanted help fighting ETA refugees in Chile during the late Eighties, now tried to dodge him. They told him in no uncertain terms that they wanted nothing to do with him. They had become commissioners, police chiefs, deputies; they had a lot to lose and little inclination to lose it. They used bullshit excuses, hiding behind their families and careers, making guilt-ridden proclamations — *What we did back then was wrong* — to cover their fear. None of the arseholes who'd hung up on him had lost more than him, but still he feigned compassion, understanding.

He didn't want to bother them, hadn't emerged from the past to burst their piece-of-shit bubbles. All he wanted was a little information about a guy who didn't add up. *Why do you want to know?* they asked suspiciously. *Better not to ask; just keep up your charade,* was his reply. *Private matter.* He worked alone now. Most of them knew he'd been expelled from the directorate over the music-teacher incident, maybe they could even guess that he hadn't been allowed to leave Pinochet's police force with a simple pat on the back. They didn't want to know the details and looked away in horror when they saw his mangled hand. *You should see what's in my pants,* Guzmán thought.

One way or another, he'd managed to gather enough information about the respectable-looking old man now heading for the garden exit with the kid trailing close behind.

If people were more observant, they'd have wondered why Dámaso bought a bag of bird food that he was now tossing into the bin, leaving the winged vermin to fight over the crumbs. Maybe someone would have picked up on the way the old man's hand encircled the boy's waist, fingers dropping dangerously close to his buttocks. Guzmán had no idea if he was married or widowed, if he had children or grandkids, if he planned to retire to a little house in the mountains when his antiques business dried up. But he did know that Dámaso Berenguer was many other things, in addition to antiquarian, or at least had been at some point in his life: black-marketeer, forger, launderer of huge sums of money, and pederast.

That last one had gotten him into trouble with the law in the mid-nineties. In a bar one night, some customers had discovered him in the bathroom with a kid who, like the one now climbing into his car — a SEAT parked beside the fence — could have been his grandson. Except that his pants were down, and Dámaso was, quite literally, giving him an arse-licking. If the police hadn't gotten him out of there, shoving and clubbing their way through, the customers would have flayed him alive. He served six months of a sentence, which was reduced to a fine.

As he drove, following Dámaso's car into an industrial area on the outskirts of Madrid, he thought of the stars in the Atacama desert, of Candela's soft skin, slightly sour from sweat and lack of bathing, of the talks they'd had on a straw mattress on the floor of the cell where he was supposed to be interrogating her, not falling in love with her. *Do you have kids?* And her reply: *No. What's the point? I wouldn't want them to suffer in this piece-of-shit world.* She used the word *shit* a lot, and over the years Guzmán realised he'd picked it up and it had stuck — shit in his mouth and on his shoes.

As Dámaso's car turned, without signaling, at an exit for Las Cárdenas Industrial Park, he thought about Bosco and his men; how, despite the horror Guzmán had been subjected to, his boss hadn't wanted to kill him. He should have done it. If he had, he'd still be alive today; instead he had a widow and three orphans in Santiago. He could have witnessed the arrival of democracy, and a Spanish judge attempting to punish Pinochet while the ex-dictator paraded around the world pathetically feigning illness and senility. *Never leave things half-done*, Bosco used to say. And he was right. He'd found that out the night Guzmán showed up at his house and blew his brains out with a shotgun.

Dámaso parked the blue SEAT, with its bumper sticker on the back window (*Visit Cuenca!*), near an industrial unit. Behind the fence, a dog chained to a cement pylon barked, baring its sharp yellow teeth. Old man and boy got out and walked into the grounds. Dámaso had a key and unlocked a gate in the fence. The dog's barking became more frenzied as it jerked violently against the chain, straining to get at them. Guzmán was terrified of dogs; he froze in panic around them. It took all the courage he could muster to conquer his fear and, after a few minutes, finally force himself to get out of the car and jump the fence, Dámaso having locked the gate behind him. Pressing himself to the wall farthest from the dog, he approached the entrance, and the animal, despite its best efforts, was unable to reach him.

The unit looked empty. It must have been a warehouse, and there were still a few pallets with copper coils in one corner. Leaning against the wall was a large *FOR SALE* sign with the phone number of a real estate agent. An overhead crane spanned the entire ceiling, its hook hanging down in the middle from an enormous chain. There was dust and filth everywhere. On the right, a narrow staircase led up to a mezzanine with a prefab module that must have served as the firm's offices when the place was in business. Through the frosted glass he could make out the silhouettes of Dámaso and his companion.

Guzmán imagined what he'd find as he climbed the metallic stairs, not caring about the noise he made. Imagining is a way of predicting the future, both distant and immediate. He was unconcerned about the scene he was about to come upon. Or what would happen after that. Guzmán knew perfectly well. The future was his to invent.

The flimsy door was buckled and in disrepair. It was broken in a few places and had a hole that looked to have been caused by a blow, maybe a fist. As if someone had taken out their rage with a gesture that probably did nothing but bruise their knuckles. Maybe whoever did it had been a worker at the old factory, unceremoniously fired from one day to the next. Or maybe it was somebody Dámaso had taken there before.

242

The old man and the boy were pressed close together. Whatever it was they were doing seemed very private, just between the two of them, even though before Guzmán burst into the room they were alone and had nothing to hide or be ashamed of. Except maybe themselves. They both looked up at him in shock, and he found their expressions both tragic and comical. The kid didn't move. He simply pulled back from the old man a few centimetres, enough to reveal his right hand clutching Dámaso's pathetically erect penis. For a split second he held onto it, as though afraid it might fall into a void. For his part, the old man made a vague attempt to do up his zipper. A handkerchief stuck out of his back pocket; perhaps he'd been planning to wipe himself off when he finished.

'Get out of here, kid,' Guzmán ordered, and the boy hesitated for a moment, looking to Dámaso for some sort of direction, a reason to refuse. But the old man was pale as wax and staring at the floor. Finally the hired-hand left, carefully edging around Guzmán, who stood blocking almost the entire doorway with his body. They heard him race down the stairs as fast as he could.

Dámaso put up no resistance, didn't even try to justify himself. Didn't ask a single question, say a single word.

And yet still, Guzmán pulled an expandable baton from his pocket, whipped it through the air to assemble it, and whacked the old man on his right carotid, just between his jaw and clavicle. The blow was so violent that Dámaso collapsed like a sack of potatoes, unconscious. Guzmán could easily have managed without hitting him, at least at first, but he felt no regret. On his scale of values — a spiral staircase he climbed up and down as he saw fit — what he'd seen merited no compassion.

He opened his eyes for a second but then closed them right away. The light bothered him. He could smell wet clothes, and the leather jacket hung over the back of a chair; he could sense an umbrella dripping and a muffled drumming sound far above his head. It must be raining outside. He heard Guzmán's voice, very close to his face. His breath was sweet, like fruit-flavoured gum. Strawberry, maybe.

'How do you feel?'

Dámaso tried to sit up, but the pain in his neck stopped him.

'Easy, don't try to move or you'll hurt yourself,' Guzmán whispered, placing a hand on his chest.

Dámaso touched his head. He had a small cut on his brow and some bruises. But the worst thing was the buzzing in his brain, the intense pain in his neck. His heart was beating too quickly, wildly.

'You're dazed from the blow,' Guzmán said, guessing the old man's thoughts, approaching from behind, and placing an amicable hand on Dámaso's shoulder. The old man saw his singed hand and amputated little finger. Guzmán appeared truly relieved that nothing worse had happened. His eyes were direct, straightforward, honest; he smiled with his mouth open wide, like a child watching a Christmas parade. And yet, there was something sinister about the way he puffed out his chest as he breathed.

They were in the basement of Dámaso's storeroom, in his private theatre. Dámaso's heart skipped a beat when he realised that Guzmán had been carelessly rifling through tapes, handling rolls of film. The idiot didn't realise how valuable the items he was mishandling were. It seemed pointless to ask him what they were both doing there and how he'd found the place. And yet he did it anyway.

'You have no right to do this. What I do in my private life is my business. If you want to report me, go ahead. But you can't do this,' he protested.

Guzmán nodded. It was true, he had no right to do *this*. But that didn't change things. If anything, it clarified them. Having or lacking the right to do something, what was just or unjust, legal or illegal … All just words, abstract concepts that weren't much good at a time like this. He got a chair and dragged it over, sat backwards on it, arms resting on the back, facing Dámaso. For a full minute he said nothing. Just stared. He wanted to make the man feel the full fear of the wait. Make him wonder: What now? What's going to happen?

'Nice little set-up you got down here. This place is better-hidden than a nuclear fallout shelter. All this just to watch Charlie Chaplin videos with your little friends? Hard to believe, I got to say. Even more so knowing your record.'

'It's none of your business. Nothing illegal goes on here.'

'Seriously? Then why did you lie to me?'

Dámaso swallowed. If this man had been a police officer maybe he could have hoped for things to turn out for the better. But he wasn't, and that terrified him.

'This is for people who want to keep their privacy. I don't know who you are or what you're looking for, but you're making a very big mistake. You're going to find yourself in some serious trouble.'

Dámaso tried to sound confident, but his voice trembled. And his defiance collapsed entirely when Guzmán reached out a hand — that atrophied hunk of flesh and wrinkled skin — and removed Dámaso's glasses. Without the magnified lenses, his tiny little mouse eyes looked petrified.

'Don't get defensive, old man. I just want to talk. We can try to be civilised.'

'What do you want? Money? Are you trying to blackmail me? You're barking up the wrong tree. I don't have a single euro.'

'Don't be an idiot. I'm not here to talk about your sick little perversions. I couldn't care less who you're fucking up the arse. I've got questions, and I want answers. End of story. Very easy if you cooperate, so there's no need to resist. I don't like to see others suffer needlessly — I'm going soft in my old age, you know?'

'What questions?'

'First: the day Magnus Olsen killed himself, he got a phone call. There was a message on his answering machine. Were you the one who called him?'

'I told you, I hardly knew Olsen. I didn't call him.'

Guzmán flexed his shoulders and, before Dámaso had time to react, punched him in the mouth, splitting his lip and throwing him back in his chair, though Guzmán reached out an arm to steady him just in time. Strangely, he was quite gentle, as though Dámaso were a frail old man who'd stumbled in the street and he a kind soul who'd come to his aid. The effect was disconcerting.

'You're not taking the easy route, Dámaso. You're heading down a dead-end street. Don't worry about what you think I know. Don't try to gauge what you should or shouldn't say, what you think I want to hear. That's a very common mistake. Believe me, my friend. I've got a lot of experience. Focus on what you know and own up, give it up voluntarily or

245

I'll have to wrench it from you. Was the voice on the answering machine yours?'

Dámaso nodded slowly.

'Much better. Now, tell me about the recording you demanded to have back in that message. Thinking about the boy who was greasing your rod a little while ago, it occurs to me that it's probably not a Harold Lloyd flick, am I right?'

Dámaso didn't take his eyes off Guzmán's fist. He could taste the blood oozing through his gums, feel it filling the gaps between his teeth, making him gag.

'I'm a collector of *special* movies. Unique films that can't be found anywhere else. I repeat, nothing illegal. But what you're doing is a serious crime. Magnus Olsen was part of the film club; I lent him a very old movie and he was taking too long to return it, so I called to demand that he give it back.'

'You're lying.'

'I swear I'm telling you the truth.'

You couldn't say he didn't give the man a chance. He'd been fair, Guzmán thought. That was what Bosco had taught him: give those you interrogate the opportunity to behave like cowards, to betray themselves, their families, their friends, their flag, their hymns and countries, their ideals. You had to give them the opportunity to surrender privately, with no witnesses, and let them know that it was okay, that pain was a useless and unnecessary ordeal — since all is already lost before you've even begun.

Once the opportunity was gone, though, you had to crush them, reduce them to dust.

Guzmán stood slowly and walked over to a metal cabinet with a sliding door. It had half-a-dozen shelves lined with reels and rolls of film, in chronological and alphabetical order. He liked movies, especially American movies from the eighties and nineties. He wasn't too demanding: Kevin Costner, Tom Cruise, Michael Douglas. People said Hollywood was commercial rubbish. But he enjoyed going to the movies, eating popcorn. He told Candela that once, in the cell, after he kissed her, when her lips were healing from the first beating she'd received on arrival at the makeshift prison. She'd never surrendered — he had.

She laughed when he confessed that he loved *Waterland* and *Top Gun*.

Candela's laugh was as wide as her mouth, and she had a slight gap between her two front teeth. He'd always imagined that kind of laugh for the protagonist of *Rayuela*, though he didn't know why. Candela laughed silently so the guards wouldn't hear and come to steal her happiness, her few drops of happiness. Guzmán was a little hurt that she'd laughed at his taste in movies, but it didn't keep him from smiling, or from thinking that she laughed like Julio Cortázar's protagonist.

'Are these the movies you're talking about?' he asked Dámaso. He had his hands on a roll of film — the original *J'accuse*. Guzmán didn't know it, but the film was priceless. It contained, in addition to the film footage itself, cuts that the French director Abel Gance had edited out. Guzmán had no idea the film was from 1919, but when he saw Dámaso's expression of horror, saw him writhing in his chair, frantic, he knew he'd hit the mark.

'Be careful with those reels, please. They're very fragile.'

Children are fragile, hopes are fragile, clouds are made of cotton. Life is a fragile balance, easily broken. Books are burned, words go up in flames, thought Guzmán. He opened the case and shredded the film. Next came *La Roue* and *Napoléon*, also by Gance. Without a trace of sorrow, in a single minute he destroyed the very films that had put France at the top of the silent film world.

In a moment of daring, desperation and idiocy (the essence of bravery) Dámaso leapt from his chair and tried to stop him, begging and crying the tears of a man witnessing the end of his world. An incomprehensible tragedy for him, a man who felt nothing at the loss of a child's innocence.

'Please, please, stop. Those are irreplaceable,' Dámaso pleaded, trying to snatch a reel from his hand.

Guzmán gave him a look of disdain, his eyes floating down over the old man like mist from the hills.

Bosco's grandfather had been Italian, a devout fascist, though more given to Hitler than to Mussolini, whom he always accused of being *too* Italian. He preferred the objective efficacy of the Germans. The venerable-looking old man once explained to his grandson that his commander in the Waffen-SS used to weep while listening to Wagner, as his men set their dogs on ragtag lines of Jews crammed into the station, waiting to be sent to extermination camps. Recalling this, the old man had cried.

Guzmán pushed Dámaso away effortlessly with a kick to the stomach. The antiquarian's mouth gasped open and closed like a dying fish.

'You're trying my patience. I can keep this up, and I will. I'll burn this whole place down with you inside it if you insist on wasting my time.'

Dámaso spat out a clot of blood. He was having trouble breathing.

'What was the film you were demanding from Olsen? Don't hold back — answer my question. I'm not going to judge you. It's simple curiosity. Don't try to justify it, we all have reasons for doing what we do or don't do.'

Guzmán thought of ripping the man's tongue out with a pair of pliers and smiled. But he decided not to, and nor did he wipe the smile off his face. The bastard would be no good to him mute.

'You've got a nice little collection here, old man. I bet it took you half your life to build it up. And now you see how easily all those years' effort can vanish.'

Dámaso closed his eyes. He was wheezing loudly, curled up on one side in the foetal position, blood and slobber puddling beneath his mouth. A brown stain appeared on his trousers: he'd shat in his pants. Holding out one arm, he pointed to the screen in front of the rows of theatre seats.

'There, behind the false wall,' he struggled to say.

At first glance, there looked to be nothing behind the screen but a low wall. But when he touched it, Guzmán saw it was a hollow plasterboard panel. On the right, half a metre from the ground, was a small, barely visible crack. Guzmán pushed and it gave way, revealing a wall-safe, which was built-in and quite sophisticated — two locks and a digital keypad.

'What do you keep in there, the original Ebola strain?'

The old man removed a key from his pocket; the other one he indicated was beneath a light socket. Guzmán slipped them both in and twisted the two locks simultaneously, then punched in a code — three letters and four numbers. The safe opened.

'You have no idea what you're doing,' Dámaso murmured, wiping his mouth with the back of his hand.

Guzmán went to the safe and casually shoved Dámaso aside. He was never afraid to walk through an open door, never worried about what he might find on the other side. Nothing could be worse than what he'd already left behind.

Inside the safe he found several dozen protective black cases, resembling book covers. Each had a sticker on the spine with a date and two letters with a dot between them. Guzmán bet that it was Dámaso's writing, and that the letters were people's initials. He opened a few of the cases; each contained a compact disc bearing the same dates and initials as those on the case.

'What are these?'

'Pornographic movies — *very* graphic.'

Guzmán understood.

'And I bet they belong to the members of your film club. And I'll wager my one good hand that they appear in some compromising positions. So what is it, child pornography? Bestiality? S & M?'

The old man gave him a grief-stricken look and said nothing. Guzmán nodded with feigned satisfaction. *Nothing new about this*, he thought to himself. *It's all been done before. Perversion becomes tedious with repetition. The rich can't be original even when they're acting like total degenerates. I can just picture them all gathered here, sitting in their theatre seats, staring at the screen, smoking cigars and jacking off, laughing, making crude comments.* Or was that not how it was? Did they maybe bring some intellectual slant to? Did they discuss angles, focus, lighting, performance?

'I imagine they paid a real fortune to see your films. Must be very rich people.'

Dámaso glowered.

'They didn't just watch the movies. Some of them paid a lot of money to take part in them. People you can't even begin to imagine. People who'd do anything necessary to keep this from coming to light.'

Guzmán gazed at the old man carefully. He knew some people might have felt alarmed by Dámaso's enraged expression, which was all bluster. But Guzmán felt nothing. He thrived on violence, saw it as his only possible path. There was nothing Dámaso or his powerful friends could do to him or take from him that hadn't been done or taken already.

'Is that what happened to Magnus Olsen? You and your little gang killed him?'

'I have no idea what you're talking about.'

Guzmán sighed deeply. His patience was wearing thin.

Slowly, he removed his leather belt. It had a large buckle. He yanked it hard at both ends, then wound it several times around his knuckles and cracked it like a whip. Before the old man had time to realise what he was going to do, Guzmán leapt and wrapped the belt around his neck, jerking it hard.

'It's terrible, when you can't breathe,' he whispered into his ear, pulling the old man's neck toward his shoulder, suffocating him. Dámaso grunted and struggled to free himself. 'Your lungs struggle to expand, searching desperately for relief, any tiny air bubble, anything to keep pumping oxygen. You could die at any moment, but your brain keeps working. You're able to respond to questions. All I have to do is very slightly reduce the pressure and let a tiny bit of air in, just enough for you to articulate an answer. That's what I think happened to Olsen, except whoever did it miscalculated and suffocated him. Then they tried to cover it up, did a poor job trying to make it look like suicide. But the police bought it. The police will believe anything, as long as it's remotely conceivable.'

Guzmán let up on the pressure, loosening the belt around the old man's neck. He let him cough and hungrily open his mouth, sucking in air, filling his lungs. Dámaso's eyes were watering and he spat repeatedly.

'The thugs you sent were so incompetent they didn't even delete the message.'

Dámaso massaged his neck. His wrinkled, flaccid skin had turned red and would soon be bruised. His eyes were popping out like a toad that's been run over by a truck. But still he refused to speak. Or perhaps his larynx was damaged. Guzmán wagged his head, looking resigned. He pulled out a switchblade and flicked it open. The blade, long and thin as a stylus, pointed at the old man's face like an accusatory finger.

'You won't be able to take it, old man. You won't last two minutes, not with what I'm about to do to you. Besides, what's the point? You're going to end up telling me what I want to know anyway and then you'll die here, alone, like a dog in your own shit.'

Dámaso pawed at the air, trying to protect his face.

'Olsen made a lot of money for us, it's true, and he earned a lot of money, too, but he also made important contacts who helped his business. He had access to the safe, to the books where the clients' personal details were kept — their real ones. The names on the tapes are pseudonyms, for obvious reasons. We didn't realise he was stealing from us until it was too late. He'd copy the tapes and then blackmail the people. Some paid him off, others placed him in positions that were useful for his *shady dealings*. But he misjudged the last man he blackmailed. I tried to make him see reason when I realised what he was doing — that's why I called that day. But it was too late. I don't know the details of what happened, and I don't want to. But there's one thing I'm sure of: I didn't kill him and no one in the club had him killed. Most of them didn't even know what was going on. If they'd even suspected it, that would have put my safety at great risk, don't you see?'

Guzmán examined the safe carefully.

'Which tapes did he copy?'

'Dozens, maybe. I never found out exactly. After his death, the club was dissolved and all the material was destroyed.'

Guzmán raised one eyebrow, pointing to the tapes in the safe.

'Those were the most important ones, the most compromising. I've never used them, but I need the people implicated to believe I could. If they didn't, I'd have been killed a long time ago. Those recordings are my guarantee of a peaceful retirement.'

'The last tape Olsen stole, was it from your top collection?'

Dámaso grew even paler, if that were possible. Tiny blue veins appeared below his eyes, like roots with no place to take hold. The faltering affirmation that came from his lips was barely audible.

'Who was on the tape? I'm willing to wager you've got a backup copy somewhere.'

For the first time, Dámaso regained control of himself. He let out a very weak laugh that slowly grew in intensity, becoming a horrific, evil cackle.

'You have no idea what you're looking for, do you? You got this far on intuition, but now you're like a blind man who's lost his cane.'

Guzmán pounced, grabbed the old man by the throat with one hand, and with the other pummelled Dámaso's face one, two, three times until he heard his septum shatter.

When he let go, the old man was no longer laughing.

'You're going to tell this blind man everything. You're going to be my guiding light, and then maybe, when I'm done with you, I'll decide to let your heart keep beating in that sick little chest of yours.'

251

On his way out of the building, Guzmán was sweating. He used his handkerchief to wipe the blood splatters from his shirt, panting. Every instinct he had told him to get in a taxi and head straight to the airport, without even stopping at his hotel — to forget about the money Diana had promised, the money Arthur owed him. He could fly to Santiago, Buenos Aires, Lima, or any other place, and hide out for the next few months.

But Guzmán only listened to his instincts when they served his purposes. Ever since he was a kid, he couldn't stand leaving crossword puzzles unfinished, riddles unsolved. But what pissed him off the most — back at school, and now on the street — was the idea that somebody was taking him for a fool, that anybody thought they could pull one over on him with no consequences.

He hailed a taxi, but he didn't go to the airport.

15

The bank manager welcomed Arthur fawningly, like a servant. As though three long years hadn't passed since Arthur had last shown his face at the bank; as if the manager were unaware of the reason for his absence. Arthur asked for access to his safe deposit box and to be left alone.

That was where he stored those things he could never allow to be associated with him: fake passports of various nationalities, so well done they were impossible to detect without exhaustive checks; cash — in dollars, euros and yuan — that was unaccounted for in any financial ledger; documents for savings accounts held in places that were lenient on fraud and tax evasion; records of industrial espionage and shell companies; tax avoidance schemes that Diana had been setting up for him for years, schemes whose plans were so intricate and complex that no tax inspector could ever unravel them without help. There was also an HK semiautomatic — and two loaded clips — for which he held no licence.

But what he picked up now was the envelope at the bottom of the box. In it was a CD. He felt its weight in his hand and his fingers trembled, as though it were heavy as an anvil and he could hardly hold it up.

When he got back to his office, Arthur sat down in front of his computer. On the screen, images flickered in the dark, their silhouettes reflecting on Arthur's intent face.

At first there was nothing but a brick wall. Toward the bottom of it, at ground level, was a ring of soot and the remains of something that had recently been burned — it looked to be a couple of broken chairs, a bookshelf and two blackened smoking doors. It was hard to make out any details — the recording was poor quality and the camera was jiggling too much, never stopping long enough to focus on anything. The cameraman's shadow was cast on the wall and you could hear his breathing, as well as a dull white noise coming from above, as though maybe it were raining. The smell must have been nauseating because the cameraman kept raising a handkerchief to his face to cover his mouth. The ground was littered with needles and a blackened spoon.

Next, a shirtless man came into view from the right, haggard, his chest hair grey, his face covered, dragging his feet. He made his way to a cassette player and turned it on.

'Is this the music you want?' His voice was guttural, his accent hard to place.

Who can say where the road goes
Where the day flows?
Only time …
and who can say if your love grows,
as your heart chose?
Only time …

Then the camera panned one hundred and eighty degrees. Whoever was choreographing the sinister scene remained off-camera, smoking in the shadows, the tip of a cigarette glowing in the dark. He pointed, indicating where the camera should focus. Nobody spoke. The only sounds were the music, the rain, and the scratchy sound of the cameraman's hand bumping against the mike.

Then the camera shifted its focus toward a corner.

Arthur paused there, freezing the image.

It was her. His daughter. Aroha. She smiled at the camera and waved, as if this were a home movie.

Arthur leaned forward, pressing his feet into the floor even though the whole room seemed to have vaporised around him. He examined his daughter's face in the grainy image, her imperfect, unfocused profile in the dim and murky light. Just a few months before then, she'd come back from Geneva and things seemed to have been going better. School was going well again, she seemed to be getting her life together — classes at the Lycée Français, horseback riding, friends in their neighbourhood subdivision. The typical, placid rich-girl existence. He recognised each of the freckles under her eyes and on her nostrils, which would flare when she laughed.

He hit play again.

She wasn't laughing now.

Now, the camera had zoomed in on Aroha's face. She looked emaciated, her hair was dirty. She didn't like having the lens that close and was trying to cover herself with a hand; that didn't work, so she crawled away like a baby, disconcerted, her movements plodding, awkward, lethargic. Her pants were unzipped and the triangle of her panties poked out. Black bra straps were showing, too, sticking out from her sleeveless T-shirt. She'd lost a tennis shoe, or maybe she'd taken it off and now couldn't find it to put back on.

'Stop it. Come on, stop that shit.' Her voice was thick and sticky, like a piece of gum you can't get off the bottom of your shoe and that stretches longer and longer, becoming ropey, tangled, twisted, incomprehensible. She was high. She'd shot up — maybe her inner thigh, which might explain why her zipper was down. Or maybe on the sole of her foot, which would explain the missing shoe. Any unexpected place, which would hide the track marks, so her parents wouldn't see. Fathers stop looking at certain parts of their daughter's bodies after a certain age. If the door is accidentally open and they see them in their underwear, they turn away in shame, stammering excuses. Mothers are different. Mothers know.

'Say something to the camera,' the voice behind the lens hissed.

'What do you want me to say?'

'Tell them you're going to be a little late to your riding class,' someone else said, emerging slowly from the shadowy corner and standing in front of her. He, too, wore a ski mask.

'Okay, enough of this shit. I want to go home now,' Aroha was becoming alarmed, fearful, dragging herself toward a filthy corner.

'Not yet. First we're going to play a little game. Like the other times.'

Aroha was a moving target. The camera followed her across the ground to where she'd pressed her back to the wall. Suddenly the recording juddered involuntarily, the shot changed. Then it went dark.

When it came back on, the camera was focused on a lopsided bedframe on the ground. Aroha's hands and feet were tied to it with twisted wire. Her naked body curved to the side, but she wasn't putting up a fight, wasn't struggling to free herself from the wire bonds. Her expression was lax, her arms and legs shiny in the artificial light of the camera. Her limbs looked almost polished, surreal, like a porcelain doll. The guy with the hairy chest was kneeling beside Aroha's head, stroking her sweaty hair with almost freakish tenderness. Arthur could have sworn his fingers were trembling as he stroked her cheek. But maybe it was the cameraman's hand shaking. The man glanced furtively at the camera, as though awaiting an order.

'Do it,' the other ski-masked figure said from off-screen.

The first one climbed on top of her and began simulating having sex with Aroha. At first, she seemed to experience nothing but mild displeasure. She looked at the camera and murmured something Arthur couldn't make out, since she was stammering. She sounded transfixed, her voice had an almost liquid hiss about it, like a fountain, or a leaky tap. Her pupils were dull, but little by little her confusion and irritation settled into resigned acceptance. It was clear that Aroha had been through this before, and not by force. But now, it was all going too far.

The other man pushed the old guy aside.

'Not like that. I'll show you.'

He unzipped his fashionably-ripped designer jeans and bent over her, the slender, delicate fingers of his right hand walloping her with a violent slap.

Seeing her image in freeze-frame for a moment, Arthur's throat ran dry and he felt as if he'd swallowed an enormous dragonfly that was now fluttering against his trachea, trying to get out.

'You've got to be violent. If you want it to look real, it's got to *be* real.'

In a flash of lucidity, Aroha realised what they were going to do. She shook her head from side to side in a cold, near-passive, drug-induced desperation.

'What are you doing? Stop. Stop it. You're hurting me.'

But he didn't stop. He picked up a stick that looked like a policeman's baton. Aroha opened her mouth wide and howled as loud as she could as it entered her vagina.

'Close your eyes,' Arthur whispered, his voice breaking, eyes stinging with tears.

It was absurd. Everything he was seeing had already happened. But by hitting play he felt like it was occurring all over again, and he wanted so badly for Aroha to close her eyes. Soon it would all be over. Everything would be forgotten. Even her unspeakable suffering.

The music blared, drowning out his daughter's cries, as the man's back filled the camera lens.

Who can say where the road goes
Where the day flows?

Only time ...
and who can say if your love grows,
as your heart chose?
Only time ...

Arthur shut his computer down but his pupils remained glued to the screen. There was something feverish, delirious in his look. The terror was reflected in his mouth, which hung open unevenly, as though he were on the verge of shouting and yet frozen, keening silently. Two fat tears, round and perfect, slid down his cheeks. It took him a minute to notice the shadow that was being cast on the screen. It wasn't coming from inside, but from behind him. Slowly, he turned and saw Guzmán, haloed in lamplight, his silhouette backlit. He didn't bother to ask the man how long he'd been standing there.

It was obvious that he'd been there awhile.

They stared at each other in silence for a few seconds, and then Guzmán walked over to the huge window overlooking Madrid. The tiny people down below, in the distance, were like little robots that couldn't decide which way to go, what to do. The muddy colours on the street contrasted with the orange, lemon, and wine-coloured clouds floating above the skyscrapers' roofs.

Arthur, still seated at this desk, could be seen reflected in the huge windows, his image superimposed over Guzmán's. That was the closest the two of them would ever get, Guzmán thought, and he couldn't say he was sorry about it. Two silhouettes, reflected as one on a pane of glass.

'I once had an instructor at the directorate, a real professional, a guy who taught interrogation techniques, and for some reason, he liked me — people like us have unusual proclivities. One of the things he believed was that feigning ignorance is a form of intelligence. You have to start from zero, he'd say, take nothing for granted, pretend you know nothing, erase what you *think* you know in order to find out what you *need* to know. Otherwise, preconceived notions will trick you, deflect your attention from the obvious. If he could see me now, here, with you, he'd give me hell, tell me I was being an idiot. And he'd be right.'

Guzmán glanced sidelong at Arthur. The man looked awful. He could imagine the devastating effect it had had on him, watching a video of his daughter being raped. He wondered how many times he'd watched it, and what kind of self-inflicted torture he went through every time he did.

'You should have told me about that video, don't you think?'

Arthur stared off into space, his lips slack, his mouth half-open, eyes wide and shiny. Guzmán walked over to a collection of porcelain figurines — a group of musicians playing instruments — and touched them.

'It was Olsen, wasn't it? He tried to blackmail you. And you killed him.'

Arthur gave him a snide look, full of hate.

'For someone so smart, you don't have a fucking clue.'

Magnus Olsen had been no one in Arthur's life, until one ordinary rainy day in late 2000. Arthur recalled having shaken the man's limp hand on one occasion, when his American subsidiary was looking for backing from some venture capitalists that belonged to a consortium Olsen represented. The guy looked like a scared puppy and was perspiring, which suggested he was afraid of getting caught in a lie. Olsen appeared surprisingly vulgar and had no visible appeal, despite sporting a gold watch and a very attractive wife.

Olsen spent the whole meeting staring at Arthur, his face red with swollen veins. Arthur could remember the man's tie — flopping awkwardly over his open shirt — and his malt whisky breath. At some point, Olsen managed to lead Arthur away from the others and into a corner. His Spanish was peculiar. He held onto each syllable before releasing it like a bubble. At first he inquired politely about Aroha. The question made Arthur uncomfortable but didn't surprise him. His daughter's repeated disappearances and run-ins made for popular gossip, and not just in the tabloid news — in the business world, too. Arthur thought Olsen was trying to ingratiate himself, earn his confidence for future deals, so he attempted to blow him off with a few nominally civil words.

'I hear your daughter disappeared a week ago.'

'The police are on it.'

'Let's hope it's just another one of her little escapades.'

Two days later, Olsen phoned him at the office. He sounded incredibly nervous and pressured Arthur to meet him in Madrid, someplace discreet. Arthur tried to give him the brush-off, but Olsen cut him off, saying he had valuable information — regarding Aroha's whereabouts. Before hanging up, he warned Arthur not to go to the police, under any circumstances.

Arthur didn't breathe a word about it to Andrea. He didn't want to upset her. His wife was hardly even getting out of bed anymore, instead just popping pills and waiting for the phone to ring. Besides, he'd had about all he could take of people contacting him in the hopes of earning some cash for tips that always turned out to be dead ends.

He did, however, talk it over with Diana, who at the time was living in an apartment they secretly shared in the chic Salamanca district.

'You should go to the police,' was her advice. 'I know Olsen. He'll try to get you embroiled in something for sure.'

But Arthur hadn't listened.

They arranged to meet on the outskirts of Madrid, on the road to Extremadura. Olsen was waiting for him inside his car, parked behind a service station. There were trucks parked at an angle, hiding him from view, but Olsen still looked uneasy. Before opening the passenger door to let Arthur in, he glanced around to make sure no one was spying on them. It was clear that his nerves were shot and he hadn't gotten much sleep.

'So, what was it you had to tell me?'

Olsen launched into a sorry tale full of debt, jail threats, and creditors making his life impossible. Arthur already knew part of the backstory — it had made the financial news. For weeks they'd been publishing the gossip, either real or invented: his wife and children's reactions, the scandal it had all caused at the firm, and all sorts of conjecture about a hidden, sordid private life. Hundreds of investors had put their trust in Magnus Olsen — and hundreds of thousands had, in turn, handed over their assets to the *investors'* companies, placing their and their families' futures in his hands. And he'd failed them. The market had taken a nosedive, and now lots of people were left hanging out to dry.

But none of that concerned Arthur. He spent ten minutes listening to Olsen's whining, his sundry excuses and his ludicrous plans to re-launch his businesses. By the time he mentioned needing money — lots of money — Arthur realised that coming had been a waste of time. The guy was a con artist who would just get Arthur tangled up in his web.

'If you've got financial problems, talk to Diana — or to Rueda, my secretary. Set up a formal meeting, and don't waste my time.'

He was about to get out of the car when Olsen grabbed his forearm forcefully.

'I know where your daughter is,' he said, sounding desperate, staring into his eyes with the intensity of a madman.

Arthur gazed at him uncomprehendingly. Olsen was rubbing his hands together as though he'd broken out in hives. His face was red, and despite it not being at all warm inside the car, rings of sweat were visible around his neckline and armpits.

'Your daughter is in grave danger, Arthur. And I can help you. I know where she is, but by tomorrow they might have already moved her someplace else.'

Arthur tightened his jaw, grabbed him by the grimy lapels of his jacket and shook him hard.

'What do you mean?'

Olsen swore that just by having met with Arthur, he was putting himself and his family at great risk, but he needed money. Lots of money, he said.

'Call me tomorrow, and have a bank transfer ready to go. I'll send you a code and an account number. When I get confirmation of the deposit, you'll get an email from an internet café containing the details of your daughter's whereabouts. And after that you won't see me again.'

This, Arthur suddenly realised, was actually full-on blackmail. He let go of the man.

'Have you lost your mind?'

'I'm afraid not, Arthur.'

Arthur felt his vision clouding over and a burning in his stomach shot up his throat like a ball of fire. Losing control, he punched Olsen in the face, hard.

'You son of a bitch! You tell me where my daughter is this second or I'll beat the ever-loving life out of you.'

Olsen dodged Arthur's fists as best he could. He opened the car door and managed to get half his body out. His bottom lip was split, his shirt covered in blood.

'Stop it. Stop it right now — if you ever want to see your daughter again,' he jabbered as Arthur beat him.

A flash of insight checked Arthur's rage. No matter how badly he wanted to rip that sick fuck to shreds, he realised that, at least for now, he was at the man's mercy. He stopped pummelling him and tried to calm down.

'I'm going to the police.'

Olsen was trying to straighten out his clothes. He opened the glove compartment and took out a little packet of Kleenex.

'No, you're not. The people who have your daughter would find out immediately and get rid of her. The cops would never find her. Believe me, I know what I'm talking about,' he said, gingerly wiping the blood from his lip.

'Did they kidnap her? What did you do to my little girl?' His voice was imploring, but Olsen wouldn't give in. At Arthur's temporary show of weakness, Olsen smiled faintly and looked rather smug.

'Tomorrow. Don't forget. Now get out of my car,' he said, before starting his engine.

When he got home, Arthur debated possibilities, over and over again. His first instinct was to go to the police, but he discarded that option almost immediately. This was the first decent clue as to Aroha's whereabouts he'd had in weeks, and he wasn't about to let it slip away. He went to the bank, got access to his safe deposit box, and took out part of the money Olsen was demanding — as well as the unlicensed HK pistol, which he slipped into his belt. One way or another he was going to get the information he needed. If he had to flay the man alive, or blow his brains out, so be it.

The next morning, Arthur sat down by the computer to wait, but he received no email. He waited for hours, until it started to get dark. And then he accepted the fact that the email wasn't going to come. On the way home, he listened to the news on the radio: Magnus Olsen had committed suicide. His wife and children had found him hanging in their living room.

Arthur parked on the shoulder and thumped the steering wheel with his fist, cursing. The only hope he had had of finding Aroha had just vanished.

'Two weeks later I got an envelope.' There had been nothing special about it, no stamp, no return address, just his name written in block letters. Inside was a clear plastic case with a CD, and a note.

Arthur showed Guzmán the handwritten note:

261

This video was made by Magnus Olsen; he's the man behind the camera. If anyone knows where your daughter is, it's him, or one of the other people in the video. I'm sorry I can't give you more help than that. I hope it's not too late.

'So, I didn't kill Magnus Olsen. And he wasn't the one who gave me the CD. I don't know where it came from. I've spent four years trying to figure out who sent it, but I still don't know. Spending the last three years in jail has made it all a little harder. That's why Diana hired you.'

'Why didn't you tell me that right from the start?'

Arthur made a fist and pursed his lips, just for a split second. And then he regained his usual composure, putting on his slightly melancholic mask once more.

'After I saw the video I realised that would be impossible. Olsen's death closed off that option. I'd automatically have been considered a suspect. Plus, Andrea would have ended up finding out what they were doing to Aroha, and it would have killed her. That's why I've concealed the tape's existence for the past four years.'

Guzmán poured himself a snifter of whisky without bothering to ask permission, and shook his head.

'That wasn't your only reason, was it? There's another one, a more powerful reason.'

It had dawned on Guzmán when he saw the tape. Dámaso had done everything he could to keep from telling him where it was hidden. But everything he could hadn't been enough. At first, Guzmán thought the old man's iron will stemmed from the fact that he was actually the one in the tape pretending to rape Aroha. But when he saw the whole of it, he realised that in fact the old man was trying to hide something else.

'You already knew, when you hired me, who the three guys in the video were.'

He eyed Arthur, sitting there at his desk. He was very still, not making a sound, gazing at the wall. His dishevelled red hair fell over his forehead, and he was breathing softly, the way a dying man does just before his last gasp.

It took him weeks to ascertain the identity of the man in the video. He watched the sickening recording again and again in search of a sign, anything that might provide a clue as to where they were, or who the people doing that to his daughter might be. In the end he concluded that the scene had not been authentically violent or unanticipated, had not been as chaotic and horrifically brutal as it appeared. Instead it had been staged, and had 'artistic' aspirations. To call them artistic was repulsive, of course, but that was the aim. It wasn't just a porn flick staring a young girl. And it wasn't exactly a snuff film, full of blood and gore. It was much more than that — or at least it was trying to be. In a sense it was a testament, a declaration of intentions, a horrifying insight into someone's world, someone who despite being forced to remain anonymous, was seeking some kind of recognition. It was the work of an expert, the work of someone who had inside knowledge about motion pictures.

He watched it dozens of times, and finally he realised something. At one point, when Aroha was being tortured, she looked into one of the masked man's eyes and murmured something, begging. She knew him. She trusted him.

Arthur watched her lips over and over, until finally he could decipher what she was saying: 'I want my mother. Ian, please. I want to go back to my mother's.'

'It didn't take long for me to find out that while Aroha was at the institute in Geneva, there was a kid named Ian there with her. His father was film director Ian Mackenzie and his mother was famous, too — a renowned violinist.'

Arthur had found out where Ian lived and went to the house, in a leafy Madrid suburb, in a very high-end housing development. He hadn't been able to get into the complex, though, with all the security. Instead, a mannish-looking woman had come to the guard booth. She said she was the housekeeper. She informed him that the woman he was looking for was on a European concert tour with the Budapest Orchestra. She'd be gone for months, maybe even a year.

Arthur was frustrated, but undeterred. And he knew it would be stupid to ask directly about the boy. Over the next few days, he found out everything he could about the kid: where he was studying the cinematic arts, who he hung out with, where he went and when.

One afternoon he followed Ian to a wooded area outside Madrid.

A dirty, grubby place where families from the suburbs went for daytrips, laden down with picnic baskets, folding chairs and playing cards, blankets on which they took uncomfortable siestas on the pine needles after stuffing their faces with every pig part known to man. In the late afternoon, as it started to get dark over the brightly illuminated radio towers in the distance, the families took off and left the woods to the Senegalese prostitutes, North African and Romanian rentboys, small-time dealers, and a random and motley assortment of night owls who all looked like they'd seen better days. As soon as it was dark enough, a long line of headlights began parading slowly past that circus of misery, seeking out their vice of choice.

Ian looked at home in that environment. Sometimes he'd roll down his car window to chat with an ageing prostitute, other times he'd buy drugs from some dealer, exchanging a friendly hug. One time Arthur saw him emerge from the bushes pulling up his pants. His face was scratched up and he wore an immensely satisfied expression. Whistling, he'd gotten into his car, lighting a cigarette, and had sat there for a minute leaning back against his seat, listening to the song playing on his stereo.

After Ian drove off, Arthur walked down to see what was behind those bushes. What he found was a girl. Little more than a child, actually, thirteen or fourteen, slightly younger than Aroha. She sat there hugging her legs, arms covered in scratches. Her head hung between her knees and she was sobbing like the child she was. Clearly, her low-cut, bone-coloured blouse and tight leather pants were designed to make her look older, as was the excessive make-up, which was now running down her face with her tears. The padded bra was no doubt for the same effect, although it now lay beside her on the ground along with a pair of stilettos, one of which had a broken heel.

Arthur asked her what had happened. The girl glanced up at him. Her face was grotesque — fake eyelashes dangled crookedly off the corner of her right eye, while her left eye was purple and swollen nearly shut, getting bigger by the second.

She wiped her nose on a forearm, sniffled, and told him she was fine. It didn't look that way to Arthur, so he told her he was going to call the police and an ambulance. She flat-out refused, and then began explaining that Ian was her boyfriend. He made her do strange things, like come to the park and let strangers do all kinds of things to her while he hid in the bushes and secretly filmed it all. And she went along with it to please him, because she loved him.

'Love? How can you say that? How old are you? Fourteen? Fifteen?'

Was that what Ian had done to his daughter, too? Had he stolen her childhood, her innocence, and made her believe he loved her?

'At least let me take you home. Your parents must be worried sick.'

The girl didn't seem convinced. It was as if there were two sides of her — one that wanted to go back to being a little girl, comforted by her family; the other preferring to be sucked in by that violent monster, trapped in his tentacles. And the two sides were at war. Finally she made a face, like the one Aroha used to make at the Feria de San Isidro biting into her candy apple because she lacked the patience to lick the crunchy coating until it went soft.

'I'll suck you off if you want, and you can just forget you ever saw me.'

Arthur would never forget the look of hatred she shot him when, despite her screaming and struggling, he handed her over to the cops at the nearest police station.

And then he decided that enough was enough.

The next morning it rained torrentially. From the window of the bar where Arthur sat, the street and clothing store on the corner were blurry in the downpour. In his head, he replayed the scene from the night before, endlessly — the girl with her eyelashes hanging off, her emaciated face, her look of hatred. The images jumbled together with those of Aroha in the video. He felt like his head was going to explode, and his chest was so tight he was having trouble breathing.

As soon as he saw Ian leave the corner shop, Arthur dropped a bill onto the table and strode out to confront him. Ian was walking toward him, completely unaware, his head protected from the rain by the hood of a camouflage sweatshirt, and he wore a leather pack strapped across his chest. He looked like a good kid, like any other kid. But that carefree, innocent-looking bastard had his daughter.

'I know who you are,' he said, stepping out into his path and pressing a hand into his chest.

Ian gave him a perplexed look. Not one of surprise, or fear, or doubt. Perplexed, as if the hand on his chest were a bug, an insect that had just fallen from the roof and landed on his sweatshirt.

'I'm Aroha's father. I've seen the tape. And you're going to tell me where my daughter is right now.'

From up close the kid's expression was glassy. Vague and unreadable.

'I have no idea what you're talking about.'

He didn't move a muscle — not even a twitch — his features betrayed nothing. Nothing but a quick blink from the raindrops in his eyebrows and lashes.

Arthur took a deep breath. *Breathe. Breathe,* he told himself. *Stay in control, or you'll lose everything.* If Ian had ever had a heart, it was now dead and buried. That's what he saw in the boy's eyes, after he turned to the street and then looked back at Arthur.

'I don't know anyone named Aroha.'

Arthur clenched his knuckles, full of rage. He wrapped his hands around the kid's neck and slammed him into the store's shutters. The impact sent the water that had been pooling on the awning crashing down on them.

'I'll kill you here and now if you don't tell me where she is, you little fucker.'

Ian looked totally undaunted. He gazed into Arthur's eyes. And then Arthur felt the cold metal of a small .22-calibre pistol against his neck. He heard Ian cock it right beside his ear.

'Let. Me. Go. Now,' the kid said, still unruffled.

Arthur released the pressure on Ian's neck but still kept hold of him. Ian himself stepped back, turning his head side to side like a boxer, before slipping the weapon back into the pocket of his sweatshirt.

'Did you think you were going to catch me off guard? You've been following me for days. Asking about me, my mother, my father. You even took one of my girls to the cops. No skin off my back, though; she's already run away again — came running back to me like they all do. Like your daughter did.'

'I'll kill you, you son of a bitch. I will.'

Ian began to laugh. It was an innocent laugh, clean and pure as a baby being baptised.

'Maybe she's already dead and buried. And you'd never find her body. You'd have no place to mourn her death. Or maybe she's still alive and

266

wondering which is better, life with you or what I offer her. You'd have to live with that.'

'I'll rip that smile off your face. I know how to make it last, and make it hurt.'

'Maybe,' Ian acknowledged. His gaze was cold and distant, like the reflection of a frozen river. And then he sauntered off as if nothing had happened, as if he and a random passer-by had just accidentally bumped into one another.

Arthur stood there on the sidewalk watching Ian's back, his camouflage sweatshirt, the leather bag strapped diagonally across it. He watched him blend into the crowd like everybody else, anonymous, as though his backstory was of no interest to anyone. When Arthur finally reacted, Ian had already disappeared and he was drenched. Rain was falling on his red hair, now a muddy brown, bouncing off his head into a thousand tiny droplets. People regarded him as though he were insane.

He began to walk very slowly, as if he'd been given some sort of paralysis-inducing drug that had numbed his legs. As if he were walking in a thick, foggy dream. He got into his car and for several minutes watched the rain beat down on his misty front windshield. Under his seat was a flask, a gift from his employees for his fortieth birthday. He hadn't touched a drop of liquor in fourteen years. He thought he'd never want it. But now there it was, loaded like a pistol, under his seat, waiting for him.

He took a long swig, drinking until he had to stop for a breath and his throat began to burn. He coughed, accidentally spitting a little alcohol onto his clothes.

He wished he were dead. Or maybe that wasn't it exactly. At that minute, leaning back against the seat, being alive seemed like a lot of work. He wondered what to do, what to tell Andrea, what to tell the police. He wondered why his whole life had turned to shit, just like that. He was a coward, that much was clear. A coward who didn't accept responsibility for his actions. That's the way it had always been. He'd always decided what to do, who to love, how to live, and with whom. He'd ruined his chance to be a poet, screwed up his marriage, and now he'd lost his daughter. Aroha hated him for everything he'd done to her mother, and to her.

She was too smart and sensitive not to realise what kind of guy her father was. A coward. And she couldn't stand it. That's why she ran away, that's why she got into trouble, flunked school — to punish him, to make him feel some of the pain he inflicted on others. He'd learned his lesson, he truly had. That's what he now told himself, letting out a nervous sob. He wanted to tell her. Sit her down and ask her forgiveness. *Forgive me, daughter. Please come home.*

The sky exploded with a deafening thunderclap. Arthur started his engine and the windshield wipers began sweeping back and forth. And then, right then, he saw Ian on the other side of the street, standing beside a bridal boutique, waiting for the light to change. He saw him through a small clear spot in the steamy windshield, the hood of his sweatshirt pulled up. Had his defroster taken a little longer to start working, had he not turned on his wipers at exactly the right time, he'd have missed him. But there he was, dead ahead. And destiny was calling.

His thinking was clouded, he was drunk. That's what Diana had told him to say when he called her a few hours later from the local police station where he'd been detained. 'Don't make a statement until the lawyers get there; I'll take care of everything.'

Diana always took care of everything, she did it fourteen years ago and she'd done it countless times since, whenever alcohol got him into trouble. She cleaned up the shit he left in his wake.

Guzmán walked around the desk and stood before a bookshelf full of commercial law tomes. Hands on his back, he glanced along the shelves. He was buying time, gathering information, formulating questions.

'It worked out well for you. Manslaughter charge, blood alcohol level as an attenuating circumstance. Diana's a smart lady. Four to five years instead of fifteen — not bad. But you made a stupid move. You let your self-interest and ego get the best of you, let an unflappable snot-nosed kid get the best of you, and when you did, you closed the only open door you had — the only way to find your daughter.'

'That wasn't the only door. There was still the third man, the shirtless one.'

'Dámaso, of course. He told me about the film club he and Olsen belonged to. Thanks to Olsen, he got Sir Ian Mackenzie, the famous director, to give a few esteemed talks, which his promising young son often attended. A few months before Aroha disappeared, Ian Mackenzie

268

stopped attending the club's meetings. His commitments were going to take him to Australia to direct a new film. By then, Olsen was a regular at his house. Before he went abroad, the boy's father went to see Dámaso, in secret. He explained that, as a child, his son had been diagnosed with some sort of mental illness. He didn't go into details, didn't tell him what kind of disorder it was. But he mentioned, with concern, that he'd been on neuroleptic meds since he was thirteen, had spent time in several clinics — always very hush-hush — in Switzerland and England. Though he was lazy by nature, for some reason he showed great enthusiasm for anything relating to the world of cinema. Obsessed over it, in fact — and that was a good thing, as far as his father was concerned. It kept him busy and away from all his father's *business* concerns. So his father had asked the old man to introduce his son to the club's more private group, and to keep an eye on him. And Dámaso did. Just as he'd been asked.'

Guzmán remained pensive, tapping his lips with an index finger.

'Funny, isn't it? His father wanted to protect his son and ended up tossing him straight into the lion's den without realising. Whoever's up there writing the screenplay of our lives has a very twisted sense of humour.

'After a few months, Ian junior discovered what Olsen and the old man were doing. It didn't take long for him to find out that the film club was actually just a cover-up for something much darker. But he didn't threaten to go to the police, or to shut him down. No. Instead, he actually demanded that they let him participate! He wanted to 'experiment' — that was the word he used. Shortly after that, he turned up with Aroha.

'They seemed pretty tight, if you get my meaning. At first, Olsen and the old man didn't think much of it. The girl seemed just like the rest of them. Ian was a good-looking kid and had the ability to get young hookers — drug addicts, girls living rough — to do whatever he wanted to keep him happy. But Aroha was special. She was educated, sophisticated but irreverent. It was obvious she was in love with Ian. And it was also becoming clear to everyone that she'd been experimenting with drugs and was starting to take things too far. Dámaso didn't give it much thought until he saw her picture in the paper and realised whose daughter she was, and that she had disappeared. He freaked out and immediately called Olsen. They had a big problem on their hands.'

Guzmán stopped talking and gave Arthur a marble stare. Arthur returned it with a questioning look.

'What did they do to my daughter?'

'Dámaso doesn't know. Believe me, if he did he'd have spilled the beans. But I'm starting to have a hunch as to who sent you that tape. Maybe you should start pulling a few more strings.'

'Enough bullshit. I want to know where Aroha is! What did they do to her?'

Guzmán turned his hand over and examined it like a pet, an ugly little dog you end up becoming quite fond of. He didn't seem to hear Arthur.

'Take a look at this. A good look. This used to be a hand, a good hand. Now it's just a tangle of flesh, useless chunks of dermis, epidermis, atrophied nerve endings, and damaged joints.' Arthur glanced at the shapeless mass without interest. 'They can make incredibly advanced implants and prosthetics nowadays, using a new material that fits perfectly into the space left by the missing digits. It's a very effective surgical procedure, but also very expensive, and guess what that means? If I want to get a fake dick and a hand to touch it with, I will have to get something cheaper, something lower quality, and that upsets me. It upsets me not to have a hand as perfect as yours, a penis that's even minimally functional, you know? You're the lucky ones, all you guys who smile at the world with your perfect teeth. But here's the thing. All your trappings — the paintings, the extravagances, the perfect teeth — they're all just disguises you use to hide behind. It all comes in the blink of an eye, but it can be taken away in the blink of an eye too. And that cycle can be repeated ad infinitum, as often as the gods so choose.'

'Why don't you just fucking come out and say whatever it is you have to say?'

'That's what I'm trying to do, but you're not listening. What I'm saying is, this tape changes everything. If the cops were to find it, it would prove you murdered Ian.' Guzmán spoke calmly, watching through the veil of his half-closed eyes as Arthur trembled pathetically, betraying his fear. 'If you tell me the truth, we might be able to reach an agreement, you and me, and no one else would have to know.'

'What do you want? More money? Bring Aroha back to me and I'll give you anything you want. Anything.'

Guzmán smiled.

'Of course you will, Arthur. Of course.'

16

They shouldn't have been there. It was dangerous and they both knew it. But their desire to be alone together was such that it made them reckless. The murky light from a bare bulb underscored the squalor of their alleyway refuge. Like a pencil underlining the dripping pipes and greasy puddles, the grime and squalor to be found behind Chang's restaurant.

Mei was staring vacantly into space. No one could be unmoved by those eyes; indeed, they had been his undoing.

'I never thought it would be like this,' she whispered.

'What would?' Mr Who asked, tucking back a lock of her hair that had fallen loose from the scarf covering her head. Mei worked in Chang's clandestine processing plant, packaging fast food. The old man didn't give them insurance, made them sleep on mattresses on the floor right next to the packing machinery, and paid them no salary, yet he still made Mei cover her beautiful dark hair with a hairnet and scarf. The world could be a sick place.

'Everything,' she said, looking down at her hands, which were grazed and raw from the plastic and preservatives. She raised her almond-shaped eyes to him and smiled timidly. Mei had a small mouth and thin lips. It occurred to Mr Who the first time he saw her, that hers was a mouth made to sing sad songs. When Mei had stowed away in a container on a cargo ship headed to a port in Spain, she spent the entire journey consoling the dozens of people who — like her — hid, cowering, some having chosen that route and others having been forced into it. She told them that Spain was a beautiful place where the air was clean and the people were always smiling. The fairy tale calmed many fears; people will believe anything if they need to, and everyone — including her — wanted her words to be true.

But Heaven's gates did not open for her.

In spite of everything, Mei thought she had no right to complain. She worked twenty hours a day, eating and going to the bathroom there in the secret factory. And she'd never be able to pay the debt she owed Chang and the men who had brought her to Europe. She didn't want to worry Mr Who, but she suspected that she might soon be transferred to another city. She'd heard people talking about a place on the southern coast, in Andalucía, where Chang and his associates were setting up brothels. They'd already moved the youngest and prettiest girls, and although nobody knew exactly where, they all had a pretty good idea.

And yet still, she couldn't complain. Her mother used to say that she was the strongest of all her siblings, the oldest and the only one she could trust. *When it all comes crumbling down,* she used to say, *you'll still be standing — the pillar of the household.* She was born under the sign of Ma, the horse. As a little girl she'd always been joyful and optimistic, always confronted problems head-on, with enthusiasm, and that made her popular with the neighbours. Though she no longer felt the keen urge to travel and have a life of adventure, to meet people and prove her worth, she managed to instill a degree of hope in the girls she was locked up with. She had to be strong when others were weak. A proverb from her native land said, *The sick are always healed, unless destiny is against them.* And she believed in destiny, always and forever, no matter what. The kind of destiny you make for yourself.

Besides, she had *him*, Mr Who; he was Mei's destiny. Maybe it was true what old people said, that you fall in love with your eyes and keep love with routine, but she didn't want to believe it. Old people were hard and intransigent — their defeats made them that way — but Mei never got tired of contemplating the face that was now just a few centimetres from hers. Before he came along, Mei didn't believe in the future; she thought only about the next step, the next order, the next minute. But a year later, she liked listening to him promise he was going to get her out of that prison, that he was going to save up money to buy them new passports so they could go back to China and start a new life together, start a family, maybe even start a business. Mr Who had a plan, he always had a plan, and it was easy to believe in his dreams. And even if they were just dreams, he was sincere.

Mr Who worked toward that goal every single day, asking her to sing him songs, to tell him about her country, and her people. He wanted to put down roots, to learn everything there was to know about being Chinese — which she was and he aspired to be. Mei indulged him without pointing out the contradiction in her having landed in Spain in search of paradise, of a future that she now saw had never existed. It was exactly the same paradise Mr Who was inventing and would end up discovering was just an illusion in China. But his dreams were something they both shared, more and more, and she was in need of a little hope. A lie is not always the lack of truth — sometimes it's about clinging to the part of reality you most need in order to keep from going under. So Mei fuelled Who's fantasies of China, and in exchange she chose to believe that this incredibly beautiful, strangely dressed young man — as sweet and sensitive as a little boy — would be able to wrench her from Chang's talons.

That night Mei had decided to go a step further in her dreamy recklessness. In the early evening, old man Chang had burst into the sweatshop and told them to run. It happened every once in awhile. The police would make raids in search of illegal workers, but Chang must have been bribing someone, because he always seemed to know in advance. Fifty or so women on the floor scrambled out, and only the half-a-dozen whose papers were in order remained. A few hours later it would all be back to normal. But, this time, the cops seemed to be taking it all quite seriously. They searched the workshop exhaustively, discovered buckets full of excrement, rolled-up mattresses tucked under worktables, and half-eaten food that had been abandoned mid-meal. The police took Chang in to interrogate him. In all likelihood, his lawyers wouldn't take long to get him out and he'd soon be back — but in the meantime, Mei could enjoy a few hours of freedom with Mr Who.

'We could run away, right now,' he said, so anxious that it was clear not even he actually believed it was an option. Not yet anyway. Mei put a finger to his lips. Her fingernail was jagged on one side, the polish chipped. It was rough to the touch and gave off an odour that no amount of water had been able to remove. But it was *her* finger, and, to him, it felt like a silk ribbon stroking his lips as softly as the laces on his mother's ballet slippers.

'Dreams that shouldn't be dreamed can hurt you,' she smiled.

Mr Who took her finger and held it in his hand. Mei didn't know much very about him — just what he needed her to know. Who preferred it that way; he didn't want to put her in danger, and certainly didn't want to scare her by telling her what he did, and what he was planning to do.

'At least Chang won't be back tonight. We've got that,' she added, her tiny body curling up against Who's torso. When he held her, he could feel her ribs beneath the baggy dress and apron, which she hadn't taken off. He felt her tiny heart trying to pound its way out, as if his chest were a wall and her heart a battering ram about to knock it down. 'I want it to be today. Now. With you,' she said almost inaudibly, her voice muffled against Mr Who's jacket.

Mei had never made love with a man before, never even seen a man naked. Even in the close quarters of the sweatshop she managed to bathe and go to the bathroom in private and hold on to her decency — that was the one thing that kept her from turning into an animal in that heaving overcrowded zoo. But she'd heard Chang talking, and knew it was almost her turn. They were going to take her, give her to a stranger — or maybe Chang and his men would rape her first, force her to take drugs, beat her, humiliate her. They were going to take the one thing she had left — her dignity — and trample it, turn it to rubble. That was why she had decided upon this one final act of freedom. She wanted to know what it felt like to be made love to slowly, with tenderness, with love, even if it was just this once.

She never imagined it could be so beautiful. The veins in Mei's throat throbbed and she opened her mouth as if to cry out in silence. Mr Who couldn't stop staring into her half-closed eyes, and he entered her with a tenderness and intensity that came from a distant, long-forgotten place. Mei was his mirror, a place he could let himself go, fall deeper and deeper into those eyes; it was a chance for salvation, poetic justice. Suddenly he felt lost and awkward, his fingers trembling uncontrollably — he, a man who fucked for a living, a man who specialised in all things kinky, now saw that life was so much more than his experiences, that it could begin again, that people are born anew each time they cross a new frontier. Mei was his New World.

She saw that Who's eyes were shining, looking like he was going to cry, and because she had no experience to judge by and also felt a supreme joy that led her to the brink of tears, she thought that that must be the language of love. So she stroked Who's face, wanting to heal him, to tell him that she was with him. That the two of them were so real they could conquer the impossible.

Orgasm flooded through them both, leaving them in a state of wonder. For a long time, Mr Who remained inside her, neither of them moving, not wanting to sever the invisible bond that held them together. They remained silent even longer, legs entwined, Who stroking the tapestry of red that had flourished on her delicate skin despite how gently he'd touched and kissed her, Mei exploring his tattoo with her fingers.

'Your heart is beating so fast. Are you in a rush to get somewhere?' she asked with a beautiful smile, free of fear and guilt. She wanted to exchange confidences, to engage in the pillow talk that follows sexual intimacy, to feel the pleasure of being able to say and hear things lovers only say and hear after making love, things and gestures that under other circumstances Mei would never have dared express.

But Who's mood had darkened. He was still there with her, wanting to stay by her side as long as possible. But the sounds of the street and the voices in his head were already dragging him, by the hair, back to the reality he lived when he was not with her. He held Mei tightly in both arms, his legs circling her hips. Mei went limp, trying as hard as she could to merge with him. She sensed the doubts churning inside him, could almost hear his thoughts. And they weren't good.

'What's the matter?' she asked with a hint of uncertainty. She'd heard that some men ran off the minute they were done having sex. And she didn't want Mr Who to be one of those.

He tried to find the right words to express what he was feeling.

'What would you think if you found out that this is not who I am?'

Suddenly Mr Who's voice was very thick. Mei propped herself up on one elbow and examined him closely.

'I'd say that I must be crazy, because that would mean that what just happened didn't happen, and I didn't really feel what I felt. If you're not the one here with me now, then you're a ghost. So I must be crazy and this must be a fantasy.'

Who hadn't yet grown accustomed to Mei's style of deductive reasoning. He struggled not to interpret her view of the obvious as naiveté.

'What I mean is, I'm more than one person. There are other people inside me, and you wouldn't like them all.'

'We open only the doors we wish to open, that the light may enter slowly,' she replied soothingly.

'Do you have always the answer?' he asked, slightly irritated.

'No, not always, although I imagine there must be one.' She wasn't stupid. She knew what Who was trying to say, but she didn't want to hear it. She hardly knew him, they'd spent so little time in one another's company and it was always furtive. They were always stealing time, blurting out what should have been said patiently, expressed over time. That night was the first time they'd ever shared a bed, spent a whole few hours together, shared the intimacy of their bodies. And even though she herself had no experience, it was clear to Mei that she was not the first woman Mr Who had loved, despite what he claimed. It was as if he were a professional ballet dancer who'd forgotten the basic steps and was trying to relearn them with her. He hadn't wanted to scare her or panic her. But now his words and questions were doing just that.

'What if you could ease one person's sorrow by causing another's?' he asked.

Sometimes questions are cast out like bait. But this wasn't one of those.

Mei shivered. She didn't want to know what was behind those doors. Not until she was sure she could handle it, or at least understand what she was going to find on the other side.

'I'm not entirely certain what you're trying to tell me,' she replied, reflecting for a few seconds, 'but transferring one person's misfortune never heals the harm that's been caused — the original harm, I mean. It simply becomes a series of errors and suffering that takes you away from the source of sorrow but not to its end.'

Mr Who realised he should say no more. She was imploring him to, and his need to be honest was not based on her acceptance of him, but simply on his need to ease the burden weighing on him. It wasn't fair.

'I don't know why I said all of that. I'm sorry,' he said, after a brief sigh.

'Of course you know, but that doesn't matter now,' she replied, closing her eyes for an instant. Her eyelashes were short and gave her a languid look. Mei sat on the mattress and began to gather her clothes. 'I have to go back to the factory now or Chang's men will become suspicious. And you have a call to answer on your mobile phone.'

Mr Who fished his phone out of the pocket of his overalls. It was a woman, one of his clients phoning. He could already imagine what she wanted. He hung up without answering.

'Nothing important.'

Mei stroked Who's cheek. He was lying again, but she felt that once again his lies were like armour being used to protect her. As long as lies can be detected in the face of a liar, all is not lost, she thought. And Who's expression was as transparent as a little boy's.

'Let's leave the insincerity to the insincere, okay?'

Mr Who went to say something, but she stopped him, sealing his lips with a kiss.

'I don't know what it is that torments you. But I do know that you can't walk forward when you keep looking back.'

When he got home, Mr Who had to face his mother's tormented look. Since the night he'd told her that he'd found and was going to kill Eduardo, they hadn't spoken about it again — as though it were a done deal, as though there were nothing to discuss. But, at dinnertime, she pushed her wheelchair to the table and stared at him as he cut his meat, served himself salad, dressed it with vinegar. Her silence was so loud drowned out the sound of their cutlery. Her expectant silence turned to disappointment every night, when Mr Who put the dishes in the sink and kissed her goodnight. *When are you going to do it?* she asked, without saying a word.

But each night when he returned home, his hands were empty. And clean.

'There's a woman, and a little girl. They love him. They're like a family.'

They were in the kitchen, having finished dinner, crumbs and the wet ring of a glass still visible on the oilcloth. Who said it without thinking — it just came out, as he wiped the crumbs and dried the watermark with a dishtowel. To avoid looking at his mother, he stared at the television. An ad for detergent. 'Spotless', they claimed, 'clean as a *paten*'. Who wondered how many people actually knew that a paten was the gold plate that held the bread during the Eucharist. Mei's skin was spotless, he thought. Her eyes, too. He would have liked to find sanctuary in them, and not have to look into his *stepmother's* — when Mr Who unconsciously wanted to distance himself from Maribel, he thought of her as his stepmother rather than his mother. In that sense, at least, the poison Chang fed him during their *sessions* had worked. When Teo used to hit Maribel (it wasn't often, in truth, but from time to time he did take out his anger on her with a slap or two) Who thought of him as his stepfather, too. Something a step away from a real father, as if his father was standing on a stool and he could kick it out from under him and watch him fall.

'What do you mean by that?'

It wasn't a question; it was an attack. *Have the guts to say what you're thinking. Tell me you're having doubts, that you don't know what to do. Tell me to my face that you're scared to avenge the death of my husband.*

Mr Who looked at Maribel. Calling her by her name was another way to distance himself from the woman leaning towards him expectantly, elbows on the metal armrests of her wheelchair. As if she could get up, as if she could leap up and attack him. He watched her try to conceal her sense of urgency and took his time picking crumbs off the dishtowel. Now there was a commercial for deodorant on — 'Natural'. *The only thing that's natural is skin. It perspires. It suffers. It dies.*

'I mean that it's been fourteen years, and people change.'

He didn't say that he was in love with a girl who was in Spain illegally. He didn't say he was afraid of going to jail; or that he was young and had a future — any future — far from the house that had turned him, too, into an invalid. Nor did he tell Maribel that he loved her, that he'd always love her, no matter where he was, and that in a way he'd never loved Teo. Or that one day she'd be a grandmother, and he'd send her photos and postcards of his house, his business, her grandchildren, who would have both Spanish and Chinese blood. And he'd teach them the songs she used to sing him when he was a child, and that he wouldn't let them smoke, not even Chinese tobacco. And that they'd never be forced to degrade themselves to put food on the table.

It wouldn't have done any good, he knew that. His words, his reasoning, would have bounced right off Maribel's stony-faced determination. He didn't want to say those things, didn't want to feel the pain of a wound reopening, one that would never heal. He didn't want to hear that his mother didn't care about her own son's happiness (oddly, Who had never called himself her *stepson*). All she cared about was her own pain. And pain was an insatiable god who demanded endless sacrifice, Who's hopes and dreams being the first of them.

Instead he simply shook the crumbs into the sink, and this time Maribel didn't reproach him, saying that's how the drain got clogged and he should use the rubbish bin, since that was what it was there for. When he turned, she'd already wheeled herself out of the kitchen. He heard her go into Teo's bedroom. A minute later he heard her wheeling herself back down the parquet of the hall. With sudden energy, she circled the table, stopping a centimetre from Mr Who. On her lap was an olive-coloured, square metal box. She placed it on the counter.

'Open it,' she commanded.

He had no need to. He knew what was in it. He'd heard the story hundreds, perhaps thousands, of times. And yet Maribel began to repeat it, opening the box for him. She struggled to speak, overcome by an emotion as intense as it was heartrending.

'Since the time he was a little boy, Teodoro was fascinated with stamps, coins and bills. He used to say that money got dirty being passed from hand to hand, but when it finally came out of circulation — which is what contaminated it — it was beautiful. That it became an object symbolising the lifelong human endeavour to quantify, to give things a concrete shape, to overcome the arbitrary nature of simple exchange. A bill like this one, or coins like these, explain part of our desire to become civilised. He liked to imagine what they smelled like, fresh out of the mint or the press; liked to wonder how many pockets they'd been in; what places they'd seen; what things had been bought and sold with them; how many lives they'd saved or ruined; how much joy or misfortune they'd caused. He had one of the best collections in the country and spent his whole life on it, but it wasn't complete — there were pieces he was missing, the very ones he obsessed over. Obtaining them was his dream, his passion.

'A man with no dreams or passions is an empty shell, and it doesn't matter whether the obsession is stamps or beer cans. When you're passionate about something, you don't stop until you've got it, no matter how absurd others may find it. It took Teo years to find the coins this box holds. He spent so much money he almost ruined us, and so much energy, it almost made him sick. You should know that, you should remember his face that morning, when he finally closed the deal. He was the happiest, proudest man I've ever seen, so full of life. I'd never seen him like that. He was practically levitating before our eyes. I think that was the moment I loved him the most. And at that very instant, the man who came to my house a few weeks ago as though nothing had happened — the man you say has the right to change — stole him from me. *I felt his blood spatter on my face! I watched the coins fall from his hands!* I couldn't react. But still, I managed to put myself between you and the bullet that would have killed you, the bullet that ruined my life. I lost everything to save you. You owe this to me. You owe me that man's life.'

'Even if it means ruining my own?'

Maribel did not reply. She stared at him fixedly. And the wound that Mr Who had tried to keep from being ripped open began to bleed.

Sometimes Sara hated her mother. In fact, sometimes she hated everybody. Everybody but Eduardo. He was always safe from that vague feeling she got that, when she really thought about it, maybe wasn't hatred exactly but more like a mounting unease she felt when she was around other people — a kind of edginess that she could *hear* under her skin, like water going down the pipes when she flushed the toilet. From time to time, the groaning sound grew louder in her head, and it got so loud it took up all the space of her thoughts. She didn't know why it happened, there didn't seem to be anything specific that triggered it. But happen it did, and she couldn't stop it. She tried to stop it, and now she had an ally — her lucky cat. She hugged him tight, spoke to him and sang him songs, pretending she wasn't hearing the sound she was hearing, that buzzing that sounded like flies trapped in her eardrum.

They only way she could explain what happened was by simile, and the doctor said that that was good, that the images she used helped others understand her better. And the sound she heard in her ear was just like Eduardo had said, when he asked, *Is it like when you trap a fly under a cup and then hear it banging into the glass trying to escape?* He'd asked her that when she had tried to explain that she hadn't kicked his bad knee to be mean, it was just that she was hearing that noise in her head and couldn't make it stop. And that was exactly what it was. That was why Eduardo was different, because he was like her.

Before running away she'd seen her mother sitting by the window.

She was smoking in her bedroom, head held high, shoulders tense. The smoke distorted her face, or maybe it made a new one, unhappy. That was the look her mother got when something made her sad. And if she was smoking by the bed it meant that soon she'd start to sob, and then she'd start drinking and her tears would turn to lava — thick, cloying, burning hot. When she saw her mother like that, the volume of Sara's rage increased and the flies started buzzing too close to her ear. And then she got the irrepressible urge to run away from home, to hide under a bench on the street — like she was now — bent over her knees, hugging her cat and covering her head with her hands until the noise stopped. She didn't run away to punish her mother, or to be mean. *Of course not, of course you don't. It's just that you have to run, and scream, because if you don't your head is going to explode*. Yes, Eduardo understood her. Years ago, he'd needed to do that sometimes, too, he confessed.

She felt better now. Really. She didn't need to keep hiding. The ground was dirty and there were cigarette butts and sunflower seed shells poking her through her socks and sticking into her shins. She could go home now; she knew the way. She'd only run a couple of blocks. She'd dust herself off, fix her hair and walk calmly home. She didn't want to go to the hospital this time. No, she was fine now. It had just been a little warning, so her mother would stop crying before she even started. When her mother was sad, Sara hated her a little bit more. And she didn't want to hate her. That was another reason she liked Eduardo. Because her mother was like a flower blooming from within another flower whenever he was around. Because she'd put blush on her cheeks and giggle nervously when she dropped her compact on the floor. Eduardo chased away her sorrows and took them for himself — hers and everyone else's. That's why he was always walking around with his shoulders slumped, like he was carrying a heavy sack full of everybody's grief.

'I didn't run away to be mean,' she said to her cat, wagging its plastic arm up and down as though it were playing yoyo. But her cat couldn't lie to her, so she covered his eyes with her hand, because she felt a little ashamed.

Sometimes you run away in order to be found. And she liked knowing that her mother and Eduardo were both out looking for her now. Together. She'd let them look a little more and then let herself be found.

'That's a nice cat.'

The voice had no face, only feet. Or rather, thick-soled boots with gold rivets, right in front of her face. Sara looked up from the ground through the gaps in the wooden bench above her. A pair of eyes looked down at her, and above them was the sky. A pretty sky, orange and purple.

'I can see you. And your cat, too.'

Curious, she stuck her head out like a little mouse scanning the horizon before venturing out of its hole.

'He's not an ordinary cat. His name's Maneki.'

'That's what I thought.' The stranger had crouched down, so the eyes now had a face. A face that Sara liked. There were faces she liked, and faces she didn't. This one, she did. Uneasy, her eyes darted immediately to the package he was carrying under his arm. She liked packages. They sometimes contained things not everybody had permission to see. 'You should come out from under there. Earthworms crawl on the ground, but butterflies fly. And it's stopped raining, so your wings will be safe.'

Sara smiled. How could he know she was hiding invisible wings that got damaged in the rain? She took the hand he held out and crawled out from under the bench.

'That's better. My name is Who. I think your cat and I are already acquainted.'

'How could that be? I never let him go out alone.'

'Well, cats are free spirits, you know. Maybe when you're asleep, he jumps out the window to patrol the neighbourhood. Maybe we've seen each other out on the streets at night.'

There was no way Maneki got out at night, because Sara would get on her knees on the bed and watch closely. Mentally, she gave him orders (cats are very telepathic). Maneki sometimes obeyed her orders, moving an arm or blinking slowly. And sometimes he didn't (that just showed his independent character). Sara had never told her mother these things. She would have said they were figments of her imagination. But Eduardo believed her, even if he did warn her not to tell other people. *Not everyone is prepared to accept certain things. People believe what they want to believe, and then what they believe ends up becoming what they call truth or reality.* Sara understood what Eduardo was telling her. If she went around telling everyone that her toy cat came to life whenever she asked

282

him to — without using words — or that she had invisible wings that got damaged in the rain, or that invisible flies buzzed inside her ears, they would give her a baffled look and assume she was dumb, or crazy. Or worse, they'd accuse her of not living in the real world and not accepting the truth.

'Why are you hiding under a bench? Why not behind a tree or in a doorway?'

Sara looked Who up and down. He was a dark spot dressed in a white spot, with messed up hair and black fingernails. His voice sounded very childlike, as if the little boy who lived inside him had not grown as quickly as his body. The opposite had happened to her — her mind grew too quickly and her body couldn't keep up, so even though she *looked* like a thirteen-year-old girl, she wasn't. And that made it hard to be respected in the adult world, where people were inclined to go by appearances. That was just one more reason she liked Eduardo so much — he accepted what really was and didn't get hung up about what things looked like. Eduardo took her seriously.

'Because if I did, they might not find me. And I want them to find me.'

'Well, are they going to take much longer? It's going to get dark soon.'

Sara shrugged.

'You found me.'

'But I wasn't looking for you. At least, not for you exactly. That must mean something.'

The evening's last glimmer of post-rain sun was shining directly into Sara's face. She held up one hand like a visor, to get a better look at him. She thought, right then, of the tin vase her mother kept in the entrance hall. It was an ugly vase, with no flowers. At least she thought it was ugly, so it must have been. A vase with no flowers. She thought of that without knowing why. That happened sometimes: she'd think of things that made no sense, for no apparent reason. She'd just get an image stuck in her mind and be unable to think of anything else. She didn't know why the image of that ugly vase with no flowers suddenly made her feel so sad. Occasionally she seemed to get sad for no reason at all. She could be walking down the street holding her mother's hand, singing a song she'd heard on the radio, and suddenly see an old person's face, or a woman with the hint of a moustache, or a dog whose ear had been bitten, or the faded awning of an ice-cream parlor, and the song would vanish, taking refuge inside her, and she'd become silent and very sad.

Out of the blue, when she saw Mr Who — or actually when she saw him switch his package to the other arm — she thought of the vase, and of home, and the music disappeared. A vase with no flowers. A tin vase.

'Would you do me a favour?' Mr Who asked. 'Would you give this package to Eduardo? Tell him it's from Teodoro López Egea.'

Sara took the package. She liked having a mission.

'And now I think it would be better if you went back home. I think that's what your cat is telling you.'

Sara stared at him wide-eyed.

'Can you hear Maneki, too?'

Mr Who smiled.

'I told you, we already know each other from the neighbourhood.'

17

Martina crossed off every day that passed with a red 'X' and circled future events in different colours — green for patients, yellow for holidays, blue for the last Thursday of the month. Why was Eduardo in a blue circle and not a green one like her other patients? Green was the colour of hope. Blue is the colour of nostalgia, the sky, the impossible. Seconds ticked by, turning to minutes, on Martina's wristwatch. 10.45, 10.46, 10.47 … And still he did not speak.

He'd said something at 10.44. He knew the exact minute because, as he spoke he kept his eyes trained on the doctor's petite, square-faced gold wristwatch. His eyes trailed from her watch-face to the fine downy hair on her forearm and paused for a second at a mark on her skin — a mole, slightly larger than a freckle, about the size of a lentil. He imagined she must have more on her body. A body covered in lentil-sized moles, which she probably had to lather with sunscreen when she went to the beach.

The doctor had jotted down what he'd said in her little spiral notebook. There were his words. He couldn't take them back: *I killed them, even though he's the only one that died.* And in order to stress them, she'd underlined the sentence with two thick lines that bled through to the other side of the paper.

At 10.48, he added, 'I went to her house to see her,' as if his earlier words were incomplete, demanding an ending.

If you discounted the two of them — discounted the office and the day-planner, the clock and the words on her notepad — it was as though the world were a lighter place, simpler, easier to bear. The last storm-front of spring was moving out over Europe, heading out to the sea. Beautiful sunlight shone down, and that unbearable heat that makes the clothes stick to your body had yet to build up. The interminable stream of economic exiles *had* not yet begun fleeing Madrid, laden with suitcases, in the hopes of discovering some prosperous new paradise. The city was a welcoming place in early May, easy to love. Perhaps the psychiatrist was daydreaming about some studio apartment she'd bought on the coast, about painters applying a fresh coat to the walls, and repairing the rusty handrails. Maybe she was making mental notes, counting off the red days left until she, too, could escape. That would explain the detachment Eduardo thought he could sense in her circumspect expression, as though the words she'd written were an unsolvable algebra problem, her eyes shining vacantly.

Why *had* he gone to see Maribel? He didn't know, he really didn't. In the almost fourteen years that had gone by, he'd never felt the need to — except once, when his nightmares had become so intense they seemed to be some sort of code, charting his guilt, speaking to him in a language he didn't understand. Often, it is only after feeling the compulsion to do something that people try to find reasons to do so. In all honesty, he'd simply turned up at the door of her apartment building, walked up the stairs, and rung her bell without thinking. He hadn't been expecting anything. He had just felt the need to do it. The need to go there.

Martina jotted something down at the top of the paper, above the underlined sentence — an addendum — the writing so small that Eduardo couldn't read it. His arms were crossed over his chest, wrapping himself in his solitude. *Stop that*, he used to say to Tania after he'd given her a talking-to and she'd taken the same defensive stance, as if sticking her hands under her armpits somehow created a shell that words bounced off, falling dead at her feet. It didn't matter how much he shouted at her. As long as Tania's arms were crossed, there was no getting through.

'How did it make you feel, seeing Maribel after all those years?'

The second he'd rung the bell, Eduardo had gotten the urge to run back down the stairs. And as soon as the door opened, he wished he were invisible, wished he were anywhere but there, but it was too late. He saw a woman in a wheelchair, legs wrapped in a plaid blanket, wearing a fake-silk kimono. Her near-white hair was scraped into a severe bun.

Did she remember him? he wondered. She most certainly did; she hadn't forgotten him for a second.

'You've taken a big step, Eduardo. Forgiveness heals wounds, but you can't expect things to suddenly be the way you want them to. It takes time,' Martina said. He felt like he was listening to a nun. One who was locked in a cloister, her only contact with the outside world a revolving hatch through which she slipped pills, prescriptions, and useless advice. The only thing left for her to do was make the sign of the cross. In the psychiatric liturgy, the equivalent was to hand him a prescription for a tranquilliser without his having to ask for it.

Eduardo contemplated her fingernails, their bone-coloured polish, above the paper. *We're making progress.* Towards what? *Forgiveness.* Whose?

'Did you want to ask me something?'

Sometimes two worlds are totally irreconcilable, they exist entirely in opposition. She held out the prescription to him.

'No, nothing, doctor.'

'Okay then, see you in June.'

Perhaps, thought Eduardo. *Perhaps*.

He decided to walk. It was a nice day and there was no reason to waste it underground on the metro. He didn't feel happy, but he bought some flowers without taking the florist's advice. 'Any kind, doesn't matter,' he'd said. Which had offended the girl, who suddenly wielded the pruning shears sticking out of her leather apron like a gun. She removed her green gloves and pointed to a few just-watered bunches on the counter: daisies, roses, verbenas. Eduardo nodded, as if to say they were all fine. He was just trying to lend some cheer to that flowerless tin vase that made Sara so sad. In the end he bought daisies, white and purple. The blue ones were more expensive. Walking down the street holding them that sunny morning, he'd have looked like a man in love were it not for how dejected he looked as he gripped the flowers, as if he was walking a poodle that insisted on stopping to sniff other dogs' pee on every streetlight. He had the air of someone who'd been rejected. Perhaps that was why some people, especially women, shot him compassionate glances.

When he got to the corner of Calle León, a crowd of people blocked the way. Fire trucks were pulling up, sirens blaring, and a dense cloud of smoke billowed from the top of a block of buildings. Ash floated in the breeze, carrying the smell of wood and plastic. Eduardo managed to push his way through the curious onlookers and saw police cars and ambulances up on the sidewalk in front of an antique dealer's. One fireman was tearing down the wooden door with a pickaxe as another was breaking the storefront window. The police were trying to control the gawkers while an emergency services worker hung a canvas curtain so the doctors could work in peace.

Behind the cloth partition could be heard distressed voices. Glancing underneath, Eduardo saw a leg hanging over the edge of a makeshift cot. It belonged to the body of a faceless man, who was still alive, moaning weakly. For several minutes, a doctor and emergency worker tried frantically to revive him. Someone brought a mask and oxygen tank. From where he stood, Eduardo could not see if the burn victim was reacting or not, but he thought all that pounding on the man's chest must surely have broken a few ribs. Two nurses and two fire fighters, their faces and helmets covered in soot, carried the stretcher out to the nearest ambulance. The police cleared the way, and then a wailing siren took off up the street in the opposite direction.

Fire fighters started spraying the antique dealer's with foam, using high-pressure hoses. Police were evacuating the apartment building next door, hustling the residents into a safety zone. A few were complaining — some people will complain even if someone is trying to protect them — others crying, one or two carrying cages with parakeets or cats in their arms, and a dog barked rabidly at the sirens assaulting his sensitive canine ears. A few people were speaking to officers, who were taking notes in their little books.

The fire had destroyed a good part of the building; apparently it had started in the basement. The piles of old clothes, furniture and paintings had fed the flames, which raged so quickly that only a few pieces had been saved. The fire fighters now dragged what they could out through the doors and broken windows: a bronze sculpture of Marcus Aurelius with a singed face; a charred baroque crucifix; spoons, plates and vases; a Louis XIV armchair. All that rushing in and out seemed just like a house being looted during the revolution.

Fifteen minutes later, the fire died down and the crowd lost interest. Only the most obstinate gawkers remained, perhaps those who derived secret pleasure from others' misfortune. By the time the fire fighters finished their work all that was left was a black stain on the building's facade and the police security tape. Nothing new.

Eduardo stepped back to pass by. His clothes were infused with smoke, and the daisies now looked sad and limp. That was when he saw Ibrahim standing among the few people still left, behind the security barrier, his head sticking out above the rest. He was watching the scene, impassive.

Ibrahim turned and saw him. They exchanged a look. Eduardo began to wave, but dropped his arm mid-gesture. As though he hadn't even seen him, Ibrahim withdrew and slipped off in the opposite direction.

When Eduardo got home, news of the fire was already on the radio. Sitting in the building lobby with her fashion magazines, Graciela was listening to a transistor radio, an absent look on her face and a half-smoked cigarette between her fingers. The announcers were grave, saying all anyone could do was regret the passing of Dámaso Sebastián, aged 72, who'd been owner of the antique dealer's for over forty years. According to witnesses, he had no family. Dámaso had died before making it to the Major Burns Unit at Hospital de la Paz — from smoke inhalation and the severity of his burns, most likely; they were awaiting results of the autopsy.

'That was just around the corner. You can smell the smoke on my clothes,' Eduardo said by way of greeting, leaving the flowers on the lobby desk beside a packet wrapped in brown paper. 'These are for your empty vase. I think Sara will like them.'

Graciela's eyes skipped disinterestedly over the flowers, but she fixed her gaze on him. She was smoking, trying to look calm, but her mouth was clamped down too hard on the cigarette and she was exhaling a steady stream of smoke through her nose.

'Did you know I pay for sex? Or at least I did, once.'

The question was so unexpected it was like a slap in the face; Eduardo felt it smack him right between the eyes.

'I don't think that's anything I need to know, quite honestly.'

Graciela put her cigarette out in the ashtray as if drowning it in a barrel of water.

'Oh, of course. I forgot — you don't need anything from me, or my daughter. You're not interested in anything or anyone, really.'

Eduardo felt taken aback by this hostility, which seemed to be coming out of nowhere. Graciela took the package off the counter and held it in her hands.

'*This* might interest you, though. Turns out the guy I paid to give it to me up the arse actually knows you. Knows where you live, knows your name, and of course he knows how my daughter and I feel about you. I doubt he knows what you feel for us, though of course that's logical, since not even you know that.'

289

Eduardo made no reply. His tongue was stuck to the roof of his mouth. He kept his eyes trained on the ends of Graciela's collar; she was wearing a beige, long-sleeved shirt, and between the tips of her collar hung a religious pendant, which quivered when she breathed. He could see her chest swelling and falling with each heaving breath, and beneath her marbled shirt buttons, the outline of a breast — just one.

Eduardo averted his eyes, concentrated instead on the daisies. Sara was right: empty vases are so sad.

He turned to Graciela and gave her a candid look, with no shame or guilt. *Forgiveness cures*, that was what Martina had said. But Martina had no idea what things were really like; she was a nun, at her revolving hatch. All Eduardo felt was a deep sense of sadness, and he wasn't even sure whether or not it was for himself. He thought about Sara and Graciela, about people like them who invented heroes to have someone to believe in, heroes who could reach out a hand and keep them from falling. Maybe they really did exist, but he wasn't one of them. Nor had he pretended to be.

'I've tried to tell you this several times, Graciela. I'm not the man you think I am. You invented your own version of me, as some sort of partner for you, as a father for Sara. But that man has only ever existed inside your head.'

'My name is not Graciela!!!' she shouted above the volume of the transistor radio. And then for a second she fell silent, as though her words had betrayed her, but almost immediately she regained her composure. 'Don't you tell me what I'm thinking, what I feel, what I believe. You don't know a thing. You're so blind ...'

They two of them stared at each other in silence. Her lips were quivering and the tears in her eyes turned into gleaming mirrors that reflected a blurred outline of Eduardo.

'I don't want to put you or Sara in danger. I'll pack my things and pay you the rest of the month's rent. I can be out of here tomorrow.'

Graciela shook her head, the anger dissipating, like the tail end of a storm heading off into the hills. And the gloomy halo of post-storm melancholy hung in the air, in a landscape still dripping with rain.

'You still don't get it, do you?' She held out the package she'd been holding in her hands. 'The guy asked Sara to give you this, on behalf of *Teodoro López Egea.*'

Eduardo examined the package as though it were some strange foreign object he couldn't figure out how to open. When he looked up, Graciela was gazing toward the half-open apartment door. Sara stood in the doorway, her face and one sock-clad foot — a pink sock with little blue elephants — sticking out into the hall. The other was hidden behind the doorframe. She had one eye trained on him. Half her cat was peeking out, too. Something about her looked different. Words overheard can alter the way you see things. Neither Graciela nor Eduardo knew how much Sara had heard.

'Go back inside, sweetheart,' Graciela said, with an urgent sweeping motion of her hands. As if that simple gesture might contain her daughter's body and keep her from slipping out, like a wounded man trying to hold his guts in after stepping on a landmine.

Before she disappeared, following behind her daughter, Graciela turned to Eduardo.

'Take care of this, whatever it is.'

Eduardo nodded. He wanted to tell her not to forget to put the flowers in the vase; they would lift Sara's sadness a bit.

The package contained a couple of very old hundred-peseta banknotes, bearing the impenetrable face of Francisco de Goya; and one thousand-peseta note, with the face of humanist Luis Vives. There were also several twenty-five-peseta bills, showing the politician Flórez Estrada. In total, thirteen hundred pesetas issued between 1944 and 1947. On first glance, there was nothing special about them. They were just old banknotes no longer in circulation, which might have held some significance for collectors — nothing of interest to him. But when he held them up to the light, he could see tiny stains, marks that seemed to suggest they had been in an explosion. There was also a note, written on a post-it. A meeting place and time. He went straight to the refrigerator, but all he found was half a bottle of some very bad wine. Filling a glass, Eduardo drank it down without stopping for breath. And then he did it again, until his hands stopped shaking.

Being punished is pointless if you don't know why you're being punished. For thirteen long years — the whole time he'd been locked up — everything the psychiatrists and wardens had done was aimed at forcing him to accept that truth. That was what Martina wanted to do, too, when she claimed she was trying to help with his *reinsertion*. Strange word. It meant that, at some point, he'd been a part of the apparatus that rules us all. That before watching Elena and Tania die, he'd been a small cog in a machine — a machine that ran smoothly, without too much friction. When his family died, the cog had broken and set off a chain-reaction of horror — more deaths, more suffering, as useless as his own. He'd been unwilling to put his faith in the law, and that was unforgiveable. More unforgiveable even than the tragedy he'd caused Teo, Maribel and their son — who were, after all, just more unimportant cogs in the machine, when it came right down to it. *We can't let individuals take justice into their own hands. That would lead to chaos; the whole societal apparatus would lose its raison d'être,* Martina had warned him.

A lunatic kills for no reason, or for reasons totally incomprehensible to others. But he wasn't one of those psychos he'd been incarcerated with in Huesca for thirteen years. Eduardo had acted in a fit of rage, a temporary *outburst*. That was another word his shrink loved scribbling in her notebook. He could be cured, she claimed. They could fix him, *reinsert* him like a shiny new object. All he had to do was keep his head down, forget the past, accept forgiveness.

But the psychiatrist was wrong.

It was seven a.m. and the park was deserted. The guard who opened the gate was stretching his limbs like a lion after a long nap. He regarded Mr Who curiously, and his brain, foggy after an uncomfortable night's sleep in the night watchman's booth, couldn't make out whether the figure was a man or a woman. Mr Who walked slowly toward the Crystal Palace, passing the first early risers who'd come in their workout gear to jog around Parque de El Retiro. The dog walkers — poo bags in hand — would arrive later, as would the newspaper vendors, delivery trucks, and police on horseback.

The artificial lake looked like a Welsh lagoon, a light mist floating over its green-tinged surface.

Eduardo was waiting on one of the benches on the south side with a vacant expression. He rubbed his wrists mechanically — first one, then the other — as though he'd just had handcuffs removed. Mr Who watched for a long while, with a mixture of disappointment and resentment. He'd been awaiting the moment for so long, had prepared for it so thoroughly that now this downcast man in the bone-coloured raincoat didn't measure up to his expectations. He was furious not to feel the hatred that he'd assumed he would. Mr Who had spent his whole life hating a shadow, and now he got the feeling that the shadow didn't even belong to this man.

Eduardo heard footsteps to his right and turned. When he saw Who, his sagging cheeks turned red. He wasn't sure whether to stand or remain seated, and ended up doing an awkward movement halfway between the two, his butt hovering over the edge of the seat and one arm over the back of the bench. *So, it's you.* Eduardo's lips didn't move, it was his face that spoke. He wasn't surprised, not really. When Graciela described Who — '… *he doesn't look like a man or a woman; it's like he's split in two, half of each …'* — Eduardo had thought almost instantly of the encounter he'd had months ago in the metro station with the young man who'd forgotten his Chinese cat. He'd remembered the unsettling feeling he'd gotten that he knew the kid, that their encounter had not been by chance.

'You've grown,' was all he could think of to say. It was an idiotic statement given the circumstances — as if they were distant relations, as if he were an uncle seeing his nephew for the first time in fourteen years and discovering that the little brat was now a man in the prime of life.

Who took a seat beside him. He was wearing a lightweight, knee-length trench coat with the collar turned up. He slipped his hands into his pockets and lowered his chin, shrugging. Who stared out at the rising mist over the lake. Through gently swirling wisps he could see the surface from time to time, the fish beneath it stirring up bubbles and gentle waves.

'I wasn't sure you'd actually come,' Who said, looking at him out of the corner of his eye, 'but something told me you would. You know, I feel like I've known you since I was nine years old. I've dreamed of you every night.' He had a sad air about him, unthreatening. A sadness that detached him from the pain that had first caused it — a distant pain that had festered like a terminal disease you learn to live with.

Eduardo took from his pocket the bills Who had given to Sara. They were carefully folded into a wad, and he placed it on the bench between them.

'There was no reason to threaten Graciela and Sara. I went to see your mother, and I knew sooner or later you'd turn up. I'd have come regardless. Whatever this is, I accept it — I'm tired of carrying around this burden.'

Mr Who tried to judge Eduardo's sincerity, but he couldn't. Did the man know he was there to kill him? Did he know he was planning to use a little .22-calibre pistol hidden in one of his pockets? He must have guessed, surely. But he didn't look like he was afraid, and it couldn't be because he thought he'd be able to talk Who out of it. In fact, deep down, he seemed to long for it.

'I wasn't trying to hurt them. I'm not like that. I'm not like you.' Who stood, looked out over the lake. He shook his head and then nodded toward Eduardo. 'Have you ever felt like a tree with no roots? That's what I've felt like for as long as I can remember.'

Eduardo avoided making eye contact, glanced away from the sun that was reflected in Who's eyes. The spite gleaming in those eyes was like a firefly trapped under a dark glass. He focused instead on the algae floating on the water's surface, swishing gently back and forth like little snakes, over by the cypress tree where his and Elena's names were carved into the bark. He wanted to tell the kid that he understood — if you have no ground in which to plant your roots, you're nothing. His ground had been his family, and without them Eduardo was nothing but a hollow trunk, rotting from the inside out, waiting for a storm to split him in two.

He knew what Who was planning to do. He'd guessed it the moment he saw the kid's hand reach into his coat pocket. He'd glimpsed the wooden butt of the gun that Who's hand now gripped. *Do it*, he thought. *Let's get this over with*. But instinctively he recoiled. No one wants to die — not even those who think they do.

'Let's take a walk,' Who said. It wasn't an order but the acceptance of something both of them seemed to find inevitable.

Eduardo nodded. He got up and glanced at the bulge in Who's pocket. There was nobody around. In the distance, a few people were jogging, way down the gravel path behind them. No one who could come to help.

'Are you going to shoot me in the back?'

Mr Who didn't reply. He gave a lukewarm smile that seemed at odds with his frame of mind, as though his lips had grown accustomed to the movement no matter what the circumstances. Then a gust of wind ruffled his black hair, and the smile vanished like a cloud. He jutted his chin out, indicating that Eduardo should walk.

Eduardo took one step, then another, and curiously his knee didn't hurt. In fact, nothing hurt. He looked at the ground, at his shoes — slightly worn on the toe — at the ants already tunneling and forming the little cones that led to their nest; at a dry leaf fluttering erratically; at a desiccated pile of dog shit.

'I've been watching you for months. You don't act like a psychopath or a lunatic. So why did you do it?'

'Your father caused the accident that killed my family. He let my daughter die. She'd have been one year older than you now, if she were alive. He left her to bleed to death by the side of a creek.'

He no longer heard Who's footsteps on the gravel behind him and turned his head to look back. Who had stopped dead. He looked disconcerted, helpless, and for a moment, amid the haze of memories both lived and reinvented, Eduardo caught a glimpse of the same little terrified boy wearing a cap and scarf that he'd almost killed. Suddenly it dawned on him that the kid hadn't known. No one had ever explained to him why it had all happened.

'You're lying. Teo would never have done anything like that.'

Eduardo turned to face him. He felt sorry for the boy, a lone reed as out of place as he himself was, equally lonely and as wounded by something that never should have happened, but did.

'You're lying,' Who repeated, and his voice sounded like a howl in the midst of a tempest.

But Eduardo wasn't lying.

'When Olga gave me your father's licence plate number and described him to me, I lost my mind. All I could feel was rage and uncontrollable fury. I'm not trying to justify myself or make you and your mother forgive me. I just want you to understand.'

Eduardo's words bounced off Who's frozen exterior. It was as though he were speaking to a pillar of salt, the empty body of someone who'd gone and left behind the hollow reflection of clothes and flesh, devoid of a soul. You can't expect someone to comprehend something incomprehensible. Can't ask them to bear the weight of their incomprehension.

'When did the accident take place?'

'The sixteenth of August 1991, in the early morning, on the road to Toledo. We were on our way back from a vacation. Elena and Tania were asleep, and your father slammed into us and threw us off the road.'

Who stared off into the distance, as though his mind were making its way through the veils of time, searching for the boy who had been seasick on a ferry that summer, the boy who'd spent his afternoons on that island exploring the walls of the country estate where they were staying, chasing the cicadas that sang in the withered meadow and watching the sea off in the distance, which looked bluer and farther away when he looked from the top of the hill, while Teo and Maribel were on their second honeymoon closed up inside the house with the blinds drawn, and a black dog barked at the butterflies.

Maribel had saved endless sentimental mementos from that unexpected vacation. Their ferry tickets, the plane tickets from Madrid, stubs from the maritime history museum where they'd spent a nice afternoon. She'd kept photographs, and still had the garishly painted shell necklace Teo had given her, which he'd bought from a German hippy who'd set up a makeshift stall and looked like he'd stepped out of another time. He could still taste the two scoops of raspberry ice cream, feel the bump he got on his head when he fell out of a pine tree trying to act like a squirrel. But what he still felt the strongest was the overwhelming sense that the trip Teo had suddenly suggested had served to heal some wounds between his adoptive parents. He heard their moans from behind the closed bedroom door, and smelled pine trees and wildflowers in the air.

'On the sixteenth of August 1991 we weren't even in Madrid. We went to an island on the twelfth and stayed until the twenty-second, six days after that accident.'

A flock of grey pigeons with white-tipped wings squabbled their way past them, chasing a sparrow with a crust of bread in its tiny beak. In the end, the sparrow relinquished its treasure and the pigeons left it hungry but in peace. *That's life*, its little eyes seemed to say, watching from a honeysuckle bush as the pigeons bickered over its bread.

The hand Who had in his pocket, gripping the cold revolver, slackened, and then emerged like a question mark.

'That's not possible. Olga said ... she described him perfectly, gave me his licence plate number.' Eduardo was babbling like a drunk whose

296

ideas had all crowded his head at once, forcing their way to his mouth. He stared at Who, eyes wide, as though the boy were an impostor, a magician who'd caught him off-guard with a trick that he was trying to figure out, desperate to know what the secret was.

Mr Who's hand became an exclamation point, his fist striking Eduardo's cheek and causing him to fall to the ground, though more out of surprise than the force of the blow. Mr Who didn't let up. When Eduardo leaned on one elbow to raise himself, he kicked him in the ribs, hard.

'Why are you making this up? Isn't it bad enough that you fucked up my entire life? Now you want to mock me, too? Are you trying to tell me you killed my father and left my mother crippled because of something someone *told* you, something you didn't even bother to find out if it was true?'

His hand returned to the revolver's grip, to the safety of the gun, which he no longer tried to hide. The barrel was aimed right between Eduardo's eyes, forcing him to stare at it cross-eyed as though his eyeballs were magnets drawn irresistibly to the metal.

Eduardo closed his eyes and clenched his teeth. He heard the gun being cocked and felt the barrel in the centre of his forehead like a finger trying to dig out his deepest thoughts. Why had Olga lied to him? Or was Who the one who was lying? Why did he believe her back then, but him now?

All of his questions froze as he heard the muffled clack of the bolt, the hammer being cocked. One, two, three times in a row, the same bang, as the cylinder turned. There was no explosion, no instantaneous searing pain, no smell of gunpowder, none of the things you're supposed to feel when a bullet hits your head.

Eduardo opened his eyes, trembling. Mr Who's eyes were boring into him. His expression seared with pain and desperation, piercing him as he cried rivers of tears like lava, sliding down his cheeks, burning them like acid.

He'd fired into the ground.

18

Arthur's eyes looked watery. Gazing at them against a backlight, they took on a greenish tone. Olga traced the outline of his pupils with one finger and felt their coldness through the paint like a riverbed full of moss-covered rocks. She jerked her hand away, startled, but the eyes in the portrait followed her. Eduardo had done a great job. In just four months he'd accomplished what Gloria had asked of him — an X-ray of the man who'd killed her son. His brushstrokes had achieved what no one else could have pulled off in such a short space of time. And yet, when he'd brought Olga the canvas three days ago, he didn't seem happy or even satisfied with the result.

'It's done. But it's incomplete, unfinished,' he'd said with resignation.

And now, contemplating Arthur's expression, seething with a fury that came from deep within, Olga thought she saw what Eduardo meant. At some point over the course of those weeks, Arthur's pose had morphed, and the result was contradictory somehow — disjointed, dysfunctional. When Arthur had found out that the portrait was for Gloria, his disposition had altered, become a sort of unspoken accusation that oozed from his every feature. And Arthur wasn't the only one who had changed. The Eduardo that Olga saw, too, was different — more despondent, emptier than usual, as though the last of his energies had gone into that painting. And still he felt no matter how many sketches he'd made, he'd failed to capture the image he had in his head.

Eduardo had asked Olga to be the one to deliver the painting to Gloria. He didn't want to see her, didn't want to know anything else about the job, or about Arthur, or anyone. He nearly left Olga's apartment without even picking up the cheque that belonged to him, and when she'd reminded him he'd looked at the piece of paper as if it were dirty. Olga thought for a second he was going to tear it up, but in the end he simply folded it slowly and slipped it into his pocket.

'I'm never going to paint another portrait, Olga. I quit. Graciela and Sara are leaving Madrid. Graciela's parents have a little house in a beach town on the Costa Brava and she's asked me to go with them. I think I might just take her up on the invitation.'

That had been three days ago. The portrait was still in Olga's studio. She hadn't dared to dismantle the frame and wrap the canvas to send to Gloria. And though she had a number of excuses for not having done it yet, the truth was that she was scared. She felt a vague but mounting fear. Olga didn't know how, but she was sure the painting was the key that was going to open those doors she'd managed to keep locked for fourteen years. She actually wondered if maybe it would be better to destroy it, and was on the verge of doing so, brandishing a pair of scissors. She got as far as touching them to Arthur's well-defined, fleshy lips. But the portrait stopped her, as though invisible fingers had gripped her wrist. *You wouldn't dare*, his angular pastel face seemed to say. And she hadn't.

It was absurd, she said to herself when she got up that morning and went to sit before the easel, drinking coffee in her robe. It was a disturbing painting, not a living thing. Arthur had no idea who she was, even if his portrait did seem to follow her all over the apartment. And Gloria was just a weird client, a woman obviously scarred by her son's death, her divorce, and the fact that the best years of her career were now behind her. Besides, Eduardo didn't suspect a thing — she'd have been able to tell. She knew him well, far better than he suspected. Maybe his crazy idea of running off with his landlady and her ailing daughter was actually the best thing for everyone. Lately when she was with him, Olga got the ridiculous urge to tell him the truth. The *truth* — the absurdity of it made her shake her head. She touched her belly through the satin of her robe, as if she could find the meaning there, tattooed onto the tiny scar above her pubic bone. The *truth* was that she couldn't have kids. That she was alone, that she felt dirty and guilty, and that no matter how much she worried about Eduardo and tried in vain to make it up to him, she could never undo what had been done.

She was only sixteen years old at the time. That in and of itself should have been enough of an excuse. Adolescence is a kind of hell that not everyone emerges from unscathed. Sometimes decisions made without thinking end up deciding a person's fate. Heaven or hell, in whatever form they take. Olga had fallen in love with the wrong man and had never stopped wondering if she'd still be in love with him today, and the answer — that it was very unlikely — tormented her, because it meant that she'd destroyed her own life as well as Eduardo's for something that wouldn't even have been worth it. But it had changed her life forever.

When she got pregnant, the woman she could have become had died. The Olga who now sat staring at Arthur's portrait, drinking bitter coffee and smoking with her knees curled under her on the sofa, was a mask that was dissolving, a façade that came closer to falling off with each passing moment. Some nights she'd get home drunk, having hooked up with some random stranger at a club. Then she'd look in the mirror and see her smeared lipstick, her dishevelled hair, her mascara running down her face. She'd try to find herself in that reflection — but all she saw was darkness. That was what the *truth* was. That was what *she* was. And telling Eduardo what she'd done wasn't going to change it.

'You should burn that portrait. In fact, I should have burned it myself.'

Olga whipped her head around, startled. Eduardo stood by the door, the keys to her apartment in one hand.

'I didn't hear you come in,' she said, but her expression asked something quite different: *What are you doing here?*

Eduardo tinkled the keys like a little bell. Olga had forgotten she'd given him a set long ago. Until now he'd never used them. He circled the sofa without taking his eyes off the painting and walked over to face it, just a metre away.

'I was sort of hoping you wouldn't be here so I wouldn't have to face up to this,' he said calmly, as if he were speaking to the painting. But he was speaking to her, although he wasn't looking at her. She could see only the nape of his neck, a thick crease above the collar of his shirt. That deep-set wrinkle had a severe look about it.

'What are you talking about?' Olga asked. She felt uncomfortable and noticed a sudden chill on her bare feet. Pretty feet, nicely pedicured toenails.

Eduardo slumped his shoulders, as if the portrait had disappointed him. As he turned to face Olga, the crease on his neck twisted into what looked like a jeer. Up until that moment she hadn't seen his black eye or swollen lower lip.

'What happened to you?' she asked, springing up from the sofa. She reached out to touch the fresh wounds on Eduardo's face, but he jerked away with a quick sidestep.

300

The wounds weren't what hurt.

'There's something I want to show you, so why don't you get dressed. We're not going far, just a little drive ...'

The sentence trailed off — Eduardo wasn't willing to finish it.

'Why all the mystery?'

Eduardo gave Olga a stony look, even colder than usual. His chapped lips were parted, gums and rough tongue showing.

'Get dressed, Olga. It wasn't a request.'

Eduardo drove toward the outskirts of Madrid and then took the Barcelona highway. Olga looked out the window every little while to mentally escape the suffocating, enclosed space of the car. She babbled nervously about trivial things, making obvious her discomfort at Eduardo's silence.

'Where are we going?'

Eduardo told her she'd see soon enough, and in order to quash any possible protest on Olga's part, he turned up the radio. On the news, they were still talking about the fire on Calle León. Apparently, new evidence discovered by the police made them suspect that it had not in fact been an accidental fire but an act of arson intended to cover up the murder of the antiques dealer, who according to the coroner's report showed signs of having been tortured before being so badly burned. The police were questioning several witnesses, among them the concierge of the building next door, and they claimed to have reliable information on the possible perpetrator. Hearing this, Eduardo thought of Ibrahim and the strange way he'd reacted on seeing him.

'Mind if I change the station?' It was just a rhetorical question; she was already turning the dial — Eighties classics: 'La calle del olvido' by Los Secretos.

Por la calle del olvido vagan tu sombra y la mía
cada una en una acera, por las cosas de la vida

Drifting down Lonely Street, your shadow and mine
Opposite sides of the road, I guess that's just life.

Eduardo clenched the wheel tightly.

'Change the station.'

'Why?'

It had been Elena's favourite song; she used to hum it constantly.

'Just change it.'

Olga snapped the radio off and studied Eduardo, clearly irritated.

'What's the matter with you, Eduardo? You're acting very strange.'

He glanced into the rearview mirror, then straight ahead. They were leaving the metropolitan part of the city behind.

'A little patience,' he murmured, as though to himself.

Traffic had thinned notably. Without realising it, Eduardo had started driving too fast, as though he wanted to get the whole thing over with as quickly as possible. Open fields now dotted the landscape, giving it a more serene aspect. The four-lane road narrowed to two — with no shoulder — and wild scrub crowded the side of the road, threatening to grow over the embankment, making it clear that at the slightest chance it would recolonise the land that nature had intended for it. The sky was clean and steely, clear and cloudless. Eduardo lowered his sunshade. Olga donned a pair of oversized sunglasses. The only thing between them was the roar of wind rushing in the half-open windows and the sound of tyres on the asphalt — asphalt which was in increasingly poor repair. At some point, the intense smell of animal hides and dyes started to fill the air, and there appeared in the distance a small town, industrial warehouses dotting its outskirts.

Olga sat up straight, suddenly stiff.

Eduardo turned off and took a back road. After a few metres, they came to a shimmering stream that ran parallel to the road, and he stopped at a curve leading off to the right — the exact place where his car had plunged into the water fourteen years earlier. He turned off the engine and dropped his hands to his knees. Unconsciously, Eduardo began to stroke his right knee through his trousers, as if by going back to the scene of the crime his wounds had reopened and were throbbing anew.

You could hear the gentle gurgling of the stream and the wind swaying the reeds close to the shore. Wildflowers lined the water's edge. A few black birds darted around, just specks in the sky — swifts maybe, or swallows, it was impossible to tell from that distance. Above their heads, high up in the sky, was the metallic glint of a plane ploughing through space, leaving a white contrail like a meteorite.

'Why are we here?' Olga asked. She was clearly feeling on edge.

Eduardo, on the other hand, felt quite calm.

'Where was it? Where'd you see that guy's car? Where did he get out?'

'I don't remember exactly. It was fourteen years ago.'

Eduardo gave her an icy stare. He himself remembered every detail of the accident precisely. He hadn't been able to forget. In fact, the details became more and more fixed in his mind with each passing day.

'When you asked me to paint that portrait, you asked me something I didn't know how to answer. You asked why I hadn't gone to the police the day you came to my house, why I didn't tell them what you told me about the driver who killed Elena and Tania. I know the answer now. But you knew it even back then, fourteen years ago.'

Olga shivered. He knew. Eduardo knew.

'You lied to me. You've never even been here, have you? You didn't see the accident — there was no car, no man, no licence plate. You made it all up. You knew I'd kill that man and you used me, to get me to do it. I was your instrument, your enforcer. And the one thing I keep wondering — the thing I've been asking myself nonstop since yesterday — is *why*? Why would you do something like that?'

Olga took off her sunglasses and folded the arms carefully. She was trembling. She thought now of the silver cross her mother used to wear around her neck, the way it swung when her mother bent down to pick her up when she helped her cross the stream.

'I know this place better than anyone. That much, at least, wasn't a lie. On the other side of the stream, behind those reeds, is a narrow path that leads to a farmhouse. When I was a girl we called it "the house of sorrow" because the man who lived there was a lonely, bitter man whose wife had run off with a vacuum-cleaner salesman from Zamora. Kids are cruel — we'd go out there and throw stones at his windows until he came to look out. Then we'd start shouting, call him a cuckold and say all sorts of mean things. We did it from a safe distance, of course, ready to take off running if he came out to chase us off. But he never did. We never got him to come out. And then one day, the Guardia Civil showed up to take him down. He'd hung himself from a fig tree.' She pointed east with her glasses. 'There used to be a granary over there, and a stable for mules and barnyard animals. When I got home from school, my mother would carry me out to feed the goats and chickens. There was this one brown duck that I really loved, I watched it hatch, and I'd come feed it by hand. One day, some kids from school were playing Cowboys and Indians out by the corral. The Indians had these arrows — they were really good, made with reeds — and the arrowheads were Coke-bottle caps filed down with a sharp stone. One of them got my duck. I buried it myself, not far from those rocks. So, this is the geography of my childhood. I thought I'd always be happy here. But this was where I learned I'd never be happy at all.'

A ray of sunlight streamed through the car window, splitting Olga's face in two — one half shiny, like polished wax, the other faded, concealed in a dark shadow.

'I knew it was a mistake to ask you to paint that portrait. I knew it, and yet I did nothing to stop it,' she said, waving her sunglasses in front of her mouth.

The night before the accident, she'd thought she was going to die. The heat was so sticky and suffocating she couldn't sleep, even with the windows open. And she'd started haemorrhaging again, the third time in the two weeks following the abortion. *Haemorrhaging* was too big a word for the blood leaking through her panties on to the mattress. But that blood meant that something was wrong, terribly wrong inside her body. Her abdomen hurt and she was running a fever. She'd lost her appetite and didn't want to stay for dinner so her mother wouldn't suspect anything. But it was too late for that; she already did.

They'd had a ridiculous fight that night over something silly — the television. They each wanted to watch different programs and her mother had put a dramatic end to the issue, seriously overreacting. She switched the television off so violently it nearly toppled from its stand. Her mother had called her wilful, spoiled, and ungrateful. She shouted from the depths of her being, clenching her fists, eyes wild. And then suddenly, unable to contain her wrath, she slapped Olga in the face.

'She glared at me, and she was so full of rage. At the time, I couldn't see straight — I was just as livid. I hated her, too. I hated her for having brought Teo home the first time, for not having seen the seduction unfolding before her eyes, the way he was making me fall in love with him. I hated my mother for allowing it to happen, for not stopping me

— a spoiled child — from playing a grown-up game and getting caught in the trap.

'I was jealous of her, crazy jealous, and secretly I blamed her for Teo having left me, having walked out on our lives and leaving that empty hole. But more than anything, I hated her for the fact that my womb was now a barren wasteland where nothing would ever grow again. How could it have happened right in front of her eyes? How could she not have done anything? In order not to lose Teo, she'd pretended to be blind and deaf, she'd humiliated herself and opted to share him with me, and share me with him. And in the end, she'd lost us both. When she slapped me, all the hatred she felt for me became just like the hatred I felt for her. And I slapped her right back, and called her a slut, and a bad mother, and a bitch. I wanted her to die, wanted a bolt of lightning to strike her down on the spot.'

'So the man who seduced you and got you pregnant is the man I killed.'

Olga nodded. Thick, fat tears welled in her eyes and then fell, dribbling streaks of mascara onto her nose and mouth. She made no effort to wipe them away, and dug frantically in her bag for her cigarette and lighter. The filter became soggy as she struggled to light it.

'You have no idea how much I hated her. Every time I felt that searing pain inside, every time I thought about that basement where I got the abortion, every time I heard my mother crying over him or saw her looking at a picture of the two of them, it made my guts churn.'

She'd imagine what his naked torso looked like that first weekend when he'd taken her virginity; imagine what he looked like after making love, with his pants on but his belt undone and zipper down, his curly chest hair going all the way down to his belly button; see his expression, so full of joy an hour before, but evasive and confused after going to the bathroom and showering. And Olga couldn't understand. She remembered that she'd feel like an idiot, trying to read his noncommittal expression, wondering if she'd done something wrong, if she'd acted in some way that made it clear she was not yet an adult, not a real woman, an expert lover like her mother.

She still cringed at the humiliation she'd felt when she'd knelt down in front of him, wanting to pleasure him, and he'd rebuffed her with a bored-looking expression. At that precise moment, she realised she'd never be happy. It dawned on her with utter clarity, and she'd wanted to cry, to get dressed and run away. But he held her back, said he was sorry, that he was nervous — came up with a thousand excuses when just one would have been more than enough, because Olga wanted to believe him, wanted to quiet the voice inside her that was telling her to be careful.

There actually *were* times when the lie had a hint of truth — that night when they danced naked on the beach with the whisper of the waves, the moon, the bottle of wine half-buried in the sand, giggling over the candles because they couldn't keep them lit. Romance was a cheap dress, easy to sew, and she liked to wear it, even though Teo hardly spoke and never once mentioned having a future together. She accepted it all impatiently.

Until Maribel, his wife, turned up. That was when she stopped believing.

'I'll never be able to erase that scene from my mind: the happy house, our own bliss; the two of us naked, play-fighting in bed; and I was so unbelievably happy that day, waiting for the right moment to tell him I was pregnant. And then she showed up, right in the bedroom, in a white gauzy dress with straps, which I thought was beautiful. You could see the silhouette of her legs and hips in the light streaming in from the window. She was wearing these earrings with unopened flowers on them — gold, like the necklace quivering around her neck — and holding a brown overnight bag with both hands. The zipper was open and there was a book sticking out, I don't remember what book it was. She stood there all silent, unemotional, resolute, in her high heels. She didn't say a word until we realised she was standing there. It was Teo who saw her first. I was on top of him, tickling him, thinking, *I'm going to tell him now and he's going to wrap his arms around me.*'

Olga was still hurt by how naive she'd been, and blamed herself. When he saw his wife, Teo hurled her off him, literally threw her to the side the way people throw off the sheets when they suddenly realise they're late for something. And all her happiness instantly vanished, sucked up by that woman, who was like a black hole in her universe. Their universe, the universe that belonged to the two of them. It was pitiful, the way he begged, practically on his knees, babbling excuses, clinging to the legs at the bottom of that beautiful strappy dress — she remembered, now, that it had mother-of-pearl buttons where the straps attached to the bodice

— ignoring Olga as though she didn't even exist, as though she'd never existed, as though he regretted her existence. Cursing her.

Olga wrapped herself in the sheet, huddled in one corner of the bed that still smelled like the fresh, hot semen of the man who had just cast her aside. But there was no protecting herself from that woman — she had such a compact, beautiful body that Olga felt cheap and insignificant by comparison. *You're nothing but a little whore who made him think he could pretend he was still young,* her eyes said. *That's all you are, a tiny speck, an affront that he'll beg forgiveness for. And I'll forgive him even though I don't forgive him, because I love him and he's my man and I'm his wife. Because you're nothing; you're no one. You don't even exist.*

Maribel told Teo to get his clothes. She didn't want to spend another second in that bedroom. And he obeyed like a little lap dog, eager and embarrassed at the same time. He dressed awkwardly, rummaging among the wrinkled sheets and Olga's underwear for his shirt, and when she tried to say something, to assert her presence, he shot daggers at her.

I'm pregnant. First she said it very quietly, struggling to find the words, to get enough air to say it. He didn't hear her and continued to dress hurriedly, buttoning his shirt wrong. And then Olga shouted it, howled it in fact. *I'm pregnant!* That time neither of them could ignore her words: Teo didn't know where to look, his eyes darting around erratically. Maribel let out a low moan, dropping the bag in her hands, and the book fell out, spine up, its pages splayed. A noxious silence coiled around them.

Maribel was the first to regain her composure. She bent down demurely — legs to one side so as not to flash her panties when she crouched — and gingerly picked the book up, wiping the dust off the cover, the invisible, bothersome dust that the wind had brought in from the beach. Then she straightened back up with the same dignity, tugging gently at the hem of her dress to smooth out a nonexistent wrinkle. *I'll wait outside,* she said blandly to Teo, who was gazing forlornly at a shoe not knowing which foot it went on.

I'll wait outside meant that she'd wait on the other side of the whole incident, that she'd chosen to turn back the hands of the clock so as to relive those minutes without that scene. It was her way of saying, *This never happened. This has nothing to do with us. We're not responsible. You're*

*nothing but a little whore, a fool who didn't take the necessary precautions —
and now you'll have to handle it on your own. We're not part of this.*

'I didn't see Teo again. He stopped answering my calls, and one day
I got a recording that said the number was no longer in service. I didn't
know where he lived — he'd never told me — but I remembered his
licence plate number. You saw for yourself how easy it is to get someone's
records from the traffic department. So I started hanging around his
neighbourhood like a crazy. I'd watch him work in his coin shop, right
below his wife's dance academy. I'd spend all afternoon watching through
the giant windows from the sidewalk, staring at her in her black leotard,
with all those disciplined little ballerinas obeying her. She looked like an
elegant swan being followed around by her little chicks — so ethereal.

'I wondered how it was possible for them to just carry on with their
lives, pretending I didn't exist. I'd take pleasure in imagining them fighting
at night, shouting and insulting one another about me, about our baby,
who would never be born. I dreamed that Maribel refused to let him
sleep on his side of the bed, that she made him sleep like a dog at the
foot of the bed, threw his food down and made him eat off the floor. I
imagined Teo tormented by his punishment and guilt, wondering what
had happened to me, missing me.

'Thinking about those things didn't bring me peace, but it consoled
me in the same way alcohol consoles people — by killing them slowly.
Fantasising about their troubles helped me feel a tiny bit less troubled.
But I wasn't even granted that consolation. Day after day, I'd see them
leave their building with that kid between them — the boy they'd adopted
who wasn't even Teo's real son, who he didn't love. And yet that little boy,
holding both their hands, was the bridge that united them.'

Eduardo had been silent for quite some time, hadn't even moved. He
was so still that it was as if he'd gone someplace else, leaving his body
behind. But his eyes were still staring straight ahead, at the stream. His
eyelids fluttered, blinking back the tears in his eyes.

'So you decided to take revenge.' His voice sounded like it was coming
from inside a hollow wall.

Olga shook her head. It wasn't that easy, though in a sense it was.
Revenge required the kind of effort and planning that she wasn't capable
of at that time. It was chance that had given her the opportunity.

'I saw you in the emergency room one day. I'd gone there because the pain and haemorrhaging were killing me. I was alone, because my mother had refused to come with me. As I was waiting on a cot, I heard a couple of nurses talking about what had happened to you, how your wife and daughter were dead and if you kept on the way you were, you might die, too. I spent one horrible night out in the hallway — but for some reason I couldn't stop thinking about you and your family. I understood why you were refusing to eat, to take your medication. You were as miserable as me — your tragedy had been as unexpected as mine. I figured that your hatred for whoever had caused the accident must be as immense as my hatred for everyone, especially Teo and his wife. As if we had no right to anything at all. In the morning, I was released, and as I was getting ready to leave, I passed your room. The door was ajar and I didn't dare open it, but I could see you. You were in bed with an IV in your arm, staring out the window, your face still all swollen from the accident. Your father was talking to you, sitting in an uncomfortable-looking chair at your side, but you weren't paying any attention. You were a mess, and as awful as it might sound, that comforted me, made me feel less alone. I went down to the florist in the lobby and bought a bouquet and asked them to send it up to your room.'

She paused for air and to gather her thoughts. Eduardo didn't hurry her.

'Months later, I had to go down to the police station for some paperwork. I was in Madrid, so I went to the Puerta del Sol station. I hadn't forgotten about you, but I had thought about you less. It was all slowly fading, as my physical pain subsided. I was learning to tolerate my life, put up with the arguments with my mother and her stubborn, accusatory silences. I'd even started fooling around with a boy from a nearby town.

'I stopped hanging out around Teo's house and assumed that in time it would all just become part of a past that I'd keep under wraps, in the deepest part of me. Anyway, while waiting to be seen by the police, I passed the time reading all the notices on the bulletin board. There were photos of missing people, criminals on the run, that kind of thing. And then I got to this one notice. The police were asking for help solving a double-homicide. It was manslaughter. I remember the word because I didn't know what it meant. It was about your wife and daughter, about the accident. They gave a general description of the vehicle that might

309

have caused the accident, a few possible letters of the licence plate, the SUV's make. Then a cop walked in and asked if I was okay. I guess I must have been pale. I debated, I wanted to say something. But I couldn't get the words out.'

As though willpower were enough, Olga had actually believed she was going to be able to put her life back together — until she saw that poster. She thought she'd start over, go to school in Madrid, fall in love with someone who wouldn't care that she couldn't have children. But willpower isn't always enough to twist the hands of fate. She left the police station still choked up by that sudden stumbling block that had been thrown in her path, her plans to forget. She started wondering if life sometimes gave you signs, signs you didn't always know how to interpret. And the answer came in the form of a greeting: *How are you, Olga?*

'It took me a second to recognise him. His face was rounder, more tanned, sort of puffy, and he'd grown a scruffy beard, speckled with grey. But it was him. Teo. He was carrying a bunch of shopping bags in his right hand — it was almost Christmas — and holding his son's hand with his left. He was a good-looking kid, whose face I couldn't see entirely because he was wearing a scarf and wool cap. The boy was looking into shop windows not paying any attention to us, and Teo smiled. *What a surprise; you look good.*

I am good, Olga had replied, though it came out in a hoarse whisper.

She couldn't breathe and had to order her heart to start beating again. Teo looked her over, looking carefree and flirty. He couldn't stop smiling, and Olga didn't know why. He talked nonstop without letting her speak, as though he didn't want to give her a chance to ruin his pre-planned script. He told her things were going well — *relatively*, he added with fake nostalgia. And then he reached out his right hand, the one holding all the Christmas presents, and tucked back a lock of her hair. Things were going well, but he missed her. *If you know what I mean*, he'd added pointedly.

Olga didn't know, didn't want to know. And as if she were still the silly naive girl she'd been a few months earlier, Teo whispered, leaning close, that they could start things back up again, see each other from time to time, have a little fun — though, he'd added with a faux reproach, they'd have to be more discreet, take measures to avoid *accidents*.

310

Olga had stared at him like he was a two-headed monster, one grotesque and the other hideous. She called him a son of a bitch. And Teo had gotten a ridiculous look on his face, like a little boy whose toy had been snatched away just when he thought it was all his.

'I spent all night tossing and turning, reliving the scene, his words, his expression, the feel of his fingers on my hair, the smell of his breath on my cheek. I threw up several times, cried more than I can say, cursed him, insulted him, and then slowly the idea of hurting him started to take form. Hurting him as horribly as he'd hurt me, causing him some kind of definitive, humiliating pain. I knew Teo had a dark-coloured SUV, and at least one of the numbers coincided with the one that had caused the accident that killed your family. It wasn't something premeditated, it just came into my head all of a sudden, like when someone solves a problem they've been studying for a long time and then all the pieces just fall into place effortlessly. And the next morning, I went to see you.'

Olga gazed at the stream, the hilly meadow, the reedbed on the other side of the shore.

'I didn't know you were going to kill him.'

Eduardo gave her a hard stare. He'd started to perspire, as if the struggle raging inside him were being sweated out through his skin, through a searing heat.

'Seriously? And what exactly did you *think* I was going to do?'

'I didn't think anything. I wasn't thinking at all, I didn't even see Teo's death as an option. I just wanted to fuck him over, show the whole world what kind of pig he was, destroy the facade of his perfect life. I didn't consider the consequences it would have for you.'

Eduardo looked at the car door on Olga's side; the dirty brown cushioned upholstery. Olga's hand was resting nervously on the windowsill. That slender hand, once, at the penitentiary, had tried to touch his crotch. They had been in a room that allowed physical contact between prisoners and visitors, no double-paned glass smudged with the fingerprints of those trying to touch one another despite the barrier. Sitting at a table beside him, Olga had slid her hand down to Eduardo's crotch and gently rested it on his penis, light as a little butterfly. She'd offered to *console* him, said she owed him at least that much. And he had let himself be consoled. And that night he'd cried until he had no more tears.

'You didn't consider the consequences. But there are always consequences, and it doesn't matter if you think about them or not. They're there.'

Eduardo's eyes had drifted to the left, to a place between the shore and a cluster of pines. Olga glanced in the same direction. A young man was approaching, walking down the hill. In Eduardo's nightmares, the young man was coming from a forest, half-naked and being chased by ferocious dogs. But that morning, there was no barking, no urgency to the young man's gait. He walked slowly toward the car with the assurance of the inevitable.

'Who's that?'

Eduardo gave Olga a look of pity. The past, the future, who knows? He couldn't hate her for what she'd done. But he couldn't forgive her, either. Martina had been wrong. Forgiveness was not a path for him.

'Teo's son.'

Olga shot him a panicked look.

'What's he doing here?'

Closing the circle, Eduardo thought.

'You can't leave me with him!'

But he could.

Mr Who stopped at the open car door. He reached out an arm and pulled Olga's out of the car. She clung weakly to the frame, like a broken marionette, shouting to Eduardo for help.

Eduardo started the car and drove away slowly, forcing himself not to glance in the rearview mirror.

19

Arthur walked into the café across the street from the National High Court. It was ten o'clock in the morning and the bar was lined with judges, lawyers, district attorneys, and plainclothes cops. Public servants who righteously imparted justice, but drank coffee, ate canapés and read the sports papers, too. Some of them went to restrooms and forgot to zip up their trousers or tuck their blouses back into their skirts. Some also occasionally had stains on their jackets, looked as if they'd had rough nights, or told dirty jokes of questionable taste, laughing in an uproarious fashion. Arthur recognised some of their faces, recalled some of their names, greeted a few with a less-than-confident handshake, gave a few nods of recognition across the room, but mostly he felt uncomfortable. He didn't like these people.

Ibrahim had walked in behind him, his menacing appearance, although tempered by a smart dark suit, catching the attention of those closest to the doorway. They eyed him with wariness, if not outright aversion. He ignored them with a defiant smile that caused the scar on his face to pull taut.

The two of them caught sight of Ordóñez at one of the tables, his back to them.

'Good morning, warden,' Arthur said.

Ordóñez looked up from the paper he was reading. Given that there was no other news of interest, the media was still fixated on the Calle León arson-homicide. The article Ordóñez had been reading was a two-page spread, its headline resembling a Marcial Lafuente Estefanía western: *On the Heels of a Killer*. A photo of the suspect accompanied the story. Arthur hardly blinked when he saw Guzmán's face. It was an old passport photo, with a caption listing various aliases as well as the suspect's background: ex-DINA agent, then mercenary. Ibrahim saw it, too, before the Meco Prison warden folded the newspaper and asked them to take a seat. He shot Arthur a brief, meaningful look, but said nothing.

'You planning to put me back in your prison, warden?' Arthur asked

Ordóñez as he sat. Ibrahim took a seat across from him so he could keep an eye on the door and his back to the wall. *Prison habits die hard*, Ordóñez thought to himself.

'What makes you ask, Arthur? Get yourself in some hot water?' Ordóñez tried to reinforce the intended humour with his Italian-entrepreneur smile. He was dressed immaculately, in a pale-coloured tailored suit that complemented his shirt and striped tie. The man more resembled upper-management at a multinational than a local prison warden.

'I'm guessing you don't ask your ex-prisoners to breakfast with great frequency,' Arthur replied, keeping up the friendly tone, but making clear the distance that separated the two of them. Maybe inside Meco Prison, Ordóñez was God, but on the outside the balance tipped a different direction.

Ordóñez adjusted his cuffs, tugging cufflinked sleeves out from beneath his jacket. He cleared his throat and glanced quickly around the room, wondering what those who saw him in the company of Arthur, and especially Ibrahim, must be thinking.

'I've got a meeting with Justice Gutiérrez in his chambers in twenty minutes.' He said it as though meeting Justice Gutiérrez in private would somehow elevate his status to that of a public servant to be envied, but neither Arthur nor Ibrahim reacted as he'd hoped, so he simply smoothed his slicked-back hair. 'I thought we could have a little chat.'

'Whatever you say.'

'The Armenian escaped yesterday during a prison transfer. He killed one of the civil guards with him and injured another. We've managed to keep it under wraps for the time being, but that won't last — the press catches on pretty quickly. I wanted you to hear it from me. He swore he was coming after you, Arthur.' He tilted his head to one side and gazed at Ibrahim for a few seconds. The man had never caused any trouble inside Meco, but he was the type of prisoner who makes civil servants uneasy. 'And I don't think having Ibrahim around is going to be enough to stop him.'

Arthur considered this piece of news, but seemed unruffled. Ibrahim looked as though the news made no difference to him.

'I appreciate the courtesy, warden. But I have a feeling that's not the only reason you asked me to come.' Arthur shrugged. 'I don't exactly think I'm the apple of your eye, and I'm surprised at your concern.'

Ordóñez scrutinised Arthur's face and saw not fear but simply exhaustion — the constant tension was wearing him down, like a soldier in the trenches, bombs landing and bullets flying overhead, waiting for the order to charge the enemy.

'Indeed, there is something else. I saw the photos of the accident, the day you ran over the Armenian's daughter and the boy. You probably don't know this, but there's a traffic camera at that intersection, on the front of a clothing store. The local police use it to fine pedestrians, and drivers who don't give pedestrians right of way at the crosswalk. Strange, but during the whole course of your hearing no one actually showed the images from that camera, which could have shed light on a few murky issues. You see, as I said, the camera isn't in fact focused on vehicular traffic but on pedestrians.'

'I don't see where you're going with this, warden. It was an accident; I served my time and was granted a pardon. *Now* you want to investigate? Maybe you chose the wrong profession.'

Ordóñez paid no attention. He reached down to the floor for his briefcase and opened it on his lap.

'This is the sequence captured by the camera, just before and after the accident,' he said, setting half-a-dozen somewhat blurry stills down on the table.

Nothing that had not already been shown in court could be seen in the pictures. The first pictures showed Ian and Rebeca, along with other people, waiting to cross the crosswalk. Then there was one that showed the hood of Arthur's car emerging, a tumult of people, the girl being flung to the right and the boy being dragged by the car until he was pinned against a building front.

'Take a good look at these three,' Ordóñez said, pushing the rest to one side. Right here you can see Ian looking straight ahead, and at his side — though it's hard to tell since there are other heads covering him — is Rebeca. In the next one, Ian's turning to the girl, speaking to her. She's making an abrupt movement, as though trying to get rid of something. Take a good look. Ian's grabbing onto her arm, holding her tightly, and she's trying to wrench free. And in the third one, taken just before your car becomes visible, Rebeca is trying to get away, moving backward, and Ian's grabbing her by the hair. I suspect they knew each other, Ian and the girl. They weren't there by chance, and if we can trust what the photos seem to imply, she was certainly there against her will.'

'What does any of that have to do with me?'

'I was able to verify that Rebeca went to school that morning, as usual. Her mother dropped her off without noticing anything strange, but mid-morning someone came to pick her up and took her out of school. According to the janitor, it was a family member, though that was never proven. In fact, when the girl's mother was informed of her death, she said that it was impossible, claimed her daughter was at school several blocks away from the accident. Rebeca never should have been there. We might suppose, and it would just be supposition, that the unidentified person who passed himself off as Rebeca's family member was in fact Ian. And if that were true, why did he pick her up from school? Where was he planning to take her? What was he planning to do with her?'

Arthur had adopted a poker face.

'I still don't see what this has to do with me.'

'There's something here that doesn't add up, too many coincidences. I know about your daughter's disappearance, Arthur, and here's what I think: that there's a connection between that, Ian's death and these pictures. Justice Gutiérrez is a good friend of mine and I'm going to tell him my hunches, and ask him to pull some strings so that the whole case gets reopened. There's something big here, something much bigger than we realised. I know it. And if I'm right, then the facts will prove that you didn't kill Ian by accident, that it was premeditated murder. And then your pardon won't be worth the paper it's written on. I wanted to warn you first, in case you had anything you wanted to say. If you know anything about Ian's past, this is the time to let me know.'

Ordóñez's stainless steel watch twinkled in the light of the chandeliers.

'Your twenty minutes are up, warden. If you don't want to be rude to your friend the magistrate, you'd better be off.'

Ordóñez looked at his watch and frowned.

'Keep the photos; I've got copies. Maybe when the Armenian finds you, you'll be more forthcoming with him than you were with me.' He stood and gave Ibrahim a curious look. 'And as for you, I don't know what your role is in all this, but if you're not implicated, I'd be thinking about getting myself another job if I were you — unless you want the shit that this is going to kick up to stick to you, too.'

Once they were alone, Arthur turned back to the photos and examined them carefully, no longer feigning the look of indifference he'd shown in the presence of Ordóñez. His eyes darkened. He was shocked, and his mouth twisted.

'What's going on?' Ibrahim asked. He wasn't upset, just wanted to be kept abreast of the situation. He had no intention of being sent back to jail, not know. 'What does all that mean, all that stuff Ordóñez just said?'

It took Arthur a minute to come round. And when he did, his eyes darted back and forth erratically.

'Ordóñez is just speculating,' he said, sounding unconvinced. 'He hates me — I'm like a fish that slipped through his fingers. He's convinced I'm guilty and he wants me to pay my dues.'

Ibrahim looked at one of the photos Arthur was holding.

'Did you kill that kid on purpose?'

It took Arthur a few moments to respond. And when he did, it wasn't with words. His oily, evasive look was almost transparent, and that was enough.

After a sharp intake of breath, Ibrahim exhaled slowly through his nose.

'You've been lying to me all this time. You told me it was an unfortunate accident. You said it over and over.'

'I couldn't tell a soul … If you'd seen what that bastard did to Aroha …'

Ibrahim scratched the scar on his face. From time to time it stung, as if the wound had reopened. Now was one of those times. *If a man betrays you once, he'll do it twice, three times, as often as he can. Traitors have no honour, no moral code, no respect. That's why they have to be rooted out; they're like a malignant tumor, bringing fear, weakness, and lies.* That was what his father had written, before he was killed, and every night his older brother had read him that letter, those very words, holding a flashlight under the sheet. *We cannot be friends with those who consider us innately inferior. A dog is not man's best friend, only his best and most faithful slave. That's how Europeans see us — as dogs — and that's what they expect from us. Not friendship, or collaboration, or loyalty. Just blind obedience and the gratitude of a servant who's been tossed a few crumbs. That's why we must fight them to the death.*

317

'Does all this have something to do with the fire at the antique dealer's? I saw the picture in the paper. The man accused is the same guy you hired to find Aroha.'

'Guzmán didn't kill that old man.'

'Then who did? Why is it you're always in the middle of everything?'

Arthur shook his head, exasperated. His red mane of hair was like fire when the sun hit it.

Ibrahim closed his eyes. He was back in Algeria, on the outskirts of Algiers, in a public square. There was a large crowd gathered around some sort of ruckus, and people were hooting and shouting their heads off. It was early 1963. Elbowing his way through the crowd, scurrying beneath people's legs, and crotches that stank of sweat and dried urine, Ibrahim made it almost to the front. Three men were being flogged. They were tied, shirtless, to whipping posts. All three were ex-soldiers from the French auxiliary forces, born in Algeria, and had borne arms in the service of France. And then France had scuttled off with her tail between her legs, abandoning them to their fate, as they did to thousands of others who were being massacred all across the country.

The poor wretches were no longer even moaning, despite their savage punishment. There comes a time when any protestation, any begging for clemency, is useless. Their backs were literally flayed, skin falling from their bodies like onionskin paper with each lash of the cane. Someone in the crowd took out a machete and carved into their bare flesh the word *vassals*. Everyone applauded when the 'artist' raised his arms aloft, machete in hand as blood ran down his forearms, as if it had been stroke of genius. Ibrahim did not laugh. His stomach roiled and he vomited, to the glee of those present. But they didn't know that the poorly stitched and still seeping wound across his face had been made by someone with a very similar machete. A paratrooper's machete, used to scar brothers in faith.

When he opened his eyes, Arthur was still there. *That could have been you — or your father, or your brother, or your mother. Men with fiery hair and green eyes, who didn't get out in time. One of the men who was martyred there could have been you, and the one carving your flesh with his father's machete could have been me.*

'Just tell me one thing. Tell me it was worth it.'

Arthur grabbed his forearm, hard. Ibrahim wanted to throw up, but stifled his gag reflex.

'Listen, Ibrahim. I am so close to finding Aroha. Closer than I've been in four years. I want my daughter back and I'll do anything to get her — *anything*. Protect Andrea, that's your job. I don't want that degenerate Armenian to even think about laying a finger on her. Leave the rest to me. This will all be over soon.'

This will all be over soon. That was what Ibrahim had said to the nearest of the three men being whipped, back in early 1963. He'd gotten up close and whispered into his ear. But the man couldn't hear — he was already dead.

Ibrahim continued visiting Andrea and she'd grown accustomed to his presence. He no longer had to invent excuses to go see her, no longer had to pretend Arthur had sent him to keep her company and nourish her hopes that they'd find her daughter.

In the afternoons, they'd take long walks through the woods by the residence. People would see them together, sitting by a fence, chatting away among the cork trees or simply walking through a yellow field, side by side, in silence. Those first walks soon became habit and Andrea looked forward to them with ill-concealed impatience. Ibrahim's presence had unwittingly broken the monotony of her indolent everyday existence. And so the two of them had had the opportunity to rediscover each other, to reinvent themselves at will.

Ibrahim spoke to her about poetry and Sufi philosophy, about the music that his virtuoso father once played, about how a man like him, fighting tooth and nail just to stay alive, could still, at times, feel close to immortality.

Andrea hung on his every word, although every once in awhile he thought she looked pensive. When Ibrahim tried to steer the conversation toward her past, she gave him a look, and clammed up. But slowly the distance between the smile on her lips and the one in her eyes was melting; the wall she had erected was beginning to crumble.

That morning they went head-to-head in a dialectical battle of the wits, speaking French speckled with Arabic at head-spinning velocity. When they engaged in verbal duels, that was the whole idea, and each of them found the other to be a sharp and entertaining opponent, quick of mind and word. They'd laugh out loud, let fly a sentence or paragraph, and the other would fire back with equal speed. A nurse acted as judge without understanding the rules of the game, so she simply smiled like a fool, gazing back and forth between the two of them.

'What are you saying to each other?' she asked Ibrahim.

'Nothing that hasn't been said before. It's a game our teachers had us play when we were in school, outside by the mosque. It was a way to encourage us to learn, a war of words. We quote each other verses. Andrea gives me Rimbaud and I reply in Berber with a Kabyle poem. She throws out Verlaine and I come back with Nouara. She tries to trip me up with Baudelaire and I retaliate with Farid Ferragui. It's fun.'

Ibrahim had brought Andrea a small gift. It was a little leather bag. In it was a small book with a cowhide cover that contained the verses of over fifty Kabyle poems.

'My father wrote them when he was young. He was a great poet, in that way some men living desperate lives are.'

If he was expecting a warm, enthusiastic response, he was not going to get it. Andrea gazed at the book of poetry timidly.

'I've almost forgotten how to read Kabyle; I hardly even remember my classical Arabic.'

Ibrahim gave her a wide smile, abysmal teeth on full display.

'So you'll dig out your old childhood songs. Poetry is what allows us to preserve serenity, and it's also what gives us hope that one day the child who once lived inside can still come back to life.'

Andrea stared at Ibrahim in shock, moved by his candid voice, his peaceful look, so out of sync with his strong body and disfigured face. The scar across Ibrahim's face was a source of strength, but she didn't dare ask him when or how he'd gotten it.

'My daughter always refused to learn the language her mother and father spoke when they fell in love. She wanted nothing to do with Algeria, with the past, with history. Sometimes I imagine that when she's back in my arms and I'm holding her tight, she'll ask me to teach her those old Kabyle songs, to tell her about the streets of Kabylia, the smells. But then I open my eyes and here I am, and I know I'll never be able to teach her anything because I've forgotten it all myself.'

Ibrahim stroked her hair, almost not daring to touch her. Such

320

tenderness from a hand like his was breathtaking.

'Children always learn the lessons their mothers try to teach them too late. She'll come back to you, and you'll remember everything about your childhood, every step you took, and you'll relive it for her.'

It was hard not to believe him. Listening to Ibrahim, her conviction that sooner rather than later her daughter would be by her side grew stronger every day. Through Ibrahim's hope, she gradually returned to an almost lively state of mind. The progress she made was not a straight course, nor was it easy; at night, when he went home and darkness descended, filling everything, she became taciturn, sordid, sad. And in those bleak moments of desperation she tried to fool herself, tell herself that all she wanted was a little peace, a little certainty. She didn't want to believe that her daughter was dead. The fact that her daughter's body had not been found in four years had taken her to the brink of madness. And if she had not yet succumbed, if she was still hanging onto sanity by the skin of her teeth, it was because ignorance allowed her to keep that fiction going — the belief that, somewhere, her daughter was still alive.

'I promise you, one way or another we're going to find her,' Ibrahim assured her.

And she held his hand tight and said she believed him. The faith of a mother pining for her daughter.

'Life is like a gambler, it doesn't play fair,' she said. 'It lays it all out within reach, makes you believe happiness is attainable, and then when you naively decide to lay your bets, it snatches everything away and leaves you unable to get up from the table, forcing you to sit there playing the same hand even after you know you can never win.'

Ibrahim looked upset. He glanced down, unable to meet Andrea's gaze.

'My life didn't turn out the way I thought it would either,' he confessed with a sudden honesty the depths of which she could not fathom.

'Who were you, before you became … *this*?'

Before I became this scar? he asked with his eyes.

He gazed at her tenderly.

This scar is you, was his wordless reply.

He'd walked a long and painful road before ending up in a place he hadn't expected. But he knew it was here, and no place else, where he belonged. Beside her.

321

'I need to ask you a question, Andrea. I need to ask, because a lot of things depend on your answer.'

Andrea gave him an anxious look, full of fear.

'Do you still love Arthur?'

She sat very still. Then her eyes fluttered as if blinking away a speck of dust, and she pulled away from him.

'That doesn't matter.'

'Of course it matters. What could possibly matter more?'

Andrea's nostrils flared as she exhaled.

There was a time when Arthur meant so much to her that each of his slights cut her to the quick. But back then she put up with his infidelities, his mood swings and night terrors as if they were simply the price to be paid in exchange for his affections and his words, which could still evoke entire universes of immeasurable beauty. Andrea would feel his arms enfold her desperately, as if she were the one certain thing in his life, the one indestructible force. And it made her happy, made her feel unique and special. But she no longer felt that. She'd stopped feeling it a long time ago.

Their marriage had inevitably slipped into a comfortable security, a precursor to the death of passion. Suddenly she realised that when they made love — less and less frequently and more and more bureaucratically — Arthur behaved like a stranger in a strange land. His expression was like that of another man, and his sweet nothings, his magic words, no longer rang true. They'd lost their power of enchantment. True love is something mystical, but his words had become rote memorisation, like a priest saying mass.

It was about that time, back before Aroha was born, that she had found out he was in love with a woman named Diana, who ran the Chicago branch of his company. He'd slept with other women before, and kept doing so later as well, but Diana was different: a beautiful black woman, ambitious and worldly. She changed Arthur forever, stripped him of his poetic aspirations and turned him into a man consumed by more immediate desires: cars, money, stocks, influence, power. And Andrea was left with the result of all that — the proxy who kept trying to make her believe he hadn't changed, a body, but no longer a soul.

One night Arthur had come home terribly upset. Andrea had been waiting up for him because she had something important to tell him, but he didn't even see her when he walked in. His clothes were wet and his shoes splattered with mud. He went straight to the garage and returned a few minutes later with an industrial-sized garbage bag in one hand. When he saw Andrea there in the living room, he startled.

'How long have you been standing there spying on me?' he asked, furious.

Andrea stared at him, infuriated. *Spying*? Had he lost his mind? She'd been up all night waiting for him to come home — happy at first, then sad, and then livid, as the hours ticked by. And now he was making her feel like a stranger in her own home.

'We have to talk,' she said, her eyes going to the bin bag Arthur held. He held the car keys in his other hand. 'Are you planning to go back out?'

'Now is not the time, Andrea,' he replied. He'd been drinking, she thought, and maybe even taken drugs. His pupils were dilated and he kept licking his lips. He smelled like a brothel.

The smell offended Andrea deeply, as did the uncomprehending look he gave her when she said, 'Aroha's had a bad night. The colic kept her awake. We have to take her to the hospital.'

'And you expect me to do that? She's four months old, for God's sake, it's normal.'

Something happened then, a confrontation between the person each of them had become at that very instant. Chaos exploded in the most unlikely of ways. Andrea began shouting, insulting him senselessly, years of accumulated resentment and reproach streaming from her mouth like a torrent — everything from ridiculous offenses to deep emotional scars, pouring out with vitriol.

'I can't stand it anymore. I'll take Aroha. We're leaving.'

Arthur glared at her, full of hatred — for himself, for her, for everything. A hatred she'd never before seen. Aroha's crying could be heard coming from the bedroom upstairs.

'Do whatever the hell you want,' he shouted. And then he left, slamming the door, and Andrea stood there in the middle of the living room, staring at the broken glass from a vase he'd hurled on his way out.

Arthur returned early in the morning. Andrea heard him come into

323

the bedroom, take off his clothes and put them on a hanger, sit down beside her on the bed and sigh. He was gazing at her, taking in her expression, but she pretended to be asleep. She let him pull her close, so close that their bodies merged, let him cry on her shoulder, let his tears slide down onto her arms and her nightgown. She listened to him beg forgiveness, explain what a terrible day he'd had, promise that he'd change, swear he'd become the same man he'd once been.

She listened to him, and she accepted his words. But deep down, on that night fourteen years earlier, Andrea stopped loving Arthur.

The reception was in full swing. Waiters glided from group to group, balancing trays of ham, salmon and cheese canapés. They were like tightrope walkers, skilfully dipping and sailing between the guests. The hotel had installed two bars out on the terrace, one by the pool and the other close to the balcony overlooking Madrid's old quarter. The Secretary of State for Culture was giving a speech from a podium that had been set up in the centre of the terrace. No one was paying any attention to him, but he didn't seem to care. He smiled for the cameras like a mediocre, B-list actor.

Arthur glanced up. Eduardo had appeared to his right. He looked awful.

'What are *you* doing here?'

Eduardo gave the drunken giggle of a man who knows how to hold his liquor. He downed a glass of wine in one gulp, to the horror of those watching — it was, after all, 300-euro-a-bottle wine. Immediately, he accosted a waiter to grab another.

'I saw Ibrahim in the hotel lobby. I told him I had something urgent to discuss with you and he walked me to the elevators. His scar is like a VIP pass. The hostess couldn't bear to deny me entry.'

'You shouldn't be here. Especially not in the state you're in.'

Eduardo glanced around with a bemused expression.

'Why not? I'm the king's official portrait artist. And this is your court, is it not? Judges, politicians, entrepreneurs, writers, actors, lawyers … Bet they all owe you something, some kind of favour. Maybe they're afraid of you. I bet some of them even despise you. You're not one of them, and yet you own them. They *belong* to you. Don't you have the right to exhibit your serfs, your lackeys, the assortment of jesters who entertain you?'

Eduardo's voice was becoming loud enough to attract the attention of those nearby, without his intending it to. Arthur shot him a furious glance, discreetly took hold of his elbow and led him off to a corner.

Red roof tiles shimmered in the dappled late-afternoon sunlight of the Austrias quarter, making it look as if it had just rained. Above the balcony, fairy lights hung twinkling from invisible strings, like at a tacky open-air dance. The bells from the Convent of the Order of St Clare were ringing in the distance. If you closed your eyes, it could have been any small town in La Mancha. The speeches were over and Schubert was playing over the loudspeakers. The contrast was almost comical.

'Have you lost your mind? Why are you making a scene?'

With a transformative skill normally seen only in mimes, Eduardo's face suddenly morphed, no longer that of a mouthy drunk. He leaned in close to Arthur to examine his face, like a short-sighted man who's misplaced his glasses. Eduardo had spent so long trying to read that expression that he knew it as well as his own. And yet he now saw what Gloria meant when she rejected those first initial sketches he'd given her in Barcelona — he hadn't captured the most essential thing, hadn't captured Arthur's true nature.

'If I were to paint you again now, you'd look completely different.'

Arthur held his gaze, unperturbed, aware of the dozens of guests who, albeit surreptitiously, were paying close attention. But beneath his artfully unflustered face there was latent rage, and scorn oozed from the corners of his mouth.

'What do you want? You've got your portrait. Go ahead, give it to Gloria, tell her what kind of monster I am, feed her all the lines she wants to hear.'

Eduardo grabbed another glass of wine and gulped it down.

Arthur was a fraud, just like Gloria, just like Olga, like Eduardo himself — so caught up in his own memories that he couldn't tell truth from fiction. Their lives were completely artificial. They obsessed over superficialities in order to cover up their emptiness. He saw women wearing expensive jewels to try to camouflage their mediocrity, though it was still blatantly obvious the moment they jammed a pinky into their mouths to free a bit of trapped food. He saw a senior official smile for the cameras, and then the second he was out of the spotlight grope the waitress' breast while she stood there, resigned. He saw the guests' phony laughter not echoed in their eyes, as they searched for someone more important to grovel to. It was all a lie full of holes nobody wanted to see. Because they were the holes. All of them.

'I just found out that I killed an innocent man, fourteen years after the fact. I killed the wrong man.' The words weighed him down like stones, but he felt the need to vomit them forth. 'I'm a fucking bastard, a bad joke.'

The man inhabiting Arthur's body took his leave at precisely that moment. He left, went far away, to a place were Eduardo's eyes couldn't trap him.

'Nobody is innocent, Eduardo. I would have thought you'd have realised that by now.'

'Exactly,' Eduardo slurred. 'Nobody's innocent. Which leads me to a terrible conclusion — whoever killed my family is still out there, mocking me.'

Arthur sliced clean through him like a knife.

'What does that matter now? Would you kill again? Take revenge? We've all done plenty of stupid things in our lives.'

Eduardo looked away. Arthur was probably right.

'If only I could be sure that his life didn't turn out better than mine ...'

Arthur looked at him with pity. All Eduardo's expression told him was that it made no sense to find things out, if you can't do anything about them.

The little hotel on the outskirts of town was no longer there. The entire landscape had changed dramatically, and the change in terrain was echoed in more profound, more personal changes, too. Arthur hadn't been back in fourteen years, and as he got out of the car, he was hit by the inevitable transformation that awaits us all in the last stage of life.

It was hard even to make out the ruins of the building, which was now overrun by scrub so tall it covered the old stone wall that once surrounded the property. Part of the gabled roof had collapsed — it looked as if a bomb had fallen on it, and the beautiful Arabic tiles had lost their lacquered sheen and were now covered in scum. Most of the windows were bricked over and the walls had become a mural of graffiti. In one corner a rusty sign proclaimed the property was for sale, although the real estate agent's phone number was so faded it was nearly illegible. The highway had been rerouted behind the hotel, so the aggravating roar of heavy trucks was constant, and they'd put in a gas station with a minimart.

That place had once been their paradise, a respite from their daily lives, a place they came every weekend, for years. There were rustic curtains — very discreet — and fresh-cut flowers on the shelves; a huge Toledan bed with dark wood headboard; baskets of fresh fruit; and an adorable dining room with a half-dozen or so other couples — often the same ones, cuddling secretively, complicit — greeting one another wordlessly, wearing expressions of suppressed joy, taking part in the same half-guilty, half-effervescent clandestine adventure.

'I bet there's no place like this in Chicago,' he'd say to Diana, boldly taking her hand, hidden behind topiary bushes pruned into bizarre animal and plant shapes, enjoying the silence broken only by birds whose nests were so high in the trees that they were hard to identify. And Diana, dressed casually in jeans and a tank top, tennis shoes in place of high heels, no jewellery, let herself be swept away by that fairy tale. She smiled at him, wrapped her arms around him fearlessly, rested her head on his chest and kissed his neck, leaving a moist, warm trail across his skin.

They went every weekend — 48 hours of stolen time that Arthur managed by weaving a tangled web of excuses for Andrea. He'd become an expert liar, very convincing. Or so he thought. And the few hours he spent with Diana were just enough to be able to pretend that what they had was special and different, untainted by the vulgarity of everyday existence.

But the time lovers struggle to procure for one another ends up making them greedy. The perfect fiction stops being enough. And there comes a time when stolen time no longer suffices. One of the two always wants to give up their slice of heaven, to take a bite of the forbidden apple with the promise of something more real, albeit imperfect. In their case, it was Diana who wanted more — more time, more days, more intensity. She wanted the legitimacy of the light of day, wanted to experience the everyday travails of an average couple, the exhaustion of cohabitation, of the compromises couples make, which are in fact a struggle in which each tries to impose their desires on the other. She wanted to savour the slow defeat of permanent coupledom personally. Arthur's mawkish fairy tale was no longer enough.

'I want to be with you when you're sick, and weak, and insecure. I want to see you absent, angry, distracted; I want to see your selfishness and your childish whims; I want to see you cry. I want to be there, by your side. I'm tired of loving a fairytale. I want to love the real you, flesh and blood.'

That was what led to the argument they'd had the last night they spent in that hotel. Fourteen years ago. The fateful night had actually begun earlier in the evening, beneath the spikey fronds of a palm tree, when Diana began complaining — in Spanish — that she was just a *fulana*, a tart. Normally they spoke in English, removing themselves even further from real life. The heat that day was as thick as hot chocolate, though without the humidity of the coast. They were surrounded by dry pebbles, desiccated creek beds, the parched earth of what was once a pond baked and cracked. Bluebottles buzzed nearby, attempting to sip at flowerpots.

It was Arthur's fault. He should never have given in to the snake-charm of intimacy, to his own deceit. They had made love pressed up against the wooden doors of an armoire, imprinting their own sweaty skin with the designs carved into the wood. Then they'd lain down, still naked, on the cold ceramic tile floor.

It was the delusion of believing you inhabit the real world that led him to commit a serious blunder — when Diana asked him what he was thinking about, he told her. What he should have said was something like, *I'm thinking of you, of how perfect this is, I'm in heaven.* Something Diana's ears were prepared to hear, something that didn't go off-script. But he didn't. He told her something far worse. The truth.

'I was thinking about a little inn on Rue Al-Mansur in Algiers, by the port. It had a fan like this one, though the air there was different — salty, almost wet, it got under your skin and left you smelling like algae, and oil, and the docks. The light was different, too, it streamed across the furniture like the gentle hand of a giant caressing its possessions. From the window you could hear the sound of the waves, truck horns on the loading dock, stevedores shouting, children laughing — Algerian kids' laughter is unlike any music in the world, you should hear it. I was thinking that my heart used to pound in that bedroom, too, because I was younger, more impetuous, more naive. I was thinking about Andrea, lying beside me, against me, the two of us all steamy and stuck together like half-eaten candies that are starting to melt. I was thinking about the road that led me from that bedroom to this one.'

He was also thinking about ending the affair he was having with Diana, with all the Dianas in his life, about putting a stop to his weekend escapes and going home, and holding Andrea.

He was thinking that on the way home he'd stop off somewhere to buy her flowers. And a little something for Aroha, too. Maybe one of those little nightlights with bears on them.

The baby had come between them like a wall being erected slowly, brick by brick. He'd first sensed it when he saw her in the delivery room, as the doctor tied the umbilical cord. Astonishingly, Arthur had trembled in a way that more resembled fear than awe. He'd wondered what that tiny bundle of flesh was, shrieking as if the whole world were hers for the asking, and she was asking for it. What kind of *thing* — that was the only word that came to him — fitted in a pair of gloved hands, hands that scooped it up like water from a bowl. *She's all yours*, the doctor had said, handing her over like an offering, like a gift. And that power scared him.

He couldn't help but think of his father in his dress uniform, a decorated lieutenant in the paratroopers — tall, strong, redheaded, a tattoo on his neck proclaiming loyalty to the homeland, an indelible mark proving where his priorities lay. *Country before all*. Was he like that too? Was he like his father, or just a hollow shell?

He couldn't avoid that sick, horrible association. Every time he saw Andrea give her breast to a mouth that was not his, he felt like an intruder. He hardly dared to touch the baby, who stared at him unseeingly, searching for his voice like a blind man with wild eyes, wrinkling her little nose in recognition when he approached the rocking chair. It was as though he didn't want to contaminate her, as though he couldn't admit that jealousy and tenderness had been waging a fierce battle inside him from the moment she was born. And it was still unclear which of them was going to emerge victorious.

That's what he was thinking as he watched the fan blades rotate slowly, while Diana stroked his chest. So he told her.

'It's over between us.'

But nothing is ever over. At least not when we think it should be, and not the way we want it to be. Life had taught him that lesson more than once — in the hands of his French cousin; in Cochard's office; in the winding road that had led him to where he sat now, a king presiding over a vast mountain of poison. But he didn't want to hear that now, didn't want to hear that pernicious voice, mocking him. He rushed to get dressed — as if the countdown had started and the apportioned time he had to win Andrea and Aroha back or lose them forever were dwindling — and as he did so, Arthur felt sure he could push back the boundaries of fate.

The road narrowed and he came to a place where cones and construction fencing reduced the road to only lane. A detour led off to the right, on a secondary road that ran through a deserted town and then continued alongside a creek for a few hundred metres. The water wasn't visible, but it was audible, gurgling under the embankment. He took the detour without slowing down or stopping at a stop sign partially obscured by brush.

That was when he smashed into a car that was, at that precise instant, going the same direction he was.

He slammed against the steering wheel and the seatbelt kept him from flying through the front windshield. For a few seconds he lost consciousness, and when he came to, he wondered what had happened. Had it not been for the evidence of the upside down vehicle on the embankment down below, its wheels spinning the wrong way, he might have thought he'd dreamed the whole thing. He stumbled out of the car, dizzy, and staggered fearfully to look over the edge.

The creek was narrower to the right. On the opposite side of it lay a body, legs floating in the water. Arthur rushed down the embankment, tripped, fell and sprang back up. He rushed to the body. It was still breathing — a girl whose life was draining away as quickly as the torrent of her blood being washed down the creek, pouring from her ears, her mouth, her nose.

'Don't move. I'm going for help.' As if her broken body could have moved an inch.

He went back to the car for his phone. No coverage. *Think, Arthur, think.* But he couldn't keep his head straight, his thoughts were swirling, his brain screaming. It was all going on at once, a series of voices all clamouring to make themselves heard. He thought of the detour, the construction workers. There must be someone back there. They'd know what to do, be able to call an ambulance. He started the car and accelerated. The road was too narrow to turn around and he decided to drive forward until he found a place to turn and go back. People always think they'll find a place from where they can turn back.

Fifty metres later the road widened. And Arthur stopped. *What are you going to do? They're dead*, the eyes in the rearview mirror told him. *You killed them. But it was an accident. Don't throw your whole life away — not now of all times.*

Many kilometres later, Arthur walked into a gas station cafeteria. The employee paid no attention when, agitated, Arthur asked to use the phone.

He didn't call the police. It didn't even occur to him. He dialled Diana's number and told her everything, his voice wracked by sobs. No, no one had seen him. Yes, he was almost sure they were dead. No, his car didn't have any marks on it.

Then it never happened, Diana had said coldly.

And his heart felt light. *It never happened.* Anything can be undone, you just have to expunge it. That was what he wanted to hear. What he needed to believe. She'd take care of everything. Diana always did. And she would that time, too.

20

The Armenian lay in bed for a few minutes, his mind blank. He liked that silent hour of the morning when the coming day still holds the promise of something new — new things that, in the end, would turn out to be the same old things, deep down he knew that, but when he opened his eyes and saw that red horizon, the whole world seemed like a mystery waiting to be unravelled. He inhaled deeply, enjoying the fleeting sense of calm, the purity of the silence, the sense of tranquillity. Marijuana fuddled his brain, and he sang the chorus of Deep Purple's 'Highway Star', enunciating each syllable.

He didn't know why he had that song in his head when he opened his eyes, though he always awoke humming something. It had been like that for years.

On the floor lay a used condom, and an ashtray overflowing with butts sat in a pool of spilled beer. At the foot of the unmade bed were his pants, a fake passport from Bosnia and Herzegovina, and a duffel bag with a few changes of clothes, and a few thousand euros stashed in a false bottom. He'd be history in a few hours. He was going to lose himself forever in the hazy borders of the former Yugoslavia, a Promised Land for men like him. It wasn't so bad, not really. He'd been in and out of prisons and detention centres for as long as he could remember, and they were his natural habitat: the smell of disinfectant, the cell walls covered in thick layers of paint, the guards who treated prisoners terribly, the other prisoners' fear disguised as bravado.

But he felt old and tired. Younger men were coming to prison, and they had new codes — no loyalty, no respect. They tried to dethrone him the first opportunity they got. He was no longer omnipotent and sooner or later he'd succumb. He wasn't prepared to let that happen: anyone who's been emperor has no desire to be ousted and end up petty king of a band of hoods. By making that jailbreak, stabbing a civil guard, he was putting an end to a legendary prison career. And his legend had to remain unblemished for all time — he wasn't going back to prison in Spain, not ever.

'This has got to end,' said the woman lying beside him. She was smoking pot, too, and resting her hand on a belly less taut than he recalled. Nor did he recall the bouquet of wrinkles on her eyelids, or the tiny creases on her upper lip. Her eyes were the colour of autumn grass; she wasn't pretty, but he still found her attractive. Her name was Azucena, and on her finger she wore a white gold band engraved with the Armenian's real name, the one he never told anyone, the one those who knew it never dared pronounce in his presence.

'It will all be over soon. In a few days some associates of mine who trade slaves and hookers will take me to Sarajevo. They owe me a few favours. And from there, who knows? Turkey, Iran, Afghanistan. There are lots of opportunities out there for guys like me. But first I have to get rid of the son of a bitch who killed our daughter.'

'It doesn't matter where you go, Eladio, or what you do. Rebeca isn't coming back, and you'll never stop running, never. You've wasted your whole life running and you'll lose me that way, too. Running from your own life.'

The Armenian felt like he couldn't breathe. He didn't want to think about life. He didn't want to respond to a woman as lonely as he was, to her fingers, trying to intertwine with his.

Azucena was a social worker. They'd met at the prison a year before Rebeca was born. She was the only person who'd ever shown him anything resembling love. She took the time and effort to teach him to read and write. And she'd given him a daughter, Rebeca, who he'd seen just once a year, on her birthday, because he didn't like for his wife to bring her along on her visits — a jail was no place for a little girl destined to become a princess. He didn't want her to grow up and remember a father behind bars. But he always carried a photo of her in his wallet and he'd show it off to everyone when he was in a good mood.

He swapped it out for a new one every once in a while, to keep up with the changes as his daughter grew. He'd read some childhood psychology books and he'd attempt to convince anyone who would listen that he was a good father, that he worried about her education. The Armenian had created his own little fiction, that of a normal family, one in which he drilled into his daughter the maxim he'd lived by: *Never mess with anyone — but if anyone comes looking for you, you let them find you.* He'd pave the way for her, keeping her out of harm's way, protecting her and at the same time teaching her to bare her teeth and to bite when necessary. He dreamed of one day seeing her go to college — something he'd never done — and become a prestigious lawyer. He even considered the ironic possibility of her wearing a barrister's robe and making it all the way to the highest rung, the Supreme Court. Why not? Self-deception is a way to survive disappointment. And for six years — as long as she'd lived — that fairytale had kept him strong and determined.

Azucena was doing up her bra, sitting on the bed. Her dishevelled hair covered her face, obscuring the bags under her eyes.

'You should turn yourself in. I've still got friends in the penal service. They can help us.'

'I'm not turning myself in, Azucena. You can get that idea right out of your head.'

'So what do you plan to do after you kill the man? How many more will you have to bring down in order to stop hating yourself, stop hating the whole world?'

When there's no hope left, you invent it. And if you can't do that, then you live full of hatred, turning vengeance into a driving force that never rests, that keeps you awake nights. It becomes an objective that pushes you to keep going when there's nothing else that can. For the Armenian, killing Arthur had become the sole purpose in his life.

'Leave your sermon for the new inmates. It's too late to do me any good. I'm already dead inside.'

Azucena gave him an exhausted look, one that foretold the inevitable.

'I can't do this anymore. I have to move on with my life. We buried her four years ago. But you won't let her go. You cling to us to keep yourself from drowning, but you're taking me down with you.'

The Armenian glanced at Azucena, indifferent. He'd lost her now, too. He didn't care, though; he'd always been alone.

'I'll do what I have to do and then clear out. Forever. You'll never hear from me again.'

When he realised the Armenian was just a few centimetres behind him, Ibrahim didn't bat an eyelid. Ever since Ordóñez had given them the tip-off, he knew it was just a matter of time until the man showed up. The

Armenian had a giant of a man — maybe thirty years old — with him. An overgrown kid, really, with his head shaved except for one strip of dark curls down the middle that made him look like a fierce Mohican. The goon had huge eyes — bulging and watery, his pupils like black holes. He'd just done a line of coke and seemed never to blink, so it looked as if someone had sewn his upper eyelids to his thick bushy brows. His arms were tattooed — a full sleeve, not a centimetre of bare skin to be seen.

'Can we speak peacefully for once?' the Armenian asked.

Ibrahim looked the thug up and down and weighed his options. He'd have a hard time taking him down and there was little chance he'd be able to do it without getting hurt in the process. So he didn't have a lot of options. Ibrahim slipped a hand into his pocket and the bruiser growled like a rabid dog. He pulled a few coins out and put them on the bar, where he'd been having a beer. Then he held up his hands in a sign of peace, and the Armenian yanked his dog's chain to rein him in.

'Let's step outside.'

The thug positioned himself to the right of the Armenian, eyes sweeping back and forth between Ibrahim and the surroundings.

'It's the simple pleasures you really miss when they're gone, don't you think? I'd forgotten what it's like to stroll through the centre of Madrid.'

'How did you escape prison?'

The Armenian lifted his shirt and showed him a nasty knife wound, about where his liver was. It had only just begun to heal and the stitches hadn't scarred over yet. That had been a close call.

'If you hurt yourself, the bastards pay attention. They can't let you bleed to death; it's against the law. So the deeper the wound, the more attention they pay. Did you know that, in the Middle Ages, self-laceration was seen by the mystics as a way to attract God's attention? Bleeding is good, it purifies. So I started a fight, purposely let them get me, and they had to move me to the hospital. Humala and his colleagues did the rest, they owed me a few favours.' He smiled, pointing to the goon.

'So what do you want?' Ibrahim cut to the chase.

'I want to start over. You know? Look, it's not like anyone ever actually *decides* to be a bastard — a soulless motherfucker. Things just happen and you end up getting swept up.'

The Armenian paused for a moment, scrutinising Ibrahim with two huge eyes that seemed to take up his entire face, as though waiting for him to do or say something. But Ibrahim didn't know what to do or say.

'Sometimes I talk a lot. It's weird because I don't usually have anything to say, but I don't like silence, you know?'

For once Ibrahim could agree, though he'd never felt comfortable talking that much.

'Why don't you just say what you've come to say and stop beating around the bush?'

The Armenian pointed at him and gave a complicit smile. He had gaps between his teeth, which were small and brown and pointy, like the teeth of a saw.

'I heard your boss hired a real badass, a pro who's asking a lot of questions about his daughter. They say the guy's fast, no bullshit. I'm touched by his interest. But that's not going to keep me from ripping the bastard to shreds. He killed my daughter. He can put an entire army in my way, as far as I'm concerned. But Arthur is a dead man. Nothing and nobody is going to stop me. I wanted you to know.'

Ibrahim looked up calmly, unflustered. He noticed his adversary's wrinkles. Like everyone else, that old fighter, too, had started to wither and was trying to pretend time had not taken its toll. He thought of the photos Ordóñez had shown them, the ones with Ian and Rebeca.

'Why are you telling me this? Your daughter's death was an accident. Arthur was drunk, he didn't know what he was doing. And believe me, if there's one thing he regrets about that day, it's her death.'

'I don't care,' the Armenian said, cutting him off. 'I couldn't care less if he was drunk or sober. I'm not one of those crazies who goes around wreaking havoc for no reason. I think things through.' He pointed a finger at his temple, as though his hand were a gun about to blow his brains out. 'I know who I am and I know what I'm doing, even if it's not right. It's just the way things are. But you ...'

'What about me?'

'I like you, Ibrahim. In fact, I admire you. We've been in and out of jails together for years, and I've never seen you lose your way. Everyone fears you, and what's more, they respect you. I do too. I know your history; I've heard the stories they tell about when you were with the fundamentalists. You're a man with scruples, in spite of it all.' The Armenian made as if to touch the jagged scar that crossed Ibrahim's face, but the man's look stopped him just in time. 'That's why I don't understand what you're doing protecting Arthur.'

'I don't know what you think you know, but what you're talking about is ancient history. And either way, it's none of your business.'

The Armenian thought he had a knack for seeing what others were hiding. People could be manipulated; he gave them what they needed and in exchange took what he wanted. So-called *honourable* people used men like him to satisfy their depraved urges. They were always seeking a little danger to liven up their boring, petty lives. All those spoiled señoritas he saw shopping their lives away in the boutiques on Calle Serrano, with their giant cars and their filthy rich, fat, old and balding husbands. They were always wanting it up the arse, or needing a line of coke, or a private fight put on for their own personal viewing pleasure, or needing to gamble, or to have an orgy. Depravity was acceptable to them as long as it was a game — a little bit of pain, a few drops of blood, some dirty talk whispered into an ear. But if he actually showed them what an animal he was deep down, they'd shit themselves. Ibrahim wasn't like them, though; and nor was he like *him*. It disconcerted the Armenian not to be able to figure out who Ibrahim was, what his weaknesses were, how to get to him. How come Ibrahim had never felt afraid of him, the way others did?

'You're right. You must have your reasons for protecting the son of a bitch. I hope they're good enough because I'm going after him and anyone else who stands in my way, and I wouldn't want that to include you. In fact, I was hoping to convince you to help me. That's why we're having this little talk. I want you to hand Arthur over to me. That's the only reason my little tattooed friend here isn't kicking the shit out of you right now.' The kid fixed his watery eyes on Ibrahim. He looked like a shark about to attack. 'I know Arthur's wife is locked up in a residence outside Madrid. I've seen you visiting her. I don't know why, but I suspect she matters more to you than she should.'

Ibrahim's face clouded over. The Armenian could almost hear the man's teeth click as he clenched his jaw.

'If you go anywhere near Andrea I will break every bone in your body.'

'Relax. I don't want to hurt her. But I will if you force me to. You can't protect her forever. Andrea — that's her name, right? — only cares about

finding her little girl, Aroha. And maybe the punk Arthur hired is good —
I've heard some terrible things about him. But believe me, he's not going
to find her. If you want to find out about pretty girls who disappear, I got
a few friends who could help you. An exchange of information. That's
all I'm asking. It's either that ... or this,' and he pointed to Humala, the
tattooed goon who was giving him an icy stare and canine smile. 'Think it
over, Ibrahim. The offer won't last. I'm sort of in a hurry to get this over
with and disappear.'

Ibrahim's father had taught him that the *tasawwuf* is the invisible
channel connecting man to God, the thing that explains his relationship
to Creation. Just like the notes he played on his *ney* when he felt lost.
It wasn't anything he could put into words, but when he felt sad and
confused he'd turned to his flute and use its music to lead him back to
the words of Mustafa al-Alawi. *Inside of every human is a piece of flesh that,
if it is strong, means all is strong, and if it is corrupt, means all is corrupt. And
that organ is the heart.* His father said he had the heart of a Rabat warrior,
and that was why he suffered, because he knew his true nature. He could
hear the old man's words now, along with the notes of a *ney*; he saw them
move his withered body, almost made of air. *I pray for you*, he used to say,
his eyes searching for a path no one could find. *I pray for your heart both
dark and light. For you to overcome your struggle; all men must find their way
and not wander aimlessly through life.*

He thought now of his father's grave, that little burial mound of
stones atop a hill, where wildflowers were whipped by the hot winds of
the sirocco. Under the leaden clouds that pulled the sky closer to earth.
A timeless sky, an earth beyond the bounds of history. He missed that
infinite tranquillity, missed something as simple as a blade of grass in the
palm of his hand fluttering in the breeze like a drunken dragonfly.

Algeria was always inside him, wherever he went. An Algeria full
of sorrow, and stained red: the first man he killed, shooting him in the
back by the Monument to the Martyrs; the bomb that went off close to
Rue Hadj Omar by the Ottoman palace that the French used as a town
hall; the tourists shot outside the National Bardo Museum; beating up
informers at the hippodrome while keeping one eye on the horses to see
if his bets came in. And every time he killed or beat someone he felt his

heart rot a little more, but he couldn't rid himself of the hatred that was making it atrophy.

There were no words or thoughts to heal him. Every time he attacked a man or woman, he saw the grinning redheaded face of Luis Fernández, saw his mother being held down by thugs, felt his flesh being ripped apart by the sharp blade of the machete. And his thoughts clouded, and he turned into what was expected of a man like him — a killer, an assassin, a degenerate, a retrograde sectarian. His victims thought they knew him. They thought they knew the man who was killing them, and why.

That was a thousand lifetimes ago. But now flags no longer waved, anthems no longer moved him, he was no longer searching for God. He expected nothing of men, nothing of himself, and the memory of his father's teachings was nothing but dust on his hands and sadness in the mirror. And a face that was still staring at him.

The *ney* was the one thing that brought him peace.

When he extracted it carefully from its leather case and showed it to Andrea, it looked like exactly what it was — a hollow reed with six holes on the top and one for the thumb. A humble shepherd's instrument that dated as far back as early man. Ibrahim encouraged her to try it. He showed her how to place her fingers, explaining that each hole corresponded to a different note. The mouthpiece came out at an angle, and the tip of it went between your teeth so you could use your tongue to guide the air.

Andrea gave it several tries but couldn't manage to make a single sound. Stubborn as a mule with a new rider, the instrument refused to budge.

Ibrahim smiled. It looked so easy, when in fact it took a lifetime to learn to play the instrument, to master the technique. He could reach three octaves and produce all sorts of different low, deep tones. When he took the *ney* in his hands, the notes seemed to flow out effortlessly, like magic.

Andrea felt her heart lurch, surprised at the mournful tune that seemed to come not from the music but the musician. As the notes were played, one after the other, they seemed to form a cloak enshrouding Ibrahim, a wayward angel who'd gotten lost along the way. The sound calmed him, transporting him to an oasis of peace where sorrow and weariness disappeared. Even the jagged edges of his scar seemed to soften.

Slowly, she realised that Ibrahim was speaking to her through the music. He was telling her things that couldn't be said with words, and she understood. She understood him. He told her of a long journey in which heaven and hell were indistinguishable, a place where memories and desires were one and the same. Without looking at her or touching her, concentrating only on the sound and not his fingers, Ibrahim took her in his arms and carried her to a meadow from which they could see the Sahara's sea of sand, its shifting dunes dancing in the wind, all the way from the Mediterranean to the Red Sea — a continent of desert, as dry as the scar on that deformed his face. And as beautiful.

He spoke to her of a man's love.

'Stop — please,' Andrea begged, hands clutching her belly as if pregnant with memories about to be born, memories that were now kicking to make their presence known.

But Ibrahim didn't stop. He couldn't, because that music wasn't his. It wasn't coming from his lungs or being played on his *ney*. The music was *sama*, the language of time, of memory, the sound of understanding and acceptance. There was no way for him to stop it; he could only accept it, as a bridge between their two souls, which were lost in time immemorial. And all they could do was dance, whirl like dervishes, spinning together to infinity, turning back to what they really were, free of all that imprisoned them. His notes became cries, borne of his wounds. Andrea could hear him shout, beg, swear and pray; she could hear him being tortured, and no matter how she covered her ears, the pain was there, shouting out until finally it began to die down and grow distant like the song of a bird as it flies away.

When Ibrahim stopped playing, when the air in his lungs had nothing more to say, he was exhausted. They'd lost track of time. It was getting dark and Andrea's room seemed to shrink as a faint darkness filtered in through the window. In the distance was the outline of the mountains, the silhouette of a nearby forest. Slowly, stars began to twinkle. A long lock of hair fell across Ibrahim's eyebrows and nose and droplets of sweat ran down his forehead along his wrinkles, while his lower lip trembled. He didn't dare look at Andrea, sitting across from him on the edge of the bed with her hands in her lap. He remained silent a few seconds, his mind blank. He needed to recharge, having emptied himself so utterly. Ibrahim was breathing deep, enjoying the fleeting sense of quietude, the purity of the silence, the sense of tranquillity, aware of the fact that when he opened his eyes he'd have to look at her, knowing the questions he'd see in her eyes.

Andrea got up and walked, silent as a barefoot shadow, to the window. Her fingers moved with the soft swaying of the gauze curtain.

'Who are you? Why have you come into my life?' she asked the horizon. And in the horizon was Ibrahim.

He looked away and his eyes fell upon a portrait of Aroha that Andrea had placed at the side of her bed. She was just a girl then who knew nothing of what was to befall her three, four, five years later. She had the arrogant naiveté of those who aren't afraid, because they don't know any better. *I could have been your father*, he thought. And that thought bled into others like an inkblot. For years after Andrea left Algiers, he kept going to a small plot of land not far from Annaba, where he'd sit on the rocks and hatch plans — the house he was going to build for them, the children they'd have, the sort of things that form the foundations of a perfect future. He was so confident that it never even occurred to him that things could turn out any other way. He was different from the rest and had been since he was a boy.

The people of Annaba were taciturn, pessimistic, their souls bent double by toil and hardship. He was not like that. Where others saw only sweat and suffering, he saw the honest toil required to build a better life. He'd planned far in advance which crops he'd plant, how he'd till the soil, where he'd buy his cattle, where he'd build the barn. He even got hold of catalogues that pictured huge tractors from the United States that could help him be more productive on the farm. Over the course of those years, he pictured himself working sun-up to sundown, strong and sturdy, convinced that each imaginary whack of the hoe would bringing him closer to his dream. He swore he'd never resign himself to his destiny, never give in to the fate of losing her.

But time passed, the plot of land was sold to some Egyptian businessmen who used it to build cheap apartments, and he forgot about his promises — or buried them under the brick and cement.

'I know a man who can help us find out where your daughter is. Someone besides Guzmán.'

Those words rekindled the flame in Andrea's eyes. And as he spoke them she felt a chill run through her entire body.

'What man?'

Ibrahim spoke to her of the Armenian. Of his six-year-old daughter who had died in the accident, of the sort of man he was.

'But he's asking a very high price …'

'I have no money, but if you speak to Arthur, he'll pay any price.'

Ibrahim corrected Andrea, eliminating her confusion. 'It's not money he's asking. He wants me to hand Arthur over to him.'

The chill Andrea had felt turned to ice.

'*Do it.*' Her voice had changed, as though it wasn't her who was speaking. But it was.

Ibrahim looked at her, perplexed, although the perplexity was only partly authentic. Why did he want a decision he'd already made to fall to her? What was he trying to do? Justify it? Share it with her to create a stronger bond? Sometimes love is twisted, sometimes it corrupts the one who loves, bringing untold misery to the beloved.

Andrea looked the other way, as though listening through her eyes and refusing to hear. The wheels of her mind had stopped turning — what Ibrahim had said had broken the chain that kept her brain from functioning.

Ibrahim pressed on. He needed to be sure that she understood what was at stake. He wasn't doing it for himself, but for *her*.

'Is this really what you want?'

Andrea pressed her hands to her throat, as though it were riddled with holes through which her good judgement was leaking.

'I want my daughter back.'

21

The gate was open and there was a moving van parked in the driveway, its back doors open. A couple of workers were loading up boxes they'd brought out from the house. Olsen's widow stood supervising the entire operation with her arms crossed, instructing them just where to place each thing. She was in a hurry to finish up as quickly as possible. Her children sat in the car, which was parked beside the moving van, and the Yorkie's head poked up between them.

'So you're leaving.'

Olsen's widow looked toward the voice, startled. On seeing Guzmán leaning with one shoulder against a desiccated pine tree, she slumped in disappointment.

'You again?' she asked uneasily. 'We had an agreement. You said you'd never bother me again.'

Guzmán glanced around and his eyes rested for a moment on the car, loaded up with suitcases, kids and dog in the back seat.

'Things have changed a little.'

Olsen's widow raised a hand to her throat, as though taking her pulse. She looked worse for wear — *a lot worse,* Guzmán thought. She'd lost weight since the last time he saw her and her clothes were dishevelled, as was her hair. She looked low-class, almost like she was doing it on purpose in an attempt to go unnoticed. If anyone had said that she was once the envy of all at high-society soirees and receptions — the most beautiful of the beautiful people — whoever was listening would have thought it was a joke.

She stepped away from the van so the workers couldn't hear.

'I already told you everything I know. Why don't you leave me in peace?'

Guzmán lit a cigarette with a match. Nobody used matches anymore, but he liked the sound of the phosphorous as the tip scratched against the striker, liked the little orange and blue flame it made. He was convinced that cigarettes tasted better if you lit them that way. Fanning his hand to extinguish the flame, he tossed the match to the ground.

'Actually, you *didn't* tell me everything you know; that's why I'm here. It seems we still haven't finished our conversation.'

Olsen's widow's eyes darted back and forth. She looked like a cornered animal. Perhaps the realisation that she had no way out was what led her to give in. Finally, she suggested they go into the house. She didn't want to upset the children. Guzmán followed her, under the watchful eyes of one of the workers, who looked as though he was puzzling over where he'd seen that face before.

The living room was almost stripped bare. There were belongings piled up against one wall, and blankets and a dolly. There were light marks on the floor, unfaded spots where chair legs and table legs and pieces of furniture had recently sat. When houses are abandoned quickly, the furniture leaves telltale signs in its wake — like the trail of a storm, or a disaster.

Olsen's widow slipped her hands into the pockets of her tight jeans and turned to face Guzmán with her jaw clenched.

'I've read the paper and seen the news. If anyone recognises you and sees you talking to me, it's going to bring me a lot of trouble — and I've already got enough of that as it is.'

Guzmán had read the paper and seen the news too. He knew he was being accused of the fire at Dámaso's antique shop. He'd been forced to leave Madrid quickly, and hadn't spent more than one or two nights in the same place since. Still, he didn't feel nervous or concerned. In a way, he'd almost been expecting something like that to happen. Someone had laid a trap for him. It could have been Arthur, or any of the cops he'd contacted to ask for help who saw him as a threat from the past, or even someone associated with the film club Dámaso was running. The old man had warned him. If he kicked the wasps' nest he was going to piss off a few wasps — and it seemed some of them were very important wasps.

It had happened before. He himself, in fact, had orchestrated smear campaigns in the past, against people they needed to get out of the way, opponents of the regime, businessmen whose interests collided with the ambitions of a member of the military junta. It wasn't hard to get someone charged — fabricated evidence, planted clues, false information leaked to the press. It was easy to create a breeding ground for public opinion that led from a witch-hunt to a false conviction. Prisons and cemeteries were full of innocent people who'd been made to look guilty. It was such an old trick, so unsophisticated it was almost tedious.

'I didn't kill Dámaso. I would have done it if I had to, but I didn't. He told me what I needed to know as soon as I tightened the screws a little.' He didn't care if she believed him or not. He knew how to handle those situations. But he couldn't stand leaving loose ends once he'd started something. 'Somebody is trying to frame me for his death, and that's going to force me to leave a little sooner than I'd planned. But first I'm going to finish what I came to do.'

'I have nothing to do with it. All I want is to get out of here, take my kids and go, forget about all this shit.'

Guzmán smiled and gazed at her in genuine curiosity. *There really are people like that,* he thought. *People who think they can just come and go as they please, do things and then walk away without facing up to the consequences, their souls intact.*

'A few days after your husband died, Arthur Fernández received a video tape in the mail. On that tape were Olsen, Ian and Dámaso — torturing his daughter. It came with an exculpatory note, as if the person who sent it were refusing to accept any responsibility for what was on the recording.' He watched her reaction — the unconscious tightening of her stomach, the rapid rise and fall of her chest beneath her V-neck T-shirt. 'You said you didn't know anything about a tape, that you had no idea what your husband was doing. But you were lying. You found that tape and sent it to Arthur anonymously.'

Olsen's widow looked up at the ceiling, crisscrossed with cracks that she'd no longer have to worry about plastering over. She was taking deep breaths trying to calm herself, to no avail. When she looked back down at Guzmán, she was like another person. Tiny, guilt-ridden, overwhelmed by something she'd never fully understood: human evil.

'I didn't know,' she murmured, sounding like she had a fly trapped in her mouth, trying to buzz its way free. And she rubbed her hands over her shoulders, searching for comfort in her own embrace.

She'd found the tape by chance, while searching desperately through cupboards and drawers, trying to guess where Olsen had hidden the money, jewellery and important documents that she felt belonged to her — she'd earned them over the years, carrying the weight of that man who, while hanging from a ceiling beam, ironically enough seemed to weigh almost nothing. The tape was hidden behind some tiles in the kitchen. She discovered it when she accidentally knocked against the baseboard and saw that it moved. At the time she didn't know what it was, but she guessed it must have been pretty important for Olsen to hide it there, so she slipped it into her bag.

She didn't watch the tape until two days later. Afterwards, she vomited several times, incredulous, unable to believe Olsen could have taken part in anything so horrific. He had children, children only a few years younger than that little girl. She'd known he was a pig, known he went to prostitutes far younger than her, and she herself bore marks on her flesh from having suffered through his perversions. But *that* was sickening, monstrous even for a monster like him.

Her first impulse had been to get rid of the tape, and she threw it in the bin and left it there for days. But she never dared to take the rubbish out. Obviously, she didn't want to go to the police either. She knew exactly what that would lead to and knew it would implicate her. Suddenly she saw Olsen's death in a new light. The images on that tape were so compromising to so many people that she had no trouble believing maybe her husband hadn't committed suicide after all. And if whoever killed him found out she had the tape, she could only imagine the danger she and her kids would be in.

She convinced herself of that, telling herself she had to look out for her children and their future, that it was her responsibility to protect them, and protect herself. After all, her only crime had been to sleep with the bastard. She wasn't responsible for that monstrosity. Besides, she couldn't do anything to stop it. But she was fooling herself and she knew it. Every night the images replayed in her head, each detail, over and over, until the bile rose to her throat. She'd go into the kitchen, pick up the tape and stare at it, and then throw it away again. Until finally she decided to do the only thing her dignity would allow, her one valiant gesture: send Arthur the tape.

Guzmán was sitting on a pile of boxed-up books that were waiting to be loaded into the truck. As Olsen's widow paced up and down the room, he followed her with his eyes, watching her stop to speak through her tears and then resume her monologue, which was riddled with defensive half-truths, grievances, lamentations, and gestures of exasperation. The catalogue of reasons she had for not doing what she should have done was as vast as human cynicism. If she was hoping he'd understand or forgive her, she had the wrong guy. Guzmán didn't judge her; nor could he grant her the pardon her eyes begged for. He was no priest, and he certainly didn't talk to God.

What he was interested in was something far different. The tape showed four people: Arthur's daughter Aroha, who'd been missing since the time of its recording; Dámaso, who was dead, and whose death he himself was being blamed for; Magnus Olsen, who may have committed suicide, but had likely been murdered by someone who'd made it look like suicide — and the list of suspects was as long as that of the victims of Olsen's extortion attempts; and Ian. With the possible exception of Aroha, they were all dead, and none of natural causes: feigned accidents, staged suicide. Guzmán had a hunch that the person responsible for all of their deaths would be the common thread that would lead him to Aroha, and that's why he was discounting Arthur. Arthur wouldn't have tried to frame him for the fire, because Guzmán was the last hope he had for finding his daughter alive.

Toward the end of his life, Bosco had contracted severe glaucoma, which left him unable to distinguish anything but dark shadows and bright light. He had to wear thick coke-bottle glasses to read. But when he really wanted to see something, he pushed the glasses up above his bushy eyebrows and let his sleepy little eyes focus on the object in question like a zoom lens. He said he could see more clearly that way, without the distraction of magnification.

That was the way Guzmán felt. He could see far better with no artifice in the way.

'I'm going to ask you one more thing: did you make a copy of that tape? Did you send it to anyone else?'

She stopped pacing erratically around the living room and bit her lip, gazing out the window. The workers were finishing up and the kids were still in the car, growing restless. Glancing at Guzmán, she nodded almost imperceptibly, using all of her effort to tilt her head.

Half an hour later, Guzmán walked Olsen's widow to her car. The workers had finished loading the boxes and were waiting inside the truck with the engine running. The driver shot him an inquisitive look and then said something to his buddy. Guzmán knew what was going on, but ignored them. His face had become too familiar. Olsen's widow took a seat behind the wheel and ordered the kids to settle down. The dog was yapping excitedly, its head out the window. They looked at each other, with nothing else to say. She nodded, put the car in gear and drove off slowly, followed by the moving van.

Guzmán stood alone in the driveway in front of the house as the wind whipped the *for sale* sign back and forth. The kids' toys — a tricycle, a deflated soccer ball, a basketball hoop with a torn net — gave the place an air of abandonment. Guzmán put on his sunglasses, as Olsen's widow disappeared into the distance with her family and her belongings — the few she had left. He wished her luck, he really did. Wherever she was headed, she was going to need it.

He walked slowly to his car and for a few minutes sat gathering his thoughts. It all made sense, he thought — it made logical sense — but far from persuading him to have any faith in the human race, it simply confirmed what his own bitter experience had already taught him.

'Human kindness — what a crock of shit,' he said, spitting out the window.

He opened the glove compartment and pulled out his mobile phone, dialled Arthur's number and waited for him to answer. The voicemail picked up. Guzmán smiled cynically. So Arthur was cutting him loose, too. Guzmán was alone and cornered, but he didn't care. Dogs fight all the more viciously when they've got no way out. And he was the worst kind of dog — a streetwise mutt.

'It's me,' he said to the recording. 'I know who has your daughter. Call me. I think it's time to make a deal.'

Two days later, Guzmán stood smoking an Argentinian cigarette. He had almost none left, but he wasn't planning to stick around until they ran out. His flight to Santiago — with a red-herring stopover in Buenos Aires — took off in less than twenty-four hours.

On Arthur's desk was that day's paper, open to the accident report.

There had been a single-car accident on the Alicante–Valencia highway. For reasons unknown, the vehicle had flipped and then caught on fire. The driver had been burned to death and was not yet identified. Police found two young children and a dog on the shoulder of the road, behind the barrier fence a few metres away. Though terrified they seemed unharmed. The circumstances were most unusual, and police had opened an investigation. Guzmán knew that one way or another, their enquiries would eventually lead to him. He imagined they'd find some conveniently placed clue or evidence that whoever was really behind Dámaso's death — and now Olsen's widow's, too — would have planted in order to incriminate him. The noose was tightening around his neck.

'You've got real balls, showing up in my office like this,' Arthur spat, pointing to the paper. He hadn't shaved that morning and he looked terrible. In fact, he looked like he'd spent the night in his office — his eyelids were puffy and his necktie hung loose around his unbuttoned shirt collar.

Guzmán smiled. If there was one thing he literally did *not* have, it was balls.

'I won't stay long. Just long enough to finish what I came to do and collect my fee. Someone's going to a lot of trouble to make me look like a killer: first Dámaso, now Olsen's widow. Someone with enough scruples to not harm her kids and dog.'

'Don't look at me like that,' Arthur admonished, 'I had no reason to want to hurt that woman.'

Guzmán nodded.

'True. In fact, you should be grateful to her.'

'I don't see why.'

Guzmán walked over to a green crystal ashtray and put out his cigarette, exhaling smoke through his nostrils.

'Magnus Olsen's wife was the anonymous person who sent you the recording with Aroha on it.' He let the surprise sink deep down inside, carefully observing Arthur's reaction. His shock seemed sincere. 'She didn't know beforehand what her husband was up to, but she found out. She discovered the recording after he committed suicide. When she saw what was on it, she realised the people involved were too powerful — many of them held respectable positions, and she knew they'd do anything to keep the story from getting out. That's why she didn't dare go to the police.' He pointed to the paper on the desk. 'She feared for her life, and for that of her children, and it seems the facts have proven her right, at least in part. But she didn't just forget about it like most other people would have. She was a decent human being, you know? Not like you and me. Every time she watched that recording, she thought about the fact that she was a mother, that she had kids too, and that they were at risk. That's why she sent you the tape, hoping you'd have the power to stop the insanity. But you didn't do it, didn't put an end to it, like she hoped you would. Instead you let yourself get sucked into the vortex.'

Arthur picked up the paper and gazed at the image accompanying the story: the flipped car, the police tape, the thermal blanket over Olsen's widow's lifeless body.

'This is madness,' he murmured.

'It is, but you're not the only one who let themselves get dragged into it. She sent a second anonymous copy of the tape to someone else.'

Arthur looked up and fixed his eyes on Guzmán.

'I suspect the other person is the one who killed Dámaso, first, and Mrs Olsen after that. Every time I've gotten a step closer to your daughter, the step has been erased by this person, trying to close all the doors that might lead me to Aroha. And they seem to have the means to do it. I'm talking about the only person who can tell us where your daughter is.'

'Who is it? Who else did she send the tape to?'

Guzmán dropped his arms, as though having to state the obvious were exhausting.

'*Her*. Gloria A. Tagger. Magnus Olsen had been a family friend ever since he helped them recover El Español, the Tagger's prized violin. He'd often go to their house, they all went out on weekends, and they all knew about and struggled with their kids' difficult characters. When Olsen's wife watched the tape for the first time, she immediately recognised Ian. And she made sure to get a copy into his mother's hands.'

Guzmán made sure Arthur was listening closely.

'Before you killed her son in that supposed accident, Gloria knew what her son was involved in. I don't know if she was doing anything about it, or was planning to or would have. Did she know Aroha was your daughter? And if she did, when did she find that out? We should ask her,

350

don't you think? I've got a feeling this whole story is like one of those esparto ropes — the more water you give it, the harder and more tangled it gets.'

The main entrance hall was bustling at Atocha train station. Sunlight filtered in through the vaulted ceiling, shining onto the tall trees in the station's botanical garden in a cascade of orange hues. A few kids amused themselves with a stick, stirring up green scum on the turtle pond to make the animals surface; there were so many they couldn't count them. A tinny voice on the loudspeaker announcing arrivals and departures blended seamlessly with the sound of heels clicking on the tile floor, of people's conversations as they talked or made phone calls. A few musicians wandered amid café tables and newsstands, playing accordion and guitar badly.

Gloria would have had to be blind not to see Arthur waiting for her at the bottom of the escalator. When she saw him in the crowd, she froze. Then she stepped back, seeking shelter among the other passengers who were descending, the way the weakest animals try to protect themselves by hiding in the middle of the flock. But the flow of human traffic impelled her forward. When she realised she had no way out, she strode firmly toward him with her head held high, daring him to get in her way.

Arthur stared at her, gauging her reaction. People walking back and forth between them blocked his field of vision, and she kept disappearing and reappearing among the other passengers on the platform.

It was Guzmán who intercepted her. He grabbed her elbow firmly and pulled her to him. They were in people's way, blocking the flow of traffic.

'We need to talk, Señorita Tagger.'

Gloria recognised him, although it took her a few minutes to place him as the journalist who'd interviewed her at her farewell concert. She shot Arthur a dirty look, and Guzmán another, wondering how they were connected.

'Let me go,' she commanded.

Guzmán obeyed with a half-smile. He liked a woman with character.

'Don't make a scene. It won't be necessary.' He escorted her over to Arthur.

It was Arthur who spoke first.

'I know everything. Guzmán figured it all out.'

Gloria writhed in fury.

'What is it that you know? That the portrait Eduardo painted is for me? None of that even matters anymore.'

Arthur shook his head. At this point Eduardo and his damn portrait were as important to him as bird shit on the sidewalk — they didn't even register. Nor did he care about Gloria's insane motives for having wanted a portrait of him to begin with. She could burn it, tear it up, or hang it on a wall in her house and spit on it every day for the rest of her life as far as he was concerned.

'Where is my daughter, Gloria?'

Gloria A. Tagger looked at him as though he'd lost his mind. She searched Guzmán's face for confirmation that he really was insane, but Guzmán just looked at her impassively.

'Why on earth are you asking me? How do you expect me to know? Maybe she's in hell, waiting to open the gates for you.'

Arthur's eyes flashed with anger. He could have beat her senseless at that moment.

Guzmán took a turn speaking.

'I know that Magnus Olsen's wife sent you a tape a few months before Ian died, right after Olsen was found hanging from his living room ceiling.'

'What are you talking about? I'd met Olsen and his wife, but she and I were never friends, and she certainly never sent me any tape.'

'She told me so herself,' Guzmán insisted, not losing his patience.

'Well, she's lying.'

'She was telling the truth.'

'How can you be so sure?'

'Because she's dead. She was killed for telling me.'

As though death were the irrefutable truth, Gloria fell silent, although she'd never received the tape.

Guzmán scrutinised that silence and a shadow of doubt fell over him. He was convinced Olsen's wife had told him the truth, but he was starting to suspect that Gloria wasn't lying either.

'That tape shows Ian and Arthur's daughter together,' he went on, ignoring the fact that Arthur was standing there beside them, mad as hell.

Gloria opened her mouth, gaping idiotically.

'That's absurd. My son and your daughter?' she said, looking at Arthur as if they were trying to convince her that the world was flat. 'What kind of a ridiculous joke is this?'

Arthur narrowed his eyes, trying to peer inside Gloria's mind, then shot Guzmán an enquiring look out of the corner of his eye. Either she was a very good liar or Guzmán was wrong.

'You're perfectly aware of the fact that they knew each other. They were at the same clinic in Geneva together. This is no joke. I got a copy of the tape, too; I've seen it with my own eyes, dozens of times over the years. I can describe every detail to you, every sound and every image of what your son did to Aroha.'

Gloria fluttered her hands fan-like before her and turned away. She couldn't process what they were trying to tell her. She refused to accept it. It couldn't be. Arthur took her by the arm. Her biceps and triceps felt soft, as though her strength had left her, and he pulled her toward him until her face was mere centimetres from his mouth. The rage he had felt was spiraling, mingling with sorrow and incomprehension.

'For exactly thirty-five minutes and fifteen seconds, your son tortured my daughter, abused her, raped her, put an iron rod up her vagina, and *demonstrated* for Olsen and Dámaso the way to hurt her so that the images would be more *dramatic*.'

Gloria stared into his wide-open eyes flashing with anger, accusing her, and she couldn't understand. The monstrous words he was speaking were too heinous for her to digest.

'You're lying!!! First you kill my son and now you want to poison me with this filth,' she screamed, swatting Arthur's hand violently away.

Gloria's shouting alarmed the nearby passengers on their way to the escalator. Some of them stared, looking panicked. Insanity terrifies people — they still seem to believe it's contagious, like leprosy. And Gloria was acting like she was in need of a straitjacket. Her face was distraught, her mouth downturned, and she was wheezing like an asthmatic, batting her hands back and forth as though there were a disgusting bug coming at her. A bug only she could see.

Arthur's rage dissolved like sugar. Gloria's reaction frightened him and surprised Guzmán, who looked on with his brow raised, like a scientist examining a white rat in a cage and noting in wonder that his experiment had yielded very different results from the ones he'd anticipated. But Arthur had seen the tape and had spoken with Ian personally. He remembered the boy's cold, cynical reaction, the cockiness he'd displayed knowing that he was protected and nothing could happen to him. No. It was impossible for her not to know what kind of monster she'd given birth to.

'I spoke to him. Before I ran him over,' he said quietly, almost whispering. She couldn't believe it and shook her head slowly back and forth. 'I just wanted him to tell me where Aroha was, what he'd done with her. That was all I was thinking. But he looked at me like I was crazy — worse, he looked at me like a clown who was there for his amusement. He was *amused* at my suffering, my impotence, my rage.'

Gloria didn't want to hear it. But Arthur wouldn't stop.

'It wasn't an accident. Do you understand what I'm saying? I saw him waiting at a light, in a crowd of people. He was smiling; he looked like a good kid, like a boy who had his whole life ahead of him — his whole life to keep using that angelic face to hurt others. I started the car and aimed straight for that monster without thinking twice. And I killed him. But it's like one of those insects you step on over and over that just keep wiggling their legs, mocking you.'

The train to Zaragoza was ready to depart from platform two. The one from Barcelona was just arriving on platform five. The humidifiers from the botanical garden were misting the plants and turtles in the pond, as they tried in vain to escape the schoolboys' mischief. The Romany musicians were taking their music elsewhere. And there beside the escalator, three people — two men and a woman — were trapped in their own silent bubble, two of them unaware of anything but their own suffering.

'I'll kill you for this! I swear to God I won't rest until you're dead,' Gloria said slowly, turning back to Arthur.

Guzmán watched the two of them. He himself was not affected by the emotions dragging Arthur and Gloria into a battle neither could win. That wasn't his job. He needed to know who had killed Olsen, Dámaso, and especially Olsen's widow. She was so different from him, so far from his world, but that woman had reminded him at times of Candela. Maybe it was just that he'd seen in her the same stubborn and at times absurd determination to cling to life that the music teacher had shown. Maybe it was that her brown eyes, too, were flecked with green and when he looked into them it was like they were like an expanding universe. Or perhaps he simply thought that both Candela and Olsen's widow had deserved better fates than the ones they got.

His meter was running — and he knew that the reasonable thing to do was get paid and get out of there. The case had left him too exposed, his face was all over the papers and there were more and more witnesses who could now tie him to those deaths. He was the ideal scapegoat — many of the people he'd made uncomfortable by knocking on their doors would be only too happy to send him like a lamb to the slaughter. But there he was, in the biggest and most crowded train station in all of Spain, in plain sight of anyone who possessed even the most basic powers of observation and a modicum of curiosity. A squad car could pull up at any moment. With his past, no one was going to believe a word he said. And yet he was intent on finding the person who'd woven that tangled web, and on beating them at their own game.

Maybe he was getting old. Maybe his cynicism was no longer thick enough to keep him from caring about the joys and sorrows of others. *The moment of guilt and regret always arrives, even for us,* Bosco used to say. *And that's when it's time to quit, and spend the rest of your life with your nightmares.* Maybe that moment had arrived for Guzmán.

'There's one thing that hasn't been cleared up: if Olsen's wife sent you the tape and you never received it, then who did?'

22

Dolores, the housekeeper, was in the kitchen making brunch — bacon and fried eggs — and quietly grumbling under her breath, as though preparing food were some unforeseen obligation that had forced her to alter her daily routine.

'The lady of the house isn't in,' she said, sprinkling the yolks with a few grains of salt.

Eduardo sat on a chair watching her bustle around, one end of the cardboard tube, containing the portrait, on the floor and the other between his knees. He'd brought it with him. If Gloria wasn't there, he wondered, why had the housekeeper called, asking him to come?

'There's someone else who wants to see you — out back in the garden,' she said, pre-empting his question as she dried her hands on a dishtowel. She put the plate of food on a tray and then added some finishing touches. 'I'll take you there.'

The sunlight in the backyard fell onto a wrought-iron gazebo at a slant. The garden was a mess. Clearly, no one was taking care of the flowerbeds, which were overrun with weeds and wild poppies. Sitting at a chipped, white wrought-iron table was a broad-backed man in shirtsleeves, frowning in distaste as he observed the fallen petals of a rosebush climbing a trellis, covered in insects. Hearing Eduardo and Dolores' footsteps, he turned, and his look of displeasure morphed into one of cordial curiosity. With boyish energy that seemed at odds with his relaxed, middle-aged demeanour, he skipped down the two steps of the gazebo to take the tray from the housekeeper.

'At least some things haven't changed. Your brunches are amazing,' he said with a frank smile. The housekeeper smiled back, timidly. It was just bacon and fried eggs, and two tomato halves that shimmered with olive oil, she thought, wondering what kind of garbage they must eat in Australia.

'This is Eduardo, sir. The artist you wanted to meet.'

'Dolores, you're never going to drop the "sir" business, are you? Is it really so hard to just call me Ian? It would help me feel less like a Windsor when I ask you for something.' He turned to Eduardo and held out one hand, the tray of food balanced precariously in the other. 'So, finally we meet. I'm Ian Mackenzie.'

Eduardo had figured as much. Parents always leave some indelible trace on their children, making them recognisable anywhere. If Ian had reached his father's age — forty? forty-five? — he'd probably have taken on that aristocratic-yet-carefree air, too, a blend of British gentleman and off-duty Californian actor.

They sat in the speckled shade under the gazebo. Ian folded his hands over the tray, elbows on the table. For a second, Eduardo thought he was about to say a prayer. But he didn't.

'So, you're the portrait artist Gloria hired. Kind of crazy. I bet you've never had a commission like that before. I don't know what she was thinking when she called you, or what her intentions were. In fact I've never really known what she is thinking. Gloria is a unique woman — I imagine you've realised that by now.'

Eduardo didn't like the self-assured way he spoke about Gloria. He'd only met the guy five minutes ago and already Ian spoke with no inhibitions whatsoever. Or maybe Eduardo was just irked by the brazen way he occupied all the space, or by his familiarity with the housekeeper and the disingenuous praise he lavished on her without having even tasted her food, oblivious to the flies landing on his egg yolks. He was annoyed by Ian's suntanned face, his just-for-show smile, his poise. It bothered him to picture Gloria in bed with him, the man's hairy fingers touching the same skin he'd savoured only once, knowing even then that it was out of pity. And he knew his feelings were absurd.

'I thought you were divorced,' he said as casually as he could, waving away a sticky fly hovering over the tray.

'Oh, we are. But that doesn't mean we're unable to come to an arrangement. I live in Australia; I moved there permanently shortly after Ian's death, but I like to come back every once in a while for a little break — I did pay for this house, after all. It belongs to me and I belong to it,' he said, although he spoke the words hesitantly, eyeing the abandoned-looking surroundings, the overgrown lawn, the dying flowers. If that place had once been his dream house, it had ended up a sad parody.

After glancing around, his eyes came back to rest on Eduardo.

'We could have been very happy here, the three of us. On occasion I think we were. But things never turn out the way you think. It's not like in the movies; you can't pick the perfect setting or direct the actors or control their entrances and exits; you can't choose the lighting or the sound. You can't cut-and-paste like in editing, so you end up with exactly what you had in mind.'

Ian had taken a seat and was perched sideways, one leg crossed over the other. He took out a box of Australian cigarettes and placed it on the table without opening it. For a few seconds he toyed with it between his fingers.

'So did you sleep with her?' he asked impassively. He might have asked if his tooth hurt for as much as his expression changed. 'I bet you did. Gloria can be irresistible when she puts her mind to it.'

Eduardo felt his ears burning. He coughed timidly, ill-at-ease and annoyed at Ian's snide expression.

'Why don't you ask her?'

'Because she wouldn't tell me. And the fact is, I don't really care.'

'Then why ask me?'

'Because you've been wanting to tell me since the moment we met. I'm guessing she didn't speak very well of me, and the fact that you made love to her makes you see me as an intruder. Gloria is very good at that, too — getting people to believe what she wants them to believe. She's both adorable and manipulative. Or at least she was, until Ian junior died.'

He spoke about her as if the whole thing were so distant and yet he couldn't let go. A story that excluded Eduardo. And he wanted him to know it.

'I'd like to see your portrait of that guy, if you don't mind. I'm curious.'

Eduardo didn't say no. He unscrewed the lid of the tube and pushed the tray of cold food to one side so he could spread out the portrait of Arthur.

He'd picked it up that morning from Olga's apartment. Eduardo wondered what had happened to her. He'd tried to get Mr Who to promise that he wouldn't hurt her, but the young man would grant him no more than an ambiguous gesture that could have meant anything. Eduardo had handed her over with no concern for her wellbeing, but he hadn't been able to shake the bittersweet feeling of guilt since.

Ian stared at the portrait for several minutes, bent over it like a field marshal poring over a battle plan. He swept his gaze carefully up and down, left and right. His eyes were shining, but Eduardo didn't know if it was in admiration of his artistic skill, or the emotion of seeing so closely the face of the man who'd killed his son and ruined his marriage. When he finished examining it he tut-tutted with a tinge of disappointment.

'An ordinary man who just explodes into your world like a ball of fire and blows it all to pieces.'

'I can assure you that Arthur is not an ordinary man, in any way.'

Ian held up his hands as though trying to deflect a self-evident truth.

'Maybe it's just my own little fantasy. No matter how far I am, there hasn't been a single day when I haven't thought about that man, tried to figure out what he was thinking, if he had feelings anything like mine.' He paused and walked to the trellis, observing the aphids making their way up a rose stem. 'Or the way you feel. It must have been really hard to spend so much time painting the man who killed your family.'

Eduardo had been rolling up the portrait carefully. Suddenly his hands froze.

'What you talking about? That's ridiculous.'

'You didn't know?'

'Know what?'

Ian traced a finger across a leaf of the rosebush, covering his fingertip with a sticky substance. He wiped it against his thumb, but all that did was give him two sticky fingers. He thought the plant needed to be pruned quite severely, but doubted even that could save it. Whatever disease it had had already spread too far. It would be better to just pull it up from the roots and plant a new shoot.

If only it were that easy with people.

He walked over to a leaky tap and washed his hand, then sniffed his fingers.

'Arthur Fernández was the man who killed your wife and daughter. It wasn't the first time he'd been involved in a fatal accident. That was the real reason Gloria hired you. Let me put it this way: Arthur is the bridge between our two shores.'

'You're making that up.'

'I most certainly am not. This portrait is the link between your tragedy and ours. Gloria knew that from the beginning. She'd thoroughly investigated you before she commissioned you.'

Perhaps the police could have pressed charges against Arthur Fernández. After the accident, the police officer who came to see Eduardo in the hospital went to a lot of trouble, despite his slothful docility. The same man was removed from service on expulsion orders a few months later, over a murky case in which the officer was charged with a crime he swore he hadn't committed. Prior to his dismissal he'd found clues pointing to Arthur. Details which, when viewed alone, might seem unconnected, but which made perfect sense — later fitting together like pieces of a puzzle for the ex-officer of the law who spent hours of his free time investigating further: receipts from a small hotel on the Toledo highway the night before the accident; a receipt for gas from a service station in the middle of nowhere — the owner recalled having seen someone very worked up on the phone, someone whose description matched Arthur's.

But shortly thereafter, Eduardo killed Teodoro on the streets of Madrid, just as that poor dogged officer had other, unrelated charges brought against him and was taken off the investigation. Inside Eduardo's apartment, the police found Teodoro's licence plate number jotted down on a piece of paper and verified that he'd gotten it by consulting the Directorate General of Traffic archives. Teo's vehicle was the same make and model as the one involved in the hit-and-run. There was even a report issued by an expert that indicated that the SUV had a dent in the bumper that had been recently repaired. As far as the new investigators on the case were concerned, it was clear from the beginning: although Eduardo never confessed his motives for attacking Teo and his family, they were certain Teo was the man who'd caused the accident and that Eduardo had taken justice into his own hands. Case closed.

They forgot all about Arthur Fernández. And about Eduardo Quintana, too. The roads were full of scumbags who committed hit-and-runs. Sometimes they got caught; sometimes they didn't. The sentences for manslaughter and failure to provide assistance weren't worth the expenditure of long-term investigations. But a murder in the centre of Madrid in broad daylight — now, that caused the sort of pandemonium on the streets that the State could not and would not accept. So they locked him up for thirteen years and threw away the key.

But the investigation hadn't ended for Gloria. A few months after Ian died, she began looking into Arthur's life. She wasn't simply searching for incriminating evidence — the police, after all, had caught him at the scene; there was no way he could claim innocence. But it was much more than that. She wanted to find out everything she could about his past, his family — anything. It turned into an obsession. Over those four years she'd spent a good part of her wealth paying private investigators, many of whom were unscrupulous, cheating and deceiving her, wheedling money out of her. She'd also ruined her marriage. Ian had tried to convince her that what she was doing was insane, pointless. But she didn't listen, not to him or anyone. She'd even auctioned off the most important part of her past — her violin. Though she'd concealed her true motivation for selling it, she had actually auctioned it off to the Ministry of Culture simply because she needed the money.

And then one day a man showed up at her house — a short, sickly, decrepit man. He had a rubber-banded manila folder under one arm, clippings and photos spilling out the sides. He smoked like a chimney and spoke so softly she could hardly understand what he said. The guy was cagey, acting like he was convinced he was being watched everywhere he went, and was unable to sit still. He had tics and tremors, and his right eyelid twitched compulsively. While explaining things, he lost the thread at times, but when the man got to the contents of that folder, which he protected like a priceless treasure, what he said was astonishing. That downcast little man was the ex-officer who'd first been assigned Eduardo's case. And just like Gloria, he was obsessed with Arthur Fernández.

Maybe the police had thought that the case was solved, and unprosec-utable — but not him. He told her he felt there had been some sort of conspiracy to get him taken off Eduardo's case. He swore to Gloria that the investigation had cost him his job on the force and six years in a Guadalajara prison, and that it had all been engineered after he disobeyed repeated orders to stop 'fucking around', as he phrased it. He'd appealed numerous times but no one had paid any attention. The proof against him was compelling, and in the end he had descended — definitively —

into the deep pit of anonymity and desperation of someone who'd been chewed up and spat out by the forces of power. When he got out of jail, he managed to scrape together a living as a two-bit private investigator. That was how he'd heard Gloria had been going around asking questions about Arthur Fernández.

Brimming with emotion, he showed her the result of his years of effort, years when he'd never stopped searching for clues and evidence against the man who was now a thousand times richer and more powerful than he'd been fourteen years ago, while the ex-officer himself was a thousand times more insignificant.

'But the tiniest germs are the ones that bring down the giants. I'm like a simple cold that turns into deadly pneumonia,' he said, laughing like a madman.

Then he showed Gloria invoices from Arthur's firm, signed by someone in the Chicago office, paying off distant relations of the officers who had been involved in the investigation back in the early days. He also managed to find out that a few months after Eduardo was locked up, Arthur's car — a black SUV — was repaired at a body shop in Pau, a small city on the French side of the Basque Country. The repairs consisted of an alignment, the kind performed after a head-on, and the replacing of the entire front right panel. Then the car was painted another colour and sold by the firm. The little man showed Gloria receipts proving that the vehicle's export documentation had been falsified.

'Eduardo fucked up,' he said, scratching his head as though he had lice. And maybe he did. 'He killed the wrong man. Arthur is one son of a bitch.'

Gloria later verified everything that man had said. She even went to the place Arthur had supposedly spent the night with someone, though the hotel no longer existed. She managed to find the gas station, where she filled up and spoke to the cafeteria owner, who corroborated what the ex-police officer had said: late that night, someone matching Arthur's description had been there and had spoken to somebody on the phone.

When she got back to Madrid, she tried to contact the ex-officer, but he seemed to have vanished from the face of the earth. Though she never learned this, the little man's name was Alberto Antequera. He was forty-six years old and hailed from a place called Villafranca de los Barros, in the province of Badajoz. At the time he was discharged from the force and sentenced to six years in prison, he was in his twentieth year of service and had a spotless record. He had two children: Alberto, who was eight years old, and Fátima, who was five. His wife, Rosa, managed to hold things together while he was in prison, but she couldn't handle his subsequent mental breakdown. She ended up leaving him and had a judge issue a restraining order. He never saw them again.

In the slums where he lived after being released from jail, they called him 'San Vito' — after Vitus the patron saint of epileptics — because he was always trembling. A few people held him in high regard and gave him token odd jobs, as a reminder of the good times, but most of them either scorned or ignored him. Two weeks after contacting Gloria, he was found stabbed to death in Puente de Vallecas. A month later, the presumed perps were arrested: two minors who were up to their eyeballs on coke and had tried to steal his watch.

Thanks to Alberto — who Gloria never found out anything about — she did manage to find out about the existence of someone named Eduardo Quintana.

She was able to get in contact with him through his agent, Olga. She'd already found out that he'd just gotten out of a psychiatric ward and was doing high-volume portraits for shopping malls, that he lived in Lavapiés, and that every morning he went to Parque de El Retiro, where he had a date with his past near the Crystal Palace. For days, she followed him and watched him sketch in a notebook and drink heavily in nearby bars. She wanted to be sure he was as broken as she was, be sure that when she proposed the job, he'd accept. And maybe, deep down, she was also hoping to find a kindred spirit. Together they'd summon the courage to do what Eduardo had done fourteen years ago. But this time, to the right man. The man who had ruined their lives.

Ian gave Eduardo a look of pity.

'You *knew* that. You had to know it somehow. Nothing in life is pure chance, but sometimes we opt to feign ignorance of certain things.'

Eduardo thought about each of the times he'd met with Gloria. A little voice inside him had told him that she was messing with him, that Eduardo was nothing but a pawn on the first line of attack, the one who struck first, driving a wedge into the enemy's defences only to be sacrificed. Ian was right. He'd known all along, but he'd denied it, even to himself, clinging to her in order to keep from suffocating, in order to keep breathing a little longer. Just a little while longer.

Ian paused the image. Without touching it, he caressed his son's face. A boy of six or seven, his eyes deep, a little sad, disconcerted. He had a naive air about him, a freckled face and a haircut too childish for his age — side part, bangs plastered to his forehead. As if nothing could ever happen to him, as if Ian would always be right there to protect him.

That was over Christmas, one year at Ian senior's parents' house in Wales. There was a river there, high above the village, which dried out in the summer, leaving nothing but pebbles, garbage and rotting sticks in its course. Only in the springtime, and the first two weeks of summer if you were lucky, could you catch anything but dead rats in that water. And yet his son loved it there. He remembered that, ever since Ian junior was a little boy, with the good looks of a grown man, he'd walk along the trail of acacias lining the river as if searching for the signs of a past he'd yet to live.

In the late afternoon the weather would change suddenly. It was always drizzling in Wales, a fine curtain of mist that blew in in gusts, dampening the washing hung out to dry behind dirty grey houses the same colour as the sky raining down on them. It was an ideal place for nostalgia. The perfect surroundings for a musician. But Ian junior didn't want to be a musician. In fact, the only thing his son seemed to enjoy was walking along the bridge above the river and staring down at his feet, lost in thoughts that took him far from wherever he was. On occasion he'd glance up, surprised, as if not knowing how his steps had suddenly led him to his grandparents' house, covered in spectacular vines, creepers full of uncertainties, full of tiny red berries and leaves that each seemed to hold a single raindrop.

Ian junior enjoyed being with Sir Matthew, his grandfather, despite the fact that their characters could not have been more different. The old man didn't mind that his grandson was Jewish on his mother's side. He was an extravagant old giant who claimed baselessly that he had Norman blood, or Moorish — or any other type, depending on how inebriated he was. He was fun and foul-mouthed like his son, and although he loved his grandson and daughter-in-law, he found them overly taciturn. He used to say he didn't want to *understand* life, he wanted to live it.

As a young man he'd played harp and loved being in a band that travelled throughout the valleys, going village-to-village during festival season. In Pembroke he met Mery, who was to be his wife for over fifty years. She was a large woman, built like a Romanesque church, and in the home movie she was seen leaning calmly over the balcony railing, in slippers and bathrobe, smoking. Mery was modern and strong-willed for her day and her environs. Her eyes gazed blankly at the fields that extended to the other side of the river, where from time to time there appeared a peasant's back, bent over the rows.

Ian junior had inherited his grandmother's melancholy nature, as well as her deep eyes and unsettling expression. Mery was always listening to music — a Chopin nocturne for violin and piano that Matthew hated. The old man complained that a melody that sad and dramatic made you think something terrible was about to happen. His grandson, on the other hand, felt his heart pound with joy whenever he approached the door knocker and held the wood in his hand, the moment before the doors opened and his grandmother appeared, smelling of flour and fresh vegetables, her mousey voice chastising him: *What are you doing wandering around the river in this cold? Don't you know the dead are out searching for a body to inhabit, silly boy?* And then she'd sit him on her knees and hum to him — the same music over and over — and tell him dark tales by the waning fire, tales of mythical creatures of the forest, of witches and wizards, tales that the boy listened to with rapt attention.

That old house had lost its former glory many years ago. Time had taken its toll, and buried Mery right along with it. One night she turned up dead, lying atop the frozen river. It was snowing out and she lay face-up in a nightgown, barefoot, arms extended, eyes gazing up at the sky. No one ever found out how she got there, or what she was doing at the river at that time of night. Or why her face had that look of horror, her pupils frozen, her mouth grimacing in agony. Matthew lost all sense of joy, drowning his sorrows in brandy, and wouldn't let a single thing be done to the house. He insisted on leaving it exactly as it had been when she died — until he too died a few years later, from cirrhosis of the liver. The remaining ruins smelled of mold and sorrow. But the river was still there, awaiting Ian each morning. As it had been for years.

It was around the time of his father's death that their problems began. And Ian junior was always at the centre of them. The arguments had turned vehement by then, and the recurring topic was the boy's character. Ian was a troubled boy, Gloria agreed with her husband about that much. But Ian senior was exaggerating, in her opinion; she could control Ian junior's mood swings, she understood his introverted, labyrinthine, overly sensitive character. It made sense, with a violinist for a mother and a film director for a father — they spent more time on planes than on solid ground. In his own way, the boy was just punishing them for their constant absence. That was all. Of course she would have liked for him to keep up with his music lessons, but he wasn't interested in music, at least not interested enough to spend all the time and effort required to be a serious pianist. But film didn't interest him either, much to his father's chagrin.

Ian remembered the last time they were together at the river house. That afternoon, his son was running around the shore with a movie camera, filming anything and everything. He'd focus in on his father and ask him to say something, and Ian senior would glance sidelong at the camera, a cigarette hanging from his lips.

'Turn that off, show a little respect. This is where your grandmother died, carried off by the dead.'

That night they saw him from the bedroom window, walking toward the river under a star-filled sky, completely naked despite the sub-zero temperatures. It had been snowing until late and his footsteps left deep imprints along the path. Ian senior raced down the stairs and out of the house and found his son on the riverbed, lying from the waist up across the frozen surface. The ice made a sizzling sound, cracking like an old man's face. In the blink of an eye, Ian senior leapt, fearful that it would give way, and fought to pull his son off its surface.

'Have you lost your mind? What are you trying to do? Drown yourself?'

His son had looked up at him as though he were a blind fool.

'I just wanted to look, to look until I could see,' he replied — he'd been gazing into the depths of the river, which had been reflected in his eyes. *Or was it his eyes that were reflected in the ice?* His face had the same cold look that his grandmother had had. The same frozen expression.

They didn't return to the house in Wales until two years after Ian's death, in Madrid. Gloria and Ian were about to be divorced. The last image he had had of the place was that of his father, Sir Matthew, putting out a cigarette on the bridge's railing, and then walking along the damp planks as though the sorrow enshrouding his soulless body were the best defence he had. Mist coiled around the reeds and oaks and swept along the smooth surface of the slimy river, concealing the bottom of the bridge's columns. Above the scaffolding loomed the outline of the house, the second storey reflecting daylight.

Promise me you'll always take care of her. That you'll protect her from herself, and from the demons that haunt her.

At the time, Ian wasn't yet thirty. And the man with bushy eyebrows and a perfectly trimmed white beard who was speaking to him was intimidating. Ian had just gotten married a few days earlier and was not yet used to the feel of his wedding band. He never thought he'd marry so suddenly, and here he was already expecting a child.

He was drinking lukewarm coffee with his father-in-law, and this was the first time they'd spoken alone. In fact, it was the first time they'd spoken. And he felt the weight of the man's deep, inquisitive expression.

He promised. Despite not understanding what the old man was asking of him.

Ian thought back to his father-in-law's words now. And he understood. Now he understood.

He had gotten married thinking he knew all he needed to know — that he loved his wife, that she was as independent a spirit as he was, that she was passionate in bed and affectionate outside of it, that she'd never get used to the Welsh climate and that his father would never like her (as for his mother, he had his doubts), but that she'd still be willing to spend time at the river house by the bridge, and put on a brave face when her drunken father-in-law started going on about his ancestry and telling stories about the family clan. He got married knowing that the child they were awaiting was going to bring them together, meld them into one, make them unbreakable, like steel. No matter what. He knew there would never be another woman in his life, knew his dalliances with aspiring actresses were over, as were his drunken nights out with friends from the set — underwear on top of the fridge, rubbish bin not being taken out, wrinkled shirts and soccer matches. He rejected everything his life before her had been; it all seemed ridiculous. And he was convinced. *Happy*.

But that wasn't enough. Not to keep them together forever. At the time he didn't know about the Taggers' past, about the photo of Great-grandfather Ulrico in his Prussian uniform, the inherited guilt of a pro-Nazi Jew that always hovered over the table at dinners and get-togethers with her family. Ian didn't understand why she insisted on keeping the portrait in the bedroom of a man they all hated, or why he sometimes found her gazing at it with an almost mystical look, stroking it as though it were a much-missed lover. And then, conversely, she'd privately become incredibly cross whenever people said that her son, Ian, was the spitting image of his great-grandfather.

But he was, despite how hard she tried to find signs of the Mackenzies in her son — as though that might save him. The truth was, that little boy was a Tagger, through and through. She didn't want to see it, and he couldn't prevent it. But he kept the promise he'd made to his father-in-law.

He'd protect Gloria at all costs. Even from herself.

23

As if able to sense the dark presence that had just entered the room, Ian paused the video.

'What are you doing here?'

Gloria's voice lashed out at him. She wasn't surprised. She wasn't happy to see him. He got up from the armchair and raised his glass of whisky by way of greeting.

'I had a few things to take care of and thought I'd stop by and see how everything was going. It's not that strange. This *is* still my house.' *And you are still my unfulfilled promise,* he thought. 'I was just reminiscing about old times, thinking about when we got El Español back. What a shame your father never got to see that.' A bittersweet smile accompanied his comment, but he hid it by taking a swig of whisky. 'I'm going back to Sydney in the morning,' he added, as though to pacify her — as a warning not to waste the few hours they had together on arguments and reproaches. But the devil that all Welshmen have inside suddenly went off-script. 'Though it would seem you're managing not to miss me.' He pointed with his glass to the portrait, now framed, leaning up against a column over by the window. 'I met your little portrait artist today. It appears that his services include a few extras in addition to the paint. Watch it, the poor man is in love with you, and that's like having a scorpion in your bed. You have to know how to handle it so it doesn't poison you with its kiss.'

Gloria stepped forward and stopped halfway between Ian and the portrait of Arthur. She looked back and forth between the two of them, as though contemplating a mirror and what it was reflecting.

'I want to see it,' she said, her voice quiet.

'See what?' Ian asked casually.

Dolores the housekeeper had an obsession — a virtue, really — about order and meticulousness. Her parents had taught her that the rich are always suspicious of their servants, that they suspect they're pilfering money and food, that they're not hardworking, that they shirk the chores they've been given to do. In order to survive in a good house (which was like El Dorado — the maximum aspiration to which people like Dolores aspired), it was crucial to always have an alibi in order to refute all of your employer's accusations.

When Gloria asked her that morning about a package that had come four years ago, the reasonable response would have been to say she couldn't remember; no one could have reproached her for that. Nevertheless, Dolores went up to her little room in the attic and rifled through the papers she kept in a shoebox until she came across the proof of delivery. She went back down to Gloria and handed it to her proudly. The signature on the bottom right of the slip was Ian's. *If you lost that package, it's not my fault,* her expression said.

'The video Magnus Olsen's widow sent. We can call Dolores if you want; she tells me she gave it to you.'

Ian Mackenzie didn't need any proof. He remembered perfectly well the day and time the housekeeper handed him a package with no return address. He was at home alone, Gloria and Ian junior had gone into Madrid and he was working on a script he wasn't quite happy with. After receiving the Medal of Arts from the Queen, his fame as a director had grown exponentially, as had the number of careerists in his life, including many desperate folks who mailed him all sorts of things in the hopes of a helping hand. Under normal circumstances the recording would have landed in the pile of CDs, résumés, and scripts he received regularly from people looking for an opportunity that would probably never arrive. But that morning Ian couldn't concentrate on his work. Olsen's death was hanging over him. The media reported the same version of events as the police: Magnus had committed suicide, unable to cope with the pressure of his bankruptcy and legal problems. The case, therefore, was not going to be investigated. But that didn't quell his fears.

He could have taken a few days off to enjoy himself — before he had to return to Australia to tackle the last part of a shoot that would require a great deal of mental effort — but he didn't. He was hardly sleeping; his arguments with Gloria were becoming increasingly heated, and they were all about the same thing: Ian junior. He needed to get back to filming, get back behind the camera, hop on a bus and cross the Australian desert. At least there he could pretend his life hadn't changed.

He popped in the tape and turned on the TV, intending to grant himself a ten-minute distraction. And a whisky. Then he'd go back to work.

Nothing could have prepared him for what he was about to see.

He'd never really liked Magnus Olsen. Maybe one reason was because of the rude, almost feudalistic way he treated his beautiful wife. Like the nouveaux riches, he possessed her without actually appreciating her. And that woman was too exquisite a morsel for the Swiss shark. He treated her like an expensive whore, openly stroking her arse in the presence of others, grabbing her by the waist as if she were a stein of beer. He felt sorry for her, and he also wanted her, had fantasies he sometimes allowed himself to indulge in, alone in the bathroom.

Regardless, Olsen was a door that men like Ian had to knock on in order to finance their films. The lie Magnus had invented for himself and was trying to live had not yet seriously begun to crack, and he seemed firmly established in his wealth; besides — and this was sheer luck — he was a real film buff who possessed truly vast stores of knowledge that surprised Ian. Olsen admired him not just because he was star-struck but also because the man sincerely appreciated his work, which inevitably predisposed Ian to get over his reticence about the man's character. And the lengths Olsen went to in order to get the Taggers' violin back finally ended up dispelling Ian's initial doubts. He opened the doors of his house to the man, agreed to give a couple of talks to Dámaso's film club and acted as intermediary so that Olsen could gain access to other directors, actors and people in the business. The club was very select — those people had enough money and power that he'd never have to put projects on the backburner over a lack of funding or over bureaucratic red tape.

It was intoxicating.

What's more, his son enjoyed those evening sessions at the club too. He watched him from the projector as they showed a Harold Lloyd film and saw that his son's eyes were taking in every detail. He asked questions that were surprisingly astute for a neophyte of his age, leaving the other attendees awestruck — and for the first time, Ian saw his son emerge from the permanent silence and cold, withdrawn air he'd had since birth.

He seemed like a different child, happier, more centred.

It had been obvious since he was a little boy that he'd never be like other kids. There was something odd about him, something that occasionally verged on cruelty. One time he'd used barbed wire to tie a puppy to a post and had then watched for hours as the poor animal struggled to get free, tearing its neck to shreds. But at the same time, he could analyse anything his twinkling eyes saw with the sort of candor that was disconcerting in someone so young — like the day he contemplated a desiccated tree and turned to look at his father, saying that things are born in order to one day die and that's just the way it is. He was seven.

Ian and Gloria were locked in a nasty and secret rivalry over the boy, each trying to be the one to govern the contradictory forces at play inside him. They sparred without realising it, pouring their hopes and fears into their son; he was the battlefield on which they waged their war. Ian senior was sure the boy would follow in his footsteps, that he'd find in film a means of expressing whatever it was that tormented him — the greatest minds often verged on the insane, and as long as his genius managed to prevail, his son had enormous potential. Gloria, in turn, put all her faith in music; she tried to force him to be disciplined with the violin and piano, claiming that music activated new parts of the brain, created neuronal associations that her son needed to fill with harmony and order.

When Ian turned down a class with his mother in order to accompany his father to see a movie with Magnus at Dámaso's film club, Ian smiled at having won a petty victory over his wife.

'I didn't realise what was going on until it was too late,' he told Gloria. He rubbed his face as though washing it with a cloth. 'When Olsen called me, I couldn't process what he was saying. It was as if I'd taken a hallucinogen; my brain could not accept it. I sat there in the hotel room with the phone in one hand, thinking it was a joke. But it wasn't. That son of a bitch told me what Ian was doing in the club, the terrible things he was taking part in.'

Nobody's forcing him, believe me. This is all coming from him, Olsen had said.

From Madrid, thousands of kilometres away, Olsen had called him in Australia to tell him that his son was a genius. A twisted, perverted genius. *I have proof. So you'd better come and take a look. We need to speak and come to an agreement. I don't like having to do this, Ian; I sincerely admire you. But my life is going down the pan and I need some liquidity.*

'He was blackmailing me. He threatened to send you the proof. I thought I was going to lose my mind, I couldn't think straight, didn't know how to react. I got on the first plane I could and went straight to his house.'

'Why didn't you tell me?' She wasn't attempting to console him, wasn't saying that together they could have handled anything — gone to the police, hospitalised their son if necessary. No, she was recriminating him for not having involved her in it, for having kept quiet all those years. Absolute contempt trembled in her voice, but she showed no other emotions.

Promise me.

He'd promised. That he would protect Gloria from everything and everyone. Even from herself. His father-in-law had looked at him, one eye cloudy with the gauzy haze over his pupil; the man was going blind. But he could still see — and he'd seen what his daughter's husband had inside, what he was capable of. Ian remembered the old man's sad, tragic smile. He was burdened by stories of war, Jews, exile, violins, secret graves. A smile revealed tartar-stained, uneven teeth — the man had always refused dentures and implants — worn down by gnawing his way through life.

Nothing more was ever said. They never brought it up again.

When Ian disembarked from the plane from Australia, foggy with lack of sleep, hair standing on end, large purple bags under his eyes, he knew what he had to do.

Magnus Olsen hadn't been expecting him so early. It was seven in the morning. He could hear the TV from behind the door, the morning news. Things were happening all over the world, but he didn't care about any of them. Olsen opened the door, half-dressed, shirt unbuttoned and belt not yet buckled. His hairy gut hung out, belly button like a spider curled up in a hairy black nest, tiny nipples poking out from his sagging breasts. Like a pig. He looked surprised, but not afraid. He looked like he wanted to say, *What's the rush? It's not that big a deal.*

Ian knew what he had to do and how to do it. He didn't hit him, though, in his neck, he felt the strain of forcing himself not to. He didn't say a word. Instead he stood looking at the man's body, calculating his weight. A hundred and ten, hundred and twenty kilos. *Nothing but a ball of fat,* he thought. A mass of blubber steamrolling over his happiness. Olsen asked him in. He was still barefoot and his toes left little marks on the parquet. There was fresh-brewed coffee, some half-eaten toast on a plate, and a cigarette smouldering in an ashtray in need of emptying. The television blared in the background, clothes were strewn on the sofa. It smelled of cheap hooker. The only window was to the right, facing the building across the street. Which was far away. A thick wood beam crossed the ceiling, dividing the open-plan space in two. It would take the weight.

'I know you must think I'm a bastard.' Olsen's voice sounded respectful and full of sorrow, but his eyes were greedy and scheming. 'You have to understand that I have no intention of harming you or your family. It's just that things have become extremely difficult for me and I need money.' He was moving with his pudgy hands — the same hands that so cockily fondled his wife's bottom — as if stroking an imaginary ball, talking, defending himself, pretending he was at the end of his tether.

Ian wasn't listening. He didn't need the prologue.

'I'll pay you, but I want to see the tape first,' he said, cutting him off.

Magnus Olsen's expression was that of a man accustomed to living a life of lies and mistrust. He was a good poker player, and a good poker player never shows the aces up his sleeve until just the right moment.

'Of course, of course, but I don't have it here right now. I'm not stupid. It's hidden in a safe place, don't you worry. When you pay me, I'll send it to you. Standard procedure.'

So he'd done this to others before, Ian thought. Coaxed out other people's weaknesses and then taken advantage of them. To him it was just a *standard procedure*. Ian changed tack. He threatened to go to the police. Olsen let out a cynical laugh. They both knew he wouldn't do that.

Olsen had become the Damocles sword hanging over his head. Ian could pay him, but there was no guarantee he'd get the tape in return, or that there weren't more copies, or that he wouldn't continue trying to extort him in the future. He knew he had to get rid of that parasite.

It was quick and violent. Silent. And the silence accentuated the surreal nature of the whole thing as Ian pounced, taking the man off-guard and hurling him to the floor with a kick to the solar plexus. Olsen stumbled backward like a disoriented bear. Without thinking, urged on by his instincts, Ian whipped off Olsen's belt and wrapped it around his neck. He fought back, pawing the air and trying to strike any which way, the blows landing mostly on Ian's shoulders. For a fat man he struggled ferociously, kicking, eyes popping out of his sockets. But Ian strangled him with a cold determination he never imagined he could possess.

Killing a human being turned out to be all too easy. And for a long time that discovery troubled him. At night, once he was back in Australia, he'd relive the scene in his mind, the sequence of premeditated movements executed with impeccable discipline. He could see Olsen's eyes go from disconcerted to irate to fearful and then finally, as the light in them grew dim, to pleading. He felt the pressure of the belt around his knuckles, heard the sound of the leather twisting across Magnus' trachea, the tapping of his heels on the wood floor and the gurgling of air escaping from his lungs.

'I didn't find the tape. I don't think he had any intention of giving it to me and I didn't have time to search. I hauled him up to the beam, knotted the belt, and left him hanging.'

Gloria stared, stunned and stupefied, at the man who had once been her husband, the father of her son, and she did not recognise him. She couldn't imagine him doing anything like that. He was too handsome, too carefree. He was a genius. Not a *murderer*. His hands, his eyes, his body were made to create things, images. Not destroy them.

'When the tape arrived, it was already too late for you and me. I couldn't explain it to you, you wouldn't have understood,' Ian said, his voice broken.

Gloria closed her eyes and pressed her fingers into them, as though trying to force her eyeballs back in, so as not to see anything else. Opening her eyes, she looked for a chair and sat down. Her body was trembling. She looked at Arthur's portrait, right in front of her, and felt infinite bitterness as she contemplated his immortalised expression. How she hated that man! How she hated the entire world at that moment.

A few things made sense now. When Ian had returned from Australia, weeks after Olsen's death, he'd been absentminded and irritable, and though he blamed it on the exhaustion of filming and on economic troubles, Gloria assumed — naively — that her husband was having some sort of affair, when in fact what was weighing on him was his conscience. Sickened, she replayed one horrible evening — the worst they'd had at that point. She had been practising, going over a few scores. Dolores sat knitting in an armchair. She liked to knit scarves and sweaters, which she then gave as gifts to people, who never wore them.

Gloria heard shouting coming from the office upstairs. Her husband sounded out of control — he was swearing in English and hurling insults that reverberated throughout the house. In the background she could hear her son's voice screaming, too, although it was drowned out by his father's booming voice. They were really fighting.

'I'll go see what's going on,' Dolores had said, looking startled, cocking her head as though that would enable her to hear better.

Gloria had already gotten up.

'No, I'll go.'

She'd walked upstairs, and on entering the office, she froze. Her husband had Ian junior cornered between the table and a sofa. His arms were aloft and from where she stood, behind them, it was hard to tell whether he was trying to hug him or strangle him. But when she caught sight of her son's contorted face and his father's furious eyes, his intentions became clearer.

Ian junior's lip was bleeding and he had a mark on his cheek. A few drops of red stained the collar of his shirt. Drops that neither father nor son had noticed but that Gloria honed in on immediately. Incredulous, she barked questions back and forth between the two of them, but neither one answered. Her son wrenched free from the prison of his father's arms and stormed out of the office, stopping in the doorway to shoot each of them a look a pure hatred.

'You're the ones who made me what I am. I wish you were both dead!'

Gloria made as if to go after him, but what he said stopped her in her tracks.

'Don't even touch me, you Jew bitch. I'm never coming back to this house. As long as he's here, you can forget about me.'

His words hit her like a blow to the stomach. The words that hurt and wound and kill the most are those spoken by the love of your life. For a mother, the worst form of betrayal, the worst sort of death, is the contempt of her child. The incomprehensible contempt.

Ian left, slamming the door so hard it rattled in its frame, but his words lingered on, rooting Gloria to the spot where she stood. She stared down at her feet wondering what they were doing there, holding her up. Slowly, she raised her eyes to her husband, on the other side of the room. He stood with his back to her, wide and broad-shouldered, with large biceps, strong enough to hang a hundred-and-twenty-kilo pig of a man from a ceiling beam. Strong enough to bear the weight of what he'd done in silence. He leant with his hands and forehead against the wall. As though trapped and trying in vain to push his way out, to escape.

'What did you do to my son?'

Ian turned slowly to face her. He couldn't look her in the eye. At that moment, he wouldn't have been able to keep up his front, to hide the tragedy already set in motion.

'It was just an argument. You know what he's like, he'll get over it.'

He might, but *she* was never going to forget it.

'Did you hit him?'

Ian swallowed hard, as though forcing down dry crumbs of bread. Bitter bread.

He'd never before laid a hand on his son. He'd never killed anybody before either. There's always a first time — and after that it gets easier.

'He needs help, Gloria. There is something *very wrong* with our son.'

She wasn't listening.

'Did you split his lip?'

Ian was exasperated. He had walked towards her, with something on the tip of his tongue. But at the last minute the words receded and sank back inside him.

'I did what I had to do.' His nostrils flared and he was panting. He didn't know whether to scream or cry. Instead he shook his head in resignation. 'You don't understand. We have to take Ian somewhere. We have to get him out of here.'

Out of his life, he should have said. *Of his sick brain and festering heart.*

'I want you out of this house,' was Gloria's reply.

Blind. She was blind. If he'd told her back then, if he'd just opened up, she could have found a way to fix things, she'd have known what to do. Ian would be alive and that sickening portrait wouldn't be sitting there.

She didn't care what it was her son might have done.

'I want to see it.' Her physical body was still there but she herself was gone — someplace where she didn't have to think, so she wouldn't go insane. 'I need to see it so that I know it's true.'

'You don't need to see the truth to admit it,' Ian replied. 'I destroyed it.'

He was lying, of course; he'd never let his wife see what the fruit of her loins was capable of. Never.

'There's another copy. Maybe more than one.'

Ian turned to this new voice coming from the direction of the door. Gloria flinched but didn't look surprised. She'd known he was there.

Guzmán had been listening from behind the door. He'd granted Gloria that much, allowed her to speak to her husband first — the same way that, before interrogating a detainee, they first let family members speak to them alone in the hopes that they might confess without having to be tortured first. It almost never worked, but he felt better at least trying.

'I'm guessing you know who I am …'

Ian recognised him immediately, though they'd never spoken before, or even seen each other up close. Over four months, Ian had shadowed that mercenary, always on his heels, erasing all trace of what he discovered. Guzmán walked over to Arthur's portrait. In it, Arthur looked as though he were full of inner turmoil, like one of those portraits of Middle Age mystics where it's impossible to distinguish ecstasy from insanity, or vice versa.

'… and you know why I'm here.'

Ian nodded. This wasn't the way things were supposed to be happening. After he'd killed Olsen, Ian had thought the whole business was dead and buried. Then, one morning, he had received a phone call from someone who spoke eloquently, requesting to speak to him, in person. The man arranged to meet him on the patio of an elegant hotel in the centre of Madrid, in broad daylight.

The man was middle-aged, handsome and distinguished. He wore an Italian suit and had gold cufflinks that matched his tiepin. His intense brown eyes twinkled wittily and his brows were subtly waxed into a perfect arch above his eyes. He never said what his name was, but from the start he made it very clear that he was acting as an intermediary for a group of people who, for obvious reasons, could not be named publically.

For obvious reasons, he repeated several times. The two of them looked like decent, civilised people just having a coffee, discussing the terms of a business deal. The man — who wore too much cologne and asked Ian not to smoke when he went to light a cigarette — claimed to be abreast of the situation Ian had gotten involved in, and added, ripping open a packet of sugar and stirring less than half of it into his coffee, that Olsen had not committed suicide. *We know you killed him. But don't let that worry you. That man would have turned into a real headache for some of those I represent. It was simply a matter of time until someone solved the problem — so in a way we should be grateful to you.*

They would make sure that Ian had no trouble with the police. And that his son didn't either. Needless to say, the club's activities had been suspended — he didn't say 'terminated'. In exchange, they asked him to forget what he knew. *Quid pro quo*, he'd said with an acàdemic smile. *You just go back to Australia and carry on with your work — which, from what I hear, is marvellous. You've got influential admirers and they'll provide all the funding you need in the future.* It was best to not even contemplate the alternative. *For obvious reasons*, he said again. He didn't need to spell them out: what today was being viewed as a suicide could turn into murder tomorrow. Evidence could be found proving his son guilty of rape, and Ian junior would never survive prison. *Kids today aren't like our generation.* Not to mention what it would do to Gloria, not just professionally but spiritually, to have the whole thing come to light. *Between you and me, the rich can't stand having to account for their actions. It makes them too like other mortals, accountability does. And they're not willing to stoop that low, for obvious reasons.*

'That wasn't the way it was supposed to happen. They said they'd take care of everything.'

'But then Arthur came on the scene,' said Guzmán, 'and he introduced a variable that neither of you had taken into account. Although, wasn't it obvious that a father like him would never stand there with his arms crossed while his daughter was missing?'

Gloria was rocking softly in her chair, a death grip on the wrinkled handkerchief in her hands. She wore the expression of someone who's just vomited. Contorted. Her eyes had turned dull black, reflecting no light.

'Arthur received a copy of that tape and saw what Ian had done to

379

his daughter. It wasn't an accident. He ran Ian over on purpose … And you knew,' Gloria said, staring straight at her husband. She understood now, and yet she did not want to understand, did not want the clarity of knowing that when she gave her husband the news over the phone, his devastation was far more heartbreaking than even her own. Because he was filled with silence, guilt, and regret. 'It was your fault.'

Ian didn't try to defend himself. Unknowingly, he'd put his own son in the firing line, not seeing that he was flinging the gates of doom wide open. There was no point telling himself that his son had a sick nature and that sooner or later the depraved Tagger side would have found another way to take hold.

'You killed Dámaso, and then Olsen's widow. You thought they'd blame me for it, the way they did with Dámaso. But you let the children live. That speaks well of your honour, but it was a mistake. Kids talk — they have good memories and they like police uniforms. I'd say it won't be long until some officers pay you a visit.'

Ian said nothing in reply. He went to Gloria and knelt before her, trying to get her to look at him.

'I didn't tell you I'd come back because I didn't want to drag you into it. I wanted to keep you safe. But when I called and you told me you'd hired the artist that that crazy police officer had told you about to paint a portrait of Arthur, I felt powerless. It was like I was stuck in quicksand, sinking deeper and deeper, and this is where I ended up. I tried to convince you to leave, but you're so stubborn. You always do things your way. And that was when I realised I had to put an end to this once and for all. Getting Olsen out of the way wasn't enough. There were other people who knew what Ian had done, people who could keep coming back again and again, threatening us, blackmailing us with other tapes. And I wasn't prepared to let them do that to you. That much, at least, I wanted you to have. Yes, I killed those people. But they were already dead, condemned even if they didn't know it. There was no way they'd have let them live, not after Arthur started stirring shit up.'

Gloria turned away in disgust. She couldn't stand the sight of him, couldn't stand his touch, his smell. He didn't understand. She didn't care what her son had done. He was the flesh of her flesh, and she'd have done the same thing — lie, betray, kill — but not to protect a memory, an idea.

She'd have done it to save his life. Her eyes focused on Arthur's portrait and she suddenly leapt up and rushed to the pencil holder on the desk. She snatched a pair of scissors and, before Ian or Guzmán had a chance to react, she lunged at the canvas and stabbed it one, two, three, four times, howling like an animal.

The two men stood staring, not daring to intervene, and waited until Gloria dropped the scissors, exhausted, and left the room.

'I'll never forgive you for this,' she said to Ian as she left.

Guzmán picked the scissors up off the floor. They were sharp. He gazed impassively at the painting, now in shreds, from which half of one eye stared out.

'I pity you, Ian. I really do. Your determination to preserve everything at any cost is what made you lose it all.'

Ian glared at him, livid. He could fight Guzmán, maybe get the scissors off him, but there was no way he'd emerge victorious. Anticipating his thoughts, Guzmán opened his mouth in reproach and pointed to the Glock tucked into his waistband.

'You shouldn't have killed Magnus' widow. She had no part in this, she only wanted to help you and forget about it all, move on with her life.'

'Nobody could move on with their life after being implicated in something like this.'

Guzmán's face hardened. He walked to the office door and turned the key that was in the lock.

'That's right. And that brings me to the part of this whole conversation that interests me. I'm in a hurry to get this over with. I've got a plane to catch. So we're just going to skip the usual protocol.'

With no warning he pulled out the pistol and fired a shot point-blank into Ian's knee.

'Where is Arthur's daughter? What did you do with her? I've got twelve bullets in this clip. And I'll fire them one by one until you tell me. Hand, elbow, foot, shoulder … You get the picture.'

Dolores arrived in the early evening that day, as she did every Tuesday, her day off. The bus to her employers' suburb was nearly empty. 'They'll shut down this route any day now,' the driver said. 'Public transportation gives rich people the willies. It's too democratic. Smells like humanity.' What would she do if they cut the only bus route that went anywhere close to their house? 'Strike it rich, Dolores,' was the driver's sardonic suggestion.

The first thing she found odd, which she later told the police, was that Señor Ian's office door was locked from the outside. He always left the key on the inside of that door. She knocked but didn't dare enter.

The second surprise made her faint, giving her a nasty bump on the head where she hit the porcelain toilet bowl. That, she later claimed, was why it took her so long to call the police. *I was unconscious for at least fifteen minutes, and the only reason I came to was because the bathtub water wet my face and woke me up.* She'd walked in to find water pooling on Señora Tagger's bedroom floor; it was coming from beneath the bathroom door. When she opened it, she found the señora naked, in the tub, arms hanging over the tiled sides.

Gloria had devised a tremendous, dramatic end to her life. She'd drowned herself in the tub, filling it with warm water and bath salts. Prior to that she'd put on Chopin's nocturne, in memory of her son's paternal grandmother. Beside the tub lay an uncorked bottle of very good wine and the remains of a joint. She'd taken the time to fold her clothes carefully. And in case she regretted her decision at the last minute, she'd also swallowed an entire bottle of strong sleeping pills. But in the end she hadn't even struggled.

24

Situated on a steep narrow street, with its awning rolled up and no sign aside from a small nameplate on the door, Chez Farida was a little slice of Algeria in Madrid's Tirso de Molina neighbourhood. The place was decorated in traditional Algerian style, and customers sat at low tables, on benches covered with colourful cushions. From time to time, the owner let Algerian artists display their work on the rust-coloured walls. Ibrahim frequented the place regularly to sate his cravings for good Machwi home-cooking, cheap platters of grilled meat, potato croquettes, and honey-drenched desserts. That day, there were very few customers. The girl waiting tables gave him an informal greeting and pointed to a table near the kitchen, where the cook could be heard bustling around with saucepans to the joyous sound of Chaabi music on the stereo, turned low.

Arthur arrived ten minutes later. He too liked the restaurant's traditional cuisine and cosy atmosphere. They met there every once in awhile, and always sat chatting awhile after their meal. But that day Arthur was in a hurry and not in the mood to talk. He refused the menu and ordered a draft beer, dropping heavily down onto the bench.

'So, what was so important?' he asked.

Ibrahim was drumming his fingers on the tablecloth to the beat of the music and staring at the black and white photos on the wall. They were all portraits of Algerians, people who life had not been kind to and whose suffering was reflected in their expressions — some unsociable, others staring into the camera with what seemed a direct accusation. Portraits of old farmers with wild manes of hair, women with the hint of a moustache visible above their wrinkled smiles, gleeful gap-toothed children in their underwear, leaping from a rock into the sea. The timeless snapshots — taken by an unknown artist hoping to sell one or two under the mistaken assumption that people find the suffering of others interesting — contrasted strikingly with the actual faces of the few customers there: young Algerians in baggy jeans and Real Madrid shirts smoking cigarettes, married couples sharing a few lamb kebabs with their ill-behaved children, who sat drinking Coke. *There are always two sides to reality*, Ibrahim thought. And nostalgia was the more ambiguous side.

'Where is your father buried?' Ibrahim asked suddenly. Arthur gave him a sidelong glance, one eyebrow cocked.

'In the common grave of a municipal cemetery in a small town in the province of Málaga, where he was killed. My mother didn't have the money to have him exhumed. And later, I chose not to. Why would I?'

'Do you ever visit him?'

'No. Why are you asking me all this?'

Ibrahim pointed to a picture hanging on the wall to the right of their table. It was a strange photo, full of grey tones that lent a certain tension to the low-lying clouds, from which emerged a hill where a Berber shepherd stood wrapped in a threadbare blanket. The shepherd and his dog had their backs to the camera and looked out at the desert horizon before them.

'Those are the hills of Djebel Adjdir. That's where my father is buried. Though you can't see it, behind that desert, out past where the shepherd is looking, is the sea. I like to imagine that my father is looking this way, that his eyes are following me wherever I go.'

Arthur glanced at the photo disinterestedly. Ibrahim wasn't often nostalgic.

'Did you know my father was a militant in the FLN? He was very active during the war of independence. For years, we had to keep secret the place where he was buried. The authorities didn't like martyrs and didn't want his grave to turn into a site of pilgrimage. If it were up to them, they'd have exhumed the body and thrown it into a common grave, but in the end, the passage of time accomplished what they couldn't do. Nobody really thinks about those days, or those heroes, anymore. There are no more pilgrims, no more flowers; nobody writes prayers or pledges on scraps of paper to leave under rocks. The heroes of yesterday make all the more obvious how mediocre the heroes of today are.'

He looked at Arthur and felt as though time had come to a standstill, as though he were no longer sitting at that table.

'I'm leaving Madrid. I want to live out the rest of my days in Algeria.'

Arthur stared at him in shock.

'You can't — when you were released, that was one of the conditions of your probation. If you leave Spain and stop going to court every two weeks, you'll be declared a fugitive of the law.'

'I have no intention of coming back.'

'You don't have a passport; you'd be stopped at the border.'

Ibrahim smiled. Papers, walls. Man-made creations can't stop the wind. People were wandering in and out of the restaurant, coming and going, burdened by the weight of their lives. They didn't realise they were free.

'I'll manage.'

Arthur was disconcerted by Ibrahim's enigmatic air.

'What are you going to do? Go back to arms trafficking? To drugs? To fighting? You're not a young man anymore, and Algeria is no country for the weak.'

Ibrahim nodded as he fingered the scar on his cheek. He wasn't the same man. Wounds can be healed. With time, with patience, with determination.

'There's something else I wanted to tell you. I've asked Andrea to come with me.'

Arthur let out a nervous laugh.

'What the hell are you talking about?'

Ibrahim took a deep breath and told him everything.

'I've been in love with her since we were children, since long before you even met her. That's the only reason you managed to stay alive in prison all these years.'

He was just a kid from the slums — dirty, sickly, shirtless, spending his days torn between fear and the need to be what he was: a twelve-year-old boy with sleep in his eyes who found the desperate urge to live intoxicating. He had already started playing the *ney* back then and claimed he knew the secrets of *sema*, the sacred whirling of the dervishes. He would talk to, look at, laugh with, and kiss any girl who'd let him. And he especially liked that shy little wisp of a girl who lived in Bab el Oued. They went swimming naked together on the beach, and it was in the surf that they first began to touch. At first pretending to dunk each other, their touching quickly became much more tender, and awkward, and direct. And there, hiding behind a barge, he kissed her with what he thought was expertise, but all she did was spit on the ground, the way a man would, and tell him she didn't like that tongue-in-the-mouth business. Later came train trips to Hydra, and afternoons spent in the reservoir to cool off and rinse away the salty seawater. And nights on the balcony gazing out over the sea, returning to Algiers with their wet underwear in a little plastic bag, her shamefaced expression and his triumph at having stolen a real tongue kiss.

He told his brother he was in love with the daughter of the owner of the Paris Bookstore, said he was going to marry her and move to France.

'The bookseller? That pig is a collaborator, a police informer — he gives the OAS tip-offs. He's a murderer!' his brother had shouted.

What did a word like *murderer* mean to a twelve-year-old? What breadth or depth could the concept of death have in his young brain? Yes, his father was dead, and he regularly heard shots fired at night, and saw his brother come home in the middle of the night with blood on his clothes that wasn't always his. He lived surrounded by violence and could chant as loud as anyone the anti-European slogans that leaders of the struggle repeated like mantras; he knew the new Algerian anthem composed by Mufdi Zakariyah by heart: *We are soldiers in the name of righteousness.* So what? The only thing he truly wanted was for Friday to come so he could go to the beach and swim naked with Andrea. He could see that, in his brother's eyes, and in the sorrowful silence of his mother, he was a bad Muslim, a bad son, a bad brother, and a bad patriot. But as far as Ibrahim was concerned, the whole world, the whole crazy world, could go to hell. He was happy.

'I don't care. I'm going to go with her and ...'

The first blow split his lower lip. The second struck him right in the nose.

'You're a traitor to your blood and to your country,' his brother hissed, still clenching his fist like a threat. Ibrahim watched the drops of blood dripping into the palm of his hand and gave his brother a look of deep rage. He felt conned, betrayed by his own kin.

'Go to your room, Ibrahim,' his mother had said, her voice trembling. Her body seemed to have shrunk, as though she were trying to become invisible.

'But ...'

'Go to your room!'

He was miserable and didn't understand. How could his desire to be happy infuriate them so? Ibrahim's childhood became the slow monotonous passage of time and the muffled sounds of the street, the passing of cars that frightened his brother if they stopped any longer than necessary close to the door. 'Ibrahim, go see who that is,' he'd whisper, always prepared to take off, running through the inner courtyards. Always on edge, waiting, overcome by fear ever since the OAS terrorists had executed his father. Now it was his brother who had taken the mantle. And when he fell, Ibrahim would be the one to continue the struggle. And meanwhile, they waited, listening to the fiery speeches of Boudiaf and Ben Bella, the heroes of the Battle of Algiers, in which his father had fought General Massu's paratroopers. But he had no desire to be a martyr for his country, like his father and brother. All he wanted was to be with Andrea.

That was when he'd heard the sound of tyres on their unpaved street — a dark car with its lights out; three men emerged. Dark cars arriving suddenly in the night with their lights out meant only one thing. Suddenly, all of their neighbours' lights went out too.

They were coming for them. Ibrahim ran to tell his mother and brother. But he got there at almost the same time that the front door — a flimsy composite-wood board — splintered and flew open. In the blink of an eye, his brother jumped out a small window overlooking the back patio, no time to put on his shirt. As he jumped, he lost one sandal, which his mother picked up, turning to face the three men, wielding it the way she did whenever she went to swat Ibrahim for whatever thing he'd done that had riled her — and there had been lots of them. But this time one of the men effortlessly snatched it away, giving her a swift kick in the stomach that dropped her to the floor with a dull groan.

The other two intruders were too beefy to slip through the window easily and they took some time getting out. The third one stayed with him and his mother. A handsome man, tall, with the olive skin of those who've spent a long time in the desert. Redheaded. On one side of his thick wrestler's neck he had a tattoo of a pair of wings with a dagger piercing them through the middle. And a slogan: *Country before all*. Rushing toward his mother, who was still collapsed on the ground, Ibrahim blocked his way, shouting his head off. The man hadn't seen him at first and was thrown off for a moment. But he reacted quickly, with a look of profound disgust. His enormous hand, hairy and calloused, clenched Ibrahim's face with excruciating force. Ibrahim's feet were lifted off the floor, and then he was hurled like a rag against the wall, once, twice, three times. Until he lost consciousness.

When he opened his eyes, he saw his shirt was soaked with blood. His mother had a black eye and her dress was torn; she covered one dark, shrivelled breast in shame, but she looked proud, almost smiling, and gazed lovingly at him. She told him to be strong. That everything comes to an end, even the most terrible pain.

The men who had gone after his brother were frustrated and sweating. One of them wielded a .38 and said that he'd shot at him but wasn't sure if he'd hit him. His brother knew the nearby labyrinthine alleyways like the back of his hand, knew every cul-de-sac and plaza and wall in the neighbourhood; he was smart and fast and hadn't been caught. And Ibrahim was happy that those bastards hadn't been able to lay a hand on his brother. They'd been thwarted and were now angry.

It didn't occur to him that that made things worse for him and his mother.

The man with the tattooed neck stepped forward.

'What's so funny?' he asked, wrapping his hands around Ibrahim's neck and rattling him back and forth as though attempting to shake his head off. He took Ibrahim's chin in one hand and stared into his face, sneering. Ibrahim wrenched his head away and managed to free himself of his cold fingers. But the redhead just grabbed him again, tighter, and forced him to show him his teeth. Teeth that until that moment had been beautiful, full of songs and stories.

'Where's your brother, handsome? I know he's around here, hiding in a pile of shit like the rat that he is. If you scream loud enough, if I make you scream, do you think he'll come out of his hiding place, or will he stay hiding and just watch you suffer? What if I start on your mother? What do you say? You love your mother. Will you ask him to turn himself in?'

Ibrahim didn't reply. He couldn't, with that hand clamped over his mouth. He didn't know what came over him, why he did it, but all of a sudden he bit the huge hairy hand as hard as he could — a hand that smelled of gunpowder and cigarettes and military shoe polish. He bit it as hard as he could until he tasted blood.

The redhead let out a howl of pain and punched Ibrahim in the face with his other hand, but the kid was like a leech, he wouldn't let go. And then the man took out a machete, which he kept in a sheath strapped to his calf. It was a long military knife, with a sharp serrated blade that curled back at the tip. The steel handle had a compass on it. Ibrahim felt the impact of that steel like a medieval club destroying his teeth. Whipped into a frenzy, the tattooed man straightened up, holding his injured hand. One of the other men kicked Ibrahim and he tasted the dog shit on the sole of his military boot. Then the tattooed man dropped to his knees as hard as he could on Ibrahim's chest while another held him down, and the third beat his mother senseless.

The child within him died that night, as two strangers held him down while the curved tip of the machete tore through the muscles in his face, shredding his skin. There — shouting through the rivers of blood clouding the dilated pupils of his eyes — the boy inside him died, staring uncomprehendingly at the trembling mass that was his mother, who no longer screamed but simply gazed at him lovingly, sacrificing herself, as though soaking up all of her son's pain, not only the pain he was already feeling but also that to come.

Mutilated children grow into incomplete men, incapable of truly feeling anything, experiencing only counterfeit love, passion, and joy. They find fleeting moments of happiness which are always hanging by a thread, lest a nightmare, a glance, or a memory suddenly pop into their heads and reopen the wound, letting it air.

Ibrahim looked at Arthur.

'That's why anyone who steals a person's childhood has to be destroyed. Because the worst crime you can commit is to steal someone's hope, destroy their soul. That's what your father, Lieutenant Luis Fernández, did to me.'

Arthur sat looking petrified, his mouth ajar. He was staring at Ibrahim, searching his eyes, shocked and frightened.

'That can't be true,' he said, his voice broken.

Ibrahim pointed to his scar.

'Here's your proof.'

Still, Arthur shook his head and swallowed.

'This is ludicrous, it makes no sense at all.'

It made perfect sense, it was destiny, and destiny is a sort of justice.

'Do you remember the first time I saw you in our cell? It was like looking at your father. You're almost identical. And when you told me about your past, I knew you were the son of the lieutenant who ruined my whole life. I'd have killed you right then, but you pulled out your honeymoon picture and put it up on the wall. You smiled and told me your wife's name. And then I saw that Allah is wise, and no matter how long the road, it always leads someplace. You brought her back to me.'

Ibrahim stood and looked at him coldly.

'The Armenian is outside. I told him you'd be here.'

Arthur tensed and then ducked sideways, cowering. The Armenian stood in the entrance with his back against the door, and behind him rose the shaved head of a giant with a tattooed neck. Arthur whipped back to Ibrahim, livid.

'You can't punish me for something I didn't do. I could never do what he did to you. I am not my father.'

'Of course you are. We're all our fathers. I look at you and I see him, and my blood boils. You have the same expression, the same red hair, the same way of twisting your mouth. You can't escape that.'

Arthur stood.

'You have no right to pass judgement on me!'

Ibrahim grabbed his arm.

'You can try to run, but if you do Andrea will never find out what really happened to Aroha. The Armenian knows all sorts of people involved in human trafficking. Nobody disappears without leaving a trace, and these men can find anyone. I made a deal with him: your life in exchange for the information leading to Aroha.'

Arthur frowned. He went pale. All he could do was glower at Ibrahim.

'Who do you think you are, making deals on my life? Guzmán is going to find Aroha, I don't need the Armenian for anything.'

Ibrahim didn't lose his cool. He let go of Arthur's arm and spread his hands to show he wasn't going to stand in his way. The decision is yours, he seemed to say: back door, or front door.

Arthur's eyes, wild with fear, glanced quickly at the door. The Armenian was ambling over, hands in his pockets, casual-like.

'It's you or Aroha,' Ibrahim repeated.

Arthur chose the back door. Fear propelled him through the kitchen door as fast as he could go. The Armenian's skinhead thug went after him. Almost immediately came the sound of plates crashing to the floor and the cook shouting, asking what the hell was going on.

'Why'd you tell him? That's not what we agreed,' the Armenian asked, half-angry and half-smiling. The regulars were eyeing him warily. He wasn't one of them; he stuck out like a black stain on a white shirt, a stain that ruined the fabric.

Ibrahim gazed at the photo on the wall of the shepherd and his dog.

'We've all got a right to prove what we're really made of. Now Arthur knows what he's made of. He won't get far, regardless. I know exactly where he's headed.'

The Armenian gave him a curious look, maybe even with a flicker of envy and admiration.

'So it's true, you really do have principles.' He said it as if Ibrahim were a leper, suffering his disease with dignity. He took a piece of paper from his pocket and handed it to him. On it was an address with map coordinates. 'You'll find the girl here.'

Ibrahim read what was on the paper.

'Alive?'

The Armenian made a noncommittal face.

'Possibly. Some things it's best not to ask too insistently. I called in enough favours as it is to get this paper. There are certain circumstances that even people like you and me shouldn't get involved in. You should go, Ibrahim. Go back to your village and don't look back. That's my advice.'

Ibrahim put the paper away. The only advice he'd ever listened to in his life had come from a man who was buried on a hill beside his father.

'I'll tell you where Arthur's headed.'

Since she was a little girl, Aroha had had trouble waking up. She was slow to get moving in the mornings and spent ages in bed, yawning and lolling around; the minute her mother turned away she'd fall back asleep as though nothing outside of her bedroom were of any interest.

Irritated and tired of calling her, Andrea would ask Arthur to get her up. He'd go into her room without turning on the light, run his fingers through her dishevelled hair and kiss her forehead, whispering quietly until, little by little, she emerged from her dream and her grogginess. He was the only one who'd had the patience required to make his daughter get up without grumbling, so she wasn't late to school every day. Aroha preferred that he be the one to take her to school, too, and back then she didn't mind holding his hand all the way up the school steps. Her friends would be there waiting, eating sunflower seeds and spitting shells all over the ground. They were a gaggle of uniforms — red polo shirts with the school's gold emblem embroidered over the chest, plaid skirts, and grey knee-socks — that swarmed like a wasp's nest when he arrived, straining to see Arthur hand his daughter her notebook and give her a bear hug, wrapping his arms around her tiny body with only part of her head sticking out.

'My friends think you're cool.' *Cool*, said with a strawberry candy stuck in her mouth, her braces turning each smile into a glinting metallic scene of torture.

His daughter's voice came to him now from far away: *You're the best father in the world,* she'd say. *The world?* he'd ask. *The whole wide world and part of the universe.* And he would respond, *That's better.* When she was a little girl, he was her hero.

But at some point she had stopped needing him to go wake her up because she was doing it all by herself, before the alarm went off, before Andrea even had to call her. There were little changes, like when he asked her to sit and talk with him for awhile, she'd make up any excuse not to and then immediately lock herself in his office to talk on the phone, sharing secrets that he wasn't privy to with a stranger. *Who?* he wondered. At first Arthur would tell himself that these things were tolerable defeats, changes that all kids go through as they grow up and move on.

He shouldn't have accepted her growing detachment without a fight. He should have paid more attention to the alarm bells that started going off that summer. *I need money.* And he'd give it to her as long as she'd just chat with him, or give him a kiss, or a hug. He was buying her affection, but any fondness on her part was increasingly scarce — and expensive. He'd ask her how school was going. *Fine.* Ask her what books she was reading. *Whatever. Are you going to give me the money?* If he asked too many questions, she'd get upset — so he stopped asking. *You'd better at least pass,* he told her. *Get off my case, I will. Are you going to give me the money or not?* He often wanted to know why she needed so much. It was always a trip to Valencia with her girlfriends, a weekend of horseback riding in the mountains, a new personal stereo. And he'd give it to her.

It was as she neared adolescence that slowly the real problems began: running away from home, them having to call the police, derelict boyfriends who were always much older, constant rebellion, arguments, fights, slammed doors, the early signs that she was flirting with drugs. Useless trips to the psychologist. Multiple expulsions from school.

Suddenly, he'd lost her, without even realising. She was no longer his little girl, no longer belonged to him. And in her eyes he began to see reproach and accusation. She'd figured out what kind of man her father was, knew that he was cheating on her mother, realised he tried to make up for prolonged absences with material gifts.

He wasn't home the day Aroha disappeared. He didn't see her brush her teeth — by then freed of their metallic corset — didn't see her brush her hair and walk out the door, never to return. At the time, there was a different woman he was seeing in the mirror, in a hotel room. A glimmering naked body that smiled at his reflection in the mirror and offered herself to him. While his daughter was on the road to her perdition, he was screwing a woman he'd never love — not the way he loved Andrea and Aroha — up the arse. And that tortured him. *Why? Why had he done it?* he wondered. He'd thrown his life away, aware of what he was doing at every step. He'd never know for certain, but maybe the answer was to be found in that inner voice, the one that called him a phony every time happiness seemed on the horizon. Maybe he didn't deserve to be happy.

It wasn't too late, he said to himself, blinking at the sun in his eyes. He got out of the car feeling convinced that Andrea still loved him, unable to believe what Ibrahim had told him was true. She wouldn't betray him like that. He just needed to see her one more time, to look into her eyes, to make her realise how sorry he was about the past. He could change — people change. Guzmán had finally found out where Aroha was, they

393

didn't need the Armenian at all. They'd go away together, the three of them, and start anew — this time for real.

His eyes feverish, his mind racing, he strode across the residence parking lot, not noticing the two silhouettes that appeared between the cars until it was too late.

The Armenian cut him off, while his attack dog hung back to make sure he had no escape route. Arthur tried to turn back, but realised there was no way out.

'You don't have to do this,' he stammered, trying not to lose sight of the enormous skinhead lurking like a hungry wolf behind him. 'I'll pay you anything you want if you let us go. Name your price, anything.'

The Armenian's eyes glimmered like a torch at the back of a dark cave.

'How much is a daughter's life worth? How much did you pay to try to get yours back?'

Without thinking, the giant goon leapt at Arthur. Arthur managed to dodge the fist roaring past his ear like a freight train, and instinctively jammed his elbow back as hard as he could, breaking the skinhead's nose. Stunned, the Armenian's thug raised his hands to his face with an animal howl, but he didn't fall. Arthur tried to use his advantage to fell him, but the man writhed in rage and clamped onto his trachea with one had, immobilising him, and then raised the other fist to deliver a single, definitive blow.

'Not here!' the Armenian shouted. The giant froze, his fist in midair, trembling with rage. For a few seconds he hesitated, but then finally exhaled and lowered his fist. 'To the car.'

He couldn't tell where they were. *Someplace in the mountains, probably,* he thought. *Far from Madrid.* Wherever he looked, all he saw were pine trees and a winding back road that disappeared behind a hill. It was getting dark. The first stars were twinkling in the hazy dusk. Warm air whispered through the tall grass at Arthur's feet. They'd taken off his shoes and socks and chained him to a rock. The sharp edges bit into the inside of his wrists, forcing him to bend over to reduce the tension. The Armenian was sitting on a tree stump with a twig in his mouth and a song in his head, humming quietly, eyes half-closed, body swaying slightly to the rhythm. A few metres further on, the Armenian's gorilla was pissing on a bush, tracing a huge arc with his stream of urine. His nose had swollen up like a potato and his face was stained with dried blood.

The Armenian opened his eyes wide and spat the sprig out.

'When I was a kid, families used to come here to get away from the city for the day. My father would load up the old SEAT 600 with folding chairs and a camp table. My mother would bring pig's snout, ear, and oxtail, and we'd stuff ourselves silly. Back then nobody worried about forest fires — everybody built campfires and they didn't make people get a municipal licence. Things were more straightforward back then. After lunch, my parents would spread a blanket out in the shade and take a siesta while I set off exploring. This stump used to be an amazing old pine tree — huge. They say you can tell how old a tree is by the rings in its trunk and this one was really old. I remember one day I tried to climb to the highest branch, but I fell and cracked my head open. My parents didn't even realise it until they woke up and saw the blood. After taking me to the clinic, where I got five stitches, my father spent the whole way home smacking me for having ruined his day out, and my mother cried the whole time.'

He gave a little laugh, as though the memory were tragically comic, and then looked at Arthur curiously.

'I bet you've never climbed a tree.'

Slowly, night fell over the countryside, enshrouding it in a veil of shadows. Everything was still there, even though it looked like it was gone. The Armenian sighed, gazing out at the bloodstained horizon.

'I've often imagined I was just a regular man. That my daughter was climbing this tree — but I wasn't taking a siesta, I was waiting down below with my arms stretched out wide to catch her in case she fell. It sounds absurd. The things a man imagines when he's spent half his life locked up; the things he thinks he'll do when he gets out. But the truth is that no one builds campfires anymore because it's against the law, and the tree was cut down long ago, and this place has become a dump, full of used condoms and cans and cigarette butts, a place where hookers and junkies come for a day out. And the truth is I no longer have a daughter to worry about her falling and getting hurt.'

He gazed sadly at Arthur and hesitated a moment, trying to calibrate the effect of his words.

'When the cup of bitterness runs over, the heart no longer suffers, because it no longer feels. I stopped torturing myself over things that never were and never will be; I gave up on the questions that no one can answer, because they have no answer, because there is no God to console me. And since that time, the only thing that's brought me any peace over these past four years has been the knowledge that one day we'd be right here, you and me, just like this, and that before I killed you, I'd speak these words to you.'

He signalled to his henchman and the giant went to the car and took from the trunk a duffel bag, with a saw and an axe handle sticking out.

The Armenian stood and began to roll up his sleeves. He showed Arthur the sharp blade of a machete, his face darkening into a scowl. The Armenian had sworn he'd take revenge, and he had to keep that promise. He'd earned a reputation and he had to keep it, because men like him needed the respect that they earned spilling blood to survive. So Arthur's death had to be remembered for years — prisoners huddling together to talk about it on the yard, wardens shivering on hearing the details, new inmates finding out who the Armenian was the second they set foot in the prison.

'I'm going to peel you like an orange, with a machete like the one your father used on Ibrahim; then my friend here is going to chop you up into little pieces, and I'll scatter your remains around this mountain for kilometres so all the vermin can feast on you. Though I think I'll save your heart and take it to your wife so that she can see it before I tear her eyes out and kill her too. I know I promised Ibrahim I wouldn't hurt her, but we both know I can't keep that promise. There will be nothing left of you, Arthur, nothing left of what you were or what you created in this life. You and your loved ones will never have existed. And the most important thing is that you're going to die without knowing what happened to your daughter, not knowing whether anything you did — the harm and suffering you caused — was of any use at all.'

25

May always left the scent of storms moving out. In the pond by the house, toads peeked out with their bulging eyes, staring at her. Olga set her suitcase on the ground, reluctant to push the door open. Coming back was a form of defeat, that's the way she felt about it. The stones on the facade welcomed her with a blunt expression; the weeds growing in a long-forgotten flowerpot greeted her mockingly. She had actually believed she could win, could get out of this place and never come back, push the bounds of her destiny and escape. But here she was again. And her brightly coloured wheelie suitcase announced that she was back to stay.

She pushed the door open and walked into the quiet room, which was painfully familiar. Almost nothing had changed. The same furniture — though it had been rearranged — the same pictures on the walls, the same dust and stillness. In the background, she heard the television, on too loud as if trying to fill the asphyxiating silence with sound.

Her mother was sitting in a wicker chair at an oval-shaped mirror, brushing her long, dirty grey hair. It fell dully over her bare shoulders, the pale skin speckled with moles. Naked from the waist up, her dry, shrunken breasts fell over her bellybutton, swinging like pendulums with the movement of her arms.

'Hello, mother.'

The old woman stopped pulling the brush through her tangles and stared at Olga in the mirror. Her dim, faded eyes flickered for an instant beneath her lashes, and then she began brushing her hair again, with determination. As though fourteen years had not passed. Olga walked to her and took the brush from her hands, taking her place like when she was a girl and her mother explained the way to do it so she didn't yank her hair. Olga gazed at her mother in the reflection. They looked too similar to have such different lives. Bound by an invisible tie. She belonged in that darkness, that smell, that mesmerising sadness where flies hovered over a basket of half-rotten fruit and her mother's old lovers posed for her in a portrait gallery above the chest of drawers. A gallery of defeats and illusions, failed escapes and promises that none of them had kept. And among them, in one corner, was Teo.

'You can't stay. You're not welcome here.'

Olga didn't have the strength to face up to her and tell her the whole truth. Truth was resentment that turned against her. Her mother had accused her of having spoiled her chance at happiness with the only man that had ever loved her. But she was fooling herself. Teo had never loved anyone but himself.

On the television, they were talking about Arthur. Dead bodies were springing up like poppies along a wheat field. Like red stains. A provincial court judge had opened an investigation that tied the deaths of Gloria and her husband to that of Arthur. The case was under sub judice rule, but press leaks hinted at a major scandal that had all the ingredients of a thriller: underage prostitution, drugs, porn flicks, and murder.

'I just need a couple of days to get my thoughts straight. Then I'll leave and you'll never hear from me again.'

She went up to her old room and found a bare mattress, no sheets or pillow. The desk was covered in dust, and on opening a drawer she found a rat had used her school notebooks as its nest. There were cobwebs everywhere, enshrouding the room. No one had been in there since she'd left. She opened her suitcase and stared down at the portfolio tucked between her blouses. After finding out about Gloria's suicide, Eduardo had refused to see her, or speak to her once Who let her go. Nor had he accepted the rest of the money he was owed for the commission.

One after the other, Olga thumbtacked the sketches to the wall and then sat on the edge of the bed to contemplate them. They created a unique sequence: in each successive drawing the lines grew stronger and more assured until finally they became something solid, as if each successive sketch peeled off another layer of the onion in order to reveal its core. And there at the centre, Eduardo had stopped. As if he'd been unable to take it any further. It was like the autopsy of a cadaver, but it made more sense now. She'd seen the pictures of Arthur on TV, flayed and mutilated in the most horrific way. But what had most caught her attention was the killers' determination to disfigure his face, as if trying to erase his existence, destroy the tangle of experiences and emotions that were superimposed in

Eduardo's work. Without those eyes staring out darkly, without that hard mouth and slightly crooked nose, Arthur was nothing.

Her mother walked in without knocking. The door wasn't locked. She stepped in and her eyes went straight to the sketches on the wall. She glanced at them, shocked because she'd never seen them before. Her mother looked displeased. She didn't like them, or perhaps she didn't like that they were hanging on the wall. Seeing Olga there, sitting on the edge of the bed with her suitcase still packed, knees pressed tightly together, hands held to her stomach, she looked like a schoolgirl. Perhaps her mother felt a slight tremor of guilt, nostalgia, and even love. But if so, it was buried too deep to reach the surface.

'What kind of trouble have you gotten yourself into?' she asked suspiciously. *What kind of trouble have you gotten* me *into*, was what she meant.

Olga glanced up, giving her mother a look of pity. Sometimes, there are people you want to love and just can't figure out how. With so many accumulated misunderstandings you end up losing the way, and it's impossible to get back on track.

'There are two police officers downstairs, asking for you.'

Olga inhaled deeply, filling her lungs with air, and nodded. Sometimes all you can do is accept things the way they are because they can't be any other way. Everything else is just pie in the sky. An illusion. Realising that made her feel light-hearted for the first time in a very long time. She was liberated by the idea of no longer fighting the impossible. And so Olga walked down the stairs free of the weight on her shoulders, and greeted the policemen.

They wanted to ask about Gloria and Ian's murders. They'd found the shredded remains of Arthur's portrait and knew she had been the intermediary between Eduardo and the divorced couple. She wasn't being accused of anything, one of them took pains to stress, they knew she was innocent.

Olga smiled sadly. Innocent. Free of blame, blessed as a newborn baby. She lifted her head and saw her mother at the foot of the stairs in her nightgown, her hair wet, wearing black socks, arms crossed over her chest. She was veiled in a soft darkness, staring at her in silence. A silence full of reproach and contempt. It was inevitable.

When Who had taken her to an abandoned house, Olga'd thought he was planning to kill her. But he didn't do it straightaway. Instead, he locked her up in a room for two days and two nights. She thought he was going to leave her there to die of hunger and thirst. Maybe, she thought during those two long nights, Mr Who was trying to make her lose her mind.

Olga spent all that time sitting in the exact same position, elbows on her bent knees, staring at the door, alert to any sound or the slightest change in the light filtering in beneath it. At first, she was so terrified she couldn't think or sleep. But slowly, she started to remember things long forgotten, brief instances that hadn't been that important to begin with but now popped into her head and made her smile, or laugh out loud, or cry the calm tears of nostalgia, or the wracking tears of desperation. As if the darkness forced her to see better, she was able to see Teo clearly, as though he — or his ghost — were sitting right in front of her, reproaching her with that condescending look he had given her for what she'd done. And it made her furious. Because that ghost, who used to jiggle the arm of his metal-framed glasses back and forth in his fingers, didn't feel guilty at all, and in fact he was accusing her.

On the morning of the third day, she heard the sound of car tyres braking outside the gate. Stunned and petrified, Olga crawled to the door to peek through a crack.

She could make out the silhouette of a woman but couldn't see her clearly through the car's dusty windshield. The woman lowered the window a couple of centimetres and looked out with a pair of brown, almond-shaped eyes that seemed to stare at her, to know that she was there peeking out the crack in the door. Olga withdrew, forced back by the intensity of the woman's gaze. She heard the car door open and the crunch of footsteps on the dusty ground, heard the rusty gate open and the metallic clink of the chain lock banging against the door as it closed. The door opened and light streamed in, blinding Olga.

It took a few seconds for her eyes to adjust.

'It's OK, I'm not going to hurt you. My name is Mei.' She held out a hand, indicating that Olga should come with her.

Olga followed her to the car unsteadily, using her hand as a visor against the brightness of the sun.

Mei opened a bottle of water and offered it to her with a look somewhere between compassion and troubled curiosity. Olga drank like a desperate camel. Water dribbled down her neck leaving streaks through the grime on her skin from the two days and nights of sleeping on the floor of that pigsty.

'Slowly.' Mei's voice was beautiful, peaceful.

Olga drank more slowly. Then she accepted the sandwich that the girl offered her, breaking it into tiny bits and swallowing them with difficulty. Olga ate, though she wasn't hungry. Her stomach had shrunk. As she chewed the ham sandwich, she stared at Mei, whose eyes were on the road, occasionally giving her a quick sidelong glance as she drove. They were on the road back to Madrid.

'What are you going to do with me now?' she asked those eyes, which were frowning — Mei wrapped up in her own thoughts.

'Nothing,' the girl replied. 'Don't worry. It's all over.'

Olga gazed at the unfamiliar hand and felt calmer. She believed her.

'Get some rest,' she said.

Olga tried to close her eyes, but she couldn't. Her heart was pounding. She felt a bit calmer — though she didn't know why — when they got to the suburbs of Madrid. Until she realised that the streets were becoming more familiar. Mei was taking her home.

When she stopped the car at her front door and asked her to get out, Olga hesitated, disconcerted. The girl who'd done nothing but look at her with a sort of curious tenderness now gave her a wide smile of encouragement.

'Good luck. Now you're going to have to pick up the pieces of your life and make something new of it.'

Olga looked at her uncomprehendingly.

'Where's Mr Who?'

The girl stroked Olga's cheek affectionately.

'No one can hurt him now.'

Mei pulled away and drove down the street, swallowed up by the Madrid traffic in no time at all.

Olga didn't see her crying.

Three hours earlier, Mei was already dead. The men surrounding her sat smoking, ignoring her, passing butts from which to light fresh cigarettes.

On the dirty glass table sat beer cans, lines of coke, and leftover pizza, as well as an overflowing ashtray. Chang's hand on her shoulder held her firmly down in a chair.

'Come on, sweetheart, try it,' he said, pointing to the white powder on the table. But Mei refused. Nor did she voluntarily submit to being groped by that old man, who squeezed one of her breasts so hard she thought he might tear it off.

'Is she a virgin?' asked one of the men there.

Chang burst out laughing.

'Are you a virgin, Mei? Do you have at least one orifice intact?'

The men ogled her greedily. They had bought her, the way you buy a head of cattle. She could do nothing but give in to their filthy mouths, their impertinent hands, which they could hardly contain. They would use her the way they'd used other of Chang's workers, and then they'd take her to a brothel in some random city, where she would be forced to prostitute herself at all hours of the day and night until she was beyond exhausted. And when she was no longer any use to them, she'd finish out her days sickly and consumptive, rummaging through the rubbish in alleyways to survive.

She wasn't planning to let that happen. Mei had decided that, at the first opportunity that arose, she would kill herself. And she felt a mixture of fear and intense sadness at the prospect of dying when she was just twenty-one, now that she'd finally found the reason for her journey in this life. She'd fallen in love with the only man for her; he was her destiny. But it was all going to be over before it began, and that seemed too cruel. Why had she been given the gift of meeting him if she couldn't enjoy the benefit of his company? Why did people like Chang exist in this world? What blows must life have dealt that man for him to end up such a callous monster?

They dragged her to the sofa and pushed her down, trying to force her to undress. When she would not do it herself, they beat her and tore her dress off. Her hands tried frantically to cover her breasts and crotch from the eyes that bored into her as they laughed. She felt as if the outside world carried on unchanged, but she was trapped hopelessly in that one instant with no way out. She tried to find refuge in her memory, in the few moments she'd been truly happy, free. She thought of Who's eyes, his smile, his promises. She thought of one day in the country, the sun on her face, the scent of fresh grass swept by a light mist that stuck her clothes to her skin and plastered her bangs onto her forehead. She remembered Who's hands, holding her face between his fingers in awe. And she closed her eyes.

The first thing Mr Who noticed when he walked into the room was the noxious air. The guy posted at the door had greeted him with a giggle, as though envious. 'They're having a good old time in there, the bastards. You're lucky Chang confers these favours on you.' Mr Who could have ripped that trained-poodle smile right off his face, kicked it out of him. He really could have.

It smelled of sour perspiration, and the sweaty backs of half-a-dozen men formed a semi-circle around the sofa. Through that wall of flesh he caught a glimpse of the pale skin of a woman, and one pink nipple. His stomach clenched.

'Ah, finally, the perfect lover has arrived.' Chang was drugged up, as were the others. His face was red, his eyes dilated. He was naked from the waist up, and the tattoo of a dragon with a serpent in its talons covered the whole of his chest and part of his stomach. His fly was down.

'Come, come, star pupil. This way,' he urged, laughing, patting his back and pushing him toward the sofa. 'We want a live show. We want you to teach us to make love. Isn't that what you tell your customers you'll do? Gentlemen, you should know that my boy here never simply fucks! No, no — he makes art, with his privileged cock.'

Who felt himself die a thousand times over, felt his body being dismembered, his brain exploding, seeing Mei's body there. She was a desolate wilderness, a prairie whose beautiful flowers had been mercilessly trampled. She turned to hide her face in shame against the sofa's leather back. It was like she was dead.

'What have you done?' Who whispered, giving Chang a look of pure hatred, unable to stop his hand from trembling as he touched Mei's shoulder, which was covered in scratches.

The old man gave the faint smile of a sick old faun.

'Nothing yet, just smacked her around a little, just warming up. We were waiting for you.' He looked maliciously at Who. 'Did you really think you could fool me? I know everything, boy. I know you've been saving up to buy two passports, and that one of them was for this little whore. I also know you've been fucking her behind my back — and I could overlook that, but not you falling in love with her and trying to leave me. You can't leave until I say so; you're my best investment — my cock of gold! And so I'm going to teach you a lesson that you won't forget the next time you get an idea like that in your head. You're going to fuck this little whore for us, and then I'm going to leave her in a brothel where they'll make her wish she was never born.'

Who felt as though an earthquake were rocking the building, the roof caving in on the room, the floor opening under his feet. After hearing Chang's words and seeing Mei hide her face in shame, he had only one idea in his head, pounding like a hammer: he was going to rip Chang's head off.

He felt the blows landing on him as they tried to stop him, but he didn't feel any pain; it was as if they were hitting a wet sack of flour. He had his prey, had a good hold on Chang's head, and wasn't letting go, clenching his teeth with rage. He wanted to rip Chang's eyes out of their sockets and see them explode. Wanted to stomp on them like they were venomous snake eggs. Then he felt a jab in his side and saw the bouncer from the door, no longer smiling but holding a long, thin knife that luckily he had not plunged into Who up to the hilt. Still, it was enough to make Who momentarily let go of Chang, who fell to his knees, red as a tomato and coughing, his windpipe collapsed.

Without thinking, Who leapt on the man with the knife, unmindful of the danger. He didn't care about anything or anyone. His only desire was to destroy everything in his path. Nobody can fight off suicidal determination, no matter how much they're being paid. Nothing can defeat that sort of desperation. Who snatched the blade off the hired goon and rammed it into his shoulder, all of his weight thrusting into the handle. The man let out a yowl and his arm fell to his side, hanging lifeless. Mr Who then yanked out the blade and turned to the others, daring them to attack. They held back. Victory would cost them too much, for now. If he wanted the little whore, he could have her. The two of them wouldn't make it far, and the men could wait to settle their score. One after the other, they filed out of the room. The last two took the wounded bouncer with them. Mr Who knew that within five minutes Chang's men in the restaurant would come for him. He shot Chang — still on the floor — a savage look. He had leaned onto one elbow and was vomiting blood and alcohol. Without thinking, Who rammed the blade into Chang's neck with the force of all the offenses he'd ever suffered, the lies and disappointments he'd been subjected to for years, when he'd actually thought of Chang as his true father, someone he admired. Mr Who had no compassion for that man.

He pulled a blanket off the sofa and used it to cover Mei, who was paralysed by fear, and stared at him as though she didn't recognise him. He didn't waste any time on explanations.

'The fire escape,' he said, rushing to open the window.

They'd gotten far enough away from Madrid to feel safe. His wound did not look good. He needed to get it stitched up, but couldn't think about that now. He couldn't think about anything. He had to pull the car over on the shoulder. His hands were trembling, he felt as if he'd just come out of a trance, and his nerves were shot. They were beside a field. Green shoots rose up, leaning toward the sun, and the poppies were elbowing their way in like spots of colour, there to break up the monotony. Whizzing sprinklers cartwheeled, shooting spirals of water that sprayed the car. He could hear a dog barking in the distance and saw the silhouette of a man bent over a ditch. Beyond that was nothing but open sky. Life goes from one moment to the next without pause, with no way to stop.

'Did they hurt you?' Who asked Mei.

She gave a quick shake of her head to say 'no' as she leaned over and lifted his shirt to inspect the wound. Relieved, she said it wasn't grave, as though she were some sort of expert. In fact it was. Her eyes were sad, humiliated. What hurt her most was her inability to comprehend human evil.

'We have to find a doctor to treat it.'

Who told her there would be time for that, and opened the glove compartment. He showed her two brand new passports and pulled out a couple of plane tickets.

'Beijing?'

He looked at her as though not understanding her surprise. Where else would they go? She contemplated her own photo in the fake passport, with a false identity. Actually, she thought it looked like someone else, not her. And the girl who'd spent months locked in a clandestine sweatshop was another person too, the one who'd almost been sold like an animal, the one who had Chang's scratch marks all over one breast. None of those women was Mei; that's how she felt, those experiences were not hers — they hadn't managed to pervade her and blot her out entirely. She reached out a hand and laced her fingers through Who's. She'd go anywhere with him, because there was nothing else she could do. Because she wanted nothing more than to do it.

Then he began to speak — slowly, allowing the words themselves to choose the form they took, not prohibiting them from being spoken. He told her everything, not holding anything back. Where he came from, who he was, what he'd been doing, what he wanted to do. He told her about Maribel and Teo, about Eduardo and Olga. He explained that he'd left her locked in an abandoned house because he didn't know what to do with her, that he trusted fate or destiny to make the call. He spoke for so long that when he was done his mouth seemed to have consumed all the world's desert, his tongue was thick and his lips cracked. And in all that time he didn't look at Mei once. Not once did he take his eyes off the green shoots and poppies and the man who moved like his own shadow in the distance.

There was a long silence. A necessary silence.

Then, after a while, Mei took his chin and forced him to look at her. She searched Who's eyes for what remained unsaid, things that did not need to be said but she needed to understand. And what she saw was enough.

'We have to go back for her.'

Mr Who said it was too dangerous to go back. They'd be looking for them; they had to run, now. Someone would find her, they'd hear her cries. He hadn't left her far from the road. They couldn't risk it.

Mei stroked his cheek.

'We have to bring her back to life, so she can be the one to decide.'

Mr Who started the car. They made it two hundred metres.

The first bullet shattered the back windshield into a thousand pieces. Then came others, exploding like fireworks. The car veered sharply and rammed into a lamppost.

'Run!' Who screamed.

He got out of the car, holding a knife, and took off in the opposite direction to Mei. He was leading them away from her. There was yelling, more gunfire. When Mei turned back to look, she saw Mr Who fighting Chang's men. One of them shot him in the back, pointblank, and Who's body was propelled forward. As though he could fly.

One night earlier, he still hadn't decided what to do with Olga. He stared at the key to the abandoned house and could not come up with a solution. Contradictory thoughts and feelings swirled through his brain. He kept wondering why he hadn't killed Eduardo, and the only answer he could come up with was that he didn't honestly want him to die. And despite it all, he didn't want to hurt Olga either. She'd told him all the details of her relationship with Teo — the child she'd lost, how she could never have children now. He understood the rage and hatred she'd stockpiled. And deep down he began to feel growing contempt for Teo himself. But another part of him said that Olga was lying, that the man he remembered — his father — couldn't have done that. He had to find some inner peace.

He told Maribel everything. He needed for her to be the one to tell him what to do, to tell him that Olga had made it all up. Or at least to show that she herself had had no idea. But far from what he expected, Maribel didn't seem shocked in the slightest.

Horrified, Mr Who discovered that his mother knew everything. She'd known the whole time. And she didn't care.

'You don't understand. Love conquers all.'

Mr Who fell silent, looking around in search of a place from which to escape his mother's scorn, escape the feeling of absolute vulnerability that was gnawing at his guts.

'Olga was just a girl. She fell in love with her mother's lover! Teo was sleeping with both of them, he seduced her — a man thirty years older than her — and got her pregnant and then abandoned both her and the child. And meanwhile he was playing happy family with us. I don't understand,' he said, shaking his head and feeling like it was going to explode. 'I don't understand how you can forgive something like that. He went to China to get me because you couldn't have children, but to him I was never anything but a pet to keep you happy — and then he goes and has a child of his own and abandons it like it was scum. And you ask me to sacrifice my life to avenge him? Don't you care at all about what could happen to *me*, Maribel?'

Maribel was furious. She banged her wheelchair arm violently and held up her urine bag, attached to a catheter.

'This is what they did to me. Do you understand that? Them, Eduardo and that thieving whore, they chained me to this fucking bag for the rest of my life. They killed the man I loved. And the bullet that broke my back would have killed you if I hadn't gotten in its way.' She gazed at him, her incomprehension bordering insanity, and then proclaimed with utter contempt, 'I wish I'd never done it. I wish it had *killed you* instead.'

Mr Who was silent quite some time before responding.

'I'm leaving, Maribel. I can't stay here. I'm not going to do it. I'm not going to kill Eduardo, or Olga. Deep down they're as much victims as me, or you.'

Maribel shouted and cursed him, but he wasn't listening. Her voice became inaudible to him as he walked out of the apartment.

The last thing he heard come out of her mouth was the word 'coward'.

26

Guzmán rubbed his eyes with his fingertips. It had been a long night and he hadn't slept. He dropped the newspaper onto the seat next to him and glanced down at his fingernails, which still had mud under them. The soap hadn't gotten it all out. He looked up at the runways through the terminal's enormous windows. The passenger walkway was being hooked up to his plane. An illuminated sign announced the departure of his flight, but he was in no rush. He could sit there and wait while families with children boarded first, then passengers with preferential seating. There weren't many people, perhaps two dozen.

For Spain, America was still a far-off continent, despite Columbus's best efforts. He told himself that in a few minutes it would all be over. This was not the time to get nervous and ruin it all at the last minute. The biggest jobs are brought down by the most trivial details — getting nervous while showing your documentation at check-in, reacting to a seemingly challenging look from the guard at the security checkpoint. Do not smile at flight attendants or offer too many explanations about your luggage. Just a businessman, tired after a long night, overwhelmed by responsibilities. That's what he looked like. Except for the dirt under his nails.

He slipped his hands into his pockets and closed his eyes, wondering what the Algerian with the scarred face was doing right now. Wondering if he'd kept his word or gone back on it as soon as Guzmán was gone. Something told him that the guy was trustworthy. One of those rare kinds of men with principles that you come across every once in a while in the gutter — the principles in the gutter, that is, not the man.

After shooting Ian in the head, he had spent quite some time contemplating the dark stain beginning to pool around him. With his head turned to the side and his eyes wide open, Ian looked like a herbivore drinking his own blood, on the lookout for predators. Guzmán didn't know why he stood there staring at the man. He'd already seen what he needed to see and heard what he needed to hear. But there he was, absorbed, watching the slow sticky spreading of that stain. He wondered why he'd killed him without actually needing to. He felt no guilt, just perplexity. *You're losing it. Over a woman you don't even know, someone who wouldn't give a rat's arse about you if she weren't in here,* Bosco had told him one night, shortly before Atacama, when Guzmán confessed that he was falling for Candela's eyes. Maybe his mentor was right; maybe he'd be right now, too: Candela didn't love him, she was afraid of him and simply clung to the hope of anything that might get her out of the DINA cells. Olsen's widow would have despised him under any other circumstances, but she'd had no choice but to trust him. *Nothing's going to happen to you,* Guzmán had promised her, and she'd believed him because it was the only thing she could do. And now she was dead. They were both dead.

He made a mental note of Ian Mackenzie's last words and walked out of the room, locking it from the outside and leaving the key in the door. Gloria was sitting on a step halfway up the stairs. She was leaning her head against the wall and rocking back and forth, her fists buried in a knit cardigan. Judging by her face, she'd lost her senses; she looked completely out of it.

'I want to see Arthur dead. I'll pay you double, triple what he paid you,' she said almost inaudibly.

'That's no longer possible, Gloria. My job here is done.'

She lifted her head and looked up at him. Her eyes and nose were red. She'd been behind the door the whole time and had done nothing to stop him, aside from claw at herself until she bled.

'I'll give you whatever you want. You don't know what it's like to lose a child. I don't care what he did or what he was. He was mine.'

Guzmán shook his head. He sat down beside her and looked at her with something that bordered, if not on admiration then at least on understanding.

'You should have hired me, not that namby-pamby painter. Now you've got two dead bodies — one that you can't get out of your head and the other in that room — and a ruined painting. In my opinion, you're going to have a fuck of a time getting over all this.'

410

He tucked her hair back from her pale sweaty face and kissed her forehead.

'It's too late, Gloria.'

He called to give Arthur the address where they should meet, but Arthur didn't answer. So he left him a voicemail with directions and told him to be there in an hour's time. He could picture the man's face, guess what he was going to say, envision his nervous gestures, the way he'd hang on whatever Guzmán said or did. Guzmán was now genuinely intrigued to find Aroha, so that he could finally see her up close.

The place wasn't far. Just a twenty-minute drive outside of Madrid on National Highway Five, on the way to Badajoz. She'd been there the whole time, a stone's throw away, almost close enough to reach out and touch. And yet an impossible distance to cover.

'When I put her in the trunk, she was still breathing. She was very high and pretty banged up. But she was alive,' Ian had told him.

To the right was a prefab unit inside a parking lot full of abandoned camper vans. They were old and rusty, with flat tyres, their trailers and licence plates all faded. Cats dozed beneath the trailers, and it was almost impossible to read the *LOT FOR SALE* sign buried in the tall grass. A chain-link fence surrounded the place, but it was full of holes and in several places had actually collapsed. Off to the right was a field full of thistles and a cement basketball court with faintly visible lines. It had only one hoop, nailed to a broken wooden panel that now served as a goldfinch nest. Further off in the distance was the crumbling roof of a windowless cabin that had once served as a changing room.

The national highway was less than one hundred metres away. Cars had sped by at all hours of the day and night for four years, and no one suspected what the place concealed. Guzmán got out of the car, leaned on the hood and lit the last remaining cigarette of his favourite brand. Tossing the empty pack down on the ground, he tried to identify the place where Ian Mackenzie senior had taken Aroha out of the trunk.

'I had no intention of hurting her,' he'd sworn. 'I wanted to get her out of the place where Ian kept her drugged and locked up night and day. It was a noxious place, worse than anything you could possibly imagine. I didn't want the police to find her in those conditions. That would have been the end for my son.'

Guzmán had a pretty good imagination. And as far as noxious places went, he was pretty sure he knew them all. He should have taken Ian on a little tour of the DINA cells, or the basement of the Directorate General of Security right there in Spain not so long ago.

He tried to picture the sequence of events. It must have been night-time. Four years ago that place would still have been at least somewhat busy during the day, the sales office for the trailer lot was still in business and the sports complex would have been full of kids who came on a minibus from a nearby suburb to use the basketball court. Ian would have made sure there was nobody around before opening the trunk. Aroha was probably out of it from the drugs, but not so much so that she didn't realise something was very wrong. No doubt she kicked and screamed, trying to escape the stranger who'd brought her there.

And then Ian had hit her over the head with a shovel.

'All I wanted to do was stun her, make her shut up so she wouldn't attract attention.' He was lying. From the start he'd decided to kill her and bury the body someplace no one would find it. Ian's only concern was to erase any sign that could tie his family to the film club. That was the only reason he'd brought Aroha to such an out-of-the-way place. To murder her.

Guzmán checked the time on his watch. Arthur was late. Maybe it was better that way. Guzmán walked around the place, stepping over piles of dog shit, used condoms and human excrement, yellowed old scraps of newspaper smeared with shit, needles, the eyeless carcass of a dead cat, its smooth cranium and sharp teeth intact. The teeth are always the last thing to go. They're too hard for worms. A flock of collared doves took off in a chaotic flurry, leaving a trail of feathers on the rotten roof of the building. From the outside, you could make out an old mattress in one corner, juice boxes and a supermarket cart full of stolen scrap metal. There were also remainders of leftover food, but no people. Perhaps whoever lived there had hidden when they heard him. Or maybe they only came back at night, to sleep.

Then Guzmán heard the sound of an engine behind him. He turned thinking that Arthur had finally arrived, but the car that parked beside his was someone else's. For a few seconds, the driver was hidden in shadow inside the vehicle, which sat with the engine running. Whoever was inside it was watching him.

Ibrahim turned off the ignition and eyed warily the silhouette walking toward the hut.

'Stay here,' he said to Andrea, opening the car door.

'Who is it?' she asked, halfway through a yawn that turned quickly to a whimper.

'Guzmán. The man your husband is using to find Aroha.' He should have used the past tense.

Andrea bit her lip.

'Then it's true … she's here.'

Ibrahim was breathing heavily. He flexed and tensed his entire body. He still harboured the diminishing hope that it was not the case. The last time she was seen was here. She was alive, the Armenian had assured him. That meant that no one had seen her dead.

'I don't know. I'll be right back.'

He still hadn't told her that the police had found her husband's body in the mountains, horrifically mutilated. He didn't know how to say it. Accepting the idea of death in theory, as something vague and faraway, was one thing; seeing the concrete real-life consequences of a decision made from a distance was something very different. Nor had he told Andrea that he'd hidden from the Armenian a piece of information that might have saved Arthur's life: he had neglected to mention the photos Warden Ordóñez had shown them in the café that day, photos that proved Ian had kidnapped the girl and that, had it not been for Arthur running her over, she would probably have had the same fate as Aroha. As paradoxical as it might seem, her accidental death had likely saved the Armenian's daughter a tremendous amount of suffering. Contemplating that was a form of deceit, he knew that. But the Armenian's mind was a labyrinth in which logic and common sense were lost. That fact might have led him to show more clemency. Ibrahim had no idea whether Arthur had told him or not, whether he'd appealed to the man's compassion as he was being flayed alive. Regardless, if he had, it hadn't done him any good.

Ibrahim was walking slowly toward Guzmán, aware that he was traversing a minefield. The hired gun might have already known what happened to Arthur, and probably didn't care, but Ibrahim had no idea how loyal he might be, or what he was capable of. He'd only seen him a couple of times, but he knew a dangerous man when he saw one — and Guzmán was one for sure. So he tread cautiously, prepared to fight. It had rained and the ground beneath his feet squished, oozing dirty mud that stuck to the soles of his shoes. But sheer will forced him to take one step after the other.

Guzmán's face was red and he was unshaven. That would have been normal for anyone flying economy, prepared to deal with the turbulence at the back of the plane. But sitting in first class, right next to the cabin door, he was conspicuous.

'Are you feeling alright, sir?' asked a pretty flight attendant with the poise of a model who'd failed just prior to achieving mega-fame on the catwalk. Nothing like the girls on low-cost carriers.

What I need, you can't give me, thought Guzmán, flashing a smile intended to send her on her way.

'I'm fine thanks. Flying makes me a little nervous.'

'Oh, you just relax, sir. We'll take off in a few minutes, and this is going to be a very smooth flight, you'll see.' *When a pretty girl tries to console you, you're more prone to believing her lies*, he thought.

He looked out the window. The ground crew was loading the last few suitcases onto a conveyor belt leading into the cargo hold. You could hear the plane's rotors revving up. It looked like a perfect day, clear and cloudless. He wondered where Ibrahim would go, what he and Andrea would do when the forensics experts confirmed that the remains they'd found did indeed belong — *what a word*, he thought — to Aroha. He looked down at his fingernails. They'd touched her, touched a yellowed femur there among the decomposing remains of matted clothes. That was the first time in his life he regretted touching a human bone.

He had watched Ibrahim approach from the distance. He had a lightness about him, and yet he was solid. *An old-school warrior*, Guzmán thought, *a man who can't be owned*. He tried to remember how many times he'd seen him close to Arthur, dancing in the wings like a restrained shadow. Two, maybe three times. They'd never exchanged more than a few monosyllabic words, greetings infused with mutual distrust. No, not distrust, more like precaution. Two dogs with their tails raised, who sniffed each other's arse and then chose to back away, each keeping to one side of the road, raising a leg to piss.

'Did Arthur send you?'

Ibrahim stopped a few metres away. From up close, he was much more fearsome, Guzmán thought. He wondered how long it would have taken to break someone like him in the interrogation room. *A tough nut to crack*, Bosco would have said. The kind of guy who clenches his teeth while the electrical current is sparking against his balls, but lets out not even a groan — the kind who looks you in the eye and strips you bare with a look that says, *you can't fool me.*

'Arthur's not coming. Not now or ever. He's dead.'

Guzmán took the news on board like the good fighter he was. Just a flicker of the eye and a slight tightening of the jaw. The news only partially surprised him. But at this stage, it didn't matter much anymore. He had the money in the car, enough to be able to stop taking on these shitty jobs.

'You shouldn't be here,' Ibrahim added, as though trying to tell him that this was their story, that it belonged to Ibrahim and the woman who — against his advice — had gotten out of the car and was watching them from behind the open door.

Guzmán looked back at her.

'Is that the wife? Did you tell her the girl is buried here?'

Ibrahim turned his head back, concern etched on his face.

'We don't know for certain that she's dead.'

Guzmán shrugged. He stared at Ibrahim's scar, the poorly sutured wound that had left him so tragically disfigured. He must have spent months unable to speak, barely able to eat solid food, before it scarred over.

'We don't know for certain that God doesn't exist, or that my new penile implant doesn't work. But you and I know that if there's one thing for certain, here and now, it's that writhing beneath our feet are millions of worms that devoured that girl's dead body. The question is: is it really worth verifying? Do we need to dig her up and see with our own eyes what we already know? Or perhaps it would be better for you to go back to the car and tell the girl's mother that you didn't find anything, that her daughter isn't here, and feed her hope that Aroha could be someplace else.'

Ibrahim gazed at the dilapidated cabin and looked down at his feet as though the image of a million writhing worms were taking shape before him, just a few centimetres beneath the ground.

'This is no longer any of your business. You got your money and the police are after you. I don't understand what you're still doing here. You need to leave.'

Guzmán didn't understand it either. It was starting to get dark and his plane was taking off first thing in the morning, with or without him. The smart thing to do would be to hide out in some roadside motel and just wait for morning to come. Get to the airport in just enough time, go through security and get on that plane without showing his face any more than necessary. But there he was, searching for something without knowing what it was.

'I don't like to leave things unfinished.' That might not have been what he was actually thinking, or what Ibrahim expected to hear. But that was what he said.

Not understanding, Ibrahim examined his face, searching for some type of motivation he couldn't see, fearing a trap. He knew guys like Guzmán. They were all over the world and they'd been around since the beginning of time. They spoke every language. Torturers were all alike, able to slash a little boy's face with a machete. But he'd never imagined them willing to risk their own hides in order to find the buried body of a little girl.

'I have a shovel in the car. I'll go get it,' Guzmán added, reading his thoughts. 'Let's get this done with, once and for all.'

Time has different magnitudes. That was what struck him as the plane finally began moving toward the runway. There he was, in a comfortable seat, his seatbelt fastened, watching the various structures of the airport go by — hangars, control tower, other planes parked on an angle as though at a shopping mall — and at the same time, he could still see the mound of overturned earth piling up on one side of the hole as it got deeper. And another part of him kept seeing the sky in the Atacama, searching for stars as his testicles melted under the heat of a blowtorch.

He was sitting on a rock beside a puddle on a dirt road in Santiago de Chile, watching a kite land, wondering why he could never get it to go higher than the antennae and the clothes hung out to dry on people's roofs. He was kissing the lips of a woman whose name meant *little fire*: Candela. He was both alive and dead. And all of it was happening there and then, at the same time.

'Who did that to your face?'

They were taking turns digging. It was Ibrahim's turn. He'd taken off his shirt and the sweat on his torso mixed in with the mud. He dug, concentrating on what he was doing.

'Life,' Ibrahim replied, not letting go of the shovel.

Andrea was just a few steps behind them. There had been no way to convince her to stay in the car. She wanted to be there, to see it with her own eyes. Ibrahim looked at her out of the corner of his eye. Through the sweat in his brows, Guzmán saw on the man's face a look that he, too, had once possessed.

'Life,' he murmured, repeating Ibrahim's words as he stroked the useless skin of his atrophied hand. *Life*, he'd said, by which he meant *Andrea*. 'Here, I'll take over for now,' he said, replacing Ibrahim in the ditch.

Up in the sky there are no plans. Everything is suspended. Clouds, superimposed with varying degrees of density, nurture the absurd feeling that anything is possible and nothing matters. Guzmán felt that even the most burdensome of things lost their weight when he was cloud surfing. Far from the ground, away from the moist earth and the worms bisected by a shovel. It was hard to find a femur when you were up in the clouds at ten thousand metres.

The pretty flight attendant had just told them they'd reached their cruising altitude and velocity. He thanked her, but still felt like asking them to go higher, and faster.

The shovel hit something solid, something stuck firmly in the ground. Guzmán knelt down and dug carefully with his fingers, like a sapper, or a paleontologist on the verge of discovering an ancient fossil. He swept aside layer after layer of dirt with his bare hands, until he uncovered the solid yellow chunk of bone. Guzmán knew something about anatomy — a basic understanding he'd picked up through experience. The femur is the longest and strongest bone in the human body, and in women its angle is more pronounced than in men in order to adapt better to the female pelvis.

Ibrahim lowered the shovel and starting digging with his hands too. Little by little the remains of what had once been Aroha Fernández began to emerge. Inevitably, as they uncovered the hardened remnants of her clothes, Guzmán thought of the cat skeleton he'd come upon a few metres away. The ribcage with just a few ribs, the metacarpals, a tibia, the cranium with its lower jaw detached and full of black earth. People are nothing without the stuff that makes them. Organs. Thoughts. Emotions. The rest is just a gruesome costume. The silent vestige of something that once was, but was no longer. He'd always found odd the human need to venerate bones — graves, tombs, cemeteries, religions — when all of those things in fact constituted the overwhelming proof of the one and only truth he'd ever read in the Bible. *Dust you are. Unto dust you shall return.* Maybe that was why he never went to visit his dead. Because they weren't really there.

'We'd better not touch anything else. The medical examiner is going to need to identify the body,' Ibrahim said, wiping the muddy sweat from his face.

Guzmán contemplated the dark cavities of the eye sockets. Where once there had been eyes there were now clumps of dirt. How much identifying did they need? Who else could it be but Aroha? Regardless, his mission was accomplished. He'd found her.

'What now?' he asked the air, gazing up at a flock of birds — what were they, swallows? — flapping wildly, feasting on insects in the dusk.

Ibrahim shrugged, gazing down at the remnants of Aroha's dress.

'The police will want to know how we found the body. They'll ask questions and inevitably your name will come up. You should leave, now. I'll lie to them to buy you a few hours. But they'll be after you.'

Andrea had approached the edge of the ditch. She gazed into the abyss and the abyss gazed back at her, both forms of darkness engaged in a mutual silent dialogue. The two men got up and left her alone, in the intimacy of her own expression, fading wordlessly away with her daughter's remains.

He pictured Aroha's remains, meticulously cleaned, no dirt or remnants of fabric stuck to them, laid out in the form of a skeleton on the shiny metallic surface of the examiner's table at the morgue. A puzzle, methodically pieced back together by the examiners — a patella here, a phalanx there. The clothing and jewellery she was wearing when she was buried — gold earrings with a little pearl, an olivine bead necklace, a silver ring — would be stored in an evidence bag. When they were finished, they'd give those belongings back to Andrea, and she could keep them or bury them with the remains that carbon testing and DNA had shown to have a ninety-six percent chance of belonging to Aroha Fernández. The report would never say that it *was* Aroha; they at least recognised that the bones were not the girl, they had simply *belonged* to her. They were something she'd had since birth, something beneath her skin that had grown year after year and should have kept growing for a number of years to come. Bones, indeed, are something that belong to us. Something that not even the worms born inside us, born of our own putrefaction, can rob us of. They remain, witness to our struggles for hundreds and thousands of years.

A ninety-six percent chance. That was a very high chance but it wasn't a hundred percent. It was as though science wanted to leave a tiny possibility to illusion. *If you want to believe, then believe. Up to you*, said the report.

Too many dead bodies, Guzmán thought. He was thinking about his life when the plane landed in Buenos Aires. He heard people applauding from behind the curtain. Here we are, safe and sound. Widespread relief. The new-age type sitting next to him applauded too, like a little kid, though his fellow passenger had said he would have liked to stay up in the air and live there in the clouds. People talk just to talk, in moments of euphoria. But really, they always opt to return to mediocrity. It's safer to have your feet on the ground. To be another face in the crowd.

It was raining and the ground crew was on the move, in fluorescent ponchos. Blue and yellow landing lights twinkled, distorted by the water. It must have been cold.

The pretty flight attendant with a tilted peaked cap had fixed her hair and makeup, adjusted her silk scarf. She was ready for inspection, fresh as a daisy. She approached him with a reassuring smile. But the corners of her mouth were trembling. She wasn't a good actress.

'I'm sorry, sir. It seems there's a small problem with your documentation. You'll have to wait for the other passengers to disembark. There are some government officials who just want to verify a few things. Nothing serious, a tedious but essential routine.'

Guzmán smiled, more than anything to calm the poor girl's nerves. They shouldn't make them do that sort of thing, as far as he was concerned. Give bad news, keep everyone calm when the plane is about to crash, demand that, in addition to leg and teeth, they show storybook courage that went against all logic.

'I understand.'

The 'government officials' were in fact federal police agents. They had a warrant for his arrest, issued by Interpol. He didn't need to see their credentials, though he made them show them to him anyway. *Democracy, what an invention,* Guzmán thought scornfully. Even guys like him had rights and could demand that the police identify themselves, and it wouldn't lead to them breaking his jaw, as it surely would have during the days of the military junta.

'Thank you for flying with us, sir. We hope to see you on board with us again soon,' she said as he walked past her, handcuffed and escorted by the two agents.

Life was a joke, and it was best to take it that way.

As they waited outside the terminal for the cruiser to arrive, one of the agents lit a cigarette. Guzmán's favourite brand.

'Sorry, could you possibly spare me a smoke?'

EPILOGUE

On one corner of the table lay the 12 June 2005 morning paper, neatly folded. Martina had set a half-drunk cup of herbal tea — it smelled like chamomile — on top of it. In the end, a judge had decided to go in with both fists swinging: it was all over the press. Entrepreneurs, bankers, a couple of police chiefs and at least one elite athlete had fallen like dominoes. Even more famous people were expected to be arrested. *The Cine Club Case* — the sensationalist name the press had given it — was going to be the soap opera of the summer.

Martina had bags under her eyes and had lost weight, but her eyes were clear. She didn't take out her notebook and instead sat with it in her lap, hands folded on top as if forcing herself not to open it.

'I suppose I owe you an apology.'

Eduardo looked at her without responding. Perhaps she expected him to cut in, but his silence forced her to continue.

'Mr Who stole the file with all your personal information. It took me a little while to realise it, and when I did, I couldn't bring myself to tell you. I was so mortified that I couldn't get over my shame. They're charging me with negligence, but that's not the worst of it. The worst thing is that now everybody knows I pay for sex.'

'I don't think that's anyone's business but your own,' Eduardo said. He really meant it. No one had the right to judge other people's means of combatting loneliness.

'What are you going to do now?' the psychiatrist asked.

Eduardo didn't know. He felt empty — emptier than he ever had. Like the most insignificant part of a story in which all the other players had used his pain to staunch their wounds. When it all died down, when the storm passed, he'd still be sitting at the foot of his bed, listening to his father's records, staring out his apartment window at the playground across the street, with nothing to fill his empty hours.

'Maybe I'll go back to painting things that interest me — faces of anonymous people, feelings floating on a landscape. Or maybe I'll just hole up at home. Honestly, I don't really know.'

'What about your landlady's offer? If I recall correctly, she invited you to leave Madrid with her and her daughter. Maybe it would be easier to start afresh someplace new.'

Eduardo saw her fingers attempting to reach out and touch his hand. To console him. He pulled his hand away and tucked it under his crossed arms, negating that possibility.

'That's no longer an option.' Truthfully, it never had been.

Eduardo looked up. Yesterday was now today. It was ten thirty-five. His last chance had left an hour and thirty-five minutes ago. Time crossed his mind and leaked out through the pores in his skin. He'd heard them walk out of the apartment, put down their suitcases, lock the door. Sara had been chattering breathlessly, excited at the idea of their trip. Graciela wasn't saying a word. She was probably looking at Eduardo's door hoping to see him appear with a backpack and a confident smile on his lips. But he didn't even have the courage to go out and say goodbye. He stood there behind the closed door, watching them walk down the stairs through the peephole. Until there was nothing there but silence.

'Do you mind if I smoke?'

Martina didn't show any opposition. In fact, she opened the top drawer of her desk and took two cigarettes out of a case. She held one out to him and lit her own, eyes fixed on the hot ash.

'I'm going to discharge you. It doesn't make sense for you to keep coming every month.'

Suddenly Eduardo felt the pressing need to keep sitting there beside her. Martina was the only real thing he had left — her and his father's records. He realised with dismay that, outside of that room, there was no longer a single person who needed him.

'I'm still having nightmares. Though they're less frequent.'

Martina smoothed her hair and tapped her cigarette into an ashtray full of paper clips.

'That's good,' she said, her expression distracted by something outside the window.

You're no longer my problem, is what she meant.

'What do you think that means?'

'Excuse me?'

422

'The fact that I don't have as many nightmares anymore. Maybe your theory of forgiveness works. Maybe Mr Who freed me from that subconscious burden. Don't you think?'

No. Of course she didn't.

'It's possible. Either way, at least it's all over.' Martina slowly turned her head to check the time on the clock behind her. Then she looked around, uncomfortable, as though searching for someone else. Something was distracting her.

'Do you have another patient?'

Martina exhaled, relieved.

'Yes, that's it. Exactly. I'm sorry, I'm on a tight schedule.'

'I understand.'

They said goodbye with a revolting, limp handshake. *After all this time together*, Eduardo thought, *this is how it ends*.

You've been drinking too much lately. He heard Elena's voice as he pointed, to indicate to the waiter how high to fill it with Glencadam.

'That's enough.'

'That's more than enough,' the waiter replied with a malicious smile.

Eduardo took the first sip, enjoying the warmth of the sun on his face as it rose over the tops of the buildings. As he set the glass down on the patio table, he listened to the sounds of children running, watched hawkers selling balloons and candy, saw mimes gesticulating silently before a group of tourists gathered in the centre of the plaza. It was a beautiful June day. His gaze caught on the two empty chairs at his table. He could imagine Tania grumpily poking at a dish of *patatas bravas* with a plastic fork, blowing bubbles in her Coke. She was probably thinking a million things, her mind filled with pre-teen ideas he couldn't relate to. In the other chair, he saw Elena leaning back, eyes closed beneath her sunglasses. She loved the feel of the sun on her skin; it relaxed her, made her happy. Maybe they'd make love when they got home, after having a vermouth. Summer always made her horny — the colours, the excitement, the heat.

That was what happiness was. Small moments in which great things were determined. Drinking a beer, sitting in a plaza.

The phone in his pocket rang. Olga. She'd left a voicemail message.

'Aren't you going to forgive me?'

He erased it and was about to put his phone away, but then had a thought. He deleted her number. Permanently. Forgetting was the best kind of forgiveness, the only kind that could be granted.

He needed to go for a walk. Eduardo stood, and for a moment thought that his knee was going to buckle under the weight of his body, and he nearly fell. The waiter who'd served him watched from the doorway with a smile. Drunks always make you smile until they became real headaches. But Eduardo wasn't drunk. Just hurt. And he wanted to forget. He walked across the plaza ignoring the stabbing pain in his knee. A drop of sweat slid down his back all the way to his coccyx. He was starting to feel self-conscious. It was time to find a pharmacy and fill the prescriptions in his pocket.

A street painter was exhibiting his work, the paintings all lined up in a row. They weren't bad, but nor were they good, Eduardo thought, giving them a passing glance.

'Want a portrait, friend?'

He didn't want a portrait. But he pressed the last dirty wrinkled bill he had into the man's hand. He was lucky, that painter.

'Be careful at crossroads; it's easy to get lost.'

The painter pushed back his beret and scratched his forehead with the tip of a brush.

'Is that supposed to mean something?'

Eduardo shrugged.

'It means that life takes strange paths and ...'

He couldn't find the words to finish the sentence. They were there, ready to be spoken, and yet suddenly they evaporated and his mind was filled with a strange vibration that drowned out everything but the sharp intense pain shooting down his back. It lasted just a fraction of a second, but it was like opening a door and having everything rush in at once: the painter's incredulous expression, his mediocre paintings, the sounds of the city, people's footsteps, the noise of the traffic, pigeons flapping around.

And then just as quickly, the door closed and he stopped feeling anything at all, except for an intense cold.

On the other side of the horizon, Sara was watching the setting sun. Waves rushed in — making her bare feet sink into the sand — and then pulled back out. A few metres away, her mother was strolling along the shore, a man's arm around her waist. Sara liked the man — he didn't ask stupid questions, he was nice to her mother, and he smelled good.

'What do you think?' she asked her toy cat.

The cat took her hand with its stiff little arm. Its toy eyes reflected the small island, a giant rock where seagulls nested in the crags.

'I think the same as you,' the cat replied without moving its moustache.

'He's not Eduardo.'

'Exactly,' the cat collaborated.

Sara found a twig in the detritus carried in by the sea. Using it like a pen she wrote on the shore, in big letters, as though someone might read the message from the sky: E-D-U-A-R-D-O.

'Do you think he can see it?'

The cat did not shrug. It was just a toy and had no joints.

'Who knows?'

Suddenly an impetuous wave, bigger than the rest, stuck out its foamy tongue and lapped up the letters, erasing them.

Sara became sad.

'It's just a name,' the cat said, comforting her.

Sara dropped her toy on the sand and took three steps back and wrote it again, in bigger, deeper letters.

'You don't understand. You're just a cat that talks.'

And the cat smiled without moving its moustache. Sara was right; it couldn't understand human beings.